CONGREGATION

RAPHAEL D. SILVER

authorHOUSE®

AuthorHouse™ LLC
1663 Liberty Drive
Bloomington, IN 47403
www.authorhouse.com
Phone: 1-800-839-8640

Published by AuthorHouse 11/18/2014

ISBN: 978-1-4969-3891-6 (sc)
ISBN: 978-1-4969-3890-9 (e)

Cover photography by Patty Williams

For JOAN

and

DINA, MARISA, and CLAUDIA

CHAPTER ONE

The car moved slowly down the narrow two-lane road that snaked from the suburbs toward the central city. On the wide plain below, decaying factories and abandoned warehouses stretched toward a downtown skyline barely discernible in the evening haze. A blanket of hot moist air had pushed in the day before and hung over Cleveland like a shroud. Eli Stone could barely make out the synagogue, its dome burnished to a dull gold, dominating a square block of aging tenements whose occupants sweltered in the unexpected heat. Inside the sanctuary, behind thick limestone walls, it would still be cool but by tomorrow, unless the heat wave broke, services would be miserable for everyone.

He steadied the pages of his sermon against the motion of the car and jotted down a few notes in the margins in an almost indecipherable hand. Eli still committed his sermons to memory. It was a lifelong habit and even though he took the pages with him to the pulpit, he seldom referred to them. He looked forward to this evening's service. There was something immensely gratifying about being in the pulpit on the High Holidays. Religion no longer held a central place in the lives of most of his congregants, but

1

no matter how far they strayed during the year they still flocked back to the synagogue on Rosh Hashanah, like birds following some ancient migratory path, seeking to reaffirm a commitment to their faith.

His wife, Rachel, took her eyes off the road for a moment. "You feeling okay?"

"I'm feeling fine."

It was an evasive response. That morning while he was shaving, the muscles in his right leg had cramped again. It had happened regularly over the past month. He found himself stumbling occasionally, the tip of his shoe catching on a step as he went up a flight of stairs, and he had begun to experience some numbness in the fingers of his right hand. He didn't say anything to Rachel about the periods of exhaustion and weakness that overwhelmed him without warning. At his annual checkup, he mentioned the symptoms to his doctor, who sent him to a specialist. There had been tests and more tests.

When he told Rachel what they had found, she broke down at first. "How long do you have?" she asked, her voice barely a whisper. He tried to reassure her. The disease followed an unpredictable path. Some people lived with it a long time.

The doctors had been more direct. "We suspect that your case may be somewhat advanced. There's no way of knowing how rapidly it will begin to affect you in a serious way."

Rachel turned the car in to the synagogue parking lot, pulled to a stop in their accustomed parking space and sat quietly for a moment, her hands gripping the wheel, the motor running, cool air still whispering from the vents.

"Will you tell them tonight?"

Eli wished she would stop pressing him. The thought of retirement terrified him almost as much as his illness, the extent of which he still couldn't grasp. He opened the car door abruptly and started for the synagogue without her. The hot air assaulted him. He could feel himself begin to perspire.

* * *

Mark Winnick, the congregation's thirty-five-year-old assistant rabbi, stood at the top of a short flight of steps that led to the pulpit from a tiny vestry under the choir loft and cracked open the door just wide enough to look out.

"Thirty-six empties, Rabbi. They're filling fast."

Mark was obsessed with numbers. He kept track of the number of times the phone rang before his secretary picked it up. He counted the number of people ahead of him in a movie line. He even counted his pulse occasionally, pretending to check his wristwatch for the time. Sometimes, when he was on the pulpit, his lips moved while he was counting. It drove his wife, Susan, crazy.

"Don't do that! It makes you look stupid."

"No one notices."

"Of course they notice."

The High Holidays were a difficult time for Mark. The rest of the year the rabbis wore dark suits to the pulpit, but

on the High Holidays they put on long black robes. Rabbi
Stone looked magisterial in his. Six feet tall, still ramrod
straight at sixty-five, a thick mane of white hair combed
back over an impressively large head, he projected immense
authority. Mark was barely five-foot eight, with short black
hair and wide eyes set in a pleasant if undistinguished
face. Each time he slipped the clerical robe over his narrow
shoulders he felt diminished. He was sure it made him look
like a penguin. Once, crossing the pulpit, he had tripped on
the hem and stumbled and there had been a slight ripple of
laughter from the congregation.

He held the door open for Eli, who brushed by him
without a word. Mark made his way to his seat on the far
side of the pulpit and, balancing his prayer book on the wide
arm of his chair, watched latecomers straggle in. He caught
a glimpse of Susan in the fourth row and tried to keep his
lips from moving. Mark had been Eli's assistant for five
years and in all that time, with the exception of the High
Holidays, he had preached only a dozen times. He would
preach again tomorrow, but the morning service for Rosh
Hashanah was always sparsely attended. At least he would
be spared the agony of having to lead the children's service in
the afternoon. It baffled him that Eli insisted on officiating
at a service where mothers brought their runny-nosed kids
and no one paid the least attention.

Mark leaned back, hands folded in his lap, eyes half-
closed in an attitude of meditation, and stared up at the
stained glass windows that circled the sanctuary dome.
Each panel depicted a different prophet. Jeremiah was his

favorite. The prophet's flowing white hair and piercing gaze reminded him of Rabbi Stone. He wondered if the prophets, as they grew older, ever thought about retiring and letting their assistants take over.

* * *

The final chords of the organ prelude echoed off the sanctuary walls. For a moment the only sounds were the soft hiss of compressed air leaking from a defective valve and the murmur of worshippers restless in their seats. Eli uncrossed his legs, placed his hands on the arms of his chair and with deliberate slowness stood up and walked toward the lectern. He took off his wristwatch and set it down carefully to one side, removed his wire-rim glasses, took out his handkerchief and polished each lens carefully before putting his glasses back on. Then he glanced toward the rear of the sanctuary where Manny Polsky, the synagogue's eighty-one-year-old head usher, a white carnation in his lapel, circled with his index finger in the air like a sailor on the flight deck of a carrier, giving Eli the signal that the congregation had settled down and that services could begin.

Eli's deep rich voice filled the sanctuary. "We will begin this evening's service with a responsive reading on page seventy-eight of your prayer books."

> *O worship the Lord in the beauty of holiness;*
> *Tremble before him all the earth.*

Come, let us bow down and bend the knee;
Let us kneel before the Lord our maker.
Righteousness and justice are the foundation
of his throne.
Mercy and truth shall go before him.
Thy kingdom is a kingdom for all ages, and thy
dominion endureth through all generations.

* * *

Linda Freling hurried down the aisle, slid into the pew next to Sally Minton and gave her arm a little squeeze.

"Have I missed anything?"

"It's just getting started. Where's Peter?"

"Working, where else? He said he'd get here later if he could."

Linda was forty-two, trim and elegant in a new dress she had bought especially for the High Holidays. She and Sally had been college roommates. They were married the same year, although Sally's marriage had collapsed when she found her husband cheating with his secretary. Linda had advised her not to go through with a divorce.

"They all do it, honey. The next one will be just like the last."

A year ago, Sally had run into Peter on a plane to New York, where her daughter was in her first year at Sarah Lawrence, and he had casually asked her out to dinner. They had a few drinks and when the dessert course came around he suggested they go back to his hotel.

She blamed herself that she had let it happen. She never told Linda about it and they had remained best friends.

"Rabbi Winnick looks as happy as if he's in his right mind," Sally whispered, noting the tiny smile that flitted across Mark's face as he shifted in his seat, adjusting the long robe that had bunched up under him.

"He should be," Linda whispered back, "considering the raise we just gave him." Unlike Sally, who found Mark unimpressive, Linda liked him. It was a relief having a pleasant-looking young rabbi at the synagogue after the succession of sallow-faced seminary graduates who had preceded him. She recalled the first time they met. He had filled in at the last moment as moderator on a panel on interfaith marriage at a sisterhood conference in Indianapolis. At the end of the day she asked him if he would meet her for a drink. She invited him to her suite, kicked off her shoes and curled up in a chair with her legs tucked under her. She was curious where things might go, but then the phone rang and it was Peter calling and by the time the call was over, Mark was at the door saying he had work to do.

When Mark's name came up as a candidate to replace Eli's previous assistant, Linda went to bat for him. Five years later, with his contract up for renewal, Mark had called her for advice and she had agreed to talk to Rabbi Stone on his behalf. She had breezed past a surprised Roz McIver, Eli's secretary, and entered Eli's book-lined study.

Eli's relationship with Linda was complicated. He hadn't wanted her to become president of the congregation. Wives of rich men were always trouble. With too much free time on their hands they sought out positions where they could swing their weight. But Linda had lobbied hard for the job and in the end a majority of the board had voted for her.

"I hope I'm not disturbing you, Rabbi," Linda said, settling nervously in a chair across from Eli and bracing herself for a difficult conversation.

Eli pushed the papers he had been working on aside. "Not at all. How are you and how is Peter?"

"We're fine, thanks." Linda paused, hoping that Eli might inquire into the reasons for her visit, but he remained silent. "Rabbi Winnick's contract is coming up for renewal and I wonder if you have a minute to talk about it?"

"Of course."

"How has he been doing in your opinion?"

"He's doing well."

Linda sensed a note of caution in Eli's voice. "If you have some reservations about him, Rabbi, perhaps we should discuss them."

Eli wasn't accustomed to having to explain himself. He remained silent, his hands folded together on his desk.

"If you have no serious reservations, I'd like to suggest that we offer Mark a five-year extension of his contract."

"I hadn't given much thought to the matter, but I would think a three-year extension is more than adequate."

Linda contemplated the consequence of disagreeing with Eli. He always listened to her politely but invariably ignored her suggestions. "Perhaps we could offer him associate status. That would go a long way toward making him feel appreciated."

"What makes you think he isn't appreciated?"

"I didn't mean to suggest that he wasn't."

"Why don't we leave things the way they are, Linda." There was an undercurrent of irritation in Eli's voice. "Mark's still young. Maybe in another year or two we can talk about it." Being an associate implied succession and Eli didn't want Mark around when the time came for the congregation to select his successor. He was planning to retire when he was seventy. That was five years off. In three years, if Mark hadn't left on his own, he would let him go. There would be no trouble finding a suitable replacement.

Linda was desperate. She hadn't promised Mark anything, but it would be humiliating to walk away empty handed. What was the point of being president of the congregation if you couldn't get a few things done your way?

"How would you feel about an increase in his salary? Would that be all right with you?"

Eli had no problem with that. There were lawyers and accountants on the board to make sure that any salary adjustments were appropriate. "Whatever you and the board decide is fine with me." Eli got up from behind his desk and extended his hand. "Give Peter my best."

It took Linda a moment to realize that the meeting was over. She felt like a schoolgirl called to the principal's office and reprimanded for misbehaving. "Well, I won't take up any more of your time, Rabbi, I know how busy you must be." She could feel Roz McIver watching her as she walked out the door in a quiet rage.

*   *   *

From the bedroom window of her tiny third-floor walk-up Liz Aurelio could see most of the synagogue parking lot. She hoped for a glimpse of Bobby Greenhut, the recently acquired center fielder of the Cleveland Indians. The sportswriters had nicknamed him Bobby G. He had been picked up on waivers in mid-season and was having a phenomenal year, and was the main reason the Indians were in a race for a place in the playoffs. One of her girlfriends worked in the Indians' front office and had offered her a ticket to tonight's game, but Bobby G. had announced that he wouldn't play baseball on the High Holidays. Liz wasn't sure he would show up at the synagogue but Bobby had promised that if he did, he would come by after services were over.

Liz had grown up in a small town near Canton, Ohio, left for Cleveland right after high school and taken a job as a waitress at the Stadium Bar and Grille. It was a ballplayers' hangout and she had met Bobby there. He waited for her after work one night and they ended up in bed in her apartment. Her girlfriends all told her that she was lucky to have a Jewish boyfriend. They weren't great in the sack, but they made good husbands if you could nail one down, and they almost never hit you. Liz wondered what her father would say if he knew she was going out with a Jewish ball player. He probably wouldn't mind since Bobby was red hot right now, third in the league in hitting and first in RBIs. She remembered lying next to Bobby in her bedroom and staring out the window at the illuminated dome of the synagogue.

"I've never been inside a Jewish church," she whispered.

"I'll take you over there one of these days and show you around." She loved Bobby's soft Southern drawl that made everything seem warm and fuzzy, and the way his callused hands roamed her body making her tingle all over.

A screech of brakes jolted her out of her reverie as Bobby's blue BMW roadster swerved into the parking lot. He jumped out and hurried toward the synagogue. Liz watched until he disappeared inside, then scurried around tidying up, in case he showed up later. She had been going out with Bobby for almost two months and he was always promising to take her places, but so far they hadn't gone anywhere. They always ended up in bed in her apartment. He said he loved her, but she was beginning to wonder. Tonight, when he came over, she would insist that he take her someplace where they could be seen together. If he refused, that would be the end of it. She wouldn't see him anymore.

*　*　*

The murmur of 2,200 praying voices lulled Sam Broad to sleep. "Wake up," his wife, Millie, whispered, jabbing him with her elbow. "You're sleeping."

"I wasn't sleeping. I just closed my eyes for a second."

"How does Eli look to you?"

"He looks fine."

"He looks exhausted to me."

Sam was a short, wiry man with a florid face and the sturdy build of an aging boxer. He had survived the concentration camps and built a new life for himself in Cleveland. In the forty years since he had founded Fabrico in the back of his garage, the company had grown from a single store to an international chain of fabric stores with 500 locations in the United States, Canada, Europe and Asia. In the late nineties the company had gone public and its stock had shot up from $4 to almost $100 a share. Now, ten years later, the market had collapsed and the stock was under $5. Profits had fallen steadily and the company had piled up massive amounts of debt. A sprawling new headquarters building was under construction east of the city. It was millions of dollars over budget and months behind schedule.

He had spent most of the past week renegotiating store leases, trying to find ways to bring costs down. If the landlords wouldn't budge, they would have to close more stores, lay off people and take a huge write-off. He pondered a call he had received from Peter Freling earlier that afternoon.

"You free for lunch one of these days?"

"Sure, Peter. What have you got in mind?"

"Nothing special. I just wanted a chance to show off our new offices."

Sam knew there was more to Peter's invitation than the wish to socialize. Peter was a venture capitalist, one of the city's richest men, and constantly on the lookout for wounded animals that he could separate from the herd. But Sam was too tired to worry about that now. The last rays of the setting sun filtered through the stained glass windows of the sanctuary and the choir began another hymn. The music washed over him. His bald head slumped forward and he drifted into a troubled sleep.

*   *   *

Eli gazed out across the congregation as Mark led them in responsive reading, his voice rising and falling in the practiced cadences of someone who applied the lessons learned in elocution class in the same mindless way he tied his shoelaces.

> *Eternal truth it is that Thou alone art God*
> *and there is none else.*
> *Thy righteousness is like the mighty mountain;*
> *Thy judgments are like the great deep.*
> *How precious is thy loving kindness, O God!*
> *The children of men take refuge in the shadow*
> *of Thy wings.*

He wondered what it was about Mark that bothered him. That he was young? Eli had become senior rabbi of the congregation when he was twenty-five. That his intellect was only average? Eli knew a lot of rabbis who didn't have much on their minds. His other assistants had always kept their distance, thrilled when he had time to talk to them, terrified that they might disappoint him in some way. Mark did his work competently, but without passion, marking time, Eli thought, until something better came along. He wondered why Mark had picked the rabbinate when there were so many other professions that were less demanding.

He noticed Sam Broad dozing in his seat. Sam had been one of his strongest supporters forty years ago when the board of the congregation had invited him to Cleveland to give a trial sermon. Their senior rabbi was retiring. The invitation had been the subject of intense debate. Eli was the rabbi of a small congregation in Boston but had already become a controversial figure. His fiery oratory had gained him a national reputation. He had been jailed working with civil rights organizers in the South and had been an early protester of the war in Vietnam. In his sermon that Saturday morning he denounced the war that was still raging and the president who seemed unwilling to bring it to a close. He could sense the discomfort of many in the congregation who had come to hear him. Later, at a private lunch with members of the board, a number of them expressed their concerns more openly. They were used to a rabbi who preached once a week, married and buried them, confirmed their children, and whose views on social and political issues were moderate and restrained. Eli told them if that was what they were looking for, he could recommend a half dozen rabbis whose views would be more compatible with their own. If they wanted him, it had to be with the understanding that he valued his independence over everything. If they were uneasy about that, then he wasn't interested in the job.

On the plane back to Boston he confided his doubts to Rachel, who had accompanied him. The board had wanted to take a look at the whole package.

"They'll never offer me the job."

"They'd be crazy not to."

"All they want is someone who won't rock the boat."

Rachel reached over and rubbed the back of his neck. "Maybe they're ready for a little spice in their life. A couple of the wives I talked to thought you were really handsome."

They had been at Sam's house for dinner a week ago. After dinner Sam took him upstairs and opened the door to a large walk-in closet filled with gift-wrapped boxes. Sam was a compulsive gift giver. He had given Eli an alligator wallet. Another time it was a pair of gold cuff links. Once he had presented Rachel with a crate of artichokes. He opened a narrow box and held up a tie for Eli's approval. "It's Ferragamo. At least that's what the label says."

Eli fingered the tie. "I went to see the doctor last week."

"I figured something was wrong when you were so quiet at dinner."

"They tell me I have Lou Gehrig's disease."

Eli could hear Sam exhale. "Jesus, Eli, when did you find out?"

"A few days ago. I'm okay for now."

"Is there anything I can do?"

"There is one thing. I don't want Mark Winnick to be my successor."

"We just voted him a new three-year contract. You agreed."

"That was before I knew I had this thing. This is really important to me, Sam. It's important to the future of the congregation."

Sam had known Eli long enough to understand that when he made up his mind nothing would change it. "Mark's made a lot of friends, Rabbi. It's not going to be easy to get rid of him. But if that's what you want, we'll figure something out."

*   *   *

Eli stood with Mark before the open doors of the Ark. Inside, four Torah scrolls nestled next to one another, each one draped in white satin damask over which hung a silver breastplate on which the Ten Commandments had been inscribed. The finials of each scroll were capped with silver crowns decorated with dozens of tiny silver bells. As Eli reached in to lift out one of the heavy scrolls, a jolt of pain shot up his left leg, so sudden and intense that he thought he was going to faint. His vision blurred as he struggled to push down the pain. Mark moved in to steady him. Then as quickly as the pain came it went away.

"I'm fine," Eli whispered as he lifted up the heavy scroll, resting it on his shoulder. He turned to face the congregation, praying that no one had noticed. Even Rachel seemed unaware that anything was wrong. He took a deep breath and held the Torah scroll aloft for everyone to see.

> *Lift up your heads, O ye gates,*
> *And be ye lifted up, ye everlasting doors,*
> *For the King of glory shall enter.*
> *Who is the King of glory?*
> *The Lord of hosts, He is the King of glory.*

*   *   *

It had grown uncomfortably warm in the sanctuary and the congregation was getting restless. Eli's sermon had gone well. It was time for the closing benediction. He walked toward the lectern and glanced briefly in Rachel's direction. Her soft brown eyes implored him to tell the congregation that he intended to retire.

"Before we close tonight's service," Eli began, "there is a personal matter that I want to share with you. This may be the last New Year's service that I will be conducting from this pulpit. My doctors told me that I have ALS. Most of you know it as Lou Gehrig's disease. As it turns out, I've had it for some time but I didn't pay much attention to the symptoms, hoping they would go away. The doctors will do what they can to slow down the progress of the disease, but there are no miracle cures. I've already been granted more miracles in my life than anyone is entitled to have. A long happy marriage to a wonderful woman, a fine son, and forty great years as rabbi of this congregation. You have allowed me the freedom to express my opinions from this pulpit and to champion the causes I believe in, even if many of you disagreed with me. For that independence I am truly grateful. I intend to continue serving as your rabbi for as long as my health permits, and when the time comes for me to step aside I know that this institution will be left in secure and caring hands and that the traditions which have been its hallmark for the past one hundred and twenty-seven years will be sustained for generations to come. Now let us all rise for the final benediction."

Eli raised his arms in the manner of the priests of old. The congregation stood, stunned and silent. A few people wept openly.

> *May the Lord bless you and keep you.*
> *May the Lord shed the light of his countenance*
> *upon you and be gracious unto you.*
> *May the Lord grant unto you and all your*
> *loved ones a year of health and happiness, and*
> *a year of peace.*

CHAPTER TWO

Josh Stone sat in his shirtsleeves staring out the window of his office in New York City's downtown financial district and waited for the phone to ring. Across the narrow street, in an office just like his, he watched a young woman slip off her shoes, lace on a pair of sneakers, stuff some papers in a briefcase, and head out the door. He glanced at his watch. It was seven-thirty. Ballard's secretary had called at six. "Mr. Ballard's meeting is running longer than expected. He'd like you to wait." It bothered Josh that he was being told to hang around like some errand boy. He thought about telling Ballard's secretary that he couldn't stay. That it was the Rosh Hashanah holiday and he was going to attend New Year's services. But the truth was that in the eight years since he had come to New York he hadn't bothered to join a congregation. Besides, this would be his first chance to spend some private time with Jess Ballard since his initial job interview six weeks ago.

He thought how lucky he had been to make the move to Parallax. Careers in the financial world had become a high-wire act with no net to catch you when you fell. He had started at Citicorp as an analyst, been promoted twice, and moved on to Merrill where they had doubled his salary. Then, just before the market crashed and Merrill disappeared, Dan Elkins, his roommate at the Harvard Business School, called to say that Parallax was looking for someone.

The interviews had been long and challenging. The money was about the same, but Parallax was a small firm with an excellent reputation and he would be working directly with Jess Ballard, the company's founder and a man considered one of the deal-making geniuses on the Street. It was an unusual opportunity.

"What's he like?" Josh asked.

"He's hard to figure," Dan Elkins told him. "Pleasant one day, cold as ice the next. He likes to provoke. Find a person's soft spot and dig in. Be careful. He'll make his mind up about you very fast."

Josh turned away from the window and waited impatiently for Ballard's call. It was almost eight when Ballard's raspy voice crackled over the intercom. "Sorry it's so late. Come on in, will ya?"

Ballard was on the phone, seated behind an antique rosewood desk, scribbling notes on a pad of yellow paper. He was about fifty, built close to the ground like a fireplug, a large head on narrow shoulders, his dark hair combed straight back above a deeply furrowed brow. He had soft pudgy hands and steel-gray eyes that stayed cold even when he smiled. Through the window behind him, Josh could see New York Harbor and the last pale colors of the sunset fading behind the refineries on the Jersey shore.

Ballard waved him to a seat. The call was winding up and Ballard's voice rose in irritation, revealing the dregs of an Australian accent. "What's he gonna do? The bank gonna bail him out? Anyway, that's as far as I want to go right now." He hung up abruptly and with barely a glance in Josh's direction, limped across a pale green oriental carpet to a bar built into a bookcase on the far side of the room. Josh had heard stories about the limp. Ballard had lost his leg in Vietnam. A shark had taken it off at the knee. He had lost it to cancer. No one knew for sure. There was a lot about Ballard that remained a mystery. He had turned up in New York twenty-five years ago, flat broke, with an Australian passport, and within ten years had established himself as one of the most successful deal-makers in the city.

"Drink?" Ballard asked.

"No thanks."

"Something to do with your holiday, right?"

"No. I just don't feel like a drink right now."

A tiny smile crept across Ballard's face. He dropped some ice in a tall glass, filled it half way up with scotch, took a long swallow and limped back to his desk. Elkins had warned that Ballard's style was confrontational. His abruptness made Josh uneasy.

"That was Peter Freling on the phone. He says he tried to hire you."

"That's right."

"Why didn't you go to work for him?"

"I wouldn't have done well there. He's got a reputation as a one-man show." Peter Freling ran a venture capital fund in Cleveland. He had wanted Josh to come to work for him after he graduated from business school but Josh heard that he courted bright young graduates, promised them roles in the decision-making process, and then generally disregarded their recommendations.

Ballard propped up his game leg on an open desk drawer and stared out at the rapidly darkening sky and the twinkling lights of cargo ships churning their way out of the harbor. "What do you know about Fabrico?"

"They went public a few years ago. Their stock was way up for a while. It's in the tank now. Sam Broad runs it. Other than that, I don't know too much."

"Peter and I are going after the company."

"Do they want to sell?"

Ballard seemed annoyed by the question and scratched at his game leg through his pants. "What's the difference? We want to buy it. Peter says you know your way around Cleveland. He says your old man and Sam Broad are buddies."

"They've been friends for a long time."

"You get along with your old man?"

"Probably about as well you get along with yours."

Ballard laughed. "My old man's back in Australia so we get along just fine."

Josh shifted uncomfortably in his chair. He felt Ballard was playing with him. "What is it you want me to do?"

"Help Peter and me with the takeover. Get your dad to give us a hand with Sam Broad."

Ballard waited for Josh's response, sipping his scotch and watching him with cold, searching eyes.

"That won't be easy."

"If you think it's going to be too complicated I'll put someone else on it."

"I didn't say it was too complicated. It's just going to be difficult. My father and Sam Broad are close, but I have no idea how he'll react when I tell him what we're doing."

"You're not gonna tell him," Ballard voice took on an unexpectedly hard edge. "You're gonna keep it quiet until we've got our five percent." Josh understood that he would be expected to keep his father in the dark until they had acquired the maximum number of shares the law allowed, after which they would have to file reports with the SEC. "You handle your old man right, he could be very helpful."

Ballard's notion that Josh could "handle his old man" was laughable. They barely talked. He was thirty-one and ever since he could remember, talking with his father had been difficult. He'd call tonight to wish him a happy New Year and that would probably be a substantial part of the conversation they would have for the next twelve months.

"I can't give you any guarantees."

"I'm not asking for any goddam guarantees." Ballard stood up, bringing the meeting to a close. "You're smart. You'll figger something out." The phone rang and he picked it up, cupping his hand over the mouthpiece. "My secretary's made a reservation for you on a flight tomorrow." He shoved a thick folder across the desk. "This'll get you started. You got any questions, check back with me."

A blast of hot air caught Josh as he stepped out onto the sidewalk. It was after nine and the heat of the day was still trapped between the office towers that lined the narrow downtown street. A few cabs trawled for passengers. The limo that Ballard had ordered was waiting for him at the curb. Josh settled down in the back seat and let the cool air revive him. As the car sped up the East River Drive he snapped on a small overhead light, opened the folder Ballard had given him and started reading. Fabrico had expanded rapidly, first in Europe and more recently in Asia, and the recession had caught the company at a vulnerable time. They had borrowed heavily to finance their growth and their lines of credit were coming due. Store profitability was down forty percent. Competition was growing. Management was getting old. There were a dozen reasons why the company was in play. Someone was sure to try to take it over. If it wasn't Parallax it would be someone else.

He knew he had made an impression on Ballard but he would have to be careful. He had hesitated when he was offered the chance to work on the Fabrico deal and Ballard had sensed his indecision. A "no" would have ended his new career before it even started. He wasn't sure how he would handle holding back information from his father. That part troubled him. He'd find a way to make it up to his father. When the time came he'd tell him everything. The important thing for now was to show Ballard what he could do. In the end that was what really mattered.

CHAPTER THREE

Mark Winnick swerved to pass a car on the narrow road that hugged the shore of a small lake surrounded by expensive homes. Susan was pregnant and had been filling the time with endless chatter about what they would do when the baby came and the nice things people had said to her about Mark's sermon that morning. Mark barely listened. Eli's announcement had changed everything. When the board offered him a three-year contract rather than the five years he expected, he understood that his future with the congregation was limited. He had sent a letter to the placement office at Hebrew Union College, inquiring about available jobs. Now he wondered if that had been a mistake. With Eli dying, the board would be looking for someone to replace him. If he played his cards right, next year's New Year's reception might be at a different place. It could be Susan standing at their own front door greeting people. They'd have to move to a larger house than the one they lived in now, but on a senior rabbi's salary . . .

Susan interrupted his reverie.

"Did Rabbi Stone tell you he was ill?"

"No. I was as surprised as anyone."

"You'd think he would have told you."

"Well, he didn't."

It bothered Susan that Mark had never developed a close relationship with Eli. She and Rachel had become friends but Mark and Eli never hit it off. Mark didn't need close friends the way she did. He didn't confide in people easily. There were times when he shut her out completely.

"Do you think he'll retire soon?"

"I don't know."

"How will they go about picking a replacement?"

"The board makes that decision."

"Do you think you have a chance?"

"I don't know." God, how he wished Susan would shut up. She didn't understand the way things worked. No one ever handed you anything on a silver platter.

They were approaching Eli's home, set back from the street behind a wide green lawn and surrounded by flowering bushes and beds of autumn flowers. Both sides of the street were lined with cars. Two off-duty cops were trying to keep the traffic moving. Mark spotted an empty space next to a fire hydrant.

"You can't park there," Susan said.

Mark rolled down the window and chatted briefly with one of the policemen. "Sure, Rabbi. Leave it. We'll keep an eye on it for you."

They started up the walk. The steps were difficult for Susan. Mark put his arm around her. "I don't mean to be cross with you, honey. It's just that with everything that's happening right now I need time to figure out what's best for us."

*   *   *

Buddy Kaplan bustled out of the kitchen, slipping his portly frame through the already crowded dining room and edging inconspicuously toward the front door, hoping that Rachel wouldn't notice. He had catered Rachel's Rosh Hashanah reception for years and they had reached an understanding. He could mingle with her guests but she didn't want him standing at the front door greeting them as they came in, or thanking them for coming as they left.

Guests streamed in, passing through the two-story red brick Georgian house to a backyard where bowls of lemon punch and trays filled with cookies and tiny finger sandwiches were set out on long tables in the shade of a pair of towering maple trees. Before the afternoon was over, more than a thousand congregants would come by and each of them would have a chance to share a moment of intimacy with their famous rabbi.

Buddy had just reached the front entrance when the kitchen door swung open and Rachel came out and spotted him shaking hands with Mark and Susan.

"I was just getting a breath of fresh air, darling. How was I supposed to know Rabbi Mark and his wife would be walking in?"

"I don't think we have enough cookies for everybody, Buddy. Maybe you should go back in the kitchen and check."

"We have plenty of cookies, sweetheart."

In all the years that Buddy had been catering Rachel's New Year's receptions they had never run out of food, but this afternoon everything was making her nervous. She wondered how Eli was holding up in the brutal heat of the synagogue. A silver Mercedes pulled up in front of the house. Linda Freling got out and hurried up the walk without waiting for Peter, who was in the driver's seat with a cell phone glued to his ear.

"Peter has a new girlfriend," Buddy whispered to Rachel.

"Where in the world did you hear that?"

"I didn't hear it. I saw it with my own eyes. She was at a party I catered a couple of nights ago. A ski instructor in Aspen. Great Nordic complexion. Legs to die for. She came with someone else but she was there for Peter. Anyone with half a brain could see it. He couldn't take his eyes off her."

"You shouldn't go around saying things like that unless you know they're true."

"Take my word for it, darling, it's true. I had a little chat with her before dinner. She's not the world's greatest conversationalist, and when I mentioned Peter's name she turned beet red. Of course if you'd rather not hear these things, I'll go double-check on the cookies you're so worried about." Buddy faked a sour look and headed for the kitchen.

Linda greeted Rachel with a hug. "We're still in shock. It was all so unexpected. How is Rabbi Stone holding up? How are you holding up?" Her words tumbled out in a torrent of manufactured concern. "And this big party on top of everything!"

"I'm doing okay," Rachel answered. She knew that Linda was a constant source of irritation to her husband, but in the minuet that was the life of a rabbi's wife, she managed a warm smile.

Peter caught up with them and gave Rachel a hug. "Is the rabbi home yet?"

"No, but he should be any minute."

"He'll get through this. I know he will. He's indestructible."

Linda and Peter disappeared inside. Other people were coming up the walk and Rachel braced herself for the same conversation all over again.

As soon as Linda entered the house, she pulled away from Peter and headed for Eli's study. She needed a moment by herself. Peter was cheating on her again. His affairs were becoming more frequent and the girls were getting younger all the time. There had been an argument in the car on the way over.

"A ski instructor for chrissake! How old is she? Fifteen?"

"How do I know how old she is? She was with Will Jarvis that weekend. Why are you always accusing me of things?"

It had been that way with Peter since the beginning. She had met him in New York when she was a student at Barnard and he was working for one of the big New York investment banking firms. Her father had taken her to dinner with some of his business associates and Peter had been there. He reminded her of her father, rough-edged and self-confident. Within a month they were engaged and they married right after she graduated. They had gone to Italy on their honeymoon. While they were in Rome she noticed him staring at a young girl in the lobby of the hotel. That night, after they had gone to bed, he said he couldn't sleep and needed to walk around. When he came back two hours later, she asked him where he had gone. "I walked all the way to the Tiber. There was a full moon. You should have come with me." When he slipped into bed next to her she was sure she could smell perfume on his body.

When they got back from their honeymoon, her father suggested to Peter that he join him in the scrap steel business. They moved to Cleveland. Her father died two years later and within a year Peter sold the business and started buying distressed companies, fixing them up and selling them. Ten years later he was one of the city's richest men.

She entered the study and stood quietly for a moment, staring vacantly at the rows of weathered volumes that lined the shelves. A voice startled her. "You okay?" Bill Palevsky was standing in the doorway. He had been her high-school sweetheart, the first person she had ever slept with. She had gone east to college and he had gone to Ohio State and then on to law school.

"Just a headache. What's happening to Eli has got me down. I was thinking this might be our last New Year's Day reception here."

"Same here. When I was a kid I used to think he was God or Moses or something. He always seemed so indestructible."

There was that word again. Linda wondered why it was that when men achieved a certain position in life nothing seemed to touch them. They did what they wanted, surrounded by admirers, indifferent to criticism, insulated from the consequences of their actions. Her father had been that way. So was Peter. So was Rabbi Stone.

"Where's Kathy?"

"She's home with the kids. They've both got colds. You sure you're okay? Can I get you something?"

Linda stared at Bill. She was foolish to let herself be humiliated. If Peter wanted to fuck some underage ski instructor, let him. Bill was plenty good looking and he still had all his hair.

"I just bought a new filly," she said. "You ought to see her. Why don't you come out to the house one of these days and we'll go riding. Bring Kathy along."

"I wish Kathy shared my interest in horses," Bill sighed. "She thinks the whole thing is a big waste of time."

"Well, if she doesn't want to come, you come on out anyway. The trails are beautiful this time of year." Linda linked her arm through his. "C'mon, it's dreary in here. Let's go outside and get some air."

CHAPTER FOUR

Pamela Dawes stared out from under the wide brim of one of her trademark hats, her narrow eyes scanning the crowd. She had spent the last two weeks at her sister's place in St. Barts getting a tan and losing, she hoped, any telltale signs of the plastic surgeon's latest efforts to peel away the years. She was sixty-four and the host of *Five by Five,* a fast-paced local TV talk and gossip show that came on five nights a week, just before the local evening news. The show had been running on Channel 2 for more than thirty years, but her ratings were off and there were rumors that some young woman reporter from the station's Detroit affiliate was being groomed to replace her.

She checked her watch. She could only stay a few more minutes before it would be time to go down to the station to prepare for her broadcast. She planned to lead off with a brief reference to Eli's illness. With the city in the grip of baseball fever, she'd find a tasteful way to link his illness with the memory of Lou Gehrig. It would strike a sympathetic note with her viewers. Two weeks in St. Barts had revived her spirits. All she needed were a few good stories to get her ratings back up and that bitch from Detroit would never get her job.

She noticed Buddy Kaplan standing in the doorway to the backyard, looking peeved, and made a beeline for him. "Buddy, sweetheart," she purred. "What have you been up to?"

"Nothing, darling. Absolutely nothing. I took a week off and went to Mustique. Had to get away for a while to collect myself before the holiday season started. And what about you? Running off without telling anyone. You look terrific by the way. Who does your work? He's an absolute genius."

Pamela and Buddy had been friends for years. He shared gossip with her in return for an occasional plug on her show. "Do me a favor, Buddy. I'm planning a piece on Peter Freling. Mostly about his new house and all the architects he's worn out getting it built. Of course I'd love to be able to say something about all his extracurricular activities. Tactfully, of course. Know anything about the new snow bunny he's pulled out of the hat?"

Buddy had just nailed down a lunch that Linda was planning to celebrate the bat mitzvah of their younger daughter. There would be two hundred guests at $250 a head and he wasn't about to take a risk with that kind of business. "I wouldn't touch that one with a ten-foot pole if I were you, Pamela. Listen, I've got to run. Rachel's got me on a treadmill. She's worse than my Pilates trainer. You'd think after all this time she'd have some confidence in what I do."

Buddy hurried off and Pamela checked her watch again. Out of the corner of her eye she noticed Bobby Greenhut walking in with a pretty dark-haired girl in tow and hurried over.

"Hi, Bobby."

"Hey, Miss D. How you doing?"

"I'm doing fine, Bobby. You want to introduce me?"

"Sure. Pamela, this is Liz Aurelio. Liz, meet Pamela Dawes."

Liz was overwhelmed. Except for Bobby she had never met a celebrity. "I'm a real big fan of yours, Miss Dawes? I watch your show every chance I get?" Her voice drifted up into a question mark at the end of almost every sentence.

"That's so nice, dear. What do you do?"

"I'm a waitress at the Stadium Bar and Grille? Right across from Gate E? We all watch your show. Maybe you'll come down some time? It would be a real thrill for everybody."

Pamela found Liz charming. "Perhaps I will, dear. Where are you from?"

"I grew up near Canton but I moved here a couple of months ago. My apartment's right across the street from the synagogue? I can see the dome from my bedroom window." She giggled and squeezed Bobby's hand. He had come over after services and they had made love and then she told him he had to take her somewhere soon or they were through. She was sure that he would get mad but he had surprised her and brought her to Rabbi Stone's for the New Year's Day reception. That's what she liked about Bobby. He was full of surprises and he made her feel special. She couldn't wait to tell her girlfriends all about it and watch their teeth fall out.

"I want you on my program, Bobby," Pamela purred. "You promised."

"When the season's over, Miss D. Right now I gotta concentrate on business. We got a big series coming up." Bobby was eager to get away before Pamela started pumping him. There were major disagreements about next year's contract and the last thing he needed was to have them aired out in public on her show. He noticed Renee Lassiter standing alone in a corner. Renee was thirty-five, tall, with short brown hair, an intelligent face and a full ripe body. She taught medieval history at the university and had been part of a small group that had invited him to lunch before proposing him for election to the board of the synagogue. Bobby hadn't met many women like Renee before. Most of the women he knew were cocktail waitresses or worked behind a hotel desk somewhere and he could read them like a book. Renee was different. She kept her thoughts to herself and her emotions under control. Bobby fantasized what might happen once he cracked through her reserve.

"Hey, Renee. How you doing?"

"Fine, Bobby. How about you?"

"I'm doing great. How come I never see you down at the ballpark? All you gotta do is let me know and I'll have them put a ticket away for you."

"That's such a nice invitation, but my classes always seem to get in the way."

"Skip them," Bobby said with a charming smile. Renee wasn't sure if Bobby understood that she taught her classes and didn't attend them. "We got a real big series coming up with the Red Sox next week and I'd be honored if you'd be my guest."

Bobby put his hand on her shoulder and Renee felt a shiver run through her body. She knew that athletes touched people a lot and that it probably didn't mean much, but still.

"Listen, Renee, I gotta go. The team's flying to Detroit tonight and if I don't get to the airport on time, they stick me with a real big fine. You change your mind, let me know and there'll be a ticket for you at the gate."

*   *   *

Rachel watched Eli's car turn up the driveway. She felt a surge of deep affection every time she saw him. She had been twenty-one, living at home with her parents and working as a teaching assistant in the Providence public school system. One of her friends had mentioned this new young rabbi who had just arrived in Boston and was setting the place on fire. She had taken the bus to Boston and a cab to the synagogue, where she sat in the middle of the fourth row. Eli was rail-thin then, tall and handsome. His sermon held her spellbound. When services were over she came forward to shake his hand. She said that she had come all the way from Providence to hear him. She thought he held her hand a bit longer than was absolutely necessary.

He called a few days later to say that he would like to see her that weekend, but her aunt was ill and she was going to New York to visit her. She was afraid it sounded like a brush-off, but a few weeks later he called again. He picked her up at the train station. She was wearing the same dress she had worn the first time they met. Their hands touched and suddenly he leaned down and kissed her. They went to a baseball game at Fenway Park and had dinner at a restaurant in Chinatown and then spent the night in a small out-of-the-way hotel. She woke up during the night and stared at him and wondered what it would be like to spend the rest of her life with him.

Eli climbed the front steps and put his arms around her. She could feel the dampness of his body through his shirt. "You're soaked clear through."

"I'll shower and be right down."

"How'd things go?"

"Everything went fine."

Mark's sermon that morning had been mercifully brief. Afternoon children's services had gone well. Eli adored talking to the children. He loved telling them Bible stories and watching them squirm in their seats and pick their noses and drive their parents crazy. Now there was just the reception to get through and then he could rest.

"Josh got here an hour ago," Rachel said.

Eli acknowledged the fact with a brief nod. He had been asleep when Josh called the night before. Rachel had picked up the phone.

"Happy New Year," Josh had said.

"You too, darling."

"I'll be in Cleveland for a few days. I've got some work to do there."

"You'll stay with us. Dad will be so pleased," Rachel told him.

"Can I talk to him?"

"He's sleeping."

"How is he?"

Rachel paused, unsure how to continue. "He hasn't been feeling well lately."

"What's the matter?"

"He went in for a physical a couple of weeks ago."

"Is he okay?"

"He was diagnosed with ALS." She could hear Josh catch his breath.

"Why didn't you call me?"

She had wanted to call as soon as the diagnosis was certain, but Eli had insisted that she wait. She wasn't sure why, but it was pointless arguing with him. For the past dozen years, ever since Josh had gone away to college, she had watched their relationship unravel. They were like two cars idling next to one another at a light, their motors sputtering, waiting to speed away from each other as soon as the light changed.

Eli stepped out of the shower. He glanced at his body in the mirror. He was still in good shape for a man his age. When the holidays were over he would visit his doctors again and they would check him out and discover that they had made a mistake. It was exhaustion or old age or something else. He opened a dresser drawer and pulled out a fresh shirt. His fingers fumbled with the buttons. He kept trying. It was a simple act that he had performed a thousand times. He managed to get the shirt open, then slipped it on and struggled to button it up. There was no mistake. One day soon, the simple act of getting dressed would be more than he could handle.

When he turned around, Josh was standing in the doorway. They embraced awkwardly, their bodies barely touching.

"How are you, Dad?"

"I'm okay."

"Mom told me." Josh wasn't sure what else to say. His father's health had always been a private matter. They had taken a family trip to Europe when he was twelve. Eli had fallen ill on a train from Rome to Venice, slumping over suddenly, his face drained of color, his breath coming in gasps. By the time they reached Venice he had recovered. When Josh asked him what had happened, his father wouldn't talk about it. When he asked his mother, she said she didn't know. Twenty years later he still had no idea what had gone wrong.

Eli looped a tie around his upturned collar. The tie was bright red with tiny dragons embroidered on its surface.

"Sam Broad gave me this tie. He'll be here later, so I better wear it."

"Need a hand?"

"I'll manage," Eli said. "What brings you home?"

"My firm gave me some work to do." Josh doubted that his father would press him for details. He seldom asked him questions about his work. He wasn't sure his father even knew that he had changed jobs.

"How long will you be staying?"

"A few days. Maybe a little longer. It's hard to tell," Josh said.

"Any chance you're free around noon tomorrow?"

"I think so."

"Good. We'll have lunch together."

They barely exchanged two dozen words, seldom looking directly at one another, the mirror arbitrating their conversation. Eli slipped on his jacket and headed for the door. Josh watched as his father started down the stairs holding onto the banister for support. A dozen members of the congregation were waiting for him at the bottom landing. Their affection revived Eli, funneling fresh energy into his tired body.

*   *   *

Brian Patzer ambled over to Josh, who was standing under one of the maple trees, sipping a glass of punch. They had been friends since childhood and had gone to Princeton together. Brian had eased through, cribbing answers to exam questions from whoever happened to be sitting next to him. At night he ran a poker game in his dorm room. He was bald, significantly overweight, talkative, and extremely likable. His decision to become a stockbroker had been the perfect career choice.

They watched a group of men gather around Peter Freling. "I used to invest for that guy when he wasn't God yet," Brian said. "I'd give my left nut to know what's going on inside that brain of his. He's up to something. You gonna be around for a while?"

"A few days, I guess."

"Let's get a round of golf in while you're here. The course is in great shape." Brian spotted someone he wanted to talk to, popped a deviled egg in his mouth and ambled off.

The men around Peter drifted away and for a moment he was alone. Josh thought how powerful men never mingled. They held court. People were drawn to them the way barnacles attached themselves to whales, looking for a free ride to wherever the whale was going. The last time he had talked to Peter was six years ago when he had been interviewed for a job.

"I need someone like you," Peter told him. "You'll be my assistant. If you're anything like your old man you'll be a winner." Josh had waited a week before he turned him down.

Peter noticed him and waved him over. "How you doing?" he asked in the casual way that people inquire about something when they have no real interest in the answer. "Jess Ballard bring you up to speed?"

"I read the file. I've got a lot of questions."

"It's way too crowded to talk here. Come by the house tomorrow around eight and we'll have breakfast."

* * *

"Get a glass of punch for me, will you?" Linda cooed. "My head's still killing me."

Bill Palevsky left her side and headed for one of the refreshment tables while Linda stayed in the shade and stared at Eli, standing in the doorway to the backyard. She had idolized Eli when she was growing up. He had confirmed her and officiated at her wedding. When she was elected president of the congregation she was sure she had finally found a place where her talents would be appreciated. But Eli had ignored her. She thought about how casually he had dismissed her when she came in to talk about Mark's contract. Her father had been the same way, pretending to be interested in her but not really caring. As a child she had listened to stories about how he started in business with nothing and how he had become successful, and she decided that when she grew up she wanted to be just like him. She adored her father and was convinced that he would help her.

The revelation came in a conversation just before she left for college. She asked him if he would teach her the business when she graduated. "The scrap business?" he answered, laughing. "Forget it, honey. They'd eat you up alive."

Later, after they were married, her father trained Peter to run the business without a thought as to how she felt. Eli was the same. He had no interest in her ideas. If he had his way, he would make sure that the board would pick someone just like him to take over when he retired and nothing would change.

She noticed Mark Winnick across the yard, watching Eli. He had the look of a child staring in the window of a candy store. How transparent his envy was. How grateful he would be if someone could satisfy his craving. She contemplated the exciting possibilities. Why shouldn't he be Eli's replacement? If she made it possible for him to become the senior rabbi, he would be indebted to her and she would be able to run things at the synagogue the way she wanted. He wasn't the ideal candidate. Someone with more class would be better, but the congregation was used to him. The board would be reluctant at first but she would convince them. One by one she would find a way to win them over. Eli would object, but he wasn't the one who would be making the final decision. That was the board's responsibility and she would bring them around. She was tired of standing on the sidelines. It was time to suit up and get in the game.

Bill Palevsky tapped her on the shoulder and handed her a glass of lemon punch. She took a long refreshing sip.

"Feeling better?" Bill asked.

"Much better," Linda answered. The splitting headache that had been bothering her all afternoon had suddenly disappeared.

CHAPTER FIVE

Josh slowed down as his car approached the ivy-covered columns that marked the entrance to Milles Fleurs. It was a brilliantly clear, cool morning. The heat wave stifling the city had broken the night before and the air was filled with the acrid smell of burning leaves.

A long gravel driveway wound a quarter of a mile through stands of towering beech trees, then rose gradually toward a sprawling modern glass and steel house that hugged the brow of a low hill. Surrounding the house, which had taken more than three years and $20 million to build, were a tennis court, a swimming pool, a glass-enclosed gym, a stable, and a small riding ring.

A uniformed maid led him across a marble foyer into a sun-drenched breakfast room. Peter Freling, just in from his morning run, was pulling off his T-shirt and toweling the perspiration from his lean body and the top of his balding head. He had the haggard look of someone for whom staying in shape had become an obsession. He motioned Josh to a table near the windows, dropped into a chair and poured himself a glass of water, drinking it down in a series of rapid gulps.

"You run?"

"I used to, but it's hard to find the time in New York."

"I run every day of my life. Wouldn't miss it. If I can't run, I work out in my gym. How old do you think I am?"

"I have no idea."

"Take a guess."

Josh thought fifty, maybe fifty-one or two, but he decided to give Peter the benefit of the doubt. "Forty-eight?"

Peter masked his disappointment with a brittle laugh. "Don't bullshit me, I'll be forty-five in December. How's your dad getting along?"

"He's doing okay."

"I love your dad. We all do. He's had a hell of a bad break."

The maid returned with a platter of fruit and a plate of dry toast. Peter speared a piece of grapefruit, jammed it into his mouth and wiped the juice that dribbled down his chin with the back of his hand.

"What do you know about Brian Patzer?" Peter asked.

"He works for Petrie and Company. He manages their Cleveland office. We grew up together."

"He's been poking around asking questions. With you in town he may start getting ideas. Petrie's short two million shares of Fabrico. They think the company's going to tank. If Brian finds out what we're doing, they'll cover their position and the stock price will go through the roof. There's no way we're gonna let that happen."

Josh could hear voices coming down the stairs. Linda entered with Stacey, their eighteen-year-old daughter, in tow.

"Hello, Josh," Linda said. "You remember Stacey, don't you?"

"Sure I do." He hadn't seen Stacey since she was a gangly twelve-year- old. Now she was tall and willowy with long blonde hair tumbling around her narrow shoulders. "The last time I saw you . . ."

"Yeah, I know," Stacey interrupted, a smile playing around the corners of her mouth. "I was twelve years old and I was wearing braces. Guess what? My braces came off four years ago." Josh had the feeling other restraints had come off as well.

"Stacey and I are going shopping." Linda barely glanced at Peter. "She needs some clothes for college. We'll be back around four. Will you be home for dinner?"

"I have a couple of meetings that might go on a while."

"Well, at least take the time to call the cook and let her know one way or the other. Jessica's still sleeping. She has to get down to the synagogue by four. Rabbi Mark is helping her prepare for her bat mitzvah. I don't suppose you could take her for a change."

Josh observed the acid interchange, wondering if they always communicated this way, exchanging schedules as a substitute for conversation.

"Your dad looked so tired at services," Linda continued without waiting for Peter to respond. "I hope he's doing everything the doctors tell him. He's taken care of the rest of us for so long, it's time he took care of himself. How about having dinner with us while you're here? Stacey's going to Columbia in a couple of weeks. She's probably got a million questions about New York."

Stacey smiled and shrugged.

"You will come, won't you?" Linda asked.

"Sure. I'd like that very much."

"I'll have Stacey call you. And tell your mother, if there's anything she needs . . ."

Linda and Stacey headed for the door. Peter seemed visibly relieved. The maid brought a pot of coffee and they spent the next hour discussing Fabrico. The stock was selling at four and a half. The tender offer would be priced between $6 and $7. They had already started buying shares quietly in the open market. They intended to pick up four million shares, which would take them to the five percent they were permitted to accumulate before they had to file reports with the SEC. They needed to be able to buy these shares without disturbing the price too much and it all depended on no one getting wind of what they were planning.

"Get together with Patzer," Peter said. "I don't want him fucking up our deal. Find out what he knows. What he makes. How much he owes. How much money he's got in the bank." Peter poured himself a second cup of coffee. "Ballard treating you okay?"

"I don't have any complaints."

"You should have come to work for me."

"I wanted to try New York for a while."

The explanation seemed to satisfy Peter. He leaned back in his chair and stared out toward the pond, where a flight of ducks was coming in for a landing. Josh prepared himself. Every successful man he had ever met had a story to tell and Peter was no exception. Always the same story. Dissatisfaction with the way other people did things. A willingness to gamble everything. If there was a car crash they were always the ones who walked away. And they were all intensively competitive. They needed to win to feel alive. Josh recalled a conversation with a man he knew who had made a killing in the market. They were sharing a cab after a dinner party given by a Wall Street banker and Josh had casually inquired if the man had had a good time. "You wanna know the truth?" the man replied. "I had a shitty time. Everyone there was richer than I was."

Peter reached absentmindedly for a piece of toast, gnawed at it, and put it down. "Linda's dad was worried about what would happen when he died. He had a partner who had a couple of sons. One was in Spain studying flamenco dance and the other one was building a biplane. You can imagine the kind of contribution they would have made to the business. My firm assigned me the job of structuring a deal for him to buy his partner out. When the deal closed, he took me to dinner. That's where I met Linda. She came along. She was still in college. Smart as hell. She could have taken over the business but her old man didn't think that way. We got married and moved back here . . ." Peter paused and glanced at his watch. "Shit, I'm due downtown in half an hour." He bolted from his chair. "Get together with Patzer as soon as you can. Let me know what you find out."

*   *   *

As Josh drove out through the gates of Milles Fleurs he put in a call to Ballard. "I just left Peter."

"How'd it go?"

"He's worried about a guy I know who works for Petrie. He thinks he may get wind of what we're doing. And there's something else I ought to tell you. My father's ill. He has ALS."

"Jesus, that's terrible news. I'm really sorry, pal. Look, if you don't want to keep on with what you're doing, just say so. Come on back. We'll find something else for you to do. I won't hold it against you."

"I'd like to stay on if it's okay with you."

"You sure?"

"Yes, I'm sure."

"Good for you, mate. But if you change your mind, just let me know."

* * *

The Accessions Committee of the Cleveland Art Museum met the second Tuesday of every month in the directors' lounge on the top floor of the museum. Medieval tapestries draped the walls. An antique oriental carpet covered the parquet floor. At one end of the room, two delicate translucent alabaster vases, each about ten inches high, were perched on twin pedestals and illuminated by pin spots from above. A screen had been set up on which a map of Turkey was projected.

Walter Bessemer, the museum's sixty-year-old curator of Near Eastern art, held an unlit cigar between the thumb and two fingers of his right hand and brushed imaginary ashes off his vest. "Sorry to be rushing this morning," he began in a heavy German accent, "but we have a great deal to cover." He stabbed at the map with his cigar. "This is where vase A was discovered last May, not so far from the library at Ephesus. Vase B, which is not so important, was found in almost the same place two years ago. Both date from the first century B.C. and show the influence of early Hellenistic design. Both are intact . . . a minor miracle. A dealer in Ankara from whom we have already acquired a number of objects has offered them to the museum."

Peter Freling shifted uncomfortably in his chair, glancing around at the other members of the committee, all of whom were paying close attention. It never ceased to amaze him how non-Jews could tolerate boredom without complaint, the way Eskimos weathered the cold. He checked his watch. He had an appointment downtown in two hours with the president of the Central Bank and Trust Company, where he was on the bank's advisory committee. There were problems with a loan the bank had made to Fabrico and he was eager to learn the details.

He stared at Antonia Petschek's ass as she walked over to one of the wide windows that overlooked the museum gardens and adjusted a venetian blind through which a tiny shaft of light cast shadows across the screen. Antonia was the museum's new assistant director. Peter had interviewed her when she had applied for the position. She was thirty years old, with gray-green eyes set in a wide, attractive face. She had grown up in Prague, studied art history at Oxford and apprenticed to the director of the Philadelphia Museum of Art. She was fluent in a half-dozen languages.

Peter visualized himself in bed with her, her shapely legs locked around him. His affair with the ski instructor was over. She had gone back to Colorado, where it was already snowing. He preferred more mature relationships anyway. Older women were more discreet. Affairs with them lasted longer and when they ended it was more like air leaking slowly out of a tire than a blowout at high speed.

Walter droned on. "Both vases have been properly authenticated and approved for export by the Turkish government. They cost $400,000 each and are being offered to us as a pair."

Antonia interrupted. "I just want to say how sorry the director is that he couldn't be here today. He's in London, but he wanted me to let you know that the acquisition of these wonderful vases will not require the use of any of the museum's acquisition funds. Our fellow board member, Max Jessel, has agreed to purchase them. They will be placed on permanent exhibit at the end of the month and Max has made arrangements for us to receive them as a bequest from his estate."

"What do I know about vases?" Max acknowledged the congratulations of the other committee members with a dismissive wave of his hand. He was seventy-one with a full head of steel-gray hair and the body of a Polish peasant. He owned the city's largest construction firm, had recently purchased the baseball team for $180 million, and was an avid collector of Oceanic art. "Most of what I buy comes from up some river in New Guinea. But when my good friend Walter called and said that these vases were available and we had to act fast, I figured it's like when the team needs a center fielder who can hit and field and all of a sudden someone like Bobby Greenhut comes along. You grab first and ask questions later."

The meeting adjourned and everyone moved to an adjoining room for coffee. Peter and Max stood together talking. "I got a call from your wife this morning," Max said. "She wants the board to get together to talk about a replacement for Rabbi Stone."

"That's Linda's world," Peter responded. "I stay out of it." He was barely listening, watching Antonia work the room. The prospect of a new affair excited him. It was like buying a company. You identified the target, did your homework, and then you made your move. He hadn't figured Antonia out yet. She wouldn't be easy.

Antonia joined them. "That was a very generous thing you did, Max," she said. She turned to Peter. "I went to an auction with Max last month. He bought half the catalogue. I never saw anyone make his mind up so fast."

"I go by my gut," Max said. "You think too long about something you never do anything."

"I wish I could operate that way," Peter said. "I worry about everything. I've got a painting at my house right now that I'm not sure about."

"Why don't you have our curator come out and have a look at it?" Antonia suggested.

"Why don't you come out yourself?" Peter suggested. "I'd love you to see it. If it's any good I might be persuaded to give it to the museum."

*   *   *

Roz McIver came out from behind her desk and gave Josh a hug. She was fifty, still trim, her jet-black hair pulled back to reveal an intelligent, oval face. She had been Eli's secretary for almost thirty years. She was indispensable to him. She transcribed his scrawl, screened his calls, handled his correspondence and scheduled his appointments. No one seemed to know much about Roz's private life. She lived alone, her life centered around the synagogue. When Josh was growing up he had developed a crush on her. Once when he was thirteen he had watched her cross her legs behind her desk. The sound of her stockings rubbing on her thighs had given him a hard-on. He was sure she had noticed.

"Your dad will be with you in a minute. He's been so looking forward to this lunch." The door to Eli's study was closed and from behind it came the rising sound of male voices. Roz glanced nervously at the door. It opened a moment later and Mark Winnick hurried out, looking pale and grim. It took him a moment to acknowledge Josh. Then he reached out awkwardly and grabbed his hand.

"Hey, Josh! How are you?"

"I'm fine, Mark."

"Home for a while?"

"A couple of days."

"Let's get together before you leave." Mark rushed out into the synagogue corridor not waiting for a reply.

*   *   *

"What was going on in there?" Josh asked as he and Eli walked toward a delicatessen a few blocks away.

"We were just going over a few things," Eli responded. His eyes were fixed on the sidewalk. Each time he came to a curb he hesitated before taking the short step up or down.

"When Mark came out of your office he looked like his world had just caved in."

"It wasn't anything, really. Nothing at all."

They sat in a booth at the back of the delicatessen. An aging waiter with parchment skin that matched the fading color of the walls came over to take their order.

"You've met my son?" Eli inquired.

"Of course I've met your son. You introduce me to him every time the two of you come in here. What'll it be?"

"I'll have the boiled beef and cabbage."

"Take my advice, Rabbi. Order the roast chicken."

"Is there something wrong with the boiled beef?"

"Did I say there was anything wrong with it? It's on the menu, isn't it?"

"I'll have the roast chicken then, since you recommend it so highly."

Josh marveled at the ease with which his father bantered with ordinary people. It had been years since they had talked that way.

"Mother tells me that you have a new job," Eli said after the waiter left.

"I started at Parallax Partners a few weeks ago."

"What do they do?"

"They look for companies that need fixing up. Then they invest in them and try to make them profitable."

The questions were perfunctory. Josh doubted that his father would probe further. The lack of interest in what he did had started once he had decided not to become a rabbi. The food came and they ate in silence. Josh wasn't surprised. Most of the lunches with his father went this way. His father didn't seem to care if they talked or not. It was just the fact that they had lunch together that mattered, a way of maintaining contact without the requirement of intimacy. Maybe all his father wanted was to be able to say to people, "I had lunch with my son today."

"I'd like you to talk to Marty Franklin while you're here," Eli said as they were getting ready to leave. "I want to be sure things are set up properly for your mother. Will you do that for me?"

"Sure I will."

The bill came and they both reached for it.

"I'll take it," Eli said.

"Dad, let me pay."

Eli let him pay. The feel of his father's hand over his gave him an unexpected rush of pleasure.

*   *   *

Mark Winnick walked past a bronze bust of Eli that had been sculpted by one of the members of the synagogue. Owing to a complete lack of resemblance to its subject, it had been tucked away at the end of a long dark corridor leading to his office. The meeting with Eli had been a disaster. He had tried to be careful, inquiring as diplomatically as he could about Eli's health and his plans for the future.

Susan had insisted. "I don't care if you don't have a close relationship with him," she had said. "Talk to him. He's ill. He'll appreciate your concern."

He had asked if there were ways that he could take some of the load off Eli's shoulders. Could he take on more responsibility with the religious school? "If you need to ease off a bit, Rabbi, I'll be glad to take on extra work."

"I appreciate your concern," Eli responded, "but I'm not planning to slow down any time soon."

Mark struggled to keep the conversation going, "What I mean is, I'd be happy to do anything I can to fill in where it might be helpful."

The conversation stalled again. "I understand that you've started looking around for another pulpit," Eli said.

Mark searched frantically for an explanation. The news of his job search had leaked out and Eli would be sure to use the information to accelerate his departure. When the word got around that he was seeking another pulpit there would be no chance that the board would consider him as Eli's replacement. "I had the feeling that perhaps you weren't satisfied with my work."

"If I weren't satisfied with your work you would have heard from me directly."

"It's just that I had been hoping that the congregation would renew my contract for five years and when they didn't . . ."

"It's your decision if you want to seek another pulpit," Eli interrupted. "If you do, I'll be happy to help in any way I can."

Mark didn't want to go back to his office yet. It was a depressingly small place with a single window that looked out on an air shaft. The synagogue parlor was directly across from the hallway leading to his office. It was a large room with double doors, a high-beamed ceiling and oak-paneled walls that were decorated with photographs of the past twenty-seven presidents of the congregation. Opposite the double doors, oil portraits of the five men who had occupied the position of senior rabbi since the founding of the congregation in 1878 were prominently displayed. Eli's portrait was in the middle and slightly larger than the rest.

Mark entered the parlor, closed the double doors behind him, and dropped down into one of the comfortable chairs scattered around the room. It was clear that Rabbi Stone had no interest in him as a successor. Nothing had ever come easily to Mark. He'd grown up in an orthodox family in Queens. His mother died when he was seven and his father had gone bankrupt running a small grocery store. They moved several times after that, always to smaller apartments in less attractive neighborhoods. He worked his way through City College, planning to become a lawyer, but his grades were average and there was no chance for a scholarship. He was wary of the business world that had destroyed his father and settled on a profession that he thought would offer him security and status. He applied to Hebrew Union College and received a scholarship that covered most of the cost of his graduate education.

The conversation with Rabbi Stone had been a dismal disappointment. On the other hand, he got along well with Linda. She had helped him once, maybe she would again. Older women had always been attracted to him. Lesta had been two years ahead of him in high school. She had borrowed her father's car and they had driven out to visit her uncle on Long Island and had sex in the parking lot behind a Howard Johnson. At Hebrew Union College he had met a thirty-five-year-old waitress from Kentucky who had just divorced her husband. She lived in an Airstream trailer with a cross above her bed. He told her that he was studying to be a rabbi but she didn't care. The beginning of his senior year at HUC, he had met Susan at a Succoth Service. She was three years older and came from a prosperous Cincinnati family in the laundry business. He decided that she would make a perfect rabbi's wife. They were married three weeks after his graduation.

He was jolted out of his reverie by a knock at the door. His secretary, Millie Pelletier, entered the parlor. "I'm sorry to interrupt you, Rabbi."

"Yes, Millie. What is it?"

"Linda Freling called. She wants to know if you could join her for lunch tomorrow. I took the liberty of checking your calendar. You're free."

CHAPTER SIX

Chez Henri was tucked into the ground floor of the Bonnaire, an elegant residential hotel west of downtown, perched on a bluff overlooking the lake. Linda arrived early. She knew the hotel manager and the maître d'. They were discreet and accommodating, and her visits, occasionally for lunch but usually at night when Peter was out of town, remained a well-kept secret. The western part of the city was foreign country to most of her friends. If they knew the area at all, it was only because they drove through it on their way to the airport.

She sat alone at a table facing the lake. It was a gray day with low-lying clouds and a steady breeze that had whipped the waves into whitecaps. A solitary freighter carved its way through the choppy waters, moving slowly toward an opening in the breakwater that protected the city's inner harbor.

As she waited for Sally Minton to join her, she ran down the list of board members one by one, wondering whom she could count on for support. Bill Palevsky would be easy. She'd go riding with him and let nature take its course. Brian Patzer was a cinch. Like so many men she knew, he was needy and insecure. She'd have Peter throw some brokerage business his way and that would probably be enough. Sally Minton was her best friend. She could count on Sally. That made three votes for Mark. With her vote, four.

Antonia Petschek was a question mark. She was one of those over-educated types who slaved away in nonprofits and probably lived for invitations to the homes of the rich and famous. She'd invite Antonia to dinner and warm her up. Renee Lassiter's ties were with the city's intellectual community. Linda had clashed with her at a board meeting over something to do with adult education. She'd try to find a way to make amends. Max Jessel was independent and unpredictable and so were Pamela Dawes and Bobby G. It was hard to tell how they might vote. Marty Franklin was the attorney for the synagogue but he was also Fabrico's attorney. When he found out that Peter was planning to take over Sam's business he would never vote her way. And Sam Broad and Manny Polsky were lost causes. Manny idolized Eli, and Sam was Eli's closest friend. Neither of them would ever do anything to hurt him.

There were twelve members on the board. She could count on four votes. She needed seven to get Mark elected. There was lots of work to do.

*   *   *

The headwaiter led Sally Minton to Linda's table. "This is certainly an out-of-the-way place for lunch. Why all the cloak and dagger?"

"I wanted a quiet place where we could talk."

"And here I was hoping maybe you'd found a man for me." Sally glanced around. What a perfect place for an affair. You could have a cozy dinner in the restaurant and then check into a room upstairs and no one would know the difference. She wondered how many times Linda had used the hotel for just that purpose. "What's up?"

"I thought it was time we started thinking about a replacement for Rabbi Stone."

"You got me all the way over here to talk about that?"

"There's no harm in making plans. Eli is dying. The board has the responsibility of selecting his replacement."

"My God, Linda, we just found out he's ill. What's the rush? There'll be plenty of time to screen candidates when the time comes."

"We don't need to screen anyone. We've got a perfectly satisfactory candidate already."

"Who's that?"

"Mark Winnick."

"You're not serious!"

"I'm perfectly serious. Mark would make an excellent senior rabbi. I've asked him to join us later so we can talk about it."

Sally barely choked down a laugh. "I don't believe you. What's Mark ever done except marry and bury people? Why would we ever want him to replace Rabbi Stone?"

"Don't be such a snob. He's young and he's talented and the congregation likes him."

"So what if the congregation likes him. We're not looking for likeable. He's a nonentity for godsake!"

"He's been stifled by Rabbi Stone."

"Oh, come on, Linda. He hasn't been stifled by anyone. Anyway, Rabbi Stone has something to say about who's going to succeed him, doesn't he?"

"The board makes that decision. You and me and the rest of the board. We're the ones who decide. It's not Eli's responsibility to pick his own successor."

Sally was stunned at the intensity of Linda's response. She had never seen her so determined. "Linda, face it. It's Eli's board. They're not going to do anything he doesn't want. Especially now that he's dying. And anyway, I hear that Mark's been looking around."

"He never would have thought about leaving if we'd offered him a five-year contract," Linda countered. "Three years was Eli's idea. Eli wants to control the selection of his successor. If we leave it up to him, we'll end up with somebody just like him."

"What's wrong with that?"

"We need someone who's young and open to new ideas."

"Like what?"

"Like different music instead of all those boring old hymns that put you to sleep. Like more programs for young people. You notice how everyone coming to services is old? I mean it's like a retirement home in there. And what about interfaith counseling? Lots of synagogues offer it. We don't. Take your daughter. How old is Alex now? Twenty-two? What if she falls in love with someone who isn't Jewish?"

"She already has. Several times."

"Well, Rabbi Stone doesn't believe in intermarriage. He wouldn't marry Alex if she decided to marry someone who wasn't Jewish. You wouldn't like that, would you?"

"I'd be thrilled if she married anybody."

"I'm dead serious, Sally."

"I need a drink. Can I get a drink around here?"

"Keep an open mind, Sally. That's all I ask. Once you get to know Mark the way I do, you'll appreciate what a breath of fresh air he could be for everybody."

* * *

On his way to lunch, Mark imagined the meeting. He assumed that Linda wanted to talk about his role at the synagogue now that Eli was ill. He wasn't sure how to play his hand. He didn't want to be seen as overreaching. He would tell her that he didn't want to do anything that might disrupt the congregation or cause Eli any discomfort. Eli's retirement presented a challenge and he would be willing to share in the planning for the congregation's future whether or not he had a role in it. He would make sure she saw him as a person concerned with the welfare of the congregation and someone on whose good judgment she could depend.

The maître d' led him to Linda's table. He was surprised to see Sally Minton there. He knew she didn't particularly like him. "I asked Sally to join us," Linda said. "I hope you don't mind." Mark had hardly eaten anything for breakfast. Now he was suddenly hungry. He glanced at the menu. The steak and pommes frites looked tempting. He was about to order when Linda ordered for everyone.

"They make a wonderful tossed salad here," she said. "Asparagus with little mushrooms and capers. Why don't we all have that?" She handed her menu back to the waiter. "And bring us a bottle of white wine, will you? Something that's good and dry."

During lunch Linda did most of the talking. Casual bits of probing. Inquiries about Susan's pregnancy. Questions about how Jessica's preparation for her bat mitzvah was coming along. From time to time she glanced at Sally, hoping she would say something, but Sally remained resolutely silent, picking at her salad, a tight smile on her face. When the coffee came Linda started in.

"We were all stunned by Rabbi Stone's illness."

Mark's gaze shifted rapidly between the two women, searching for clues. "I remember mentioning to Susan that he was looking tired lately, but when I asked him how he was, he said he was feeling fine."

"What do you think the Rabbi's plans are?" Linda asked.

"My guess is he'll stay active as long as he can," Mark said.

"What about your own plans?"

"I want to be as helpful as I can."

Sally interrupted. "I understand that you've been looking around for a new position."

Mark covered the best way he could. "The last five years have been a tremendous opportunity for me, but with

Rabbi Stone ill, I thought it might be best for everyone if I looked around."

"Why best for everyone?"

"What I mean is, the board might want to consider alternatives without the burden of my contract to worry about."

"Are you planning to leave or not?" Sally demanded.

Mark was confused. He hadn't expected the third degree. Linda rescued him. "I wonder if you've given any thought to the possibility of presenting yourself as a candidate for the position of senior rabbi? There are a number of us who think you would make an excellent choice."

Mark could hardly believe it. The first small indication that he might have a chance. Forget about Sally Minton. Focus on Linda. That's where the power was. "I'm flattered that you would consider me, but Rabbi Stone hasn't mentioned anything about retiring and I'm not sure that he's that eager for me to be his successor. I wouldn't want to do anything that would make him feel uncomfortable."

Linda despised the empty posturing. What was Mark worried about? Eli was on his way out. Someone else would be taking over. Here she was trying to do Mark the biggest favor of his life and all he could talk about was how Eli might react.

"Of course," she continued, her tone hardening, "all of us want Rabbi Stone to continue on as long as he can, but it's the board that decides who the next senior rabbi is going to be." Linda's blue eyes bore in on Mark until he looked away. "I realize it may be difficult for you to contemplate the possibility right now, Rabbi, but think it over and let me know if you want to be considered." Linda motioned impatiently for the check.

* * *

"Well, you certainly gave him a hard time," Sally said as they watched Mark heading for the door.

"He deserved it, the little shit. Here I'm practically offering him the job of senior rabbi and he's playing mind games with me. And why didn't you speak up? All you did was sit there and watch him make a fool of himself."

"It looked to me like you were doing fine on your own."

"You just watch. He'll think it over and by tomorrow he'll be calling me, pleading for the job."

"I wish I understood what you see about him that's so special."

"I need you with me on this, Sally," Linda said as she paid the check. "It's important to me. Don't let me down."

* * *

Mark drove off in dismay. The confidence he had felt at the start of the lunch had given way to an avalanche of self-doubt. Linda frightened him. She was like one of those big waxy flowers that lure insects into their delicate centers and then absorb them into their digestive system. But it was Sally Minton's reaction that really bothered him. As far as Sally was concerned he was just another one of those rabbis whose names appear in small print in wedding announcements in the back pages of the Sunday paper. If her opinion was shared by others on the board, he could forget about the job. The congregation would never pick him to be their leader. A rabbi's reputation rubbed off on a congregation. Being a member of "Rabbi Stone's congregation" meant something. Who had ever heard of Rabbi Winnick? He began to think that maybe the best idea would be to move on. Start over someplace else, where the cards weren't stacked against him. It was impossible to compete with a legend.

He drove back across one of the bridges that spanned the narrow river that divided the city. The stadium loomed ahead, flags flying from a dozen masts. The Indians were only a game and a half behind the Red Sox in their race for a playoff spot in their division and Bobby G. was leading the league in batting with a .327 average with 107 RBIs and 34 home runs. There was a certain comfort in numbers. You could count on what they meant. People were different. They said one thing and meant another. He could feel the tension in his neck and shoulders ease a little. He had been a baseball fan all his life. He and his father had gone to games together. It was the only time he could recall ever seeing his father happy. But the sport he remembered as a child had changed. The important battles were no longer waged on the field but with the networks willing to pour millions into the owners' pockets. The insides of the stadiums were like giant cereal boxes, plastered with ads. Tickets cost so much that the ordinary fan had to think twice before taking his family out for an afternoon at the ballpark. The sport was manipulated by people for whom ownership was a trophy and not a public trust. Drug scandals, greedy agents demanding millions for their clients, all were all undermining the game. He had talked to Bobby G. about it.

"Baseball isn't part of the American dream anymore."

"I don't know, Rabbi. People still like to go out and watch us play. Anyway, baseball's a business like everything else. Nothing's going to change it."

Mark wasn't so sure. People cared more about baseball than they did about religion.

One day, if Eli gave him half a chance, he'd preach a sermon about what was wrong with baseball and how, if enough people demanded change, the sport could be redeemed and returned to the fans who cherished it. One sermon like that would put him on the map. But the way things were going he would probably never get a chance to deliver it.

The road back to the synagogue passed through a desolate neighborhood where blocks of aging tenements had been demolished. Only a few scattered houses remained. Here and there tiny flower gardens flourished, testimony to the resilience of the human spirit. Mark remembered reading in a self-help book somewhere that "*no* is never final . . . it's only *yes* that's final.' He wanted to believe it. He knew that anything was possible, but his instincts told him that the lunch with Linda had ended whatever chance he might have had to take over Eli's job and make his dreams come true.

CHAPTER SEVEN

Marty Franklin met Josh in the lobby of Burkett, Burden and Wilkoff. Unlike most lawyers who prided themselves on their appearance, Marty worked with his shirt sleeves rolled up, his collar open and his necktie hanging loose around his neck. He was forty-four, with a full head of curly hair that had turned prematurely white. His pants, held up by suspenders, were an inch too short and his red socks flashed like semaphores as he preceded Josh down a long hallway. He talked rapidly in short energetic bursts. "I can't tell you what a shock it was to learn your dad was ill. When I first came to town I was kind of floating around and your dad took a shine to me. He had me out to your house for dinner a couple of times. I guess you were away at school. Your mom and dad were like second parents to me. How's he getting along?"

"He doesn't talk much about his illness so it's hard to tell," Josh said. "He asked me to find out about the terms of his employment agreement. He wants to be sure that everything is in order as far as my mother is concerned."

They entered Marty's office. His desktop and the windowsill behind it were piled high with files and folders.

"I envy you working in New York. I almost went to work there myself, but old man Wilkoff got hold of me and convinced me to come to Cleveland." The whole time he was talking, Marty kept searching through the papers on his desk. He pushed a button on his intercom. "Hey, Nan, you got those papers on Rabbi Stone?"

"They're right on the windowsill where you left them."

Marty spun around and kept on looking. "I understand you're working for Jess Ballard. I represented him once. I doubt if he'd remember me. He got you working on anything special?"

The questioning seemed casual enough. Josh doubted that Marty could have any idea that Ballard and Peter Freling were planning a run at Fabrico. "Nothing yet. I just started there a few weeks ago."

Marty found what he was looking for. "I went through your dad's employment agreement. He has a lifetime contract. It was entered into a number of years ago on the occasion of his twenty-fifth anniversary with the congregation. He can retire any time he wants and his pension will continue for the balance of his lifetime at 60 percent of his current salary. When he dies, your mom gets half of that for as long as she lives. There's a significant amount of life insurance that the congregation pays for and your mom is the beneficiary. There's a medical plan that should take care of your dad's medical requirements with an overall cap of $2 million, so there's a risk that if his treatment carries on for a number of years, the benefits could be exhausted. But let's assume for the moment that's not a problem."

"There is one interesting thing, though," Marty continued. "If he retires voluntarily, everything's the way I described it. But if the board decides that he's become incapacitated and he won't retire, they can have him examined and if the doctors say he can't handle his workload any more, the board has the right not only to terminate his contract but they can also limit the amount of benefits he and your mother are entitled to receive."

"Why is that in there?"

"Because sometimes a rabbi won't retire when he should, and those provisions are in there to encourage his retirement. Negative incentives I guess you'd call them. I doubt if your dad has the slightest idea what these provisions say. Knowing him, he probably never even read the contract."

"What happens if he won't retire?"

"Well, the amount of his pension benefits and the number of years he would be entitled to receive them could be significantly reduced. Some of his perks, like an office and a secretary, could be taken away. Your mother's benefits on his death could also be reduced. The board of the synagogue can decide to waive the penalties, but the decision is up to them." Marty shoved the documents back in the folder. "I wouldn't worry about it. It's in there just in case. Your dad's a sensible man. He'll work as long as he can and he'll step down when he can't."

As soon as Josh was back in his car he checked his cell phone for messages. Ballard had called. Josh called him back.

"I was thinking about Patzer," Ballard said. "We're not sure he knows anything, are we?"

"Peter's worried. That's about it."

"Go slow with him. Let's not arouse his curiosity. What else is going on?"

"I just got out of a meeting with Marty Franklin."

Ballard exploded. "He's Fabrico's attorney, for chrissake! Why the hell did you agree to meet with him?"

"My dad asked me to talk to him. He handles his personal stuff."

"Does he know you work for me?"

"It's not exactly a secret."

"He ask you what you were doing in Cleveland?"

"I told him I was here to see my father."

"He believe you?"

"Why wouldn't he?"

The phone went dead for a moment. When Ballard came back on the line his voice was cold and vaguely threatening. "Go easy, boyo. I don't want this thing blowing up in our fucking face."

* * *

It was Antonia's turn. She had invited Renee Lassiter to lunch at the museum cafeteria. They had both joined the synagogue as a way of easing into a new community and both had been invited to serve on the synagogue board. Each expected that after a few years she would move on to New York or Boston. Someplace where a more challenging intellectual and social life was possible.

"Bobby Greenhut invited me to a ballgame." Renee said. "Can you believe it?"

"You're going, aren't you?"

"I haven't decided."

"Of course you're going. He's single and he's cute and he makes three million a year."

"What would we talk about?"

"Maybe you won't have to talk about anything," Antonia smiled wickedly. "Listen to this. Peter Freling made a pass at me. Right after the meeting of the accessions committee. I'm waiting on the coffee line and he comes up behind me and gives me a pat on my butt and whispers in my ear, 'You've got a great ass.' I mean he's so damn blatant about it and I've got to be nice to him because he gives all this money to the museum. I can't imagine how his wife puts up with him."

"She called me today," Renee said.

"Yeah, me too. She asked me what I thought about Mark Winnick."

"What did you tell her?"

"I didn't know what to tell her," Antonia answered. "I've heard him preach a couple of times. It was pretty meager stuff."

*　*　*

Leo Bookman waited anxiously for Linda Freling to arrive. She had left word that she would be at the synagogue by two and she wanted to see him. Leo was executive secretary of the congregation, in charge of the day-to-day business that kept the synagogue going. His salary was $57,000 a year, plus health benefits and a modest retirement package. He was fifty-three, unmarried, with thinning brown hair and light hazel eyes. He wore off-the-rack suits that hung loosely on his slightly stooped figure. In a crowd he was as indistinguishable as a pebble on a beach.

Leo attended all synagogue board meetings and served as recording secretary. He would arrive early, sit in a corner of the parlor, notebook in hand, and listen to the casual conversations that preceded the meetings. When board members talked about stocks, he would jot down the names of the companies they mentioned. Later, in his one-bedroom apartment near the synagogue, he would go to his computer and research the companies.

If he thought they had potential he would buy a few shares. He timed his purchases and sales with the precision of a watchmaker.

Eight years earlier, at one of the board meetings, Leo had overheard Sam Broad and Marty Franklin discuss the initial public offering of Fabrico. He cashed in everything he owned and bought 60,000 shares of Fabrico at $5 a share on margin. He sold out a year-and-a-half later at $97 and kept on trading. He had been prudent enough to avoid the worst of the recent market collapse and his portfolio, mostly in U.S. treasuries, had grown to more than $12 million. He never discussed what he owned with anyone, content in the knowledge that he was probably worth more than most of the members of the board, whose questions about synagogue finances he answered with unfailing courtesy.

Over the last few months he had watched the stock of Fabrico drop like a stone. He was convinced that the stock was unlikely to go much lower and had begun accumulating shares again. He now owned three million shares of stock at an average price of $3.80 a share. When he checked the price that morning, before leaving for work, the stock had moved up another eighth to four and a quarter. He was $370,000 richer than he had been the day before.

He rose to greet Linda as she entered his small office.

"I have a small favor to ask, Leo."

"I'll be glad to help if I can, Mrs. Freling."

"Does the synagogue keep a copy of Rabbi Stone's employment contract on file?"

"We keep copies of everything in our safe."

"Would you make a copy for me?"

It was an unusual request. The originals of all important documents were kept in a safe deposit box downtown with a backup copy in the safe in Leo's office. No one was entitled to have access to the documents without the consent of Marty Franklin, the synagogue's attorney.

"They're not supposed to go out of here without Mr. Franklin's approval."

Linda fingered a bright yellow silk scarf that was wrapped loosely around her neck. "I'm aware of that, but I need a copy now and I haven't got much time," she said. "I'll call Marty later and tell him I asked you for it. Get it for me, will you? I'm late for a meeting and I don't want to have to stand here all day arguing with you."

Leo had no desire to antagonize Linda. She was president of the congregation and could make his life miserable. He spun the dial on the massive steel safe that occupied a corner of his office. The door swung open and he removed a thick packet of documents held together by a wide rubber band.

"I'll make a copy for you right away. It won't take but a minute."

While Leo ran off a copy of Eli's contract, Linda walked down the hall to Mark Winnick's office. Millie Pelletier greeted her as she entered.

"Is the rabbi in?"

"He's in the building somewhere, Mrs. Freling. Shall I page him for you?"

"No, that's not necessary. I was just wondering if he's been able to straighten out the arrangements for Jessica's bat mitzvah?"

"I'm not sure," Millie responded. "I know he's been working on it." Another boy was scheduled to have his bar mitzvah the same morning and Linda had asked Rabbi Winnick to shift the boy's bar mitzvah to the following week.

"Well, tell him I came by and have him call me." Linda had expected Mark to get in touch with her by now and apologize for his behavior at the restaurant, but he hadn't called and she was getting anxious. She headed back to Leo's office. He handed her a copy of Eli's contract.

"You'll call Mr. Franklin and tell him, won't you?" Leo asked.

Linda took the contract without a word and left. She didn't need a fifty-thousand-dollar-a-year accountant telling her what she could and couldn't do.

As soon as she was gone, Leo went into his office and closed the door. This wasn't the first time Linda had spoken to him this way. It bothered him that he didn't have the nerve to say anything to her about the way she treated him. He hated direct confrontations, preferring to resolve personal conflicts in his mind. He sat down, closed his eyes and visualized Linda walking to her car, fishing out her keys, opening the door to her silver gray Mercedes, sliding behind the wheel and turning on the ignition. Then, in a fiery explosion that could be heard for miles, the car lifted off the asphalt and disintegrated into a thousand fragments of red-hot steel. When the dust settled, all that was left was a pile of twisted metal, a puddle of radiator fluid, and a tiny shred of fabric from her yellow scarf. They wouldn't even find her teeth.

CHAPTER EIGHT

Dr. Munroe, the head of neurology at Lakeshore Hospital, glanced over Eli's medical records, closed the thick folder and pushed his glasses high up on his forehead. He stared at Eli for a moment with the practiced gaze of someone accustomed to observing and recording the tiniest details.

"How are you feeling, Rabbi?"

"I'm feeling all right."

"Any new symptoms?"

"I've stumbled a few times. My left arm is a little weaker than the last time I was here and I'm more tired than usual."

Rachel had insisted on coming. She knew that Eli would never tell her what the doctors said and she was determined to find out exactly what lay ahead. She sat next to him, holding his hand. Medical diplomas and board certifications covered the walls. She wondered why doctors felt the need to display their qualifications. She distrusted doctors and their diplomas. She felt safer in an elevator, where the inspection certificate at least guaranteed that a safety check had been completed within the last six months.

"I'm glad you're here, Mrs. Stone. What has the rabbi told you?"

"Only that his condition may be somewhat advanced. Beyond that, I'm pretty much in the dark."

"Well, I'll try to fill you in. We don't know much about what causes ALS. What we do know is that an excess of a neurotransmitter called glutamate clogs the synapses of the motor cell nerves and prevents the transmission of neural impulses to the muscles. That's a complicated way of saying that the brain doesn't get its messages through to the muscles the way it should, hence stiffness, muscle twitching, shaking, weakness, and a whole range of related symptoms."

"Which get worse with time?"

"Unfortunately, yes." Dr. Munroe turned to Eli. "Have you noticed any problems with your breathing?"

Eli was only half listening. "What?"

"Have you been having any problems breathing or with your speech?"

"Not yet."

A nurse entered the room and handed the doctor a slip of paper. A phone rang and was left unanswered. Doctor Munroe kept on talking. Eli felt as though he was hearing everything through a thick blanket of fog . . . "mental acuity intact . . . bowel and bladder control . . . sexual functions unaffected . . . heart will be fine . . . David Niven had it . . . Catfish Hunter . . . Stephen Hawking has been living with it for more than 40 years." His thoughts drifted back to his years in rabbinical school. He studied all the time. He had practically no social life. He made few close friends. After he graduated, he had been offered a pulpit in a small community near Boston. Eligible young women were paraded past him.

Ruth, who intended to become an important poet and had already had a poem on Chanukah published in the *Boston Globe*. Leila, who had just returned from a year in India with a silver ring in her nose. Penny, who preferred the company of women and was only going out with him to keep her parents off her back. When Rachel came along he had fallen in love with her at first sight.

"Pain?"

"What?"

"Have you been experiencing any pain, Rabbi?"

"The muscles in my legs keep cramping up."

"That's to be expected."

"ALS isn't contagious, is it, Doctor?" Rachel asked.

"No, it's not contagious."

Eli was glad Rachel was there. It saved him having to listen to the clinical assessment of his condition. He already knew what it was. He was going to die. What did the specifics matter?

"Is it hereditary?" Rachel asked.

"It's generally not hereditary. Only about 10 percent of the cases are. What did your parents die of, Rabbi?"

"My father died of old age at ninety-four. My mother had a heart attack when she was ninety-one."

"I wouldn't worry about the hereditary aspect, Mrs. Stone. The possibility is remote. What your husband has is sporadic ALS. What we term "limb onset" ALS. It starts with weakness in the legs and arms. For some patients those are the first symptoms. For others it's their breathing."

Eli tuned out again . . . "Expected progression" . . . "wheelchair" . . . "lose the ability to write" . . . "feed yourself" "difficulty swallowing." The words blurred into a wall of meaningless sound.

"Will it affect his speech?" Rachel asked.

"Eventually. As the muscles of the mouth and the tongue weaken, speaking will become more difficult. But the ability to think and to reason and to hear is seldom impaired."

"How far has it progressed?"

"It's hard to judge. Usually when a patient begins to notice neurological symptoms more than half the motor neurons in his brain may already have been destroyed."

Rachel felt light-headed. The enormity of Eli's illness overwhelmed her. "Is it always fatal?"

"So far we haven't found a cure."

"How long does he have?"

"The average life expectancy is approximately eighteen months. Some patients are willing to prolong their life through the use of a ventilator. If they're willing to do that, it's often possible for them to live a few extra years."

"Do many of them choose to do that?"

"Frankly, most don't. It's fairly intrusive as far as the quality of life is concerned."

Eli wondered how doctors managed to issue death sentences with the detachment of a clerk working checkout at the local supermarket. He had a sudden vision of himself locked in a wheelchair unable to move, breathing with the aid of a respirator, unable to speak.

*   *   *

On the way out of the hospital he stopped by to visit Molly Blaustein. Molly was ninety-two. She'd broken her hip in a fall and it wasn't healing properly. She lay in bed watching a soap opera on TV, her thin arthritic hands resting lightly on a blanket that covered her frail body. "Oh, Rabbi," she said, grasping Eli's hand tightly with her bony fingers, "I don't like it here one bit."

"Of course you don't, Molly. Nobody likes hospitals. As soon as you get better you'll be going home."

"I hope so."

"Just let the doctors take care of you."

"What if I don't get better?"

Eli had heard the question a thousand times. When you were old and sick it was the only question that really mattered.

"You'll get better, Molly. Nothing's going to keep you down." He felt her fingers relax their grip. How easy it was to offer hope to others. How difficult it was to hold onto it yourself.

Rachel took his arm as he came out into the hospital corridor. "How is she?"

"She's a tough old bird. She's hanging in there."

They walked out to the parking lot. It had been raining and a breeze from the lake brought with it the smell of damp earth. "At least now we both know what to expect," Rachel said, gripping Eli's hand tightly. "We're going to get through this, sweetheart. We're going to do just fine."

*   *   *

When Josh came home that night, the door to Eli's study was closed. He entered quietly and sat down next to him. Eli glanced up from his work, the pages of his sermon spread out across his desk. "Did you have a chance to talk to Marty?" he asked.

"Yes, I met with him this afternoon. We reviewed your employment agreement with the congregation. Everything's in good shape. Mom's well taken care of."

"Anything special I need to know?"

Josh told his father about the portions of the agreement that dealt with what happened if he didn't retire and could no longer work effectively. "You're planning to retire, aren't you?"

"Eventually."

"Then there shouldn't be any problems."

Josh stared at the books that lined the study shelves. On weekend afternoons when he was a small boy he would sit at the bottom of the stairs outside the study and wait for his father to call him. He would read a chapter of the Bible in Hebrew and would try to translate it into English. His father would help him out when he got stuck. If he stumbled over the meaning of a word, his father would reprimand him.

"You know that word. You've heard it before."

Sometimes they would stop at a particular spot in the text and Eli would reach for one of the books behind him and read what some biblical scholar had written about the passage he was struggling with. Josh tried to concentrate but there was a school nearby and he could her the noise of children playing. The lessons continued until he left for college.

Eli reached for a cup of tea that was sitting on the corner of his desk. "How did your work go today?" he asked.

"It went fine." Josh noticed that his father's hands were shaking as he picked up the cup and moved it to his lips.

"What sort of work are you doing?"

"Just some research for my company."

Josh found it awkward lying to his father. He wanted to tell him that he had been sent to Cleveland to negotiate a takeover of Sam's company. That Fabrico was in trouble and that Parallax was willing to pay a fair price for control. Instead, he changed the subject.

"Mom told me you went to see the doctor today."

"It was just a regular visit."

"What did he say?"

"Nothing I didn't already know."

An awkward silence followed. Eli went back to work, his hand shaking, his handwriting scrawling messily across the page. Josh watched him for a moment as he wrote, then he got up and left his father's study, quietly closing the door behind him.

CHAPTER NINE

Stacey's long blonde hair, pulled back in a scrunchy, hung almost to her waist. She gave Josh a quick self-conscious hug. "I'm really glad you came. I've got a ton of things to ask you about New York." She grabbed his hand and pulled him inside. "Mom's not home yet. Dad's in the living room with some woman from the museum."

The living room was fifty feet long, with walls painted bone white and a floor made of polished bluestone blocks fitted seamlessly together. A series of narrow floor-to-ceiling windows along the outside wall offered tantalizing views of green lawns, the pond in the distance, the stable, and the riding ring. Three large canvasses by Franz Kline, Clyfford Still and Willem de Kooning dominated the wall opposite. At the far end of the room a white leather couch and four white leather armchairs were grouped together in front of a massive stone fireplace against which a large abstract oil painting was propped.

Peter slouched in one of the chairs, his leg thrown casually over an arm.

A vague look of annoyance crossed his face as Josh entered the room.

"Josh is here," Stacey announced. "Mom invited him for dinner, remember?"

Peter didn't bother getting up. He rattled off introductions with the indifference of a train conductor calling out the stops. "Josh, this is Antonia Petschek. She's the new assistant director at the museum. Antonia, this is Josh Stone. He's Rabbi Stone's son. He's in from New York for a few days."

"You look just like your father," Antonia said. "I suppose everybody tells you that."

"I'm used to it by now."

"How is he?"

"He's doing okay."

"I envy you. When I was a little girl growing up in Europe, I dreamed of living in New York. What sort of work do you do?"

"I work for a venture capital firm."

"Like Peter?"

"Not exactly. I'm just a working stiff."

Peter had been pleasantly surprised when Linda announced that she had invited Antonia home for dinner. Now Josh was here, getting in the way. "What do you think of the painting, Josh?" he asked, barely able to conceal his irritation.

"I don't know much about abstract art."

"I wasn't asking how much you knew. I was just wondering how it made you feel."

Antonia interrupted. "I've been trying to convince Peter that he should let our curators have a look at it. I'm an administrator, not a curator. My opinion doesn't mean much, I'm afraid."

The tension was broken by the sound of a car crunching up the gravel driveway. Stacey ran to the window. "Mom's home."

Linda entered, barely glancing at Peter as she set down her parcels. "I'm bushed." It had been a busy day. There had been a message on her cell phone from Mark Winnick saying that he needed to talk and she had called Buddy Kaplan to say she wanted white asparagus, not green, for the salad at Jessica's bat mitzvah party. On her way home she'd bought two new dresses and stopped at the beauty parlor to have highlights added. She would turn forty-three in two weeks, but from the way men looked at her she could tell that they still found her attractive.

She greeted Antonia warmly. "I wanted us to have a relaxing meal and here Peter's making you sing for your supper. Josh, I'm so pleased you could come. Stacey, go get Jessica. Where is she?"

"She's upstairs with her door closed."

"Well, tell her to come down. And tell Maria we're going to eat right away. I'm sure everyone is starved."

*   *   *

"We have to say a blessing first," Jessica said as they all sat down. She was a spindly thirteen-year-old, her adolescent figure camouflaged under layers of baggy clothes. She wore a green sweater with holes in the elbows and a knitted wool cap pulled down to her eyebrows.

"Jessica's going to be bat mitzvahed next month." Linda said, smiling.

"I'm going to be a rabbi," Jessica announced proudly, pushing her tiny wire-rim glasses back from the end of her nose. She glared at Stacey, who was rolling her eyes. "What's wrong with wanting to be a rabbi? Women can be rabbis if they want."

"Of course they can, sweetheart," Linda interrupted. "It's just that one day you might want to change your mind."

"I'm never going to change my mind."

A maid came in with a platter of sliced filet of beef surrounded by a ring of peas and roast potatoes. "How about we have some dinner?" Peter suggested.

"We have to say a prayer first and we have to all hold hands."

Stacey slipped her hand into Josh's with a look that said, "We go through this every night."

Peter cleared his throat. "Let us thank God for His many gifts and for the friendship of those who have joined us for this meal."

"You have to say something about the family," Jessica demanded. "Rabbi Stone says that family is the most important thing there is."

"And we thank God for the gifts that He has bestowed upon this family and all who are gathered here. How's that?"

"Can we eat now, dear?" Linda asked. "I think Clara is getting tired holding that heavy tray."

"Daddy hasn't said the blessing over the bread yet."

Peter intoned the ritual blessing. "*Baruch atah Adonai melech ha'olam hamotzi lechem min ha'aretz.*"

"Okay," Jessica said, "We can eat now."

*   *   *

"Peter tells me you've been absolutely indispensable at the museum," Linda said as the dinner plates were cleared away.

"I'm hardly that," Antonia answered. "I work with the director on administrative issues. Staffing, budgets, programming. Things like that."

"Is raising money part of what you do?"

"It's an important part of my job. Our admissions and the museum shop and everything else barely cover half of our annual expenses so we depend on the generosity of board members and others to pull us through. My real interest is opening up the museum up to the larger community. We need to get young people to take a more active interest."

"The director says you've had a spectacular career."

"I've had the good fortune to work for top-flight people most of the time."

"You say that as if you've had problems."

"You'd be surprised at the number of museum directors who like having a smart woman around, but not too smart and not too ambitious."

"What would you like to be doing someday?"

"Running a museum I guess. It's a dream of course."

Linda watched Peter stare across the table at Antonia with hungry eyes. She had wondered at first if it had been a mistake inviting her to dinner, but she needed to cultivate

Antonia's friendship and it was obvious from the way she handled herself that she was much too smart and self-assured to be taken in by Peter's clumsy flirtations.

"I'm planning to major in art history," Stacey said.

"Why don't you come down and we'll have lunch before you go away to college," Antonia suggested. "I'll show you around. Maybe next summer you can work at the museum. We've got a great intern program."

Jessica had been silent through dinner. "How did your bat mitzvah session go today, honey?" Linda asked.

"It went okay."

"I got a call from Rabbi Mark's secretary. She said it's all been worked out. You'll have your bat mitzvah all to yourself. Rabbi Mark talked to Billy's parents and they said they didn't mind."

"You made them move Billy to another day?"

"I thought you'd be pleased."

"I can't believe you did that. I wanted to have it the same day as Billy. That was the whole point."

There was an embarrassed silence. Linda glanced at Peter, hoping he would intervene, but he didn't. "We're having cherry pie for dessert, sweetheart," Linda said. "It's your favorite."

"I think what you did was so mean and unfair," Jessica cried, pushing her chair away from the table and storming out of the room. A moment later her door slammed shut upstairs.

*   *   *

Linda and Antonia stayed in the dining room while Peter led Josh into the den and switched on the TV. The Indians were playing the Colorado Rockies and the game was tied at two all in the bottom of the fourth. Bobby G. was in the batter's circle, swinging a weighted bat. Peter poured himself a brandy and handed one to Josh.

"Find out anything about Patzer?"

"He's divorced. He's still paying alimony and child support. His wife got the house and the condo in Arizona. He rents a small apartment. My guess is he's strapped for cash."

"Get together with him. We need to find out how much he knows."

"We're playing golf tomorrow."

"Good. How's everything else going?"

"I'd feel a whole lot better if I could tell my dad what I'm doing."

"Don't worry. I'll let you know before we do anything. You'll have plenty of time to tell him." Peter took a sip of brandy. "Antonia's smart as a whip, isn't she? The museum was lucky to get her." Josh wondered where the conversation was heading. "I wouldn't like to see her distracted. She's got her hands full at the museum and you've got your own work to do."

Peter settled back to watch the game with the contented air of a fox that had just pissed the boundaries of its territory. There was a knock on the door and Stacey entered.

"I thought maybe Josh would like to take a walk around and see the place."

"Good idea," Peter said. "I've got some calls to make."

*   *   *

Stacey led Josh through a pair of sliding doors onto a wide brick patio. It was a cool night and she wrapped her arms around herself against the chill. "I'll bet anything Dad was talking to you about Antonia. He was, wasn't he? Mom's got to be out of her mind to invite her here. I don't know how she stands it. Dad has all these affairs and Mom just sits around and takes it."

They reached the swimming pool, lit by underwater lights, the surface rippled by a slight breeze. "You know," Stacey continued awkwardly, "I had a crush on you the whole time I was growing up. You probably didn't even know I was alive."

"I remember the pigtails."

"God, I must have been a mess."

"You were like what, twelve when I left for New York?"

"Something like that," Stacey laughed, "but I'm eighteen now." She reached up and put her arms around his neck and kissed him. He could feel her firm breasts push against him.

"Look, Staccy, we better get back."

She kissed him again and pulled him toward the pool house. Through the window of the den Josh could see Peter slouched in a chair, talking on the phone. "You worried Mom and Dad will find out? I don't care if they do. C'mon, nobody's going to miss us. Mom's in the dining room talking to Antonia and Dad's watching the game."

Josh pulled her arms gently from around his neck. "Look, Stacey. It's just . . ."

"Just what?"

"It's just that it doesn't seem like such a good idea."

"You still think I'm a little girl . . . I'm eighteen."

"It's not that."

"You work for my dad and you don't want to get in trouble. That's it, isn't it?"

Stacey's deep-throated laugh surprised him. "Well, okay for now, but I don't give up easy, so watch out."

*   *   *

Josh eased his car down the long driveway leading away from Milles Fleurs. Antonia sat next to him. Peter had offered to drive her home but Linda quickly squelched the idea. "Josh can take her. It's on his way."

"I've never seen anything like it," Antonia said. "Everyone in that family has their own agenda."

"It's not hard to figure Peter out," Josh said.

"He's pretty transparent, isn't he?"

"And little Jessica wants to be a rabbi," Josh said.

"And not-so-little Stacey wants Josh to pay attention to her. I watched her at dinner. She couldn't stop staring at you. Where did the two of you disappear to?"

"I was given a tour of the grounds."

"I'll bet you were." Antonia's warm laugh put him at ease.

"Anyway, we both seemed to have come through unscathed. What were you and Linda talking about?"

"Mostly about your father. She's worried about what will happen when he's not around anymore, and she wanted to know what I thought about Rabbi Winnick. I didn't know what to say. What do you think of him?"

"I hardly know him."

"What about your father? What does he think of him?"

"My dad and I don't talk all that much." Josh turned onto the highway. The lights of the distant city cast a dim glow into the dark night sky. "What brought you to Cleveland?" he asked.

"I was born in Prague. I went to school there, " Antonia said. "Then I got a scholarship to graduate school in London, where I met this guy. He worked in finance like you. He got offered a job with a Wall Street firm and I went to New York with him. Then I got offered a museum job in Philadelphia that I wanted. He didn't want me to go, but I went anyway."

"What happened?

"What always happens. He met someone else and I was offered this job in Cleveland. That's about it. What about you? Are you and Peter working on a project together?"

"Something like that."

"Don't want to talk about it?"

"I can't tell you exactly what it is."

"You like what you do?"

"Most of the time," Josh said. "What about you?"

"I love the work I do. I don't always like the people. There's always some guy like Peter who thinks because he's made all this money he can have anything he wants."

"How do you handle it?"

"Once I actually had to change jobs," she said.

They were approaching a group of apartment buildings on a quiet tree-lined street near the museum. "Here's where I live. I always seem to end up in places like this. The rent's cheap and I can walk to work. I'm a creature of habit." Josh expected Antonia to get out of the car but she didn't. He put his arm around her, pulled her to him and felt the warmth of her lips against his. He slipped a hand under her blouse. She didn't push his hand away. He kissed her again and could feel himself getting hard.

* * *

It was almost four o'clock when he woke up. Antonia was curled up next to him naked under the sheets. He ran a hand across her breasts and down her belly. The steady rhythm of her breathing and the slow rise and fall of her body made him want her again. She woke up slowly, stretching like a cat.

"I told myself we'd be doing this," she whispered hoarsely. She reached for him and began laughing gently.

"What's so funny?"

"I was thinking you were probably all worn out from your tour of the grounds with Stacey, but I guess I was wrong."

CHAPTER TEN

It was two-thirty in the afternoon and a heavy rain was falling. Linda greeted the members of the board as they entered her home, tramping their muddy boots on her polished marble floor. She had invited them out to Milles Fleurs so they could meet away from prying eyes. Bill Palevsky had been asked to review Eli's contract, particularly those sections dealing with the powers of the board in issues dealing with his retirement, but Linda had no intention of telling the members what she knew. All she wanted for now was to get them to start thinking about the issue of succession.

A last car pulled up and Pamela Dawes hurried toward the front door through the rain, saying, "Sorry I'm late, darling, I just couldn't get away." She had come from a meeting at the station, where she had been introduced to Cindi Li, the reporter from Detroit who might be replacing her. She had expected her to be young, but was unnerved to discover that she was also highly intelligent and exceptionally attractive. Pamela left the meeting in a state of depression, acutely aware that the best plastic surgery in the world couldn't compete with the unlined face and the brain power of this stunning Asian American beauty.

As soon as she had herded everyone into the sunroom, Linda rapped on a coffee cup. "I appreciate that you all took the time to come out here in this terrible weather. Both Rabbi Stone and Rabbi Winnick know about this meeting but I didn't think it was appropriate for either of them to attend. I didn't ask Leo either, so we won't be taking minutes. It's going to be an informal meeting where we can all speak our minds and I hope we can all agree to keep these discussions private and confidential."

Marty Franklin interrupted. "Linda, I think someone should be taking notes. Even if this isn't a formal meeting of the board, none of us want anyone thinking we're discussing important synagogue business in secret."

"Not 'in secret,' Marty. Just informally."

"Even so, it would be a good idea for someone to take notes."

Linda was determined to appear neutral and objective. The important thing was to get the issue of succession on the table and find out where everyone stood. "Of course you're right, Marty. Any volunteers?"

Renee Lassiter raised her hand. "I take the minutes at our faculty meetings. Not that anyone ever reads them."

"Well, let me try to frame the issue," Linda began. "We all feel the same way about Rabbi Stone. We wish he could be our rabbi forever. But one of our responsibilities is to insure the continuity of leadership for this congregation, and we have to make sure there is a plan in place for succession."

"I don't get it." Max Jessel's gravelly voice filled the room. "Eli says he wants to keep on working as long as he can. He seems fine for now. So what's the rush?"

"I thought that way too at first, Max. But I took the liberty of speaking to a neurologist who is familiar with ALS and he told me that in many cases the onset of debilitating symptoms can happen very fast. Sometimes on the order of six months or less. I know that's hard to deal with, but those are the facts. At some point Rabbi Stone isn't going to be able to carry on and it seems to me that under the circumstances, we have to plan for the future." She paused and glanced around the room, waiting for reactions. "We all want him to keep on as long as he can, but that isn't something over which any of us has control. We have to be prepared in case something happens to him sooner rather than later."

Sam Broad was indignant. "I'm surprised you consulted a doctor about Eli's condition. You had no business going behind his back."

"I wish you wouldn't characterize it that way," Linda replied calmly, "I felt it was my responsibility as president of the congregation to find out what I could about his illness and bring the facts to everyone's attention."

Manny Polsky's thin voice was barely audible above the steady thrum of rain on the roof. "I've been on this board longer than anyone," he said, "and I think Rabbi Stone is entitled to make up his own mind about when he wants to retire. I'm sure he'll let us know when he's ready and we'll have plenty of time to decide what happens next."

RAPHAEL D. SILVER

"I appreciate that, Manny," Linda said. "But we have to look at this thing realistically. The fact is that Rabbi Stone is critically ill, and we have only one assistant rabbi and he's already started looking around."

The news that Mark might be leaving surprised everyone.

"We just gave him a big raise," Max shouted, his booming voice drowning out the sound of the rain pounding on the roof. "What's he trying to do, blackmail us?"

"That's not what he has in mind at all," Linda responded. "He's just concerned about where he stands now that Rabbi Stone is ill. He doesn't want to find himself out on a limb."

"How's he out on a limb? We just signed a new three-year deal with him. What's he think he is? A free agent?"

"Absolutely not, Max, but he feels insecure right now."

"Then let him go to a shrink for chrissake," Max grumbled. "He's got a contract with us. He's not going anywhere."

"What do you suggest, Linda?" Pamela inquired.

"I believe we need to urge Rabbi Stone to announce a specific date for his retirement so we are free as a board to consider what happens next."

"Have you spoken to him about it?"

"I wanted to get the board's approval before I did anything."

"What about a search committee? Isn't that the usual way to find a replacement?"

"Yes it is," Linda answered, "but it's awkward since Rabbi Stone hasn't given us any indication of when he plans to retire. It's hard to offer a job to someone when you can't tell them when it might be available. Unless we make arrangements soon, we could find ourselves with no rabbi at all."

"Seems to me," Antonia observed, "that the first thing we ought to do is make sure that Rabbi Mark stays on for a while. It's not like he has to look around right way. And in the meantime someone should sit down with Rabbi Stone and get a better idea of his plans."

Linda glanced in Sally Minton's direction. She had met with Sally an hour before the meeting and got her to agree to introduce the possibility of Mark as Eli's replacement. It had taken some heavy coaxing.

"What about Mark Winnick? Is he a possibility?" Sally inquired. "He's been with us for five years. Is he someone we might consider?"

"Save yourself the trouble," Max growled, shifting uncomfortably in his chair. "Who wants him, anyway? I sure don't."

Manny Polsky nodded in agreement. "You ever watch when he gives a sermon? Half the congregation falls asleep. He's better than Sominex."

Pamela's hearty laugh filled the room. She'd never heard Manny utter a harsh word about anyone before. "I agree. Rabbi Stone is a national treasure. If we have to replace him we need to find the best rabbi in America. Mark's a nice young man but he's a cipher."

"He's certainly not a cipher," Linda's voice rose angrily.

Renee glanced up from the yellow pad on which she was busy scribbling notes. "Does anyone know how to spell 'cipher'? Is it with an 'i' or with a 'y'?"

Bobby G. was slouched in a chair at the back of the sunroom, staring at Renee from behind dark glasses that he wore everywhere. He wondered what she looked like naked. "Either way is acceptable," he said. "It's an arithmetic symbol meaning zero."

Renee had always assumed that Bobby's reading habits were limited to the sports pages of the morning paper with comic books as a probable chaser. "How do you happen to know that?" she asked.

"I do crossword puzzles," Bobby answered, sliding his glasses up to the top of his head and giving her a broad smile. "We have a lot of free time on the road."

The tension broke and a vote authorizing Linda to meet with Rabbi Stone passed seven to three with two abstentions. Sam Broad, Max Jessel and Manny Polsky voted "no." Marty Franklin and Bill Palevsky abstained and everyone else voted "yes."

After the meeting adjourned, Linda asked Bill if he would stay a while. "You're not in a rush to go home, are you? I want to show you my new filly."

It had stopped raining and the late afternoon sun cast long shadows on the lawn as they walked down the grassy slope behind the main house toward the stable.

"I appreciate your going over those papers for me, Bill. This whole thing is really awkward."

"You want Mark to be Rabbi Stone's replacement, don't you?"

"Why not? He's young and he's open to new ideas. I think he'd be an excellent choice."

"But why put pressure on Rabbi Stone now? He'll announce his retirement soon enough. The congregation's not going to fall apart if we wait a while."

Linda felt herself getting angry. Why was everyone so concerned with how Eli felt? The congregation had been led around by the nose for so long that they'd forgotten that Eli was a hired hand. It was their congregation, not his. Rabbi Stone had been elected to occupy the pulpit. He didn't own it.

"It would be a mistake to put everything off until Rabbi Stone can't handle his work load anymore. Besides, I like Mark. He'll be good for the congregation and anyway, I don't think we have the luxury of sitting around doing nothing."

She pushed open the doors to the stable. The smell of decaying leaves mixed with the sweet odor of damp hay. Light streaming in from a series of tiny cobweb-covered windows traced spidery patterns on the sawdust-covered floor. Linda's coal-black filly stamped in her stall. As they approached, she pushed her head forward to nuzzle Linda.

"She's a beauty, isn't she?"

"Where'd you get her?"

"Peter bought her for me at an auction a couple of months ago. It was his way of apologizing."

"For what?"

"It doesn't matter." Linda took Bill's hand. "Remember the night of our senior prom when we snuck off to that motel?"

"That was a while ago."

"Not so long that you can't remember."

"We were both a little drunk."

"You weren't exactly reluctant as I remember."

Linda moved closer to him until their bodies were touching. "I didn't want a dull life then and I don't want one now." She reached up and kissed him, her lips lingering on his. Then she took his hand and led him to a small room in the back of the stable where the saddles were kept. They made love on an old battered couch and when they were through, Linda's plans for Mark's election to replace Eli as senior rabbi of the congregation had inched one small step closer to consummation.

CHAPTER ELEVEN

Josh entered the sprawling clubhouse of Rolling Ridge Country Club, hurried down a flight of stairs, past a glass-walled squash court, through an oak-paneled bar and into the men's locker room, where overweight men shuffled out of the shower room, paper sandals on their feet, pausing to weigh themselves on a scale set five pounds light. Brian Patzer was waiting for him.

"Manuel, fix Mr. Stone up with a locker, will you?"

"Sure thing, Mr. Patzer. He can use Mr. Matson's locker. He's in Florida. Leave your shoes by the locker, Mr. Stone. I'll have them shined up for you by the time you leave."

*   *   *

They hit a few balls on the practice range, then grabbed a cart and headed for the first tee. "How about we play for twenty dollars a side and twenty for the eighteen," Brian suggested. "I'll give you two strokes a side. We can adjust later if we have to."

By the seventh hole Josh was two strokes up. "I thought you said you didn't play much anymore," Brian complained.

"You stay two up through the turn, we're gonna have to adjust." Brian glanced around to make sure Josh wasn't watching, then nudged his ball up on a tuft of grass and hit a five-iron onto the green. "You moved over from Merrill in the nick of time. Ballard make you a partner?"

"No, but I've got a shot at it in a couple of years."

"I'll be ready for retirement before Petrie gets around to making me a partner."

Josh's second shot ended in a trap and he blasted out. He watched as Brian marked his ball on the green, cleaned it and put it down six inches closer to the hole. He wasn't sure how much Brian knew about their plans for Fabrico, but the longer he hung around Cleveland the more suspicious Brian would become. Sooner or later he was bound to figure out what was going on. Then he would tell Petrie and they would rush to close out their short position, and the price at which they hoped to acquire Fabrico would go through the roof.

"I heard about you and Patsy," Josh said.

"Yeah. She met this asshole from Chicago who owns a bunch of Ford dealerships. She took off with the kids, but she hasn't married him so I'm still paying alimony and child support. I'll probably be on the hook forever. The last couple of years have been absolute shit for me. The brokerage business sucks. It's not like the old days when everyone was making money."

"Why don't you bring us a deal to look at?" Josh asked.

"You think your guys would be interested?"

"Why not?"

"You pay finder's fees?"

"We wouldn't do much business if we didn't," Josh said.

"It's not like I'd be taking anything away from Petrie," Brian mused. "They keep saying they want to do deals but the fact is, they don't do much of anything anymore. I brought them a terrific deal six months ago and they hardly looked at it." Brian took off his golf cap and wiped the top of his bald head with his handkerchief, lined up his putt and sank it. "You're only one up now."

On the next tee, Josh asked casually. "What about Peter Freling? You said you thought he was up to something."

"Peter's always up to something."

Two hours later Josh still wasn't sure what Brian knew. He answered questions the way he played golf, shading the truth a little. But he was certain of one thing. Brian needed money. A couple of times Brian seemed on the verge of suggesting that he was willing to do just about anything to make a buck, but then he would pull back, run his handkerchief over his head and change the subject.

They were on the eighteenth fairway waiting for the group in front of them to move off the green. Josh had won the first nine and they were even on the second. If he won this hole he'd win all three sides of the bet. They had both driven well and their balls were about the same distance from the green.

"How about we double up?" Brian asked. He was first to play. His ball sailed over a small pond and landed on the edge of the green about twenty feet from the pin. Josh's ball landed on the back of the green and skidded off. He chipped back, making sure to leave himself a long way from the hole, putted first and missed. Brian holed his putt and won.

"You owe me twenty bucks," Brian crowed. "You won the first side. We split the eighteen and I won the back side and the press."

They stayed at the club for dinner. "I should have gone to New York when you did," Brian complained as they lingered over drinks. "You can be anyone you want in New York and no one knows the difference. Here you meet somebody and right off they know your whole life history. How much you're worth. What hospital you were born at. Where you went to high school. Who you screwed before you got married and who you screwed after. It's a fucking fishbowl. I've been living a monk's life the last couple of years. Things have got so bad, I have to get off on other people's affairs."

There was something endearing about Brian. He was like an overgrown child who had taken too big a bite out of life, and it had given him indigestion. The conversation drifted back to business. "There's something going on with Fabrico," Brian continued. "I'm sure of it. I keep poking around but no one's talking. You hear anything?"

Josh played dumb. "Nothing, why?"

"I've been thinking about what you said about doing something with your firm," Brian said. "How would I go about it?"

"You'd have to come down to New York and meet with Ballard."

"He'd meet with me?"

"Why not? He's always looking for new ideas."

*   *   *

By the time Josh got home it was after ten. He came in the back way, through the garage. There was a light on in Eli's study. He was asleep at his desk, a book open in front of him. Even in repose he seemed powerful. It was hard for Josh to believe that after winning so many battles in his lifetime, his father was being vanquished by an unseen adversary as he slept.

Josh was careful to be quiet climbing the stairs to his room. He closed the door and lay down on his bed. His head was spinning. He'd had too much to drink. He pulled out his laptop and sent Ballard an e-mail. "Played golf with Patzer. He's pretty sure something is going on. Don't know how much he knows or how close he is to finding out."

He was about to shut down his computer when he noticed a message waiting.

"Get him down here," the message said.

"When?" Josh e-mailed back.

"Tomorrow," came the reply.

Josh woke Brian up at home. "I just talked to Ballard. He's available tomorrow if you want to meet with him."

"Jesus, that was fast."

"I gave you a big build up," Josh said. "We'll take the eight o'clock plane. You'll be back home in time for dinner."

*   *   *

The plane flew low out over the lake and then banked sharply, heading southeast toward New York. The downtown gave way to the suburbs and then to a patchwork of small farms and rolling hills as the plane climbed above the clouds. Brian seemed unusually nervous. He was a loose cannon, Josh thought. At least Ballard would be the one deciding what to do with him. If something went wrong, Josh wouldn't get the blame.

"When do I get to meet him?" Brian asked.

"We're meeting him at the Regency at eleven-thirty."

"What am I going to talk to him about?"

"Just talk with him. See what develops," Josh said.

They grabbed a cab for the city. Josh still got a thrill every time he saw the skyline of New York.

He had gone back to Cleveland following his graduation from business school. After turning Peter down, he had taken a job as assistant to the president of a large industrial company. The city closed in around him. He began to regret having come home. After four weeks he quit. When he came home that night, he told his father he was going to New York.

"What will you do there?"

"I'll get a job," Josh said.

"Doing what?"

"I'll get a good job, dad, don't worry."

"You just gave up a good job," Eli said.

"It wasn't right for me."

"You didn't give it half a chance."

It was the first time Josh understood that his father had no interest in his future. All he wanted was for him was to be safely tucked away somewhere out of trouble. He knew then that he would have to break away from his father or be paralyzed by the need to please him. That same night he shoved everything he owned in the trunk of his car. At dawn he was on a highway in New Jersey looking across the Hudson River at the towers of Manhattan, their windows blazing with the reflection of the rising sun.

*　　*　　*

They were sitting at a table in the dining room of the Regency Hotel when Ballard's secretary called to make apologies. He would be a few minutes late.

Brian picked at a callus on his hand. "Maybe this wasn't such a good idea," he said.

"Relax, Brian. Everything's going to work out fine."

Ballard spotted them and headed for their table, limping across the room, stopping to greet a couple of men he knew. He reached their table, leaned across and shook Brian's hand. "Josh says you're a hell of a golfer," Ballard said. "I used to play in Australia. I wasn't any good but I loved the game."

He asked Brian questions about his background and seemed genuinely interested in what he had to say. Brian relaxed. Josh wondered how long it would take Ballard to get to the point. Finally, after the waiter had cleared away their salad plates and brought the main course, Ballard threw out the bait.

"Josh tells me you'd like to do something with us."

"I don't have anything specific right now, Mr. Ballard, but Josh suggested I come down here anyway and meet you."

"I'm glad you did. We're always looking for new ideas and new folks to work with." Ballard's steady gaze locked on Brian's eager face. "I understand your firm has a big short position in Fabrico stock."

Brian's eyes darted frantically to Josh.

"Peter Freling and I are planning to make a tender offer for the company. "Didn't Josh tell you?"

"No, he didn't."

"I'm surprised he didn't fill you in. We've been buying stock for a couple of weeks. We want to be sure the price doesn't spike before our offer."

"I'm not sure I understand."

Ballard's narrow mouth twisted into the semblance of a smile. "Sure you do, Brian. A couple of weeks is all we need. You keep your people shut down for the next couple of weeks and you'll be a whole lot richer than you are right now. How's that sound to you?"

Josh marveled at the way Ballard bulled ahead. "What have you got now?" Ballard continued. "A job that's going nowhere, a salary that doesn't cover half what it costs you to live. A shitpot full of alimony and child support. Fabrico's stock is in the toilet right now and that's where I want to keep it. A million dollars, Brian. That's what I have in mind. How does that sound to you? A million bucks to keep your mouth shut."

Brian knew he should protest.

"Your people suspect anything?" Ballard asked.

"As of now they don't."

"Of course they don't. They don't know a goddam thing about what we're doing and you're gonna make sure it stays that way."

"I can't do that," Brian stammered.

"Do what?" Ballard demanded. He wanted to make sure that Brian understood exactly what he was talking about.

"Not tell the people in my firm what's going on."

"Sure you can, Brian. It's not that complicated. You keep your eyes open and your mouth shut for the next couple of weeks and I'll guarantee you get a million bucks no matter what happens. Petrie pay you that kind of money? No? I didn't think so." Ballard forked a chunk of steak into his mouth, leaned back in his chair and wiped a spot of gravy off his chin.

"You're taking a chance talking to me about this, Mr. Ballard."

"I'm not taking any chance at all," Ballard continued smoothly. "The way I see it, you're the one with your tit in a wringer. You tell Petrie what's going on, we'll know right away. We'll sell the stock we bought and move on to something else. But before we do, I'll get the word out that you asked for this meeting. That you came in special to New York to tell me you were willing to sell out your firm. Who are they going to believe? You or me?"

Brian slumped down in his chair staring at the food he hadn't touched. "You don't have to lay out a red cent, Brian," Ballard said. "Where's the fucking risk? All you got to do is keep Petrie from figgering out what we're up to for the next couple of weeks."

"What if they start covering anyway?"

"Why would they, unless you spill the beans? Fabrico's in bad shape. They owe the banks way too much. They're closing stores left and right. Next quarter's earnings are in the shitter. You keep Petrie off our backs for the next couple of weeks and you're home free."

Ballard gulped down what remained of his drink.

"You got any questions, you work them out with Josh," Ballard said. "Just let him know what you decide before you get back on the plane. If you can't make up your mind, I'll figger your answer is no. If that's what you decide, okay, but I still wouldn't tip Petrie off if I were you. They close out their short position, I'll know you're the one who told them. That happens, I'll make sure everybody knows about this meeting and you'll be out on your ass without a dime to show for it."

Ballard wiped his mouth with his napkin and let the message sink in. The waiter took their plates away and brought coffee. "You play ball, Brian, so will I. You don't. I don't. It's that simple." Ballard got up to leave, struggling out of his chair, his napkin still tucked under his chin. "Josh ever tell you how I lost my leg? I was fifteen. Went surfing near Sidney. Shark took it off at the knee. They found the shark washed up on the beach. Died of indigestion, so the story goes."

Ballard limped across the room. Just before he got to the door, he pulled the napkin out of his collar and tossed it on an empty table.

"Jesus!" Brian gasped. "You work for that guy?"

"I had no idea he was going to do that."

"That's bullshit! You knew it all along. You set me up."

"Believe me, Brian, I didn't set you up." Josh knew it was a lie. He had put Brian in a coffin. All Ballard had done was nail the lid shut.

The taxi ride back to the airport was a nightmare. The traffic on the Triborough Bridge was creeping along at five miles an hour. Brian folded himself against the door, staying as far away from Josh as he could get, tormented by visions of what he could do with the money if he went along with Ballard and terrified of the calamity that would befall him if he didn't.

"I'm going to miss my plane," he whined.

"We've got plenty of time."

"I guess it's pointless to ask for something in writing."

"You'll get a fair shake, Brian. I promise."

"From that guy?"

"It's going to work out fine," Josh said.

They were at the airport in time for the flight. Josh walked Brian to the security checkpoint.

"What's it going to be? You in or out?"

"I'll call you when I get back to Cleveland," Brian said.

"That won't work. Ballard wants to know one way or another before you get on the plane. You won't get a second chance."

The misery on Brian's face reflected his confusion. "Do you trust him?"

"I trust him," Josh said. "He'll come through, I promise."

"Then I'm in, I guess."

Josh stayed long enough to watch Brian disappear into a crowd of travelers. Then he put in a call to Ballard.

"He's in."

"Sure he's in. I could have told you that the minute I sat down."

*   *   *

Brian sat slumped in his seat staring down at a sea of white clouds. He emptied the contents of two scotch miniatures into a glass filled with ice and downed the drink in one long gulp. What did he owe Petrie anyway? All he had to show for his years at Petrie was "Senior Vice President" stenciled on his office door. He had cut his living expenses to the bone, but with the need to maintain a decent front and his country club dues and alimony and everything else, he needed a windfall to pull himself out of the hole. A million bucks would buy him a new life. All he had to do was keep his mouth shut. When the news of the tender offer broke, Petrie would be upset that he hadn't been able to give them any advance warning. He would find a way to convince them there was no way he could have known.

The scotch calmed him down and he began to consider the possibilities. He could do better than just keep his fingers crossed and wait for Ballard to come through with the million. Fabrico stock was bound to go up on the tender offer. He'd buy calls on the stock. Twenty thousand dollars would buy him calls on 40,000 shares. It would take all his savings but if the stock ran up a couple of bucks on the news, he'd make a quick eighty grand on top of what Ballard promised him. He would handle the whole thing through outside brokers. No one would ever know.

* * *

Ballard limped across his office to the bar and poured himself a drink. "This whole thing bothers you, doesn't it?"

"I haven't been able to tell my father what I'm doing," Josh said. "That bothers me a lot."

"You'll have plenty of time to tell him before anything happens."

"And I don't want Brian getting hurt. He's a friend of mine."

"Brian's got nothing to worry about."

"He's convinced you'll go after him, even if he plays ball."

"Let him run scared for a while." Ballard downed his drink and poured himself another. "You see his eyes light up when I told him there was a million bucks in it? Watch the eyes, boyo. The eyes tell you everything you need to know even when someone's trying to blow smoke up your ass."

Ballard walked to the window. The sky had cleared and across the harbor the Statue of Liberty stood out in stark relief against the glowing colors of an autumn sunset.

Ballard's voice took on a distant tone. "You wanna know how I really got this bum leg? I was a kid of fifteen. I had a job working for some guys in Sydney. Small time crooks. They lent out money and if you didn't pay them back on time, they worked you over. My old man was into them for a few hundred. I tried to cover for him. I told them he was sick and couldn't pay, but after a while they didn't believe me. They came after him. They took me along and I stood there watching while they beat the shit out of him. I never was close to my old man. He was a drunk and he was never much use to me, but he was my dad and that meant something. After a while I couldn't stand it any longer. I went after them and one of them took a bat and broke my leg in a bunch of places. I just lay there with my leg broke and watched them beat the living crap out of my old man. He was never the same after he came out of the hospital. He hardly said a word to me after that. He was sure I set him up."

Ballard caught the look on disbelief in Josh's face.

"You think I'm bullshitting you, don't you?"

Ballard hobbled back to where Josh was sitting and pulled up his pant leg, exposing a right leg laced with ugly scars. "I got a word of advice for you, pal," he said. "You want to make it in this business don't spend so much time worrying about other people. Cover your own ass and let the other guys watch out for theirs."

CHAPTER TWELVE

Stefan Belzner opened the door to his West End Avenue apartment and stared at Josh through thick horn-rimmed glasses. He was a diminutive, sixty-five-year-old Belgian émigré who had been Eli Stone's political confidant for thirty years. Josh had met him a number of times, usually cloistered with his father, discussing matters of Jewish interest. His father said that Stefan, who had never married and lived an almost monastic existence, understood the dynamics of Jewish communal life better than anyone he had ever met.

From the tiny vestibule, Josh could see into the living room. A pallor of neglect had settled over everything. The paint on the walls was cracking. The lamp shades were torn and shredded. Heavy curtains were drawn across the windows as if to seal in ancient memories.

Stefan padded ahead of Josh down a narrow hallway, his slippered feet poking out below the folds of a terry cloth robe that hung almost to the floor. "You look more like your father all the time. How's he getting along? He never mentions his illness when we talk, but that's in character, isn't it?" They entered a small book-lined study and Stefan

119

motioned him to a couch. "You said you wanted to talk to me about him. What is it you want to know?"

"There's so much I don't know," Josh said.

"You're not the only one. I've known your father all my life and I can't really tell you what he's like. We talk almost every day, but I can't say that I was ever close to him." The skin around Stefan's pale blue eyes wrinkled as he talked and there was the constant hint of a smile on his lips that suggested he knew more than he was willing to reveal. He rummaged through his desk and brought out an envelope stuffed with photographs, some old enough that the edges had turned yellow and begun to crack. One was of a group of boys, around eleven or twelve years old, sitting on the stoop of a dilapidated tenement on the Lower East Side of Manhattan. Eli was seated apart from the others, who were huddled together laughing, their arms around each other.

"That's your father on the right," Stefan said. "We all lived in the same building. Your dad lived fourth floor back."

"Was he always like that?" Josh asked.

"You mean serious like in the picture?"

"I mean keeping himself apart from everybody."

"It wasn't that he was aloof," Stefan said. He could be warm and friendly, but there was a part of him you couldn't reach. We used to talk about it. We were a little wary of him. I think we were in awe of him."

"That's a strange word to use about a twelve-year old."

"I'm not so sure it isn't appropriate. He always seemed to have his emotions under control. He didn't talk much.

He listened. I've never met anyone who was able to listen better than your father. When he made up his mind, that was it. He never backed down after he had made up his mind about something. You ever hear him speak? I mean in front of a big crowd. I remember once, at a peace rally in New York, this crazy man comes down the aisle shouting, 'I am the Messiah! I am the Messiah!' He walks right up to where your father is speaking and screams up at him, 'I am the Messiah! I am the Messiah!' And your father, calm as a cucumber, looks down at him and says, 'I knew you were coming but I never expected you so soon.' The crowd went wild. I've only seen him lose his temper a couple of times. You don't want to be around him when that happens. You get along with him?"

The question caught Josh off guard.

"Not always."

"I'm not surprised."

There was something about this tiny, intense man that put Josh at ease. Josh told him why he had gone to Cleveland and why he had found it necessary to keep his father in the dark about the real reasons for his being there.

"Keeping things from your father? That doesn't sound like a good idea to me," Stefan said. "He doesn't like to be kept in the dark about anything. One time I had some information I didn't give him. I don't remember what it was any more. Some news I didn't think he needed to know. Anyway, he found out about it from someone else and he cut me off. Turned cold as ice. He didn't want me anywhere near him. It was a month before he was willing to talk to me again."

"What was his family like?" Josh asked.

"His mother was this wonderful, uncomplaining woman. She kept the family together. His father was a teacher," Stefan said. "A very austere man. He'd been a rabbi in the old country. I don't think he made a living over here. He was Orthodox. In shul most of the time. He never understood why your dad wanted to become a Reform rabbi. There's a phrase from the Talmud that says, 'The knee of the father is the son.' What that means is that the knee is the one part of the body that can make a man look tall or short. So a father must stand tall as an example to his son, but a son must also stand and act in a way that makes his father proud. I know your father felt that he let his father down. I wouldn't be surprised if that's the way he'll feel about you if you don't tell him what you're doing."

"It's not easy to talk to him."

"I'd tell him anyway."

"I'm not sure he'll listen," Josh said.

"He'll listen. How much time has he got left?"

"I'm not sure."

"Then I wouldn't wait too long."

On the way back to his office Josh kept thinking what a mistake he had made not to tell his father, but it was too late now. In another week they would have accumulated the shares they needed and he would tell him then. He would try to explain why he had taken on the assignment and why he had chosen to keep his father in the dark. He hoped his father would understand.

*   *   *

The evening at Milles Fleurs had been a welcome relief from the tedious round of cocktail parties and dinners with museum patrons that had become the staple of Antonia's social life. Privately she chided herself for having gone to bed with Josh so fast. She knew that it fed the sense of entitlement that men carried around with them like Boy Scout merit badges. But she had been attracted to him and saw no reason to be coy. She expected to hear from him, but two weeks had gone by and he hadn't called.

At their weekly lunch she told Renee about the dinner at Milles Fleurs. "Linda's so goddam devious. The whole thing was a setup to get me to start thinking about Mark as a replacement for Rabbi Stone. That was pretty much all we talked about and then Peter wanted to drive me home. Thank God Josh was there."

"What's he like?" Renee asked.

"Self-absorbed. Sure of himself. Like most of the guys who work on Wall Street."

"Is he cute?"

"Yeah, he's cute," Antonia admitted. "The minute he walked in I wanted to go to bed with him."

"You going to see him again?"

"He's back in New York."

"For long?"

"I don't know."

"Does he call you?" Antonia shook her head. "Why don't you call him?"

"That never works. Anyway, it doesn't matter."

Renee noted the wistful look on Antonia's face. "Yeah, I can see it doesn't bother you one bit."

* * *

Bill Palevsky followed Linda into Eli's office. Roz McIver waited at the door. "Will you be needing me, Rabbi?"

"No, Roz. I don't think so."

Linda's fingers tapped nervously on the arm of her chair as she stared at Eli, trying to detect any visible effects of his illness. "I'm not sure exactly how to begin, Rabbi. We had an informal meeting of the board at my house a few days ago."

"I'm aware of that."

"We discussed the fact that you would be retiring at some point and most of us felt that there were some things that we needed to talk directly with you about."

"There's no need to be so formal, Linda. Just tell me what's on your mind."

"Bill explains these things better than I can. Bill, why don't you start?"

"Rabbi," Bill began, "we're here to discuss the matter of your retirement. The board is anxious to know if you've reached a decision about when you might retire?" He paused, hoping for a response, but Eli sat quietly in his chair, waiting for him to continue. "We'd like to know what your plans are so we can start making provisions for your replacement whenever it is that you decide to step down."

Eli had no desire to make Bill feel uncomfortable. His questions were straightforward and deserved an answer.

"My understanding is that the time I pick to retire is up to me."

"It is, Rabbi, but we think because of your health problems, we need to take steps to prepare the congregation for the future."

Linda sensed the momentum slipping away. "What Bill is trying to say is that we're all worried about your health and the fact that at some point you may not be able to carry on with your duties. From what I understand, the progress of your disease can be rapid and the diagnosis is often not made until well after the disease is under way."

"I see you've done your homework," Eli said.

Linda was determined not to let Eli get under her skin. "The board feels that an announcement of your plans for retirement would make it a lot easier for us to find a replacement."

"I'll step down when I can't handle the work load any more. Right now that's not a problem."

"But at some point you'll consider stepping down, won't you?" Linda asked.

"When that time comes I'll let you know."

"I don't mean to offend you, Rabbi," Linda continued. "It's just that it's difficult for us to attract suitable candidates if you don't set a specific date for your retirement."

Eli marveled at her persistence. She was like an augur boring in. "This is a choice pulpit, Linda. I don't think there will be a shortage of qualified candidates to succeed me when the time comes."

Eli was getting the best of her again, sitting behind his desk, waiting for her to run out of steam. She had watched her father negotiate with scrap dealers. There was a time when you had to take the gloves off.

"We were hoping that we could have a productive discussion, Rabbi. It would be to everyone's benefit if we could find a way to agree on the timing of your retirement. We're not anxious to exercise the rights we have under our employment agreement with you."

"I'm familiar with the terms of the agreement," Eli responded evenly. "But I haven't decided when I plan to retire. I'll be glad to let you and the board know when I do. And I'll be glad to work with you to evaluate suitable candidates. I believe that's the process, or is there someone in particular that you have in mind?"

Linda was startled by the question. She hadn't intended to discuss her plans for Mark with Eli just yet, but she despised the way she was being treated. "Would Rabbi Winnick be a suitable candidate in your opinion?"

"Is that what the board wants?"

"A number of us feel he's well qualified. It might simplify matters all around. He could stay on as your assistant for as long as you plan to remain active and then he would be in a position to take over when you decide to retire."

Eli glanced at Bill Palevsky. What hold did Linda have on him? Bill was a levelheaded lawyer. Why was he part of an effort to force Eli into retirement? "If you want my cooperation, Linda, set up a search committee. I believe that's what the by-laws call for. Find out who's available. When you have a full list of candidates I'll give you my opinion on all them, including Mark. If, after that, the board decides that Mark is the one they want, I won't stand in your way when the time comes."

"You don't object to our starting a search?"

"I encourage you to do it."

Linda's mind raced ahead. With Eli's approval she could now have the board issue a formal notice that it was seeking a new senior rabbi. The wording would make it clear that no specific date for a transition had been set. That restriction made it highly unlikely that many qualified candidates would apply, but it was progress. In the meantime she'd keep working on the members of the board and find a way to swing the vote Mark's way when it came time for the board to make a choice.

*   *   *

Eli left his office and headed down the marble corridor leading to the sanctuary. The meeting troubled him more than he cared to acknowledge. He had devoted forty years of his life to the synagogue. He had raised it from obscurity to national prominence and now, with his health failing, one misguided woman was threatening his hopes for the future of the congregation.

The sanctuary was in shadows. Soft light filtered in through the stained glass windows around the sanctuary dome. Eli walked up the sloping floor and reached a pew in the back. He sat down and ran his hands over the polished wood and gazed across the rows of empty seats that funneled toward the pulpit and the Ark. The vast emptiness of the sanctuary wrapped itself around him like a shawl.

He had grown up attending a tiny shul many times smaller than this one, watching his father in his tallith, rocking back and forth, transported by the hallucinatory incantation of ancient prayers. From the time he was a small boy the synagogue had fascinated him. He was moved by its rituals and by the devotion of the worshippers in his father's shul, most of them old men bent with age. There had been orthodox rabbis in his family for generations and he was expected to follow in the family tradition, but as he grew older, the limits of his father's narrow life began to trouble him. He wanted to practice his faith in a way that would let him participate in the world around him. When he told his father that he planned to become a reform rabbi it had caused a rift between them that never healed. His father had lived long enough to see him rise to prominence both as a rabbi and as a social activist, but he had never fully forgiven him.

A burst of organ music startled him. It was the day that the synagogue's organist came to practice. Eli closed his eyes and let the haunting sounds of a sixteenth-century

Kaddish sweep over him. For a moment he was able to forget about his failing health and Linda's determination to elevate a mediocrity to the spiritual leadership of a great congregation.

As the last chords of the Kaddish echoed off the sanctuary walls, he left his seat and began the long walk back to his office. In the corridor just outside his office, the muscles in his left thigh began to spasm. The pain shooting up his leg radiated through his body. He stumbled and fell. His head hit the marble floor. As he came to and his vision cleared he saw Mark standing over him, talking to someone.

"Are you okay, Rabbi?" Mark said.

"I'm a little dizzy. What happened?" Eli asked.

"You passed out."

Roz appeared. "Should I call a doctor, Rabbi?"

"I don't need a doctor, Roz. I'm fine. I just lost my balance for a second." He shook off the hands that helped him up and walked unaided to his office.

Mark rushed back to his office. "Millie, get me Linda Freling on the phone."

"He fell again." Mark breathlessly relayed the news to Linda. They were on speaking terms again. He had apologized for the way he behaved at lunch and she had forgiven him.

"Where did it happen?"

"Right outside his office."

"When?"

"Just a couple of minutes ago. The janitor got there first and then I got there and then Roz. I don't know if anyone actually saw him fall."

Mark was getting anxious. Nothing much had changed since the night Eli announced to the congregation that he was ill. He was still coming to the synagogue every day and there was no indication that he had made any plans to retire. If Linda was doing anything to hasten his retirement, Mark wasn't aware of it.

"How long is all this going to take?"

"Be patient, Mark," Linda answered. "These things takes time. Everything is going to work out fine."

*   *   *

Rachel brought Eli his supper on a tray.

"How are you feeling, sweetheart?"

"A little headache, that's all."

Rachel marveled at Eli's ability to shunt concerns about his illness to some distant corner of his brain. She couldn't do it. His illness obsessed her. She scoured the Internet every day for information about ALS and read every article she could get her hands on, determined to find some new treatment that would offer a glimmer of hope. On their way home after his last visit to the neurologist, she had suddenly begun bombarding him with questions. How could the doctors be so sure he had ALS? She didn't trust doctors. Maybe they were wrong. Why had he been so passive? Why did he just sit there, during the examination, saying nothing?

Eli had waited until she calmed down. "You know what I want?" he said. "I just want to keep going for as long as I can and talk about it as little as I have to."

He finished eating and pushed the tray away. "I'll tell you what's weird."

"What?"

"When I came to, Mark was standing over me and I swear I heard him say to someone, 'I wonder how many times I'm going to have to pick him up off the floor.'"

"You're imagining things, honey. Why would Mark ever say a thing like that? I wish you'd pick a date for your retirement. What's the point of acting like you have all the time in the world?"

CHAPTER THIRTEEN

Max Jessel had just finished reading the sports pages and was glancing through the front section of the morning paper when his eye caught an item on the editorial page. It was a letter addressed "To the Commissioner of Baseball." Next to the letter there was a photograph of Mark Winnick wearing an Indians' baseball cap and a caption that read:

Rabbi Reads Riot Act to Baseball

Dear Commissioner:

I have been a baseball fan all my life. Over the years the game has reflected the highest ideals of our society and has inspired generations of young Americans to a lifetime of achievement and excellence.

Along with millions of other fans, I have been saddened to witness the decline of our national pastime. The senseless use of drugs to enhance natural talent, the misconduct of some of our favorite players both on and off the field, the greediness of owners, and the incessant commercialization of the game are contributing to the rapid deterioration of the sport. Baseball, which should be revered as a national trust, has become the plaything of the rich and powerful.

It's time to stop the erosion of values that is currently undermining baseball. Baseball is the cherished patrimony of every American. It reflects what is best in American popular culture and represents the best of our great Judeo-Christian tradition.

I know that you must be as concerned as I am about what is happening. If, in your deliberations, you should decide that a strengthening of the moral and spiritual foundations of our national pastime is overdue, I would be pleased to meet with you to discuss this important matter.

Sincerely,
Mark Winnick
Assistant Rabbi,
Shaaray Emunah Synagogue

Max jumped up and pushed the paper across the kitchen table to his wife, Ellie, who was scrambling eggs for his breakfast.

"You see this?" he asked.

"What is it, dear? I left my reading glasses upstairs," Ellie said.

"It's a letter to the editor by that putz, Mark Winnick. We're supposed to be figuring out whether he's qualified to be Eli's replacement and the whole time he's angling to set up prayer shop in the commissioner's office. They even have his picture in the paper with a goddam Indians' baseball cap on his head!"

"You're getting yourself all worked up, Max. It's not good for your blood pressure. Sit down and eat your breakfast."

Max shoveled a forkful of egg into his mouth. The gall of that little schmuck, he thought. Before I'm through with him he'll be sorry he ever learned to write.

*   *   *

Mark was proud of his letter. He had read it over a dozen times before he sealed it in an envelope, addressed it to The Editor, Cleveland Plain Dealer and dropped it in the mailbox. He hadn't said a word to Susan about it. When he showed her the editorial page she turned white.

"What did you do that for?" she asked.

"I've been thinking about doing it for a long time."

"Did you talk to Rabbi Stone about it?"

"Why should I?"

Why was she always worrying? People wrote letters to the editor all the time. They spouted off about everything from health care to global warming. None of the letters did any good. The people who could change things didn't care. They did what they wanted and lied about it later. But his letter was different. Americans were hooked on baseball.

The President tossed out the first ball at the start of the season. Congressmen and senators attended ballgames with their wives and mistresses. People would read his letter and reflect on what was happening to the game. They would demand action and the men who owned the teams would listen and changes would be made.

He put on the baseball cap he always wore on his way to work, got in his car and headed for the synagogue. At a red light a car pulled up next to him. The driver shouted something and gave him a thumbs-up sign. Before he reached the synagogue two more drivers had honked their horns. One man rolled down his window and called out, "Way to go, Rabbi."

When he got to his office, Millie was waiting for him. He had never seen her so excited. "The phones have been ringing all morning. I can't keep up with them. Mrs. Freling wants to talk to you right away."

"Well, that was certainly a surprise," Linda bubbled. "Why didn't you tell me what you were planning to do?"

"You're not upset?"

"Why would I be upset?"

Pamela Dawes was on the other line. Mark cut short his conversation with Linda.

"Rabbi," Pamela purred, "I was wondering if you'd be a guest on my show tonight. I want to talk to you about that letter . . . You'll do it? . . . Wonderful. Try to get down here by four-thirty. We'll have a chance to chat a bit before we go on the air."

The phone kept ringing. Millie fielded all the calls. Mark picked up an extension and listened in.

"We used to take our kids to the ballgame two, three times a year but with ticket prices where they are, we can't afford it anymore. Tell the rabbi that we support him one hundred percent."

"Me and my husband used to be big fans until all those steroids and the other stuff. Tell the rabbi to give 'em hell. It's about time someone let them assholes know which end is up."

Mark spun around in his chair and stared out the single window of his small office. A bird was trapped there, flapping its wings trying to escape. There was no way they would keep him holed up here. His letter to the editor had been an inspiration. If the congregation wanted someone of stature to replace Eli, he would give them what they wanted. Pamela Dawes had invited him on her show. Soon everyone in the city would know his name.

*   *   *

In his skybox above the baseball field, Max Jessel sat alone, staring out into the night. It was raining lightly and the grounds crew was huddled in the Indians' dugout waiting for the rain to stop. Max enjoyed the quiet time before the crowds streamed in. There was a solemn grandeur about an empty stadium. Acres of green grass mowed to a perfect checkerboard pattern. High intensity lights that made everything look like a movie set. Max had grown up in a crowded orphanage in London during the Second World War and had been brought to Cleveland by a childless middle-aged couple named Jessel. His adoptive father had been a house painter and his adoptive mother worked in a grocery store near the synagogue. Max revered them. When he bought the ball club he renamed the stadium Jessel Field in their honor. He dreamed of bringing the city a pennant after a drought of sixty years. If he was successful, his name and the name of his parents would be remembered long after he was gone.

He knew he had overreacted to the letter. How many people read the editorial page? And even if they read it, they would probably get a laugh seeing Rabbi Winnick with a baseball cap stuck on his head. Today's newspaper would be wrapped around tomorrow's garbage and the letter would be forgotten.

He switched on the TV to watch *Five by Five* as he did every night. Pamela Dawes sat in an armchair in front of a backdrop of the city skyline with Mark Winnick seated across from her.

"Rabbi, what in the world motivated you to write that letter?"

"I've been a baseball fan all my life, Pamela. When I was a kid I collected baseball cards. By the time I was ten I knew the batting average of every ball player in the major leagues. The game has always meant a lot to me, but it isn't the same game anymore. If you're a wealthy corporation you can buy a skybox for a couple hundred thousand dollars, but if you just want see a game now and then, you're lucky if you can afford a seat in the bleachers. If you want to watch your home team play on TV you have to subscribe to a premium channel."

"But you're a rabbi. Why would want to get yourself mixed up in something like this?"

"Because baseball is a religion for most Americans and it's being threatened by the greediness of management and by the behavior of certain stars of the game. The game doesn't belong to the fans any more. It's just another big business and the fans are the last thing anyone ever thinks about. I felt an obligation to speak out."

"You said in your letter that you hoped the commissioner would talk with you. Have you heard from him?"

"Not yet, but I hope I get the chance. I've got a lot of ideas I'd like to discuss with him."

"And what about our own team? Isn't its owner, Max Jessel, a member of your congregation?"

"Yes, he is."

"How do you think he's going to react to your letter?"

"I hope he'll be open-minded and understand that I'm trying to help the sport."

Max switched off the TV and stared silently at the screen. Then he grabbed a phone and punched a button with his stubby finger. "Has Bobby G. come in yet? Tell him to get his ass up here as soon as he comes in."

* * *

Amanda Johnson, Max Jessel's smartly dressed secretary, ushered Bobby G. into the chairman's skybox. "Max stepped out for a minute, Bobby. He'll be right back. He asked me to see if there was anything you wanted."

"Just you, hon, but I guess that's out of the question."

"Sit down and behave yourself," Amanda chided. She was married to Deshawn Johnson, the team's head trainer. "You want me to tell Deshawn that you're flirting with me again? He'll turn the temperature in your whirlpool up so high your ass will fry."

Bobby laughed. "I'll take a cup of coffee if you got some."

"Cream and sugar?"

"Black is fine with me, honey. Always has been."

Amanda gave him a mock-angry look and headed for the door. The sight of a good-looking woman always set Bobby's mind to contemplating the possibilities. You let them know you were interested and if they were available things followed naturally. Most of the ballplayers felt the same way. When you were flying to a different city every few days and under constant pressure, you needed easy relaxation without complications. Even the married ballplayers would tell you that when they were on the road, "away doesn't count."

Bobby had met Liz Aurelio that way. She brought him a beer and lingered at his table for a moment. She had been an ideal playmate for a while, but it was time to move on and he had stopped calling her. Now it was Renee Lassiter who fascinated him. He had a feeling they would get along if she gave him half a chance, but he would have to wait until the season was over before he could spend the kind of quality time with her that he knew she would demand.

Under the bright lights, Bobby watched the grounds crew strip the protective tarpaulin from the infield. He disliked being called to management meetings. The last few years, as he moved from club to club, a call from the front office usually meant a handshake and a "thank you, but we won't be needing you anymore." He was sure the meeting with Max wasn't about that. Max had picked him up when he was down and had given him a chance and Bobby had delivered. But Max was putting pressure on him to sign a short-term contract for a lot less money than he thought he was worth. He enjoyed being with the Indians, but at thirty-seven he wasn't getting any younger. This was his last chance to make the kind of deal that would guarantee him a comfortable retirement.

Max barged in, a cigar clamped between his teeth, and dropped down in a chair across from Bobby. He pushed the morning paper across his desk, open to the editorial page.

"You see this?"

"Yeah, I saw it."

"What did you think of it?"

Bobby hadn't paid much attention to the letter. Mark was naïve about baseball. It wasn't a sport anymore. It was big-time business and the players and the owners were paid accordingly.

"I just got through watching that little putz on *Five by Five*, Max sputtered. "Spouting off like he knew what he was talking about. What's he think he's doing?"

"He's a baseball nut, Max. He knows the averages of every player who played in the last twenty years."

"I don't care if he knows what time of day they take a crap," Max bellowed. "Where does he get off talking like that? He's a rabbi for chrissake. He's not a fucking sports writer." Max's temper was legendary. It erupted as regularly as the fireworks that exploded over the grandstand when someone hit a home run. "We gotta be careful," Max continued, turning suddenly sober and reflective. "First of all he's one of us, you know what I mean? Second, he's a rabbi, which makes it worse. And third, he's a fucking troublemaker. The media gets hold of this, they'll blow it up out of proportion and all of a sudden it's not about baseball. It's about us and them and there's a hell of a lot more of 'them' than there are of 'us' and who knows where it goes from there? You gotta get him off my back."

"How am I supposed to do that?"

"You're his friend. Talk to him."

"We're not that close," Bobby said.

"Tell him to back the hell off."

"Why would he pay attention to me?"

Max crumpled the newspaper and threw it on the floor. "I got a team that's maybe gonna make it to the playoffs. Maybe all the way to the World Series. I want you to tell that son of a bitch that he's not doing himself or me or you or the sport of baseball any good with all this mouthing off. He admires you. He'll listen to you."

"What if he won't?"

"Then we'll think of something else," Max said.

"I can't promise anything."

"I'm not asking for a promise. Just find a way to do it. It would mean a lot to me."

"Like how much?" Bobby responded with a wide smile.

"I'm not talking about your contract, for chrissakes! This is something bigger than that. There's only a few of us in the game and we gotta stick together. We don't want some misguided schmuck fucking things up. That's more important than any contract, which is something we can talk about later. Now get the hell out of here and win us a game tonight."

CHAPTER
FOURTEEN

When the television interview was over, Pamela invited Mark to join her for a drink. She wanted to show him off. There had been a meeting at the station that afternoon where Cindi Li was introduced to everyone. Cindi had handled the meeting brilliantly, saying how pleased she was to be at the station and how eager she was to "fit in." Pamela wasn't fooled. It was only a matter of time before the ax would fall, and she was determined do everything she could to keep her job. The excitement over Mark's letter would probably die down in a day or two, but in the meantime it couldn't hurt to be seen with someone the whole town was talking about.

They drove down to Carnavale, a new restaurant that had opened in the Flats, an area along the river where freighters used to unload iron ore for the city's steel mills. When the steel mills closed down and the terminals were abandoned, the riverfront had been turned into a popular spot for dining and late-night entertainment. It was already dark and the lights of the stadium a quarter-mile away cast a brilliant halo in the sky. A muffled roar reverberated across the river valley.

"That's a hometown roar," Mark said. "Either our pitcher struck out somebody or else we scored."

"You really do care about baseball, don't you?" Pamela said.

"I would have been a baseball player if I had any talent."

"What are your current plans? There's talk that you're looking around for another job."

Mark was careful with his answer. "I have an employment agreement with the synagogue for the next three years."

"I just thought that with Rabbi Stone ill, you might be concerned about your future."

"I hope that my future will be with the congregation."

They entered the crowded restaurant and the hostess came over to seat them. She was tall and slim, her long dark hair piled up on top of her head. She wore an elegant black silk dress with spaghetti straps and a hem of black lace. "Hi, Miss Dawes, remember me? Liz Aurelio? We met at Rabbi Stone's house? On New Year's Day? I was there with Bobby G.?"

Pamela vaguely remembered a dark-haired girl in an off-the-rack dress with a charming lilt in her voice who had come in with Bobby. "Look at you!" Pamela exclaimed. "The last time I saw you, you were a waitress in a bar across from the stadium and now here you are at the fanciest restaurant in town. Say hello to Rabbi Mark Winnick."

"Omigod," Liz exclaimed. "I just watched you on *Five by Five*. You were amazing."

Mark realized that people were staring at them. There was a buzz in the room as Liz led them to a table with a river view.

"This table okay, Miss Dawes?" Liz asked.

"It's perfect, dear. We're just going to have a drink and then I have to get back to work," Pamela said. "Are you and Bobby G. still going together?"

Liz managed a brave smile. Bobby had been a total shit. He had dumped her for someone who taught at the local university. One time he had actually brought the woman into the restaurant and when she seated them, Bobby had acted like he didn't know her. "I'm not seeing him anymore. I have this new job that I really like and I'm looking around for a new apartment."

Liz gave Mark the once-over. He was cute. A little on the short side but he had a pleasant face and attractive brown eyes and he smiled a lot. She remembered seeing him at Rabbi Stone's house the day she went there with Bobby. "I watch you get out of your car sometimes, Rabbi. I live right across from the synagogue. You always look like you're in a rush to go somewhere." She glanced toward the door where more people were coming in. "Oops! I better get back to work or my boss will kill me. Nice to see you again, Miss Dawes. Really nice meeting you, Rabbi. If you come in again, be sure to say hello."

"What a delight," Pamela exclaimed after Liz had left. "The next time we come in here she'll probably own the place."

Mark watched Liz walk away. It had been a long time since a good-looking woman had paid that much attention to him. He wondered if she really found him attractive or if it was only because she had seen him on Pamela's show. A couple stopped by to shake his hand.

"How do you like all the attention?" Pamela asked.

"I don't know yet," Mark said.

"You'll get used to it."

"You think so?"

"I'm sure of it." Pamela noted the gleam in Mark's eye. There was nothing like a little celebrity, she thought, to bring out the worst in people.

*   *   *

On his way home Mark switched on the late-night news. Cleveland had ended up losing in the bottom of the ninth. He felt bad for the team. They were fighting for a spot in the playoffs and had lost their last three games. But on a personal level he was elated. He had taken a chance writing the letter to the newspaper and it was paying off. People knew who he was now. He could feel it. The stares. The buzz. And Liz Aurelio had suggested that when he came down to Carnavale again, he should be sure to say hello.

When he got home, Susan was asleep and there was a note taped to the refrigerator door.

"Bobby G. wants to talk to you."

He poured himself a glass of milk and called Bobby. They chatted about the game for a while. Bobby sounded as if he had been drinking. "That letter you wrote to the paper, Rabbi. I didn't think much of it and I didn't think much of the TV show either."

"I'm sorry you feel that way, Bobby. I thought we shared some of the same views."

"That was just the two of us talking, Rabbi. I got my ass handed to me by the front office today and some of the guys on the team are giving me a hard time. They figure since you and me are friends, I must have put you up to it."

"Up to what?"

"Knocking the game."

"I'm not knocking baseball. I'm just trying to point out some things that might make it more appealing for the fans."

"Well, that don't mean shit, Rabbi, if you'll pardon the expression. Do yourself and me a big favor. Cool it, okay?"

"It's just my opinion, Bobby. A lot of people feel the way I do."

"Yeah, well maybe they do and maybe they don't, but what you're doing is making a lot of people real mad."

Mark crawled into bed next to Susan. She lay on her back, snoring lightly, her pregnant stomach pushing up the sheets. He was glad he had written the letter. If it made some people angry he didn't care. His letter had touched a nerve. You had to take risks to get ahead. From now on no one would ignore him. Even Rabbi Stone would pay attention.

CHAPTER FIFTEEN

That same night Leo Bookman finished his favorite TV dinner, Stouffer's baked chicken in a white wine sauce. A bottle of Chateau d'Yquem 2000 sat half empty on his kitchen table. It was the priciest bottle in the small collection he kept in a twenty-eight-bottle thermoelectric wine cellar in his hall closet. Fine wine was his sole indulgence and he had promised himself that he would keep this bottle for a special occasion. Tonight there was reason to celebrate. The three million shares of Fabrico he owned had closed that afternoon at $5.55 a share. He was worth more than $15 million.

It had been a trying day in other ways. After Mark's letter had appeared in the newspaper, reporters from the TV stations started calling and the synagogue switchboard had been swamped. He was aware that a certain frostiness had developed between Mark and Rabbi Stone. The meeting at Linda's house, to which he had not been invited, had significantly heightened the tension, but he wasn't sure what it all added up to. He worried that the stable routine of the synagogue was being disrupted and that was never a good thing.

Most of his thoughts were focused on his portfolio. The size of his investment in Fabrico was beginning to make him nervous. Until recently his net worth had been an enjoyable abstraction. He lived a simple life. He still rented the same one-bedroom apartment he had lived in for twenty years. He owned a new Apple laptop and had recently purchased a fifty-four-inch flat screen TV. Otherwise his life hadn't changed much since the time he had gone to work at the synagogue sixteen years ago.

Leo had charted Fabrico stock over the last three years and read everything he could about the company. He had confidence in Sam Broad. He believed the steps the company was taking to stem its losses would be effective and that the market overall was probably heading up. Sam Broad and Marty Franklin had been particularly upbeat about the company at the last meeting of the synagogue board. He had overheard Sam mention that he thought the company would start reporting profits by the end of the second quarter of next year. That was encouraging news. Still, he had never had so much riding on a single stock and wondered if it wouldn't be a good idea to talk to someone about it.

The following morning Brian Patzer ushered a nervous Leo Bookman into his small office. He couldn't imagine why Leo wanted to see him. Perhaps he had managed to squirrel away a few thousand dollars and was coming in for some investment advice. If that was the case, he would chat with him for a couple of minutes and turn him over to one of the younger salesmen who would recommend one of the mutual funds that Petrie & Company handled.

"How are you, Leo?" Brian asked.

"I'm very well, Mr. Patzer. Thank you for seeing me."

"Brian, please. What can I do for you?"

Leo tugged nervously at a loose thread on his sleeve. He had almost decided not to come. He hardly ever left his job during the day to attend to personal matters. If he did, it was for a doctor's appointment or a visit to the dentist, and he always told someone where he was going. Today, he had slipped away quietly, hoping no one would notice.

"I have some questions about an investment matter and I thought you might be able to help me," Leo said.

"Sure, Leo. Shoot."

Leo had debated with himself whether or not it made sense to talk to Brian. He was eager to preserve the anonymity that he had guarded successfully over the years and worried about what might happen if it became known that he had made all this money. He executed his purchases and sales through a half dozen online brokerage houses, where his identity was a secret. The trades were handled by computer and the extent of what he owned was known only to himself.

"I've never had occasion to discuss what I have with anyone so I hope we can keep this conversation private."

"Of course we'll keep it private, Leo. What's on your mind?"

"I've done a little investing over the last few years and I own some shares of Fabrico. I'm worried that I may be over-invested and that maybe I should lighten up a little."

"Well, that's a legitimate concern. Diversification is always a good idea."

"I've noticed that the volume of trading in the stock has been rising lately and the price has been moving up."

Brian nodded agreeably. "Sounds like you take a solid professional interest in your money. How much Fabrico stock are we talking about, Leo? Give me some idea so I can try to be helpful."

"I'd rather just talk about the company's prospects, if that's all right with you."

Brian smiled. Most small investors were reluctant to talk about how much stock they owned. They were afraid that their negligible net worth made them unattractive candidates for investment advice. "I really need to know a little more, Leo. How many shares do you own? A few hundred?"

"A bit more than that."

"How much more, Leo? I really can't help you if I don't have an idea of what we're talking about. We're just as interested here in the small investor as in the big one." Brian glanced at the clock on the wall. It was almost nine-thirty. The market would be opening in a few minutes. He was anxious to get Leo out of his office so he could go to work.

"I own over three million shares."

Brian wasn't sure that he had heard Leo correctly. "How many?"

"Three million fifty-one thousand shares to be precise. I bought them at an average price of $3.80 a share and the stock is up to $5.50 and I'm wondering if I should sell or at least lighten up some." Leo communicated the information with the same detachment with which he advised the board of the size of each year's impending deficit, but he couldn't help deriving a little satisfaction from the look of astonishment on Brian's face. "You're the only one I know who's in the business and I thought you might be able to give me some advice."

"Three million shares, Leo! That's fucking incredible! And all this time I thought you were this quiet guy who sat in our board meetings and took minutes and then went home to watch reruns on Turner Classics. How in the world did you manage to keep this quiet all this time? Who does your trading for you?"

"I use a number of online brokers."

"And how do you decide when to buy and sell?"

"I do my own research and I listen to what people say."

Leo's absence of ego made Brian smile. Most of the people he knew who were worth half of what Leo was thought they were geniuses. "Three million shares, Leo! That's $15 million!"

"Fifteen million seven hundred and eighty thousand, to be exact."

"How long have you been at this?"

"I've been investing for the last twelve years, but I've never let it interfere with my work at the synagogue."

"I'm sure you haven't."

"I've been very rigorous about that. I made a lot of money on Fabrico when it first came out and I have this feeling that the stock has bottomed out so I started accumulating shares again. I thought that you might help me evaluate what's going on and advise me whether I'm in too heavily."

The nine-thirty start of trading had come and gone. Brian closed the door to his office and for the next hour they discussed Fabrico. Brian told Leo that Fabrico was having a tough time but that Sam had a decent shot at turning the company around. He didn't mention Petrie's short position or anything about the tender offer that he knew was coming. He suggested that Leo sit tight with what he had. He would keep his eye on the company and tell Leo if there were any changes that might affect his position. "And you don't have to worry about my talking to anyone about this, Leo. I understand your desire for privacy."

"I appreciate that," Leo said as he stood up to leave. "I feel I can count on your discretion."

Brian watched as Leo made his way to the front door. He couldn't help smiling. This inconspicuous little man was a major player in a high stakes poker game that he didn't even know was going on. Leo would be his insurance policy. Somewhere down the line, knowing that Leo owned three million shares of Fabrico stock would come in handy.

*   *   *

It was the height of the baseball season and the story of an unknown midwestern rabbi challenging the baseball establishment caught the attention of the media. Mark's letter had been reprinted in more than one hundred fifty major city newspapers. Excerpts from his interview with

Pamela Dawes had been picked up and rebroadcast by dozens of stations across the country and he had been invited to appear on the Letterman show.

"All this incredible stuff is going on and it doesn't mean a thing," Mark complained as he got ready to leave home for the synagogue. "I'm doing twice as much work as I used to because Rabbi Stone's not down there half the time. I get more mail in a day than he gets in a month and I'm still holed up back there in the boonies with just one secretary to help me with everything."

"Be patient, honey," Susan urged. "Give people a chance to digest what's happening. I'm sure that's the best thing to do right now."

"I'm going to talk to him."

"About what?"

"About how I feel."

"You'll just get him upset. What will that accomplish?"

"I want him to take me seriously."

"I'm sure he takes you seriously."

"No he doesn't. He treats me like I'm a nobody."

Mark knew he should make allowances for Susan, whose pregnancy was making her nervous about everything, but he hated the way she was always undermining him, urging him to be careful.

"I don't want you getting into trouble," she pleaded.

"I'm not going to get into trouble. I'm just tired of hanging around, waiting for things to happen."

Mark started for the door to the garage. Susan noticed that he was walking strangely. "Are your shoes bothering you, honey?"

"No, my shoes are fine." Mark gave her a quick kiss and hurried to his car. The lifts he had just purchased took some getting used to.

* * *

Roz McIver greeted Eli as he came in. "How are you feeling, Rabbi?"

"A little bump on my head, that's about it."

Eli had taken a few days off after his fall. His ribs still ached. He was tiring more easily and his voice was occasionally hoarse. Once or twice he felt that he might be slurring his words. He could feel the syllables gathering in his mouth like loose marbles. He settled down behind his desk and Roz brought him his mail.

"I need you to be totally honest with me, Roz. You know how this thing is. If you hear me slurring my words, even a little, I want you to tell me."

Roz refused to answer him directly. "Let's go over your schedule for today, Rabbi. Adam Burwell is coming in to review the organ music for this weekend's service and Jessica Freling is scheduled for her bat mitzvah talk with you at four. Then Rabbi Winnick wanted to know if he could see you for a few minutes. I told him after lunch, if that's okay with you."

"I'd rather see him now."

Roz called Mark's office and spoke to Millie, who relayed the message. The last meeting in Eli's office had been a disaster. Mark preferred a more neutral meeting place. "Millie, see if the Rabbi will meet me in the parlor," Mark said.

The answer came back immediately. "Rabbi Stone prefers to see you in his office."

*   *   *

Mark settled in a chair across from Eli. "I suggested the parlor, Rabbi, because I thought it might be easier for us to talk there."

"That's perfectly all right, Mark. What's on your mind?"

"I'm embarrassed by all the mail that's coming in."

A sack full of mail addressed to Mark was coming in every day. *People* magazine had sent a reporter and a photographer to do a story on him and he had agreed to pose in front of the synagogue with his Cleveland Indians baseball cap on his head. A number of members of the congregation had called in, expressing dismay that he was using his position as a rabbi for things that had nothing to do with his religious responsibilities, but others, mostly the younger members, were surprisingly supportive. Eli had decided that the best thing to do was to pay as little attention as possible. The storm of interest generated by the letter would blow over in a week or two and things would return to normal.

"I had no idea my letter would generate this kind of a response. I know it's putting a burden on everybody."

"That won't last forever. We'll deal with it. What I do object to is your use of the synagogue as a backdrop for publicity photographs."

"I'm sorry that happened. It was a mistake. It won't happen again." Mark tried to gauge Eli's mood, but Eli remained impassive, his hands folded quietly on his desk, waiting for Mark to get to the point.

"Is there something else you wanted to talk to me about?"

"There is one matter I would like to discuss with you, Rabbi. I'd like to be considered as a candidate for the senior position here when you decide to retire."

Ever since his meeting with Linda and Bill Palevsky, Eli had been expecting Mark to come in. "There's nothing that I'm aware of that would keep you from applying for the position," Eli said.

Mark shifted uncomfortably in his chair. "I think if I had been a rabbi somewhere else for the last five years and was applying for the job, I'd be considered a promising candidate, but the way things stand, it's impossible for me to get a fair hearing. The fact is, Rabbi, that without your support my candidacy is extremely difficult."

"It's not my intention to support any particular candidacy," Eli responded.

"Why are you so opposed to me? Don't you think I'm qualified?"

Eli had been around long enough to know that all sorts of people aspired to positions that exceeded their abilities. The lure of power was a compelling aphrodisiac. There was nothing wrong with ambition. He had plenty of it himself, but it required more than ambition to hold a congregation of two thousand members together. By the time he was Mark's age he had walked the streets of Birmingham with Martin Luther King, he'd been an early and constant critic of the Vietnam War, and had lobbied senators and presidents in support of the young State of Israel. And in between he'd kept on studying and learning. Leading a congregation required maturity and tact and thoughtfulness and compassion and a dozen other things that Mark was lacking.

"It doesn't really matter what I think, Mark. I don't make the final decision about who succeeds me. The board does that. It's the board that will decide if you're qualified or not. Not me."

Eli was trifling with him again. He wasn't a nobody any more. More people would see him on the Letterman show than had ever heard of Eli. Why should this dying man, whose reputation had been made years ago in struggles that hardly anyone remembered, block his chance to get ahead?

"You're making a big mistake, Rabbi. I'm qualified to lead this congregation regardless of what you think and there are a lot of people around here who share that opinion."

"If that's the case," Eli said, "you should have no difficulty in achieving your objective. Now if you'll excuse me, I have some work to do."

CHAPTER SIXTEEN

From where Sam Broad stood at the top of the winding marble staircase, he could look into the members' dining room of the Founder's Club where tables were set far apart and intimate conversations drifted up into the high coffered ceiling. The club, a pile of grime-encrusted granite on one of the main avenues downtown, was the preserve of the city's power elite. For most of its one hundred fifty years, decisions that affected the city's future were hashed out around tables in its private dining rooms. Sam was one of the first Jews invited to become a member. The first woman member had been accepted ten years ago. It had been a close vote and several of the older club members had resigned in protest.

Tom McCarthin, the new president of the Central Bank and Trust Company, bounded up the winding marble staircase and greeted Sam at the top of the landing. "Sorry I'm late, Sam, I hope you haven't been waiting long."

Sam had been a client of Central Bank ever since he started Fabrico. It was a small bank then, specializing in loans that the larger banks wouldn't touch. A national banking syndicate had bought control of Central a year ago and a group of young executives had been sent in from New York to run things. He had been invited to the syndicate's hunting lodge on Chesapeake Bay for a "get-to-know-you" weekend. Each morning he crouched in a duck blind with a group of the bank's younger officers and shivered in the cold. In the afternoon they tramped through dusty fields, flushing pheasants from stands of withered corn. At night, over friendly games of poker, there was endless talk about golf scores, trips to the Caribbean, and the merits of various private boarding schools. Sam came away from the weekend with a bad cold and a conviction that his company's relationship with the bank was about to undergo a fundamental change.

The maître d' sat them a table near the window. "I thought we could talk about our joint goals for next year," McCarthin said as the waiter placed steaming bowls of clam chowder in front of them. McCarthin was thirty-four, with prematurely gray hair and penetrating steel-gray eyes. His voice carried the remnants of a Boston Back Bay accent. "Tell me something about your plans."

"We're closing a number of unproductive stores and renegotiating some of our leases," Sam said. "We're going to concentrate on expansion in the U.S. and in Europe, where we see the best opportunity for growth. It's been a rough couple of years but we're going to pull through."

"What's your guess about how long it's going to take your company to reestablish profitability?" McCarthin asked.

"We're about a year away. By the middle of next year we should be profitable. We'll take a hit the next couple of quarters but after that we'll be a leaner operation and a profitable one."

"And what about your new headquarters building?"

The building was a sore subject and Sam had hoped to avoid it. "It's coming along."

"I talked to Max Jessel," McCarthin continued. "He says it's likely to be six months before it's finished and it may end up costing five million more than the original estimate."

"There's no question it's going to cost more," Sam said, choosing his words carefully. "There are times when I wish we hadn't started it when we did, but we're spread all over town and when the new place is finished we'll have a totally centralized purchasing and distribution system. We'll be able to track the performance of every store and every single item on a daily basis."

McCarthin spooned up the last of his clam chowder, wiping the corners of his thin lips with his napkin. "It's the construction loan that's got us worried, Sam. We've tried to lay off some of it on other banks, but given the way things are, they've turned us down. If times were better maybe, but they're worried about your company and so are we. Our loan department thinks we need additional collateral if we're going to advance you the money you need to finish the building."

"You already have five million shares of our stock," Sam said.

"Yes, but it's way below the price we took it in at, plus this will be the third consecutive year of losses for your company. If it was up to me, I'd let things go the way they are for a while, but I've got New York on my back."

"You want more stock?"

"We have too much of that already," McCarthin smiled at Sam with everything but his eyes. "What we want is more working capital in the company and we'd like you to personally guarantee the overrun on the construction loan."

"I won't do that," Sam said, picking nervously at the Cobb salad that the waiter had slipped in front of him. "More working capital is one thing, but personally guaranteeing the construction loan is something else. You're lending to the company, not to me."

"I understand your position," McCarthin said. "But you're going to have to do something. Your company's credit line comes up for review this month. We need to find a mutually agreeable solution. If we can't protect ourselves we'll have to consider cutting your company's line of credit. One way or another my instructions are to get our exposure under control. I'm sorry to have to be so blunt about it."

"How would your bank possibly benefit by shoving us against the wall?"

"That's an unfortunate way of characterizing our position. We're not interested in shoving you against the wall. Frankly, Sam, we hadn't planned to advance more money for construction than we originally anticipated. We're happy to maintain a relationship with your company but we've got to find a way to put things on a firm financial basis. How you decide to do it is up to you."

"I'll need some time," Sam said.

"We'd like an answer as soon as possible."

"I'll need a couple of weeks."

"A week would be better," McCarthin said. "I wouldn't want to stretch it any further."

*   *   *

The offices of Calypso Partners, Peter Freling's investment company, occupied a high floor of a downtown office building. Secretaries scurried down carpeted hallways. People spoke in hushed tones. Computers whirred noiselessly. The smell of money was everywhere. Peter and Marty Franklin sat across from one another at a glass-topped conference table in one of the firm's small conference rooms. There was a Hans Hofmann on the wall and a Giacometti on a pedestal in the corner and, out the window, a breathtaking view of the downtown skyline and the lake. A waiter brought in plates of curried chicken salad, set them down and left.

They had both come to Cleveland the same year. Peter had gone to work in his father-in-law's scrap steel business. Marty was hired by Burkett, Burden and Wilkoff, one of the city's most prestigious law firms. The firm represented the estate of Linda's father, and Marty had been assigned the task of sorting out a disagreement over a large amount of money that had been loaned by Linda's father to a close friend just before his death. Peter, as executor of his father-in-law's estate, wanted to sue to get the money back. Marty urged him not to. Even if he won, the financial benefit would be offset by a damaged reputation.

"You remember when Linda's father died?" Peter asked. "You gave me some good advice then."

"I remember," Marty said.

"I'm considering something equally sensitive and I need your advice again."

"As a lawyer?"

"As a friend."

"Shoot."

"Jess Ballard and I are planning to make a tender offer for control of Fabrico."

Marty wiped the corners of his mouth with his napkin and continued eating. Peter suppressed a smile. The only time you got a rise from lawyers was when you questioned them about their bills.

"We're prepared to make an offer that we think Sam will find attractive and we'd like the opportunity to talk to him about it."

"What would you do with the company, liquidate it?"

"That's not our plan at all. The company had tremendous potential but not the way it's going. We'd close down some stores. Get out of some dying markets. Tighten up the company's marketing strategy. We've got some ideas about new product lines. We're prepared to invest a substantial amount of fresh money in the company. Maybe down the line we'd merge it with a couple of companies that we have interests in, but not right away."

"What about management?" Marty asked.

"Sam's key people will get significant severance packages. We'd like him to stay on for a while in a consulting capacity."

"What kind of price are you talking about?"

"We think seven dollars is a fair price. That's more than 30 percent above current market."

Marty wished he had picked the signs up sooner. He had an inkling that something might be happening when Josh came in to see him about his father, but he had put it out of his mind. "Is Josh Stone part of your team?"

"Yes, he is. Ballard sent him here to help out."

"Have you set a date for the offer?"

"We'd like to talk to Sam first."

"Let me talk to him. I'm sure he'll meet with you, but I can pretty much predict what his answer will be."

* * *

As soon as the lunch was over, Marty called Sam. "I figured it was only a matter of time until someone took a shot at us," Sam said. "Peter Freling? Well, I guess I shouldn't be surprised. He called me a couple of weeks ago and wanted to have lunch. Never got around to it. How much time do we have?"

"My guess is they're close to announcing the offer. They want to meet with you first."

"What do you think?"

"I'd meet with them. You've got nothing to lose."

"Who is this Ballard guy?"

"He runs a takeover firm in New York called Parallax. Josh Stone works with him."

The phone went dead for a moment while Sam absorbed the news. "Jesus! I figured he was in town to be with his dad."

"So did I. Do you think Eli knows?"

"I doubt it. He would have said something to me if he did."

"Someone better tell him."

"I'll tell him myself," Sam said. "I sure as hell don't want him hearing about it on the evening news."

* * *

Jessica sat in a chair in Eli's office, her green wool cap pulled down over her ears. "I love the part where Miriam sings this song about how the Jews escaped from Egypt and made it across the Red Sea. Do you think it really happened that way?"

"What do you think?"

"I think it's a cool story, but I don't think it's true."

Eli made a habit of spending a half hour with each child before his or her bar mitzvah. It was pure pleasure for him. Children were so unpredictable. They could make you laugh or leave you dumbfounded at the profound insights they expressed in simple ways. Most sat across from him, shifting uncomfortably in their chairs, communicating in grunts, eager for the meeting to be over, but Jessica was a delightful exception.

"How's the preparation going?"

"Rabbi Mark has been working with me on my Hebrew. It's coming along okay."

"What about your talk?" Eli had heard almost everything in the few minutes each child was given to address the congregation. Most of them talked about how they planned to make the world a better place and then thanked their parents for "bringing them to this day." But there had been notable exceptions. Once a boy had delivered a string of one-liners about getting ready for his bar mitzvah with the timing of a borscht-belt comic. The only thing missing was the drum roll after the punch line. Another time a girl had talked about a summer spent on a kibbutz in Israel and how she had used desert flowers to make perfume. She brought an atomizer to the pulpit and sprayed perfume at the congregation.

"I started writing something about wanting to be a rabbi," Jessica said, tugging at the edges of her cap, "but it drives my mom and dad crazy when I talk about it, so I'm writing something about my family instead."

"That sounds like a good idea. Have you gone over your speech with anyone?"

"Do I have to?"

"You don't have to. It's just a suggestion."

"Do you go over your sermons with someone?"

Eli smiled. "That's a fair question. Not usually. But sometimes I talk over what I'm going to say with my wife. You might want to do the same thing with your mom or dad. Sometimes people get nervous up there on the pulpit and it can help to try their speech out first on someone."

*   *   *

Adam Burwell, the synagogue's young organist, stretched out his long legs under Eli's desk. He was thirty-five, taught piano at the Music Institute, and had been the organist at the synagogue for the last three years. "We've kind of worn out the old standards, Rabbi. I was planning to play some Rossi this week if that's okay with you."

"Eighteenth century?"

"Late seventeenth century, actually. I did some research. Until Rossi came along no musical instruments or voices were used in the synagogue. It was a sign of mourning for the Temple in Jerusalem after it was destroyed. He brought music back into the service. The authorities in Venice thought so much of him that they exempted him from having to wear the yellow star."

Eli often wondered what it would be like to have this kind of relationship with Josh. He could talk with Adam about anything, but when he and Josh got together there never seemed to be anything to talk about. It had been that way with his father. Once he had made the decision to become a Reform rabbi, the intimacy he had once enjoyed with his father was replaced by a cold detachment.

"As for the recessional, Rabbi, I thought maybe some Bach, if that's not going to bother you too much."

"Bach is fine. No reason to let the goyim have all the fun."

* * *

As he was getting ready to leave for home, Roz called in. "Sam Broad is on his way over. He'll be here in a few minutes. He said it was important."

When Sam arrived they chatted briefly about the weather and the chance the Indians had to make the playoffs. Eli recognized the signs of someone who was having trouble coming to the point.

"Something's bothering you, Sam."

"You ever hear of a company called Parallax?"

"Sure. That's where Josh works."

"I just found out they're planning to make a tender offer for my company," Sam said.

Eli was stunned. The idea that Josh was working for someone who was trying to take over Sam's company was hard enough to understand. The fact that his own son had kept him in the dark about it was incomprehensible.

"He never said anything to me about what he was doing."

"I know that, Rabbi. I just didn't want you to hear about it from somewhere else."

"I'll take care of it," Eli said, the cold calmness in his voice masked the utter desolation he felt inside.

"It's not the end of the world, Rabbi," Sam urged. "Don't do something you'll regret."

*   *   *

Ballard poured himself a drink and handed one to Josh. Parallax's floor broker had just called to let him know that they had picked up another fifty thousand shares of Fabrico.

"We've got our 10 percent," Ballard crowed. "Now we can move."

The phone rang again. It was Peter calling. Ballard switched on the speakerphone. "I just got back from lunch with Marty Franklin."

"How'd it go?"

"I told him we were making a tender offer."

"How did he take it?"

"He didn't blink an eye. I doubt if they'll go for it. I set up a date for us to meet with Sam Broad this Wednesday afternoon."

"The news get out yet?"

"Not yet, but it won't be long."

Josh listened in shocked silence. Peter had promised to let him know in advance so that he would have a chance to tell his father before the news got out.

"Josh is here with me," Ballard said.

"Hey Josh, I meant to let you know, but things got kind of hectic around here and we had to move fast. And I bumped into Tom McCarthin at Central Bank. He says he knows you."

The call ended and Josh rose numbly from his chair, his mind flooded with images of the impending confrontation with his father. Ballard wrapped an arm around his shoulder and walked him to the door. "Peter's not the most considerate guy in the world, but I guess you figured that out already. I know you wanted to tell your dad first, but these things happen. You're doing a first rate job, pal. Keep it up. I'm counting on you."

*   *   *

Josh stood at the window of his office and watched a squall sweep in from the northwest, sheets of rain gusting in the narrow Wall Street canyons, drenching everything. In the building across the way a maid was vacuuming an empty office. The desk was bare and the pictures on the wall were gone. Maybe the young woman he had seen working there had been fired. Or maybe, fed up with the grind, she had just packed up and gone back to Illinois or Indiana or wherever she came from, her empty office waiting for the next person ready to stake out a temporary claim. Peter had let him down and so had Ballard. He could quit now but what would be the point? The financial world was littered with the wreckage of flamed-out careers. People would say he had moved too fast. That he had been pushed beyond the limits of his ability. One thing was sure. If he quit now, someone else would be at his desk tomorrow, ready to grab at the chance to work with Ballard. What was the point of losing everything? He'd get on a plane and fly to Cleveland and meet with his father. Maybe his father would understand.

CHAPTER
SEVENTEEN

By the time Josh arrived at Linda's the following afternoon, a number of cars were parked around the oval driveway. She had called the night before. "We've been talking about your dad's plans for retirement and some of us on the board thought you might be willing to help us." Josh had assumed that his father's retirement would be trouble free. A date would be set. There would be a celebration honoring his years of service. A new rabbi would be installed. "We've been trying to work through some of the issues related to an orderly transition and we've found it difficult talking to your father about it," Linda had said. "We want to do everything we can to make the transition as comfortable for him as possible. Will you come and talk to us?"

Linda led him into the sunroom, where Sally Minton, Bill Palevsky and Brian Patzer were waiting.

"I think you know everyone."

"Are there others coming?"

"It's just the four of us. This isn't a formal meeting, Josh, just a few of us trying to figure out the best way to move forward when your dad retires." Josh glanced around the room. No one seemed happy to be there. Bill Palevsky shifted uncomfortably in his chair, Sally Minton seemed distracted, and Brian Patzer was barely paying attention.

"Bill and I met with your father," Linda continued, "and we're reluctant to trouble him again. Bill, why don't you explain?"

Josh wondered what was coming next. Negotiations always started this way. First, an expression of goodwill, then a recapitulation of where things stood, and when that was over a list of demands inevitably followed. Josh wasn't surprised that Linda had asked Bill to continue. He was a lawyer and lawyers had the drill down pat.

"Josh, you know we have the highest regard for everything your father has meant to this congregation," Bill began, "but we have to make some hard decisions about the future and to be blunt, your father hasn't made it easy for us. We met with him last week and he suggested that we interview applicants for the job of senior rabbi. We're eager to do that, but your dad has been reluctant to announce a date for his retirement so we're not able to tell prospective candidates when the position might be available. We thought you might be able to give us some idea on how to move ahead."

"What did he say exactly?"

"He said he hadn't made up his mind when he planned to step down."

"We're not trying to pressure him," Linda interrupted, "but we have a responsibility to the congregation and we don't know how much time we've got. From what we understand, the course of your dad's illness is unpredictable. He's reasonably healthy now, but his condition is bound to deteriorate. Rabbi Winnick has expressed a willingness to stay through a transition, but he might not stay unless we can give him some idea of when your father plans to retire. He's been looking around, and with your father ill, the congregation would be in an extremely vulnerable position if he left. Fact of the matter is, the best thing would be for your father to announce his retirement as soon as possible. He'd be doing everyone a favor, including himself."

"Why is that?"

"I don't know if you're familiar with the terms of your father's employment agreement, but the board has a number of ways to encourage his retirement. It's the last thing we want to do, but we have to find a way to move ahead."

"If I know my dad, he'll announce his retirement when he thinks he can't do his work anymore."

"I understand," Linda continued, "but we have to take the congregation's needs into consideration as well as your father's. He's already collapsed a couple of times at work. Fortunately, there were people around to help him. And he's still teaching confirmation classes. There are a number of members of the congregation who don't think it's right for their children to have to watch his condition deteriorate. It's difficult for us to understand why he hasn't announced his retirement. It would be so much better for him to pick a date and let everybody know."

"Does the whole board feel this way?"

"A number of us do."

"How many?"

Linda's voice took on a firm edge. "Enough to take the necessary steps to force him to retire unless we can arrive at some accommodation."

It angered Josh that they were using him to get to his father. "If you expect me to suggest to my dad when he should retire, forget it. You want my advice, let him set his own schedule. He will anyway. He's not going to be pushed around by you or me or anyone."

After the meeting broke up, Josh walked Brian to his car. "What the hell was that all about?"

"Linda's got a bug up her ass. She wants Mark to take over when your dad retires, and your dad isn't cooperating. I thought you knew."

"How the hell did you get mixed up in this?"

"I do business with Peter. Linda asked me to come to the meeting and I couldn't very well say 'no.' How's the deal going?"

"The deal's going fine," Josh said.

"When's it going to happen?"

"Soon enough. Sit tight."

"I've been sitting tight for the past two weeks," Brian said. "I hope Ballard realizes that."

Josh wasn't listening. The news that Linda was conspiring to make Mark the next senior rabbi was bad enough. In less than an hour he would be meeting with his father, and the prospect of trying to explain his actions during the past two weeks terrified him. He drove home taking the back roads, anxious to postpone the inevitable confrontation. His mother met him at the door . Any lingering notion that his father might be unaware of what he had done was immediately dispelled.

"Why didn't you tell Dad what you were doing?"

"I wanted to tell him. I didn't think he'd understand."

"He's your father. You had an obligation to tell him."

Josh had never seen his mother so upset. He wanted to tell her that he didn't know how to talk to his father anymore. That he was frightened of him. Not in a physical way, but in the way a child is frightened of coming into a dark room at night and not being sure what he'll find when he gets inside. A car turned up the driveway and Rachel disappeared upstairs. The back door opened and Eli came in, barely glancing at Josh as he hung his coat in the front hall closet and walked slowly to his study.

After a moment Josh followed him. Eli was seated at his desk. Josh had always been amazed at how much larger than life his father seemed up close. His presence seemed to suck all the air out of the room. "I understand that the company you're working for intends to take over Sam's business." The even tone of Eli's voice masked a deep undercurrent of anger. He refused to look at Josh, staring instead at his own hands.

"I was planning to tell you."

"When? When it was all over?"

"I should have told you sooner."

"Why didn't you?"

"They didn't want me to talk about what I was doing."

"Who's they?"

"My company. We were trying to acquire a position in Fabrico stock before it became public knowledge and I was asked to keep quiet about it."

"And you agreed?"

"I would have preferred another assignment, but this is the one I got."

"You could have turned it down. Why didn't you?"

"They would just have given it to someone else. Don't you understand, Dad? Sam's business is in trouble. It's not being well managed. Somebody's going to buy his company. If it isn't us it's going to be someone else."

"Did it occur to you that what you were doing was wrong?"

Josh felt a sudden urge to lash out. "If I thought it was wrong I wouldn't have agreed to do it. We're not stealing the company. We're making a bid for it. I know you don't have much respect for what I do, but there are a lot of people whose jobs will be saved if we're successful. And Sam will walk away with more money than he has any right to expect."

"And that makes it right as far as you're concerned?"

"It's not a moral issue."

"Just another business decision, is that it?" Eli's words cut into Josh with the precision of a surgeon's knife paring away offending flesh.

"I know I should have told you what I was doing. I'm sorry that I didn't. Not that it would have made any difference." Josh's voice trembled as he spoke. "I didn't choose this assignment. It came and I took it and I'm going to do the best I can to make it work." He heard a door open at the top of the stairs. Rachel was listening. "I know you don't think much of what I do for a living. The only thing you ever cared about was that I might turn out to be a failure and that would embarrass you, instead of which I'm a success and you can't deal with that either. You want to make me feel inadequate? You want to belittle me? Go ahead. You've been doing it all my life. I've never had your approval for anything I've ever done, so I guess we can both deal with one more disappointment."

For a moment Josh thought his father was going to reach across the desk and hit him. Instead he picked up a pencil and Josh watched it slip out of his hand. He picked it up again and it fell out of his hand again and Josh saw his father's eyes fill with hopeless rage. Then he picked the pencil up a third time and snapped it in half. The sound of the pencil breaking shattered the silence like a rifle shot.

"I want you out of this house," Eli demanded in a voice thick with rage.

"I'll clear out tomorrow."

"I want you out of here tonight," Eli thundered. "If you want to act a stranger, live like one."

*   *   *

Rachel entered Josh's room and sat down on a corner of his bed. She had been crying.

"Please go downstairs and talk to him."

"There's nothing more to talk about, Mom."

"Just tell him that you're sorry."

"He's not interested in my apology."

"He's upset about everything that's been happening."

"Why didn't he tell me about what was going on at the synagogue? Why didn't he tell me he was sick?"

"He didn't want you to worry. Go down and talk to him. It's not right for the two of you to be fighting all the time."

Josh zipped his suitcase shut and tried to give his mother a hug but she pulled away.

"Don't worry about me, Mom. I'll be okay."

"I'm not worrying about you. It's your father I'm worried about."

He started down the stairs, pausing for a moment at the bottom of the landing. The door to Eli's study was closed. He wondered what would happen if he walked in and said he was sorry. He doubted that his father would even listen. He hurried through the house and out the door, tossing his suitcase in the trunk of his car. As he backed down the driveway, he stared up at the house and saw his mother watching from her bedroom window.

He drove around aimlessly for an hour. The cold fury with which he had been ordered out of the house left him drained. His father had discarded him as easily as he would throw away a pair of worn-out shoes. He wanted to believe that his father had acted out of frustration with his own diminishing vitality, but he knew the real reason was that he had deceived his father and there would be no reprieve.

It was after eight when he parked his car in the museum parking lot and headed for the side door. A camera stared down at him. The door opened and a uniformed guard took his name. A few minutes later an elevator hummed in the distance.

Antonia seemed irritated at the interruption. "I wasn't expecting you. I'm right in the middle of a lot of work. We've got a new show opening this weekend."

"Is there someplace we can talk?"

She led him up a flight of stairs to the main floor of the museum, where they sat on a bench overlooking the Armor Court. Soldiers in chain mail stood guard in the corners of the gallery. Heraldic banners hung from the wood-beamed ceiling. Longbows, pikes and shields decorated the stone walls.

"I should have called you sooner."

"You don't have to apologize." Antonia sat impassively, her eyes avoiding his.

"I meant to, but things kept getting in the way." Josh could tell that she didn't believe him. "I'm making a mess out of this, aren't I?"

"You're doing a pretty good job of it."

Josh stared at a pair of knights in armor who sat astride wooden horses whose flanks were covered with plates of polished steel. "This isn't the easiest place to talk."

"It's as good a place as any." Antonia's eyes followed his. "They're called 'free lances'—warriors who have no particular allegiance to anyone. They travel from one battle to the next, wherever they can make the best deal. They're extinct now. Basically empty suits. You pry their visors open and there's nothing there."

"Is that the way you see me?"

"I think you're an opportunist. Why did you come down here anyway?"

"The whole time I was in New York I kept telling myself to call."

"Why didn't you?" Antonia's voice was cold and unyielding.

"I want to see you again."

"I don't like to be taken for granted."

"I don't take you for granted."

"Look, Josh, I have to get back upstairs. I've got a ton of work to do. Maybe we can finish this discussion some other time."

Antonia stood up and headed for the elevator. Josh waited until the doors had closed, then found his way out to the parking lot and sat in his car staring at the gray granite museum walls. He knew Antonia was right. If you cared about someone you stayed in touch. It had happened before. He would meet someone and as soon as the relationship started going somewhere he would do something thoughtless and the relationship would end. It had never bothered him before and he had never tried to understand it. There was always someone else to fill the gap. He had treated Antonia as if she didn't matter and now that he wanted to see her again she was no longer interested in seeing him.

He needed a good night's sleep. He checked into a motel and was about to crawl into bed when his cell phone rang. He didn't immediately recognize the voice on the other end.

"It's me, Stacey. I heard you were in town. I need to talk to you."

"What about?"

"I can't tell you over the phone."

"Can we talk about it some other time, Stacey? I'm really beat."

"It's important. Please say you'll meet me somewhere."

He remembered a restaurant near the motel.

"I'll be there in half an hour," she said. "Please be there, Josh. Don't let me down."

* * *

Stacey entered the restaurant wearing blue jeans and a faux military jacket over a tight black sweater. She hurried over to the booth where Josh was sitting. "I bet myself driving over here that you wouldn't show."

"Your folks know you're here?"

"I wish you'd stop treating me like I was still twelve years old." She ordered a beer. The waiter didn't ask questions.

"What did you want to talk about?"

"I was home when you and mom and the rest of them were having that meeting. She wants Rabbi Winnick to get your dad's job when he retires and she's trying to get the board to go her way."

"I know that."

"I bet you didn't know that she's been pushing my dad to give more money to the museum so she can get Antonia on her side and she's made him send Brian Patzer some business, and I think she's having an affair with Bill Palevsky. What has your father ever done to her? And Rabbi Winnick is such a jerk. He taught my confirmation class. He spent most of the time staring at our tits." Stacey's words spilled out with the frantic urgency of a moth beating its wings against a windowpane. "I think what she's doing is so mean."

The waiter brought their drinks. Stacey gulped down her beer in a few quick swallows. It seemed to calm her.

"You gonna show me around when I get to New York?"

"You'll probably find a million things you'd rather do."

"I want you to show me around." Stacey reached across the table and put her hand over his and left it there. "You promised me, remember?"

*   *   *

Josh glanced at the clock by the side of his bed. It was two-thirty in the morning. Stacey lay next to him, curled off on the far side of the bed, her clothes draped over a chair, her zippered boots on the floor with their tops flopped over. She was wide-awake and staring at him.

"It's late. You better be going home."

"You don't have to worry, I'm not going to tell anyone. I bet you will though. I'm probably just another notch in your belt."

It occurred to Josh that he was probably just another notch in hers.

CHAPTER EIGHTEEN

Josh followed Tom McCarthin into a handsomely appointed office overlooking the Central Bank's landscaped atrium. "Not exactly the cubby hole we had at Citicorp," McCarthin said, "but I'd rather be in New York any day. I miss the action."

It had been six years since they had worked together on the trading desk at Citicorp. Josh remembered McCarthin as a relentless careerist with a brilliant mind that latched onto your thoughts before you had a chance to express them. Now he was president of the bank that held all of Fabrico's loans, and it was Josh's job to find out how the bank might react to a possible takeover.

A secretary brought them coffee. "I bumped into Peter Freling the other day," McCarthin said. "He told me he was working with you guys on something."

"We're thinking of making an investment in one of your companies."

"Which one?"

"Fabrico."

"What sort of investment?"

"Modest for now. We'd like to get some idea of whether your bank would welcome us getting more involved."

McCarthin leaned back in his chair and stared at Josh with the calculating air of a poker player trying to decide whether to call or raise. "We like the company. They've been a customer of ours for a long time."

"Does that mean you wouldn't encourage an outside investment?"

"We'd need to know more about the size of your investment and what sort of plans you have in mind." McCarthin's smile radiated all the warmth of an Arctic sun.

"We think Fabrico has a lot of unrealized potential," Josh replied, "but we're not sure that current management is making the right decisions about the future."

"Sam Broad says they expect to return to profitability soon."

"So you're comfortable with the way things are going?"

"We're never completely comfortable with anything. What you really want to know is what our position would be if you tried to take over the company. We'd need to know a lot of things first. What your plans are for the company? Are you going to run it as a going concern or are you just looking to liquidate it? We've got a lot of money tied up in Fabrico. If we're going to contemplate a change, we have to understand how it would impact our lines of credit and our construction loan."

"What about the shares you hold as collateral?"

"What about them?"

"I assume you'd be happier if they had a higher value than they do right now."

"What kind of price are you talking about?"

"We haven't decided yet," Josh said.

"I'll lay it out for you." McCarthin responded. "Fabrico is short of cash and our bank is overexposed. Anyone tendering for the company's stock and seeking our cooperation has to bear that in mind. We're interested in reducing our exposure, but it would take a very creative offer to get us to side with a new group. Sam has been a customer of ours for a long time. As things now stand we're sticking with him."

*   *   *

Josh watched Ballard's private jet touch down and taxi to a stop in front of the lakefront terminal. It was only a short drive to the offices of Burkett, Burden and Wilkoff.

"I was thinking about you on the way over," Ballard said as they walked to Josh's car. "I called Peter right after you left. There was no excuse for what he did. He was supposed to give you a heads-up and he knew it. You talk to your father yet?"

"I talked to him."

"How'd it go?"

"He threw me out of the house."

"I'm sorry, pal. I wish it hadn't happened the way it did. I'll try to find a way to make it up to you."

It was hard to figure Ballard out. Most of the time he was cold and distant, but there were times when he seemed almost paternal. It was hard to tell if he was truly sorry for what Peter had done or if he was just covering for him.

* * *

The air conditioning in the conference room at Burkett, Burden and Wilkoff was on full blast, but the heat of the afternoon sun baked through the wide windows overlooking the lake and it was uncomfortably warm inside. Promptly at two-thirty a door opened and Sam Broad and Marty Franklin entered. "Jesus, it's hot in here," Sam exclaimed as he took off his jacket, draped it over the back of his chair and reached across the table to shake Jess Ballard's outstretched hand.

"You're Jess Ballard."

"I am."

"I understand you're Australian."

"I'm from Sydney. Please call me Jess."

"We do a lot of business in Australia." Sam reached for a carafe in the middle of the table and poured himself a glass of water. He was wearing a short-sleeved shirt and the concentration camp numbers tattooed on his arm were clearly visible. "What brought you over here?"

"Opportunity, I guess. I wasn't from the right side of the tracks. People over here are much more forgiving."

"Not all the time," Sam responded. "Well, the clock's running. Let's get down to work. Marty says you guys have a proposal to make. Let's hear it."

Peter started in. "Sam, you've done a remarkable job with your company, but times are changing and we think there's a need to reshape the company, reinvigorate it and help it regain the leadership it once enjoyed."

"Cut the bullshit, Peter," Sam interrupted. "Get to the point."

"The point is we want to buy your company. We're prepared to offer seven dollars a share for all the shares. That's a 30 percent premium over current market. We think that's a fair price and should be attractive to you and your shareholders."

"I give you guys a lot of credit for seeing an opportunity," Sam responded, "but from where I sit it's the wrong time to sell. We're just turning the corner. At some point I might want to sell, but not right now."

Ballard interrupted, speaking so quietly that Sam had to lean forward to hear him. "It's a matter of perception, isn't it? You see the glass half full and the level rising, but the banks and the market don't see it that way. The way they see it, without fresh capital and new leadership there's a good chance the glass will end up empty." Ballard placed his short forearms on the table, his stubby fingers linked together, his eyes locked on Sam's. "You've done a fantastic job with the company, Mr. Broad. You built the business up from scratch and you've made a lot of money for a lot of people. But people have short memories. You're planning a big write-off this year. That'll make a third consecutive year of losses. Your new headquarters building is six months behind schedule and millions over budget and the bank is getting nervous. Your credit lines are coming due and the rollover isn't automatic anymore. And a number of your principal suppliers are cutting back and tightening their terms. Josh, which ones did we talk to?"

Josh rattled off the names of a half-dozen suppliers, mostly in Asia and South America, who were owed significant amounts of money. It was ammunition they would use when they made a tender offer for the company. Lawyers and accountants and public relations advisors would use the information. When they were through, even people who had confidence in Sam's ability to turn his company around would begin to wonder if it might not be a good idea to sell, rather than risk the chance that the share price would keep dropping and they would end up with nothing.

"We know pretty much everything there is to know about your company, Mr. Broad," Ballard continued. "We do a lot of business around the world. You'd be surprised how much you can find out when you've got the right connections. Maybe you are turning the company around but most people don't see it that way."

Ballard sat back in his chair and waited for a response. Marty intervened. "I think you'd have a hard time convincing the company's shareholders that the price you've offered is a fair one."

"We don't set the price," Ballard answered. "The market does, and right now they don't share your optimism about the company. We're offering your client and his shareholders a way out. Why not take advantage of the fact that there's someone willing to take over the risks and pay a hefty premium for the privilege of running his company for the next few years?"

Sam's normal calm exploded. "Run Fabrico for the next few years? Who do you think you're kidding? You're not fooling anybody. You're partnered with Peter. He's a goddam liquidator. I've spent my whole life building this company up. I'm not about to turn it over just so the two of you can tear it apart."

"That's not what we're planning," Ballard interrupted smoothly. "We intend to grow the company, not sell it off piece by piece. You have my word on that. That's the only basis on which I agreed to come on board. Peter understands that. We'd like to keep as many of your people on as we can, and we're prepared to offer attractive severance packages for those who won't be staying. We'd like you to stay on as a consultant. It goes without saying that we'd construct a severance package that you would find attractive."

For a long moment the room was quiet. Josh watched Ballard, his eyes fixed firmly on Sam's face, which remained flushed but otherwise impassive. The only sound was the noise of the air conditioner struggling to pump cold air into the overheated room.

"If you need an answer right away," Sam said quietly, "my answer is 'no.'"

"I was hoping we could get a favorable answer while we were here," Ballard responded, his quiet, even tone turning insistent and demanding. "Take a day or two to think it over. If we have to make a hostile tender offer it will be at a significantly lower price than what we've offered today. And if we have to go that way, all bets are off as far as what we do with management, yourself included."

"That's a decision for you to make," Sam growled as he heaved his heavy bulk out of his chair, sweat stains showing under the armpits of his shirt. "I think we're finished in here, Marty."

Josh followed them to the door.

"That's some bunch you've thrown in with," Sam muttered.

"It's a fair offer. I hope you'll reconsider," Josh said.

"Don't worry about me," Sam answered, barely looking at Josh as he walked out. "I'll do just fine. It's your father you should be worried about."

* * *

"You were pretty quiet in there," Ballard said as Josh drove him back to the airport. "It must have been uncomfortable for you, with him being your dad's close friend. You think he'll take the offer?"

"I doubt it."

"I don't think so either. He's a tough old bastard. He made sure I saw those numbers on his arm." Ballard's cell phone rang. It was Peter calling. "Yeah," Ballard said. "I don't see much point in waiting either. Tell our lawyers to file first thing tomorrow. Let's set the price at six-fifty a share." When the call was over he turned to Josh. "You don't think much of Peter, do you?"

"I think he's a horse's ass."

Ballard laughed. "He's our partner in this deal."

"That doesn't mean I have to like him."

"No, but you have to work with him. I want the two of you to get together with McCarthin tomorrow. Tell him we're going ahead with the tender offer. Tell him we expect his bank to be helpful and that I'd like to keep on doing business with their parent in New York. He'll get the point. And see if you can get your father to talk to Sam. Maybe he can soften him up a little."

"My dad threw me out of the house. I told you that."

Ballard wasn't listening. He was a racehorse with blinders on, focused on the shortest way to the finish line.

"Yeah? Well talk to him anyway."

When they got to the terminal a sharp wind had come up and the skies were growing dark. The pilot of Ballard's plane was waiting. "We better get going, Mr. Ballard, while the weather's holding up."

"What about Brian?" Josh asked.

"What about him?"

"When can he expect to get paid?"

"Let's hold off for a while."

"What does that mean?"

Ballard didn't answer. Josh walked him to the gate. The door was open and the roar of the jet engines drowned out further conversation. Ballard grabbed his briefcase and hurried to his plane.

*　　*　　*

Josh watched the jet take off and disappear into the low-lying clouds. He wondered what Ballard meant. If he had decided not to pay Brian, then Brian was in big trouble. When the tender offer was announced, the stock would run up and Petrie would take a beating on its short position. Brian would probably lose his job and when he went to collect, Ballard would deny that he owed him anything. If he threatened to expose Ballard, Ballard would claim he had tried to extort money from him.

He took out his cell phone and punched in Brian's number. "We need to talk."

"What about?"

"I'll tell you when we get together."

"Why all the mystery?"

"Just tell me where you want to meet."

"Carnavale. It's in the Flats. I'll be there in twenty minutes."

* * *

It was a little after three when Josh reached the restaurant. The storm that had been threatening had broken over the city and pedestrians hurried by, hunkered down under their umbrellas. Carnavale was empty. Two waiters were setting tables for dinner, which would begin at six o'clock. Liz Aurelio led him to a booth in the back where Brian was waiting.

"Liz, this is my pal, Josh Stone. He's from New York."

"Hi, Josh. I saw you at your father's New Year's reception," Liz said. "I understand he isn't well. I'm sorry."

Brian watched Liz walk toward the kitchen. "She's something, huh? She used to go with Bobby G. but he dumped her and now everyone's hitting on her. I've been trying to get her to go out with me, but she won't give me the time of day. What's up?"

"I think you should tell Petrie to close out their short position."

"You guys going ahead with the tender offer or what?"

"All I can tell you is that if you get Petrie out now, you'll be better off than if you don't."

Josh hoped that Brian would take the hint. If Brian warned Petrie before the tender offer was announced he'd lose his payday, but since it now seemed likely that Ballard had decided not to pay him, at least he wouldn't lose his job. Brian was about to ask for a fuller explanation when the restaurant door opened and Mark Winnick entered.

"Hey, Rabbi," Brian called out, "C'mon on over and say hello."

Ever since he had met Liz, Mark had been coming down to Carnavale. Always in the mid-afternoon when the restaurant was empty. He would order a cup of coffee and they would sit in a booth in back and talk. It flattered him that Liz enjoyed his company. He didn't expect anything to come of it, but it had been a long time since an attractive woman had paid attention to him.

"Hi, Brian. Hello, Josh." Mark seemed ill at ease. "I'm supposed to meet some people here, but I don't suppose they'll be coming downtown in this kind of weather."

Brian pulled out a chair for him. "Sit down for a minute, Rabbi. Take a load off."

"Thanks, but I better get back to work. I don't think anyone's going to show."

The door to the kitchen opened and Liz came out, "Hi Mark," she exclaimed. "I wasn't expecting you." Mark's eyes pleaded for cover and Liz guessed immediately the source of his discomfort. "Mark's one of our best customers," she said. "He has a lot of meetings here."

The phone up front started ringing and Liz hurried to answer it. Mark stood up abruptly, glancing at his watch. "I better get going. So long, Brian. Nice to see you again, Josh." He made a beeline for the door, barely stopping long enough for Liz to hand him his umbrella.

"You notice she called him, 'Mark'?" Brian said.

"I noticed."

"Lucky bastard. I should have been a rabbi."

"For chrissake, Brian, stop staring at her like she's on the menu. Focus on what I'm telling you. Call Petrie and tell them to close out their short position. I don't want you getting hurt."

On the way back to his office Brian struggled to make sense of what Josh had told him. Why was he so eager to have Petrie close out their short position? Maybe Ballard had no intention of making an offer for the company. What if he had bought a ton of cheap stock and all he wanted was to make a quick profit? If Petrie closed out their short position, the shares would run up and Ballard would unload his stock and make a killing. Then Ballard would claim that he had broken his word and wouldn't pay him. The more he thought about it, the more certain he was that Josh's warning was a trap. Josh had played him for a sucker once. He wouldn't let it happen again.

When he got back to his office there was the usual end-of-the-day call from Petrie, which he returned with a "nothing new to report." He put Josh's warning out of his mind. All he had to do was keep his mouth shut until the tender offer was announced and he would have his million dollars. He thought about what he would do with all that money. And he couldn't get his mind off Liz Aurelio. She had that great smile and that great ass.

CHAPTER NINETEEN

Eli watched the green diode on the car clock blink on and off. He glanced over to be sure Rachel wasn't watching and tapped his right index finger on the arm rest as many times as he could in ten seconds. It was a test he had been using to gauge the progress of his disease. Two weeks ago he had been able to tap fifty times. Now he could barely manage thirty. He had noticed some stiffness in his right arm. That was the way it went. One leg to the other, then one arm to the other, next his speech would be affected and finally his breathing. That morning just before they left the house, a cup of coffee had slipped from his hand and spilled over his suit, and on his way upstairs to change, he had stumbled on the steps and almost fallen.

They were approaching a neighborhood of imposing old houses that overlooked the city. The area had been fashionable once, but the families had cleared out to distant suburbs where the air was cleaner and the complexion of the neighbors more predictable. Most of the houses had been taken over by fraternities and sororities from the local university. A few remained in private hands and one of those, a gray shingled Victorian pile with a wide front porch, housed the Ausenheim Clinic.

The clinic had been founded by three brothers who had fled East Germany in the mid-sixties. They had located their first clinic in the basement of an abandoned church in the center of the city. There they treated patients with ultraviolet light and applications of mild electric current. Their unorthodox procedures were ridiculed by the medical establishment but they managed to find a small clientele, mostly women of a certain age, who swore by them. When the church building burned down, a group of these women, including Rachel, had purchased the Victorian house Rachel and Eli were now approaching and donated it to the clinic. Dr. S. Ausenheim, the only one of the brothers still alive, maintained his practice there and kept an aging nurse on hand to assist him.

As far as Rachel was concerned, Dr. S. was a saint. She had gone to him thirty-five years ago after every other doctor had told her that her high blood pressure was not responding to the treatments available at that time, and that she should avoid stress and resign herself to a life of rest and only moderate activity. Dr. S. had examined her and when the examination was over he said, "I sink ve can do better."

Over the next year Rachel visited the clinic once a week. She endured the discomfort of narrow light-emitting tubes poked up her nose. Each session ended with twenty minutes in a chair fitted with brass knobs through which low-voltage current passed through her body. By the end of one year with Dr. S. her hypertension had disappeared.

"He's a quack," Eli grumbled as Rachel parked their car on the street in front of the clinic.

"He is not."

"Well, why won't the medical profession recognize him?"

"They don't understand what he does."

Twice a year Rachel invited Dr. S. for dinner, during which he tormented Eli with endless tirades against the Russians. "Mark my vord, Rabbi, zey vil attack again. Ve should never have reduced our stockpile of nuclear veapons. It vas a big mistake." If Eli argued with him, he would say, "Rabbi, you are maybe an expert in ze religious vorld but in ze real vorld you are a naif." The meals Rachel prepared each time Dr. S. came to dinner were equally dispiriting. Dr. S. subsisted on thin soups, boiled vegetables and yogurt for dessert.

"You remember when you almost cut off the tip of your finger in the kitchen?" Eli asked as they approached the clinic steps. "You made me drive you here instead of going to the hospital?"

"Dr. S. sewed up my finger for me."

"I sewed it up for you. His hands were shaking so much he had to keep them in his pockets."

"You're exaggerating."

"I'm not exaggerating. I was there, remember? He had that crone of his bring him some alcohol, then he made me do the suturing. 'Rabbi, I vil show you ver ze staples go und you vil push them in.'"

"Stop making fun of him. He cured me. Maybe there's something he can do for you. You'll be out of here in less than an hour."

Dr. S. waited for them at the top of a short flight of steps. He was a short man, slightly bent over, who wore a stained hospital coat over a gray vest and a pair of rumpled striped gray pants. Wisps of white hair fringed the back of his head.

"Gut to see you, Rachel. Und you too, Rabbi."

He ushered them into his private office, a dimly lit room with blinds that were kept perpetually closed. Eli glanced around. He recognized a chair from their living room and a desk that had been in his study years ago. Even the couch they were sitting on looked familiar. He nodded his head in the direction of the couch. Rachel glared at him.

"Eli has been diagnosed with ALS," Rachel began. "I thought you might have a look at him."

Dr. S. rolled his chair forward and took Eli's hands in his. He examined the backs and fronts of them carefully. He made Eli stick out his tongue. He pushed Eli's eyelids up and stared into his eyes.

"Vat haf zey told you, Rabbi?"

"Zey haf told me I haf ALS."

"Cut it out, Eli," Rachel warned.

Dr. S. ignored Eli's behavior. "Haf zey given you any medications?"

"I take a pill now and then to help me get some sleep. There are some exercises they gave me."

"Your eating habits, haf zey changed?"

"I'm not as hungry as I used to be."

"Und your bowel habits?"

"They're pretty much the same as always."

"Follow me, Rabbi."

Eli followed Dr. S. into a room bathed in the gray-green glow of fluorescent light. Thick drapes covered the windows and a web of electrical cables hung from the ceiling like damp spaghetti. Eli could hear the low buzz of a generator somewhere. Dr. S. motioned him to a straight-backed chair with brass knobs at the end of each arm.

"Zit down und wrap your hands around ze knobs."

Dr. S. threw a switch and a motor hummed. Eli felt a pleasant tingling sensation course through his body. The procedure lasted a few minutes and then the motor shut off, leaving a slight chemical odor in the air.

Driving away from the clinic, Eli couldn't stop smiling.

"What's so funny?

"You vil feel a zlight tingling zenzation."

"You're behaving like a child. Dr. S. saved my life."

"Und maybe he vill save mine alzo."

As upset as Rachel was about Eli making fun of her beloved Dr. S., she was thrilled to see him laugh. He hadn't laughed in weeks. "Maybe he will save you," she chided. Eli leaned over and kissed her cheek. He adored Rachel for the fierce determination with which she was fighting for his life. He had accepted the inevitability of death as soon as he heard the diagnosis, but she wasn't willing to give up so easily.

"How's it going with Linda?" she asked.

"She has her mind set on Mark taking over."

"Is there anything you can do about it?"

"We'll have to wait and see."

"You don't owe them anything. Why not announce a date for your retirement? Let the board fight this thing out. You can't control everything."

Eli didn't answer and Rachel's thoughts drifted back to the night Eli had ordered Josh out of the house. He had come upstairs after Josh left, still white with rage. She was waiting for him when he entered the bedroom.

"You had no right to do that."

"He lied to me."

"You should have talked to me first. He's my son as well as yours."

"I don't want him staying here and I don't want him coming back."

"You don't have to worry about him coming back. He's as stubborn as you are. He's gone and he won't be coming home again."

They drove on for a while, lost in their private thoughts. The golden dome of the synagogue loomed ahead.

"What about you and Josh?" Rachel asked.

"He disappointed me.'

"Maybe you disappointed him," Rachel responded. "Did you ever think of that?"

CHAPTER TWENTY

Brian sat in his office with the door closed, staring through a glass partition at the electronic tote board that recorded the ebb and flow of the market. Nothing unusual had happened overnight. A record trade deficit had been announced for the thirty-seventh consecutive month. The markets in Europe were slightly higher. The president was going to Moscow on a state visit. The Indians had won again and were only a game and a half away from a wild card spot in the playoffs. He placed some orders for Peter's trust accounts and then, at precisely ten-thirty, as he was about to leave his desk to get a cup of coffee, the announcement of a tender offer for 100 percent of Fabrico at six-and-a-half dollars a share came across the screen.

Moments later, blocks of the company's stock were trading at six and three-quarters. The stock moved in great tidal surges. Four hundred thousand shares came across the screen at six and seven-eighths. Another million shares traded at $7 and the price kept rising. Brian sat in his chair, mesmerized by the strings of numbers that raced across the screen. The stock reached seven and a half. He felt a strange exhilaration. The waiting period was over. Ballard and Freling had made their move. The phone rang. It was Charles Petrie calling in a panic from New York. Brian had been rehearsing for this moment. He knew exactly what to say.

* * *

Across town in the executive offices of the Central Bank and Trust Company, Josh and Peter Freling were ushered into a small conference room. After a moment, Tom McCarthin entered. From the expression on his face they knew that he had heard the news.

"Well, you guys are a surprise. A couple of days ago it was just a small investment and now you're going after the whole company."

"We're anxious to know how the bank views our offer," Peter began.

"It's too early for us to have a position. Personally, I think the price you've offered is on the low side, but that's just me."

"Your collateral is worth a lot more today than it was yesterday," Peter added. "You must be pleased that we've put a floor on the price."

Josh was only half listening. He wondered how much of a beating Petrie was taking and whether Brian would be able to keep his job. And he wondered about Ballard. Maybe he had been wrong. Maybe Ballard would pay Brian after all.

"We've been talking with a number of institutional investors," Peter continued. "Most of them are getting tired waiting for the company to turn around. We think the majority of them are going to tender their shares. We're reasonably sure we'll get the shares we need to close the deal."

"What about other bidders?" McCarthin asked.

"There's always a chance that someone will show up and bid against us. We'll have to wait and see," Peter said.

"Will you be putting more working capital in the company?"

"We're prepared to do that."

"What about the construction loan?"

"We're willing to take a portion of it off your hands."

"What would you expect from the bank in return?"

"We'd like the bank to issue a statement that it's reviewing its relationship with Fabrico. Something along the lines that the bank is concerned about the company's financial condition and that its credit lines are under review. That should help us shake loose any institutions that are still undecided about whether or not to tender their shares."

"And if we don't?"

"We do a lot of business with your parent in New York," Josh answered. "Mr. Ballard hopes you'll see the value of cooperating."

"I appreciate your candor," McCarthin said irritably. It was usually the bank that turned the screws, not the other way around. "I can't give you an answer right away. I have a board to consult with."

When they were in the elevator, Peter turned to Josh. "My guess is he'll come back with something. It won't be what we want but whatever it is, there'll be a price tag on it. What do you think?"

Josh barely looked at Peter. Maybe he had to work with him, but he didn't have to be friendly. "What does it matter what I think? I'm just the water boy around here."

* * *

"You're so nice to see me on such short notice," Pamela said, as she sat down across from Peter. As soon as she had heard the news of the tender offer she had hurried over to his office. "I know how busy you must be, but I want you on my show tonight. Your offer to buy Fabrico is big news and my show is the perfect place for you to let everyone know what your plans are for the company."

She had tried to get Peter on her show before but he had always refused.

This time he accepted. "On one condition, Pamela. No personal stuff."

"You have my word." His consent nailed down, she turned to other business. "I guess my departure's been decided by now, except for someone getting around to telling me."

"I wish it wasn't happening, Pamela. You know how Linda and I adore you, but the station's under pressure to find a younger audience and I'm just one member of the board."

"A pretty influential one."

"Not as influential as you might think."

"I wish they'd reconsider, Peter. My ratings are up and I've got all sorts of new ideas. Can't you do something for me?"

"I wish I could, but I have to pay attention to what management says. They say we need a younger audience and that we've got to cater to it. I know it isn't fair, but that's the way it is. I've urged them to make you an offer to consult."

Pamela knew all about those consulting deals. Fifty percent of what you were making for a year. Pointless meetings where everyone listened politely to your suggestions while they looked at their watches. Then a farewell lunch and a plaque in the lobby, if you were lucky.

"Think about it, Peter. There must be something you can do."

"I can't do anything, Pamela. If I could, I would, you know that." He walked her to the door.

"Well at least you're coming on my show. Come early, will you? It'll give us a chance to chat. My makeup person is unbelievable. She'll make you look like you don't have a care in the world."

*   *   *

Leo Bookman arrived at the synagogue a little after ten-thirty. He had been to the dentist for a loose filling. He greeted the secretaries, picked up his mail and hurried into his office. He closed the door behind him and switched on his computer for a quick check of the markets before he went to work. It was a routine he followed every morning. More than seven million shares of Fabrico stock had traded. The stock had been as high as $8 and had settled back just under $7. He stared slack-jawed at the screen, then picked up the phone and called Brian Patzer. "Brian, what's going on?"

"You lucked out, Leo," Brian said. "Somebody decided that the company was worth a lot more than what the market said."

Leo had always based his decisions on the careful study of facts and figures. Now all that information was useless. The price of Fabrico shares was being determined by forces unrelated to the company's business. He had planned to get out when the stock hit $7 a share. It was there now. "I'm thinking of getting out," he said.

"Sure, if you want to, Leo."

"Is there any reason why I shouldn't?"

"How long have you owned the stock?"

"I bought most of it over the last four months."

"Why not sit tight for a while and let the gains go long term? You'll pay a whole lot of taxes if you sell now."

"But if the deal doesn't go through, the stock will go back down."

"Look, Leo. I know the guys who made the offer. I went to school with Josh Stone. He's Ballard's right-hand man. And I do business with Peter. From what I understand they've got it locked up. There's not a chance in hell the deal won't go through. Worst case, you tender your stock and get six and a half. Best case, someone else comes along and bids a whole lot more. I wouldn't bet against the stock going to

$10 before it's over. If you want my advice, hang in there. I don't see how you can get hurt."

*　　*　　*

Linda stretched and yawned. It was almost five-thirty. The drapes were open in her ninth floor lake-view suite at the Bonnaire. The sun was setting and a warm glow filled the room. The afternoon reminded her of the way it used to be with Peter when she would meet him in New York and they would go to his apartment and make love all night, until he had to leave for work and she had to head back to Barnard for classes. For a while after they were married, he had been an ardent lover. She even managed to convince herself that she had been mistaken to think he had cheated on her during their honeymoon. Then they moved back to Cleveland and he took over her father's business and devoted himself to building an empire. Stacey and Jessica were born. She turned thirty. Peter ran every day, worked out in his gym, and traveled around the country chasing deals and women. Linda wasn't aware of his first affair, denied the next few, tried to ignore the ones that followed, and finally, when she turned thirty-five, began to take on lovers of her own.

Bill Palevsky had been a pushover. You could always tell when someone was bored and ready for a change. They showed up at parties without their spouses. There always some excuse. The wife was ill or the kids had colds. Kathy had been attractive when she was younger but she had let herself go and Bill had told Linda in confidence that she didn't like sex that much anymore. Thank god, Linda thought, for wives who wouldn't give their husbands head. Since that afternoon at the stable, she and Bill had been seeing one another regularly. It was unlikely that Peter would find out. Men who screwed around seldom worried that their wives might be doing the same thing. And even if he did find out, she didn't care. He had always taken her for granted. Now at least he was being useful.

She hoped Peter's significant pledge to the museum's outreach program would bring Antonia around. And he had thrown some business Brian's way. That would lock him in. She remained confident of Sally's support. Sally didn't think much of Mark, but she and Sally had been friends forever and she knew she could count on her when the time came.

Bill Palevsky walked out of the bathroom with a towel wrapped around him and flopped down on the bed.

"What about Bobby G.?" Linda asked. "Where does he stand?"

"I talked to him the other day. I'm pretty sure he'll vote for Mark. And once we get him, we've got Renee. They've been going out together."

Sally, Bill, Brian, Bobby G., Renee. She had five votes locked up. With her own vote, six. All she needed was one more. Antonia's vote would be decisive. She checked her watch. She was in no rush to get home. Peter was working late again. She moved close to Bill, slipped her hand under his towel and wondered if he was good for one more time.

*   *   *

"That was an excellent interview, Peter," Pamela said as the red light flashed on, indicating that the program was over. "You were great."

"To tell you the truth, I was worried about coming down here. You've got a scary reputation," Peter said.

"I only go after people I don't like." The cameras had moved to another part of the studio where the local news was under way. "Anyway you don't have to worry. Somebody else will get to work you over next time."

"I wish it didn't have to be that way."

Pamela gave him a quick hug. "Me too. This station's been my second home for the last thirty years. I feel like I'm part of the wallpaper. Well, youth and beauty always trumped old bags like me. Matter of fact, when I got started I knocked off somebody twice my age, so I guess I shouldn't complain. Have you had a chance to meet my replacement?"

"Not yet."

"Would you like to?"

"Sure."

They walked down a long corridor to an office not much bigger than a closet. A young woman was sitting with her back to the door, watching the local news on a monitor.

"Cindi, this is Peter Freling. Peter, meet Cindi Li."

Cindi spun around and stood up to shake Peter's hand. She was an inch taller than Peter, with long straight jet-black hair. She wore a tracksuit that accentuated her trim athletic figure. "I was just watching you guys on TV. You looked pretty relaxed out there," she said. Her engaging smile lit up the room.

"To tell you the truth I was scared to death," Peter said. "Pamela can be pretty daunting."

"She's kind of an iconic figure around here."

Pamela winced. *Iconic.* How skillful Cindi was, buttering Peter up and trying to bury her at the same time. A relic. The remnant of a bygone era.

"I've got to go," she announced. "I'm sure you two will find something to talk about." She gave Peter a quick hug and lobbed a cold smile Cindi's way. "Peter, please think over what we talked about."

"I will, I promise."

"Make yourself comfortable, if you can," Cindi said, indicating the only other chair in her tiny, cluttered office. She shuffled through some papers and smiled at Peter with the confidence of an attractive young woman who knows the effect she is having on an older man.

"You a runner?" Peter asked.

"There's a track on the roof. I go up there every chance I get. You run?"

"Every day of my life. Looks like you're swamped."

"I was just getting ready to call it quits for the day."

Peter was intrigued. He had given up on Antonia. The few times he suggested they have a drink together, she came up with excuses. And Linda was looking over his shoulder all the time. Cindi was new in town and Linda didn't know about her yet.

"You're one of the owners of this place, aren't you?" Cindi asked.

"A small one. You getting along okay?"

"Except for Pamela, I'm doing fine. She'd like to kill me. I don't blame her. I've admired her all my life. She's kind of the gold standard for the rest of us and now they bring me down here to replace her. It doesn't seem fair, does it?"

*   *   *

Pamela gathered up her things to leave. When she got to the garage, the attendant was waiting with her car.

"Evening, Eddie. Have you seen Cindi Li?"

"She left a couple of minutes ago, Miss Dawes."

"Alone?"

"No. She was with Mr. Freling."

Pamela drove home through deserted streets. Except for those nights when the Indians were in town, the roads were empty, traffic signals shifting from red to green and back again without a single car passing though. The city was like a giant reservoir, filling up each morning with streams of workers pouring in from the suburbs, and emptying out at night as they flowed home again. She reached in her purse, took out her cell phone and punched in Buddy Kaplan's number.

"Buddy, darling," she cooed. "Peter Freling was just on my show. Were you watching?"

"Of course I was watching. I never miss it. What I wouldn't give for just a little taste of his money. Why is it that some people get rich while the rest of us slave away, cooking for them?"

"Bad day?"

"Listen to this. I'm getting ready for Linda's bat mitzvah party. You're going? Of course you are. And she calls and says they're having two hundred and fifty people, not two hundred, and she wants squab instead of duck, and green asparagus, not the white kind she told me about last week. I'm going to kill myself. Will you come to my funeral?"

"Buddy, I need a favor," Pamela said.

"Sure, if I can," Buddy said. "What is it?"

"We have this new girl at the station who's taking over for me, and after the show Peter said he wanted to meet her. So I introduced them and I was wondering if you would keep your eyes open?"

"For what?"

"For the usual."

"Peter's a wonder, isn't he? Our own little Energizer Bunny."

"I'm afraid I can't do much for you in return. No more free plugs. Those days are gone forever."

"Listen, darling," Buddy cooed. "If there's anything to find out, I'll find it out for you. And as far as tit for tat is concerned, forget about it. We can't be commerce all the time, can we?"

Pamela snapped her cell phone shut. There was still a glimmer of hope. She had baited the hook. She hoped it wouldn't be long before Peter took a nibble.

* * *

It was after eight when Antonia came down from her office on the top floor of the museum and found Josh examining one of the armored knights that stood on raised pedestals and guarded a corner of the Armor Court.

"I wanted to finish our conversation," Josh said.

"I thought we had."

"You've got these guys in the armored suits all wrong. They weren't all opportunists."

"Oh no?"

"Some of them guarded their lady's honor. They protected her virginity."

Antonia laughed. "It's a little late for that."

They walked around the pond in front of the museum. It was a warm night. In the distance, the gold dome of the synagogue was silhouetted against the dark night sky. Josh told her everything. He told her that Ballard had offered him the chance to work on the Fabrico deal and that he had jumped at it. He told her about his trip to New York with Brian and the angry meeting with his father. He even told her about the night he spent with Stacey.

"So she nailed you after all," Antonia said.

"It wasn't her fault."

"I'll bet."

"It was a mistake."

"Some mistake. What about your dad? Did you tell him you were sorry?"

"I've tried to call him. He won't talk to me."

"You love him, don't you?"

"Of course I love him."

"Have you ever told him?"

Josh thought about how long it had been since he had hugged his father and how many years had passed since he had told his father that he loved him.

"It's okay to take the armor off every now and then. It doesn't hurt to tell people how you really feel."

They continued their walk around the pond. Josh thought about how much he wanted the woman who was walking next to him.

"How come you never called me?" Antonia asked.

"I should have. I'm sorry. I don't have any excuse."

"I was hoping that you'd call."

"I'd give anything if we could start over."

Antonia put her arms around his neck and kissed him. "Where are you staying?"

"At a hotel downtown."

"Come with me. I've got a better idea."

CHAPTER TWENTY-ONE

Most of the 2,200 seats on the main floor of the sanctuary were filled. All of Jessica's schoolmates had been invited, along with Linda's friends and many of Peter's business associates. Linda and Peter and Stacey sat in their usual pew a few rows back from the pulpit. Jessica had just finished a flawless reading of her Torah portion. There was a brief organ interlude and then it was time for her speech. She walked confidently to the lectern, removed her wire-rim glasses, cleaned them carefully, and put them back on slowly. Then she paused and looked out over the congregation, waiting for them to settle down. There was a ripple of laughter as many in the congregation recognized that she was imitating Eli.

"This is an important day for me," she began. "First, I want to thank my mother and father and my sister for putting up with me all these years. I know I've been a real pain sometimes. And I want to thank Rabbi Winnick for helping me with my Torah portion, and I want especially to thank Rabbi Stone for everything.

"The Torah portion I read this morning means something very special to me. It's the Song of Miriam. A song that she sings to God for saving the Children of Israel from the Egyptians. They have just crossed the Red Sea and escaped from Pharaoh's army, and the Bible says, *And the Lord brought back the waters of the sea upon them, but the children of Israel walked on dry land in the midst of the sea.*

"I figure they must have been really scared. All of a sudden they were at the edge of this big sea and the Egyptians were chasing them and Moses told them to follow him and not be afraid, and he led them through the Red Sea to safety."

"We all need someone to help us through hard times. Sometimes I've got some big problem. At least I think it's big, and I need someone to help me find my way. I always look to my mom and dad when I get confused. I know they care about me and want to help me. I trust them and I count on them for advice and support."

Linda grabbed Peter's hand and whispered, "She's so self-confident up there."

"When you're growing up, your parents are the ones you want to model your life after. You look to them as an example. You know they're interested in your future and you want them to be proud of you. My mom and dad are both very successful people and I admire them for what they have done. They expect a lot from me and I know that I have disappointed them sometimes. I don't do it on purpose. I hope they know that, but it's confusing because sometimes what they tell me I should be doing is so different from what I see them doing."

Jessica glanced briefly at her parents. Linda sat stiffly in her chair. Peter stared straight ahead. Stacey was smiling.

"Mom and Dad, I wish you wouldn't be so wrapped up in your work and everything. I know what you do is important, but I get so little chance to talk to you and there are so many things I want to ask about and you're hardly ever around. I wish we could spend more time together and not just dinner a couple of nights a week when there's usually company around. And I wish you wouldn't make fun that I want to be a rabbi. I know you think it's silly and that I'll change my mind, but more than anything that's what I want to be when I grow up. And most of all I wish you could find a way to be friends again. I know you love each other, but you spend so much time arguing about everything that it doesn't leave much time for anything else, and it makes me feel really sad.

"I know this isn't what you expected me to talk about, but I've thought a lot about what I wanted to say and what I want more than anything is for us to be a happy family. Rabbi Stone says that being part of a happy family is the most important thing that can ever happen to you, and I keep thinking about how great it would be if we all tried really hard to make that happen. That's what I wish for on my bat mitzvah."

Jessica walked back to her seat on the pulpit. An embarrassed hush fell over the congregation. People shifted uncomfortably in their seats, glancing at one another. A few of Jessica's school friends started giggling. Stacey shot Jessica a "thumbs up" sign. Peter tugged at his collar while Linda struggled to keep her face from collapsing.

Eli walked slowly to the lectern and waited for the congregation to settle down. In all his years as a rabbi, Jessica's bat mitzvah speech was absolutely unique. He thought about his brief meeting with her and realized that he had missed the signals.

"You read your portion beautifully, Jessica," he began. "And saying the things you did couldn't have been easy for you. Growing up is difficult. There are lots of disappointments along the way and it's easy to get frustrated because there doesn't seem to be much that you can do about them. But talking about the way you feel is always a good idea and that's what you've done so courageously today. Your parents are extraordinary people, Jessica. I know they have listened to you and I am sure that the bonds of affection that you all share for one another will grow stronger with every passing day. So, Jessica, we congratulate you on your bat mitzvah and we hope that in the years ahead, all the things that you wish for will come true."

* * *

A long line of cars snaked its way up the tree-lined driveway toward the portico of the Rolling Ridge Country Club and disgorged an endless stream of luncheon guests.

"I heard all about it," Buddy Kaplan whispered to Pamela Dawes as she handed her coat to the cloakroom attendant. "You think it's cold outside, you should have felt the chill a couple of minutes ago when Linda walked in. Listen, I've got something really important to tell you but it'll have to wait. I've got two hundred fifty squabs in the oven. After what happened at the synagogue this morning, Linda will kill me if this lunch isn't perfect."

Pamela was in a foul mood. She had been formally notified the night before that she was being let go. Her program would go off the air in two weeks and Cindi Li would be anchoring a new show, to be called *Cindi at Five*. The station manager, whom she despised, had given her the news.

"I know what you're thinking, Pamela, but it has nothing to do with age. It's all about format. So I wouldn't go around complaining publicly about our decision, because we haven't signed off yet on the terms of your separation agreement."

The reception line had formed at the far end of the country club's parlor. Linda and Peter greeted their guests in front of a cavernous fireplace filled with baskets of pink and white carnations. Stacey stood with her arm around Jessica, who was smiling proudly. No one knew exactly what to say. "What a lovely service." "Wasn't Jessica delightful?" "You must be very proud."

Linda stood ramrod straight, a tight smile pasted on her face, while Peter, who had already bolted down a few stiff drinks, beckoned a passing waiter and exchanged an empty glass of scotch for a full one. Linda, who seldom drank, struggled to smile, her eyes full of anger, the chords in her neck standing out like the fluting on a vase.

As soon as the reception line thinned out, Peter headed for the bar. Linda made a beeline for Mark, who had just come in with Susan.

"I need to borrow your husband for a minute," Linda announced, not waiting for Susan to respond. She grabbed Mark by the arm and pulled him into a corner of the parlor, where they were partially obscured behind a large potted fern. She pushed her face up close to his.

"How could you have let that happen?"

"Believe me, Linda, I had no idea what Jessica was going to say."

"You should have gone over her speech with her."

"That's not my responsibility. My job was to help her with her Hebrew."

"She would never have done something like that on her own. She was coached. I'm sure of it. Eli must have put her up to it. Did you see the way he patted her on the head when she was finished?" The words spat out of Linda's mouth like spent casings from a machine gun.

Mark made no attempt to answer. He had problems of his own. He was no longer confident that things were going his way. His appearance on Letterman had been a disaster. The moment he was introduced, he realized that Letterman was determined to make fun of him. Letterman had started the interview by insisting that the Old Testament had been the first to recognize the importance of baseball.

"Isn't it true, Rabbi, that the Book of Genesis begins with the words *In the big inning*?" Things had gone downhill from there. When his brief appearance was over, Letterman hurried him off with a cheery, "Rabbi Mark Winnick, ladies and gentlemen."

By the time he got back to Cleveland, Mark noticed a subtle change in the way members of the congregation regarded him. He was sure that Linda would drop him like a hot potato once she sensed the momentum shifting. At the first sign of trouble she would cut and run and he would end up a conversational appetizer at one of her dinner parties. "Can you believe Mark actually expected to succeed Rabbi Stone? I mean, really!"

Linda was still holding Mark tightly by the arm, staring across the room at Eli, who was talking with some friends. Where did he get off treating her like that? If it was the last thing she did, she would find a way to avenge the public humiliation he had intentionally inflicted on her.

*   *   *

Bobby G. and Renee Lassiter arrived at the party arm in arm. Renee had taken Bobby up on his invitation. She hadn't been to a baseball game since she was eight years old, when her father had taken her to watch the Yankees play. She could still remember how bored she had been, but she had to admit that watching Bobby was exciting. He got her a seat behind the Indians' dugout and tipped his cap to her as he trotted out on the field. It was a night game and the Indians were playing Kansas City. The game was tied going into the ninth and Bobby had come up with two men on base and hit a single. A run scored and the Indians won.

She found herself screaming along with everyone else. They had gone back to his place that night and made love, and when he took her back to her apartment the next morning, he kissed her on the doorstep and said, "I hope this wasn't just a one-night stand."

"I bet you say that to all the girls."

"Not all of them," Bobby had responded with a loopy grin. "Just the ones I really care about."

Antonia joined Renee and they watched a crowd of young boys surround Bobby, clamoring for his autograph. "I don't know how he deals with it," Renee exclaimed. "They never leave him alone."

"Are you kidding? He loves it. Who wouldn't like all that attention? So, what happened last night? Tell me everything," Antonia said.

"I had a good time at the game and then we went out for a couple of drinks."

"And then?"

"And then we went back to his place. I almost missed my first class the next morning. We talked about all sorts of things. He can talk, you know. He doesn't express himself the way you and I do, but he's interesting and he's sexy and he's lots of fun."

"Are you serious about him?"

"He's a baseball player and I lecture on the effects of the Black Death on the papacy in the fourteenth century. He's on the road half the time. Who knows what he's doing when he's away. I couldn't live like that. What about you and Josh? He call yet?"

"I saw him."

"You did? And?"

"And he's all wrapped up in his work and he's got problems with his father." Antonia glanced across the room and saw Josh talking to Stacey, who was standing in the reception line.

"You don't have to marry him," Renee said.

"Don't worry," Antonia said, "there's no chance of that."

* * *

Until early that morning Brian Patzer had thought he was home free. When Fabrico shares shot up after the tender offer, he had closed out his options and made a fast $40,000. He had weathered the first round of criticism from the partners in New York. They had taken a loss of $11 million on their short position. The phone conversations had been awkward but he was confident he had been convincing. No one could accuse him of negligence. He had told them of every conversation he had with people in and out of Fabrico who might have known something. He had even mentioned Josh's trip to Cleveland and suggested that they check around to see if anything was going on with Parallax. He was sure that he had convinced them that the tender offer had come as a complete surprise. Now all that was left was to collect the money Ballard owed him and figure out what to do with the rest of his life.

Then the phone rang and it was Charles Petrie saying that they were letting him go. They regretted the decision.

He would be given six month's severance. They wished him good luck and would he please have his desk cleared out by Monday. After the shock wore off, Brian reflected that there had always been the risk of getting fired. Petrie had to find a way to save face and he was the logical fall guy. Anyway it wasn't all bad news. He still had a million-dollar payday coming. He would take a vacation. He hadn't taken one in years. Then he would take his time figuring out what to do next. He had a wealth of knowledge about the markets and he would find a way to get back in.

He spotted Josh standing at the bar and joined him. "I got canned this morning," he announced almost casually. "I guess it had to happen. They had to lay the blame on someone."

"I'm sorry. I tried to tell you to get them out of their short position."

"What would have been the point? It would have cost me my deal with Ballard. When do you figure I'll get paid?"

Josh paused before he answered. "I'm not sure."

"What do you mean 'you're not sure'?"

"He told me he wanted to wait a while."

"What does that mean?"

"I did the best I could to warn you. You should have listened."

The bartender put a drink down in front of Brian. He picked it up, but his hands were shaking and half the drink spilled on the bar.

"I lost my fucking job over this, Josh. That money's mine. I'm counting on it. What's Ballard's number?" Brian pulled out his cell phone and Josh watched him punch in the number.

"Can I speak to Mr. Ballard. This is Brian Patzer calling. Yes, I'll wait." He bolted down what was left of his drink. "Mr. Ballard, this is Brian Patzer. We met in New York a couple of weeks ago . . . at the Regency . . . The exact date? No, I don't remember the exact date." Brian stared at Josh with a disbelieving look. "Josh Stone was with me, remember? . . . Yes, that's right . . . I'm calling to find out when you're going to pay me." The conversation stumbled on for another minute, Brian's expression turning rapidly from disbelief to despair. "No, I'm not threatening you, Mr. Ballard. I'm just telling you that you owe me a million dollars. You can take that any way you want."

When the call was over Brian stared into the mirror over the bar. "You knew all along, didn't you? All that bullshit back there at Carnavale. Why didn't you just tell me straight out what was going on?"

"I couldn't," Josh said.

"Why not?"

"I still work for Ballard."

"You're a prick, you know that?"

"I'm sorry, Brian. I did the best I could."

*   *   *

Josh found Peter standing alone in a corner of the country club parlor nursing a drink.

"Gotta hand it to Linda," he mumbled, a glazed smile creasing his face. "Planned this whole thing herself. Didn't have a thing to do with it except write the check." He drained his glass and grabbed another drink from the tray of a passing waiter and looped a limp arm around Josh's shoulder. "Coupla' more weeks we'll have our deal locked up. Then we can really celebrate."

"Brian got fired," Josh said.

"Thas' too bad."

"And Ballard's not going to pay him."

Some of Peter's drink dribbled down on the front of his shirt. "You get tired working for Jess Ballard, you come back and work for me. Should'a done it the last time you had a chance."

Josh tried to shrug Peter's arm off his shoulder. "Goddam it, Peter, Brian did everything he was supposed to do and Ballard's hung him out to dry."

Peter's eyes narrowed as he contemplated the bottom of his empty glass. "Hey, pal, this is a party. Loosen up for chrissake. Don't be such a fucking bleeding heart." He waved a limp hand in Antonia's direction. "What are you complaining about. You got Antonia, don't you? Look at her over there. Great tits. Greatest ass I ever saw. You don't know what a big favor you're doing me, taking her off my hands. Linda got really pissed when I went after her."

*　*　*

Sally Minton wondered what a party like this cost. A catered lunch for two hundred fifty people. Champagne. Flowers. An eight-piece band. Seventy-five thousand? More? She had heard about the tender offer at the beauty parlor when the woman next to her mentioned it to her manicurist. As soon as she got home she had switched on the TV and caught the end of Pamela's interview. Peter sat across from Pamela, looking tan and confident, his arm draped casually over the back of his chair.

"Peter, you've built your reputation as a liquidator. Is that what's going to happen to Fabrico? Are you going to chop it up and sell off the pieces?"

"We have no intention of doing that. Fabrico's a sick company but it's not dead yet. We're going to revitalize it. We think there's an opportunity for the kind of change that will reward shareholders who have watched the value of their shares drop down to almost nothing. Sometimes management gets entrenched and radical change is the only way out."

Sick companies? Entrenched management? Sam had built Fabrico from scratch. Sally adored him. He had given her a job after her marriage fell apart and paid her enough so that she didn't have to sell her house or take her daughter out of private school. On his advice she had invested her modest divorce settlement in Fabrico stock when the company first went public. When the stock soared, Sam insisted that she sell and the profits she made had provided her with financial independence. The notion that Peter was trying to take over his company offended her. He had so much money already.

Why did he need more? And why did he have to pick on Sam's company when there were a million other companies he could have gone after?

The lights in the parlor flickered and the guests started moving toward the dining room. Sally waited until Sam was alone for a moment and then walked over to him.

"I feel so bad about what's happening, Sam. I wish there was something I could do," she said.

"Hi, sweetheart," Sam said, giving her a warm hug. "Don't you worry about it. I can take care of myself."

"I know you can, Sam, but it all seems so wrong to me."

They watched Jessica tug on her father's arm, urging him away from the bar. "Get a load of that," Sam said. "I'd be half smashed myself if I'd gone through what he went through this morning."

*   *   *

Linda caught up with Eli and Rachel as they were putting on their coats. "You aren't leaving, are you, Rabbi?"

"Rachel thinks it's time for me to go home. She's the boss."

"We only planned to stay through the reception," Rachel added. "It's a lovely party, but Eli needs to get some rest."

"Please let him stay, Rachel," Linda said. "Just for a few more minutes. I'll call on him as soon as we sit down and then you can leave. It would mean so much to all of us if the rabbi would say a few words. Won't you let him stay at least that long?"

* * *

Silver and blue balloons festooned the ceiling of the dining room and sprays of white and pink carnations decorated each table. The band was playing show tunes. "Hey, can we get the music to hold up a little?" Peter said. He stood up, tapping his spoon against his glass. Linda tugged at him to sit down. "I just want to say how happy I am that you're all here to celebrate Jessica's bat mitzvah with our family. This isn't a time for speeches and anyway you already heard the best speech anyone is going to make today and that was the one Jessica made this morning. So I want you all to raise your glass to Jessica. Jessica, where are you? Oh, there you are, right next to me. And also to my darling wife, Linda, without whom none of this would have been possible. For those of you who don't know it, Linda and I will celebrate our twenty-third anniversary next week."

"Twenty second, dear," Linda hissed behind clenched teeth. "Sit down. You're making a fool of yourself."

"I'll sit down in a minute, honey, but first I want everyone to know what a great day this has been for our family and how happy we are that you're all here, and I want to . . ."

Linda yanked Peter down and stood up. "I just want to add to what Peter was saying. Most of you have known us for a long time and you know that next to our own family, the family we care the most about is our synagogue family. We've been blessed with the leadership of Rabbi Stone for so many years. He has been a guiding light for all of us and I know that you share our love for him. I asked him earlier if he would say a few words. I know you're tired, Rabbi, and Rachel, I know you want to get him home, but Rabbi, would you? Please?"

Eli rose with difficulty, leaning on the back of his chair for support. "After listening to Linda's over-generous introduction, I'm reminded of a story. After Stalin became the leader of all the Russians and Trotsky had been sent into exile, Stalin stood on Red Square in front of thousands of his followers and read a telegram that had just been handed to him. It said. 'You were right. I was wrong. You are the true heir of Lenin. I should apologize.' Signed, Trotsky. The crowd cheered. Then a little old man at the front of the crowd called up. 'You haven't read the message right, comrade Stalin.' . . . 'Come on up here, comrade.' Stalin commanded. 'You read it to everyone the way you think it should be read.' So the man climbed up on the platform and took the telegram from Stalin's hands and cleared his throat and sang out. "You were right? I was wrong? You are the true heir of Lenin? I should apologize? Trotsky."

After the laughter died down, Eli continued. "We get so used to people saying one thing and meaning another. Jessica is an unusual young woman. She says what she thinks. She has an independent and inquisitive mind and she isn't afraid to use it, and that's a rare quality these days."

Eli could feel his voice weaken. His words were slurring, coming out thick and indistinct as if coated with a film of oil. He had attended a recital once where an elderly pianist had stopped in the middle of a passage and stared silently at the keyboard, unable to remember what came next. He had never forgotten the look of utter desolation on the man's face as he realized that the skills he had relied on all his life had deserted him.

At a nearby table, Antonia gripped Josh's arm, her eyes communicating the agony she knew he was feeling as he watched his father struggle. Every noise in the room had stopped. At the head table, Linda's eyes darted around, checking to see how Eli's difficulties were registering with her guests. Eli paused and started again, but the slurring was worse and after a moment he sat down.

Josh rushed to his side. "Dad, are you okay?"

"I'm a little dizzy."

Friends crowded around. Eli tried to wave them away. Linda hurried over. "Are you all right, Rabbi?"

"He's fine," Rachel responded sharply. "He just needs some rest."

"I should never have asked him to speak," Linda said. "Please go home, Rabbi, and take it easy. And thank you for the lovely things you said about Jessica. She'll never forget it and neither will we."

*   *   *

As guests huddled under the club portico waiting impatiently for their cars, hardly anyone spoke. Jessica's bat mitzvah party had taken on the characteristics of a wake. Pamela was already worrying about the lead in to her next show. How could she tactfully combine a mention of the Freling party with what had happened to Rabbi Stone? Buddy Kaplan saw her and hurried over.

"I was afraid you'd left," Buddy said.

"I'm in a rush, Buddy," Pamela said. "What was it?"

"You'll absolutely die when you hear this."

"Tell me quickly. I've got to run."

"A certain mutual friend of ours has been meeting at a restaurant downtown with a young lady who is definitely not his wife."

It was the news Pamela was hoping for. Peter had fallen into the trap she had laid for him. "How perfectly marvelous. Well, you can't say we didn't expect it. We can always count on Peter."

"It's not Peter, sweetheart. It's Rabbi Winnick. Is that not the most delicious piece of gossip you ever heard? Our junior rabbi in a tryst with a restaurant hostess. And she lives right across from the synagogue. How convenient can you get? I know you wanted me to find out something about Peter, but this is the best I've got right now. Be patient, darling. I'm doing the best I can."

*   *   *

Linda was slumped in a chair in the parlor, staring at a blue balloon that had floated up to the ceiling, its taffeta tail swaying in the draft of the air conditioning. What had happened to Eli had been the unexpected climax to an exhausting day. It had cast a pall on the party, but now everyone knew just how sick Eli was. It would be a matter of time until even his closest friends would tell him that retirement was the only option.

She closed her eyes for a moment, enjoying the comforting sensation of things falling into place. When she opened them, Josh was standing over her.

"Oh, Josh. I thought everyone was gone by now."

"Why did you make my dad give a talk? You knew he was tired."

"I just asked him if he would say a few words and he agreed. I've had a long day, Josh. I'm really not up to having an argument with you."

"You were looking around the whole time to see how everybody was reacting. It was almost like you were enjoying it," Josh said.

"That's ridiculous and demeaning. I was doing no such thing. How dare you suggest that I was enjoying it?"

"What has my father ever done to you?"

Linda's composure snapped. "The same thing you're doing right now. Getting in my way. And that little Stalin joke he made. It was insulting. Suggesting that I wasn't being honest in what I said about him." She pushed Josh away and stood up, her face close to his. "Look, Josh, I'm extremely tired. This has been an exhausting day for me. I'm sorry about your father. I'm not responsible for his illness and I resent the fact that you're implying that what happened today is my fault. Why don't you just concentrate on the work you're doing for Peter? That's what you're here for, isn't it? And if you want to be helpful, tell your father that it's way past the time for him to announce his retirement. The congregation needs to get on with the business of selecting his successor. Now if you don't mind I want to get out of here and go home and get some rest."

*   *   *

What had begun as a sunny day had turned stormy. Josh drove away from the Rolling Ridge Country Club, inching his car through pools of water that had flooded the highway. In his mind he kept seeing his father struggling to speak and the expression on Linda's face as she watched him. He had wanted to hit her. Make her pay for what she had done to his father.

Antonia sat next to him and put her hand on the back of his neck. "I know how miserable you must be feeling," she said.

Josh pushed her hand away. "You have no idea how I feel," he snapped. "Why didn't you tell me about Peter?"

"What are you talking about?"

"All that crap about being so upset because I didn't call you from New York. Why didn't you tell me you were having an affair with him?"

"I never had anything to do with Peter. I never had an affair with him."

"He told me he's glad I'm taking you off his hands. He said you had great tits and a great ass."

Antonia pushed herself as far away from Josh as possible. "You know what? I've spent half my life trying to stay away from men like you. I'm sorry for whatever's gone wrong in your life but don't take it out on me. Go get drunk. Go find Stacey and get laid again. I don't care what you do, just take me home."

The rest of the drive passed in silence. When they reached Antonia's apartment she hurried out of the car without a word and ran up the steps in the pouring rain. Josh watched as the front door closed behind her. The events of the past few weeks churned around in his mind like cloudy water in which the sediment refused to settle. He had deceived his father and ruined Brian's life and now, in a paroxysm of self-loathing, he had driven Antonia away. He gripped the steering wheel and stared through the windshield as rain hammered on the roof and the slap-slap of the wiper blades punctuated the feeling of hopelessness that engulfed him.

CHAPTER
TWENTY-TWO

Linda had been awake since five, mulling over the events of the past twenty-four hours. Jessica's bat mitzvah speech had been a disaster and Peter's drunken behavior at the country club had embarrassed her, but a significant portion of the congregation was now aware of the extent of Eli's disability and the word would spread. Only the confrontation with Josh troubled her seriously. She poked Peter and woke him up.

"What time is it?" he mumbled.

"It's almost six. I need to talk to you." She reached across him and switched on the light by his bedside table to make sure he stayed awake.

"What about?"

"It's about Josh. Do you trust him?"

"Why wouldn't I trust him?"

"He came up to me after the party and insulted me. He said I knew that Eli was exhausted and that I took advantage of him. He accused me of forcing him to speak. Where does he get off talking to me like that? If someone like that worked for me I'd get rid of him."

"He works for Jess Ballard. I couldn't fire him if I wanted to."

"Then tell Ballard to fire him. It's demeaning to me to have people know that he's working with you. You can imagine what he's saying about me behind my back. I want you to talk to Ballard about him."

Peter had no intention of talking to Ballard. Josh was a pain in the ass but he was useful. There were already signs that some of the institutions they had counted on to tender shares were planning to sit out the tender offer, and he needed Josh's help to keep the deal on track. He would do his best to keep him out of Linda's hair and hope that her own efforts on Mark's behalf would keep her occupied. With her attention focused on the synagogue he would be able to focus on Cindi Li.

He and Cindi had already met several times at out-of-the-way places where they weren't likely to be recognized. She was ambitious and exciting. She talked about her education at an elite private school in Hong Kong, her year at Oxford and her plans to be the next Diane Sawyer. She flattered him. Did he have any advice for her? Did he have any suggestions for her show? Did he know anyone at the network level who might help her career? When he suggested that he would like to go to bed with her, she surprised him. "I was wondering when you were going to get around to that," she said. They reached an understanding. She would sleep with him and he would help her with her career.

* * *

Mark got up at seven and dressed quietly, trying not to wake Susan. He made himself a cup of coffee and tried to relax. A call had come in the day before from the office of the Commissioner of Baseball. The commissioner had agreed to meet with him. They would fly him to New York and get him back the same day. Susan had expressed her usual misgivings.

"Are you sure meeting with the commissioner is a good idea? It makes it seem like you're more interested in baseball than you are in your work as a rabbi."

"I'm trying to keep the pressure on, honey. If I don't keep the pressure on, we'll be right back where we started."

"We have a good life here. I just want you to be careful."

"I am careful."

By the time he got to the airport, a reporter from the newspaper was already there. "Rabbi, what will you and the commissioner be talking about?" Mark started to answer but the commissioner's assistant, an intelligent looking young man in his twenties wearing a plain black suit with a white button-down shirt and a thin black tie, tugged at his sleeve. "We're on a tight schedule, Rabbi."

"My name is Duane," the assistant said, as the Gulfstream IV gained altitude and headed toward New

York. "The commissioner is looking forward to his meeting with you."

"Have you been working for the commissioner a long time?"

"A while."

"I don't suppose you know what he wants to see me about?"

"No, I don't."

Mark remembered seeing young men like Duane in Europe on a trip he had taken with Susan the year after they were married. They were everywhere, on the subways, on the trams, always smiling, never saying much, always dressed the same way, handing out pamphlets.

"You a Mormon, Duane?"

"Yes, I am."

"Are most of the people who work for the commissioner Mormons?"

"Some."

It made sense that the commissioner's office would hire Mormons. The inner workings of baseball were a closed book and Mormons were the most closed-mouth, dedicated people he had ever met. He gave up trying to make conversation, leaned his seat back as far as it would go, and imagined what life was like for people who crossed the world in private planes, were picked up by limousines, and spent long weekends at second homes in Aspen or St. Barts. He glanced out the window at the shadow of the plane skimming the clouds and thought about Liz Aurelio. He had gone down to Carnavale again last week, calling ahead this time to make sure that no one he knew was there. When he had mentioned his meeting with the commissioner she had been excited for him, not cautious and disbelieving like Susan. "You must be driving them crazy. There were a couple of guys from the Indians' front office in here the other day. You should have heard what they were saying about you."

"You can tell me. I've heard it all before."

"One of them called you a fucking weasel," she said blushing. "And that wasn't all they said. Aren't you afraid to meet the commissioner?"

"Why should I be afraid?"

"I'd be scared to death."

She had been standing next to the booth in the back where they always met, the front of her thighs pushing against the rim of the tabletop, close to where his hand was wrapped around a glass of beer. He watched her thighs move and he thought about what lay between them. From time to time the phone would ring and she would run off and when she came back she would tell him who had called and what she knew about them. A bond had developed between them. He could feel it in the easy way she talked about herself. She told him that she had gone out with Bobby G. for a while and that he had ditched her for an older woman who taught at the local university. "I could have gone to college," she told him, "but after I got out of high school, the last thing I wanted was to sit in another classroom."

When he talked about his ambition to become the senior rabbi when Rabbi Stone retired, her enthusiasm was immediate. "Of course you should take over. You've been there five years. They owe you something." He particularly liked the fact that when he talked about his plans she never tried to undercut him. "I like it when you come in here," she said. "Most of the guys I know don't want to talk. They just want to have a couple of drinks and take me somewhere."

"Do you go with them?"

"Are you kidding? I only do that with people I really care about."

Mark wasn't sure if Liz intended that as an invitation. Maybe when he got to be senior rabbi he would find a way, but for now, just being with her was enough. They talked until the restaurant started to get busy. Then he left through a side door and headed back to the synagogue.

*   *   *

The plane landed at the Marine Air Terminal at LaGuardia and another young man wearing a black suit, button-down white shirt, and narrow black tie met the plane and escorted Mark to a waiting limousine. "My name is Walter," he said. "The commissioner is looking forward to meeting you."

After a half-hour's drive into the city, during which Walter sat in the front seat next to the driver and Mark was left alone in the back with his thoughts, he was ushered into the commissioner's office on the twenty-seventh floor of an office building on Park Avenue. Colin Steadworth greeted him, heaving himself up from behind his desk, his two-hundred-fifty-pound frame squeezed into a rumpled pinstripe suit with a wide green paisley tie knotted loosely around his size-nineteen neck. Mark had seen Colin Steadworth's picture on the covers of *Time* and *Newsweek* and had watched him interviewed on *60 Minutes*, but he wasn't prepared for the overwhelming presence of this sixty-five-year-old ex-trial lawyer from Chicago.

"Let's sit over here, Rabbi," Steadworth said, leading Mark to a conference table at the far end of the room. The walls were covered with photographs of past commissioners and Hall of Famers posing with movie stars and politicians. A male secretary sat in a corner taking notes. "Some of my associates told me that this meeting would be a waste of time, Rabbi," Steadworth began, "but I can see that you're a thoughtful person and I know we'll have a productive visit. I've got Max Jessel on the speakerphone. I thought it would be good to have him join us. Max? You there?"

"I'm here," Max answered, sounding tired and irritated.

Steadworth sat back, the stubby fingers of his large hands locked together over an immense gut, and stared at Mark with the look of a toad wondering if it had room in its stomach for one more bug. "So, Rabbi, what's on your mind?"

"I've been a baseball fan all my life," Mark began. "I hope you and Mr. Jessel are willing to listen to my ideas from that perspective. I want to be constructive."

"Wouldn't have it any other way," Steadworth responded. "I've watched you on TV. Read the letter you wrote. Max and the rest of us appreciate what you've been saying. There's no question that some of the problems you talked about need attention and we're happy to explore what might be done, but we'd sure as hell like to find a way to work it out without all this religious stuff getting in the way."

"I'm not sure how all this 'religious stuff' can possibly be a threat to baseball," Mark replied.

"It's a question of priority," Steadworth continued. "How you and I feel about religion and how we act as baseball fans are two different things. What I mean is, there's a place for religion but it sure as hell isn't at the ballpark. I go to church Sunday mornings same as you do, but when I come out and head for the ballpark, I want to eat hot dogs and cuss and holler and watch the pretty cheerleaders' skirts fly up their ass, if you'll pardon the expression. You bring religion into the ballpark, Rabbi, you take all the fun out of the game."

"That's certainly not my intention."

"Max, you want to say anything?"

"No, Colin, I'm just listening."

"Max has called me more than once to complain that all the fuss you started up there in Cleveland is having an effect on his team. And I can tell you for a fact that it sure as hell is having an effect on us down here. The kind of thing you're doing, it just basically confuses people."

"I'm not sure I follow."

"It has to do with who says what. If the President makes a speech and says the country is going to hell in a handbag, that would confuse people, wouldn't it? It's the same with baseball. I mean, if I got up and made a speech and said that baseball was in the shitter, what effect do you think that would have? People like you and me, Rabbi, we got to be careful. We're in leadership positions. People pay attention to what we say. Sure the fans want things to get better. But they also want to know that if things need changing, the people in charge are smart enough to know it and make those changes."

"I don't see how things get better unless people like me speak up."

"My point exactly, Rabbi." Steadworth glanced in the secretary's direction to make sure he was taking everything down. "I just want to find a more constructive way for us to look at the issues and not get into a pissing contest in the press or on TV. That doesn't do anybody any good."

Max's weary voice crackled out over the speakerphone. "My team is fighting to get into the playoffs and right in the middle of everything, I have to deal with all this bullshit. I don't know what else to call it. It's time to lay off, Rabbi. We've lost our last three games. You want to kill the best chance we've had in years to bring a pennant home? Colin, we got a game tonight. You work something out with the Rabbi, fine. You don't, let me know. I'm hanging up."

Steadworth pushed back from the table. "Bottom line, Rabbi, we'd like you inside the tent, not out."

"I'd welcome the opportunity to cooperate."

"We'd like you to consider consulting with us. That way you'll be providing the fans with a real service. What we have in mind is for you meet with all the owners a couple of times a year. Share your ideas. No big publicity about it. We'd pay you a consulting fee, of course. Our demands on your time wouldn't be heavy. What do you think, Rabbi? We making sense here?"

"Would I be able to keep my current job?"

"It's not a problem as far as we're concerned. We just need to reach an agreement that any ideas you have about baseball, any personal appearances you make on the subject of baseball, that sort of thing, gets cleared through this office first."

"I'm flattered," Mark responded, "but I'll need some time to think it over. I want to talk to my wife and see how she feels about it and I have to talk to the board of my congregation."

"You do that, Rabbi," Steadworth said as he walked Mark to the door. "But don't wait too long to get back to me."

Mark was elated. If he played his cards right he might end up with Eli's job plus a consulting agreement with major league baseball. If that happened he would become the most envied rabbi in America.

As soon as he left, Steadworth put in a call to Max. "I offered him a consulting job. He's gonna let me know."

"I wouldn't trust the little prick farther than I can throw him," Max answered. "But I appreciate the help."

*   *   *

Max hung up the phone. Maybe the commissioner would have some luck keeping Mark Winnick out of his hair, but he doubted it. Amanda popped her head in the door.

"Bobby's here."

"Tell him to come in."

They stood together staring down at the green expanse of stadium grass that was being groomed for a night game with the Red Sox. Max took a long pull on his cigar and blew the smoke up toward the ceiling

"So, where are we with the salary thing, Bobby?"

"I don't know, Max. You tell me."

"I thought we'd have a little talk and try to work things out."

"Fine with me," Bobby said. "Got anything to drink?" Max pushed a buzzer. Amanda entered.

"Bobby wants a drink."

"What'll it be?" Amanda asked.

"I'll have a diet coke."

"Diet coke coming up."

"Put a little rum in it, will you, honey?"

"Sure, Bobby." Bobby watched Amanda's hips sway out the door. Nice.

Max moved from the window and dropped into a swivel chair behind his desk. "I got an idea that might solve both our problems. But I want to tell you a little story first."

"I like a good story." Bobby said. "Shoot."

"A couple of years ago we're building this warehouse on the docks where the old stadium used to be and this teamster guy comes over. I never met the guy before and I'm in my car with the door open and he leans in and says

I have to hire four more guys. I ask him why, since the job has already started and it will cost me another ten grand a week to hire four more guys. And he says, 'Because I say so.' So I tell him, 'I already got the number of men I'm supposed to have on this job. I go by the book.' And he says 'Whose book?' and I say, 'Your fucking book. The one that tells me how many men I gotta hire.' But he keeps pushing me. 'All I'm asking for is another four guys and they'll work their balls off for you.' I tell him, 'You can take those four guys and shove them up your ass.' My car door is open and he's leaning on it. 'Get your fuckin' arm off my car door,' I tell him. 'I just bought this car.' But he won't let go, so I floor the gas and I drag the son of a bitch fifty yards along the asphalt until he lets go."

Bobby sipped his rum and coke and kept on listening.

"That afternoon, Kelleher, the president of the local, calls me. 'What the hell's going on, Max? You busted up one of my guys real good.' 'The prick leaned on my car', I tell him. 'I told him to get off and he wouldn't.' Then Kelleher says, 'How many more guys he tell you to put on?' 'Four more, besides the ones I got already.' 'How about we settle for two?' Kelleher says. 'How about none?' I say. 'How about we split the difference?' he says. 'Okay,' I tell him. 'One more guy, but next time don't send me some wet-behind-the-ears goombah who can't tell his rear end from second base.'"

Max leaned back, stubbed out his cigar and waited for Bobby's reaction.

"That sure is an interesting story, Max. What's the point?"

"Point is, Bobby, there's always a deal to be made as long as both sides are reasonable and no one tries to take advantage of the other. You're looking for a three-year deal with the team, right?"

"That's the general idea."

"We got a good thing here. The team makes money. You and the rest of the players are doing fine. Then this little prick, Winnick, comes along and makes trouble and the worst thing is, he's got the fans on his side. The owners are all over me. I got the commissioner calling me every day. You know Winnick. Do something."

"I don't know him all that well. He's a baseball nut. He can tell you everybody's batting average going back to 1950."

"I don't care if he can recite the Talmud blindfolded with his thumb up his ass," Max bellowed. "I want him off my back."

"I tried already."

"Well, try again. You find a way to get that son of a bitch out of my hair and we'll be a hell of a lot closer to a deal than we are right now."

CHAPTER
TWENTY-THREE

Josh spent most of the week sitting in the office Peter had provided for him, talking with institutional investors, answering questions about the tender offer and trying to convince them to tender their shares. A number of institutions were holding back, waiting to see if someone else would step up and make a better bid. When the daily calls were over, he would walk into Peter's office and they would sit and have a drink and watch the sun set over the lake. Linda, Eli, and Antonia never entered into their conversation. All they talked about was the deal. How many shares the institutions had already delivered. How they could shake more shares loose. What they would do with the company once they controlled it. All Peter wanted from Josh was another couple of weeks of work and then he would get rid of him. All Josh wanted was for the tender offer to be over.

By eight o'clock, Josh would walk back to his hotel and have dinner. A movie one night. A baseball game another. He kept trying to reach Antonia. Her answering machine at home was always on but she didn't return his calls. When he called her at the museum she was never in. Once he thought it was her voice on the line but when he asked for her by name, the line went dead.

He tried calling his father at the synagogue. Each time Roz would tell him gently, "He's not able take your call." She urged him to keep trying, but her tone suggested that it was unlikely that he would get through.

He and Peter met with McCarthin again. This time the bank was more forthcoming. Subject to reaching an agreement on how much fresh money they would put into Fabrico and what sort of arrangements they were willing to make to reduce the bank's exposure on its construction loan, the bank was prepared to issue a press release. It would state that the bank had reviewed Fabrico's finances and was considering a reduction in the company's line of credit. Once the news came out, virtually every institutional shareholder would tender its stock rather than take the risk of seeing the value of its investment erode further.

At the end of each day there was a conference call with Ballard.

"Where are we with the bank?"

"We're almost there," Peter said. "We still have to agree on exactly how much of the loan on the headquarters building we're willing to pick up. We've offered to pick up half. They're stalling. I guess they figure maybe another buyer will come along and they'll get an auction going."

"What do you think, Josh?" Peter asked. Josh's thoughts were a million miles away. "You there, pal?"

"Yes, I'm here."

"What's your take on the bank?"

"My guess is that if no one else shows up by this time next week, they'll cut a deal with us."

*   *   *

One morning his mother called and said that she wanted to see him. When he got to the house there was a note taped to the back door. *Taking Dad to work. Back in a half hour.* Josh entered the house and looked around. There were handrails everywhere. A chair elevator leading to the second floor had been installed.

When his mother returned they sat in the kitchen drinking coffee.

"How is dad?"

"He can't handle the steps anymore."

Rachel's fingers played nervously with the handle of her coffee cup. "He was always so strong physically. That's the hardest part for him. Not being able to do things anymore. I think that's why he ordered you out of the house. To prove to himself that he could still make something happen." She poured herself another cup of coffee. "You remember his mother and father?"

All Josh could remember was an old photograph of his grandfather, a tall thin man with a beard who wore a yarmulke, seated on a straight-backed chair with his grandmother standing behind him, her hand on his shoulder. They were both young in the photograph. A wedding picture, probably.

"By the time I knew them," Rachel continued, "they were already old. Your grandmother was a tiny woman. She had gentle eyes. Your grandfather's eyes were like the eyes of someone who expected more out of life than he got. They had no money, and dad made it possible for them to move to Israel shortly after we got married. We went over to visit them a few times. Your grandfather's health was failing. Once, before we left, dad bought him a new hat and took it with him. Your grandfather had worn the same hat for fifty years. He wore it everywhere. Inside the house and out. It looked disreputable, but he wouldn't buy a new one. It wasn't that he couldn't afford a new one. He just wouldn't do it. So your dad bought him this beautiful new Borsalino in New York, and we took it with us to Israel and he presented it to his father. His father never opened the box. He just took it and put it in a closet. Six months later when we came back for his funeral, the box was still there, in the closet, unopened. I remember how upset your father was. He had chosen a way of life that was different than the one his father wanted for him, and his father had never forgiven him.

"What do you want me to do?"

"I want you to talk to him."

"He won't even pick up the phone."

"Go and see him."

"I don't think he'll see me."

"Of course he will."

"I can't change him, Mom."

"I don't want you to change him. I just want you to talk to him."

* * *

Eli glanced at the typed draft of his sermon. He was no longer able to write out his sermons longhand. He dictated them into a tape recorder and Roz transcribed them. At home he would practice reading them aloud to Rachel. When he spoke slowly he could handle the words, but when he tried to talk at a normal speed the words came out garbled and indistinct.

Roz knocked on his office door. "Manny Polsky is here to see you."

"Send him in."

Manny entered with a tin of cookies and set it down on Eli's desk. "My granddaughter baked these for you, Rabbi."

"How thoughtful of her. Thank her for me, Manny. Come on in and sit for a minute."

"I don't want to bother you."

"You're not bothering me at all."

From the time Eli had first appeared on the pulpit, Manny knew that he was in the presence of someone special. The retiring rabbi's work had been mainly pastoral. His sermons were like comfortable geography lessons. You learned a little about Jewish life in a country that the rabbi and his wife had recently visited. Occasionally he gave a bird's-eye view of a different religion and its customs.

His lectures never strained your mind or interfered with whatever else you might be thinking about. When Eli arrived, the spiritual and intellectual content of the services changed. His sermons demanded attention. He challenged members to think about their faith rather than just claim it as a part of their inheritance. His sermons often made people uncomfortable. Manny had been an usher for ten years when Eli delivered his trial sermon. On that Saturday morning Manny handed each board member a 3x5 card on which to record their comments. There was a line for Content and another one for Delivery and one for Pulpit Presence. Manny collected the cards after the service. Every Saturday morning since, with the exception of two weeks when he was hospitalized with pneumonia, he recorded his private comments on a 3x5 card, which he left face down on Eli's desk after services. Eli always made a point of looking at it. It was a private joke they had kept going for forty years. On the way home after services Rachel would ask, "Well, how did you rate with Manny today?"

Manny sat perched on the edge of his chair like a bird on a branch. "You've meant a lot to me, Rabbi. I don't suppose you remember how you helped me get through the loss of my wife. That was a long time ago."

"Of course I remember. Helen was a wonderful woman. Rachel and I still talk about her."

"I don't think I could have kept going without your help. You know, Rabbi, my hearing isn't what it used to be, but I can still hear every word you say from way in the back, clear as a bell. You got a problem, I'd be the first to tell you."

"I appreciate that, Manny."

"I know you're worried about what happened at the country club the other day, but I talk to a lot of people and they all understand. You just keep doing things the way you've always been doing them and we'll take care of the rest. We've got everything under control."

Despite what Manny wanted him to believe, Eli knew that things were not under control. What happened at the country club had given Linda a big lift. He had talked to Sam Broad just that afternoon. "She's scheduled another board meeting for next week," Sam told him. "She's trying to wear everyone down so they'll vote for Mark just to get this thing behind them."

"How's she doing?"

"I used to think she didn't have a chance but I'm not so sure anymore," Sam had said.

Eli had read the notice that had been sent out seeking applicants for his job. Linda had made sure the wording was vague. It stated that the congregation was seeking applicants with more than five years of experience in congregations of more than a thousand members. No date was given for when the position might become available. Eli had looked over the half-dozen resumes that had come in. None of the applicants had suitable backgrounds or experience.

"What's her next step?" Eli asked.

"She plays her cards pretty close to the vest." Sam answered. "I wish I knew."

*   *   *

"I'm so glad you're here," Roz exclaimed. "I've been telling your father to take your calls but he's like an ox sometimes. Don't tell him I said so." She motioned Josh toward his father's office, where the door was closed.

It had only been two weeks since Josh had seen his father, but already he seemed diminished. His clothes hung loosely on his frame. His face was drawn. He sat stiffly in his chair, his hands folded in front of him, fingers locked to keep his hands from shaking. Under his eyes were deep circles whose intensity had not diminished, and Josh found himself squirming under his father's steady gaze.

"I've been calling you almost every day, but I couldn't get through."

"I've been busy," Eli said. His voice seemed tired and he spoke slowly, measuring each word.

"What I did was a mistake. I should never have taken the assignment. I know you'll never understand, but it wasn't my intention to hurt Sam, or you or anyone else. I feel miserable about what happened."

Eli remained silent, hardly moving.

"Won't you at least talk to me?"

"Of course, I'll talk to you."

"Mom says the reason you won't stop working is because of what's happening with Linda. She's worried about you. She says you won't slow down."

Eli smiled wanly. "I am slowing down. I don't have much choice about that."

"You know what she means."

"I'm doing the best I can."

"Why is Linda so determined to have Mark succeed you?"

"Because she wants to be in a position where she can control the future of the congregation. She's chosen Mark as her vehicle. He's an opportunist and she's a predator. They make a perfect team."

"Can you stop her?"

"I'm not sure anyone can."

Eli shuffled some papers aimlessly. His hands shook more than Josh remembered.

"Why don't you let the congregation know how you feel? If the members of the congregation knew what she was up to, they'd never stand for it."

"I wish it was that easy," Eli said. "You get a fight started in a congregation and no one ends up a winner. You'd be surprised how fast people take sides. That's why there's a board, to keep things like this isolated from the membership so that they don't start a war that can't be stopped. The synagogue's not a battlefield."

"But if she has her way, Mark will take over."

"I hope that doesn't happen, but if it does, it's not the end of the world. I'm not going to tear the congregation apart to prevent it."

"What happens if she wins?"

"Every so often, rotten apples get in a barrel. Congregations catch on fast. Eventually the rotten apples get thrown out."

Josh could see that his father was getting tired. "I'm sorry about everything that's happened."

Eli nodded.

"Doesn't it matter to you that I'm trying to tell you that I'm sorry?"

"Apologies don't mean much." Eli's eyes held Josh in their steely grip. "I've made a lot of them myself. They have a way of making you feel better for a while but they don't change things."

"What is it that you want from me?"

"I don't want anything from you," Eli replied. "It's what you want for yourself that matters." He rose slowly from his chair, leaning on the desk to steady himself. The visit was ending as formally as it began. It had been one of the longest conversations that Josh could remember having with his father, but there had been no hint of forgiveness. He wanted to reach over and hug his father but there was a desk between them and Eli stood quietly behind it, waiting for him to leave.

CHAPTER
TWENTY-FOUR

As soon as Josh left Eli's office he called Brian. "I need to talk to you."

Brian was sitting on the floor of his apartment sorting through the contents of several cardboard boxes that he had salvaged from his office. There was a half-empty bottle of scotch open next to him. "I think I'll take a rain check. The last time we talked it didn't work out so good for me."

"You're drunk."

"Goddam right I'm drunk."

"I've got something important to tell you."

Brian mumbled something and Josh heard the sound of boxes being pushed around. "Look, Brian, I'll be at Carnavale in an hour. If you show up, fine. If you don't, okay."

* * *

By the time he got to Carnavale, Brian was already at the bar. Liz Aurelio led them to a table in the back. "You see the pitiful look she gave me?" Brian muttered as he watched

Liz walk away. "She must have heard I lost my job. It's all over town. This whole thing has been a fucking nightmare."

"For both of us," Josh said.

"I'm the one who's out of a job. You seem to be doing fine."

"I'm quitting Parallax."

"I don't believe you."

"And I've got a plan to make sure Ballard pays you."

"Yeah. Ballard's gonna be so pleased you're leaving that he'll pull out his check book and write me a check for a million dollars." Brian gulped down the rest of his drink and managed a bitter laugh.

"I'm gonna tell him that if he doesn't pay you, you'll go public with the fact that he tried to bribe you."

"He'll just deny it."

"Not if I back you up. He'll pay you what he owes you rather than take the risk of his reputation going down the drain."

Brian was silent for a moment. Even through the haze of too many scotches, some of what Josh was saying was getting through.

"You'd do that?"

"I just told you I would."

"No one walks away from the kind of job you've got."

"I don't care about the job anymore."

"Why not?"

"I'll tell you some other time when you're not drunk."

"What happens if Ballard doesn't buy it?"

"Then we're both fucked, I guess. What have you got to lose? You're already out of a job. If it works, you get your money. If nothing happens you're no worse off than you are right now. I'll be in New York tomorrow. Call Ballard at five. Tell him you're going to let everyone know he tried to bribe you and I'll take it from there."

*   *   *

The plane banked sharply, turning toward LaGuardia. Josh remembered the thrill eight years before when, after a long overnight drive from Cleveland, he had parked his car on a bluff overlooking the Hudson and stared across the river at the towers of Manhattan silhouetted against an early morning sky. The city seemed so full of promise then. This morning, with the sun obscured behind a scrim of low-lying clouds, the city seemed a cold forbidding fortress.

Why had he ever taken the assignment from Ballard? He had known the risks but he had rationalized them all away. He lived his life among people who spent their waking hours looking for slim openings beyond which glimmered the promise of advancement and financial gain. As a child, he had been fascinated by the men in his father's congregation who made a lot of money. None of them seemed burdened with guilt about the past. They did what they had to do to get ahead. Success was its own absolution. If you were tortured by the process of getting rich, you had better not start the journey.

*   *   *

"Don't be an asshole," Dan Elkins warned him over lunch. "Ballard's not going to lie down and roll over just because you don't like the way he does business."

"He promised to pay Brian."

"Be smart, Josh. Ballard doesn't give a shit about Brian, and he never will. If you don't like it here, wait until the deal goes through. Then tell him you decided to do something else with your life. He'll understand that and he'll send you off with a bonus and a letter of recommendation. You leave now, in the middle of everything, he'll never forgive you. He's an elephant. He never forgets."

*   *   *

A conference call in Ballard's office was winding down. Peter's voice came through the speakerphone. "I met with McCarthin this morning. They're giving Sam until Friday to come up with a proposal. If the bank doesn't get what they want from him, they're ready to go with us."

"What's the bottom line?" Ballard asked.

"We put twenty million of new money in the company and take over half the bank's construction loan. That's the deal. We do that and the bank will go along," Peter said.

"How soon can we close it?"

"I told them we'd be ready to close on Wednesday. Our lawyers are drawing up the papers."

The call ended and Josh checked his watch again. It was after five and Brian hadn't called. Ballard noticed a worried look on his face. "You thought closing this deal was gonna be easy. Well, it never is. It's like the first time you get laid. You want it in the worst way but you're not sure it's gonna happen. It's the anticipation that makes it all worthwhile." The analogy seemed to please him. He rolled up his pant leg and scratched his calf. Josh could see the crisscross of surgical scars that laced his leg. "Goddam leg itches like crazy sometimes."

A light flashed on Ballard's console. He switched on his speakerphone.

It was Brian.

"Yeah, what is it, Brian?"

Brian's voice was shaky and uncertain. "You owe me a million dollars, Mr. Ballard. If you don't pay me I'm going to let everyone know exactly what happened."

Ballard's face remained an empty mask. "I don't think that's such a good idea, Brian, but if that's what you want to do, you better find yourself a damn good lawyer because I'm going to sue you for slander. As a matter of fact the first thing I'm going to do after we hang up is call Petrie. I understand they took a beating on account of you and after I tell them why you came down here, I wouldn't be half surprised if they decided to go after you as well."

"But you owe me money," Brian stammered.

"For what?"

"For the help I gave you."

"What help was that?" Ballard stared directly at Josh as he spoke. His voice was missing the polite veneer he affected when he talked to people he wanted to impress. What was left was the ugly snarl of a man brought up in the backwater slums of Sydney, ready to do whatever was necessary to survive. "I don't owe you a goddam thing and I don't appreciate blackmail. If I were you, I'd think real long and hard about what I was gonna do."

Ballard hung up and swung his chair around and stared out the window.

"Brian told me he was going to make this call," Josh said.

"Why didn't you let me know?"

"He doesn't understand why you're not paying him."

Ballard spun his chair back around, facing Josh. The worry lines in his face gave way to a tight ironic smile. "I didn't know you were a fucking romantic. You pay guys like him, you never hear the end of it."

"He can make trouble."

"What's he gonna do? Start a war? Who's gonna believe him?"

"Lots of people."

"How do you figger that?"

"Because I'm going to back him up."

Josh watched the color drain out of Ballard's face. For a moment the only sound in the room was the hard tapping of Ballard's foot on the floor. "You're as much involved in this as anyone. You're the one who brought him down here."

"That's my problem. Brian's yours. After he talks, I don't think anyone's going to have a problem figuring out what really happened."

Ballard's eyes searched Josh's face for clues "We're both a little hot under the collar, boyo. Let's think this through before either of us does something he'll regret."

"I want Brian to get paid."

Ballard relaxed. "That's not a problem. We can work that out."

"And I want the tender offer called off."

The expression on Ballard's face hardly changed. "I thought it was Brian you were worried about."

"If you don't pay him and call off the tender offer, he's going to tell everyone what happened and I'm going to back him up."

"I guess I had you pegged all wrong. I thought you liked the business."

"I like the business fine. I just don't like the way you do it."

Ballard's body seemed to compress. His hands balled into small tight fists and his leg began jiggling up and down so violently that Josh could feel the floor vibrate. "Don't start preaching morals to me, you little shit. If you don't like the way I do things around here, then get the hell out."

"I'll call you at four tomorrow," Josh said as calmly as he could. "You can let me know then what you've decided."

"I'll look forward to your call," Ballard growled. "I'll be expecting it."

*   *   *

As soon as Josh left his office, Ballard put in a call to Peter. "I had a feeling about him. I should've trusted my gut and not that bullshit resumé and everybody telling me what a hotshot he was."

"He's upset because we aren't paying Brian."

"No one throws away his career just because a friend got screwed."

"Maybe we should have given him a chance to tell his father."

"It's not that either," Ballard snapped. "He would have quit earlier if that had bothered him. It's this demand that we drop our tender offer. Where the hell did that come from?"

As they talked, Peter did the math. They owned six million shares of Fabrico at an average price of just under $6.00 a share. Insider trading restrictions would keep them from selling their stock in advance of a formal cancellation of their tender offer, and if they cancelled, the stock was sure to drop to $4.00 or even lower. They'd be out at least $12 million. On the other hand if Brian talked and Josh backed him up, Ballard's reputation would go down the drain and the deal would probably go with it.

"It's your call, Jess," Peter said. "You want to call it quits, we'll get out. I'll go along with anything you want to do."

"He says he wants an answer by four tomorrow."

"You think he'll do what he says?"

Ballard thought for a minute. "Yeah, I think he will."

*   *   *

Brian lay on his bed fully clothed, flipping aimlessly through the channels on his TV. It had been a struggle to decide whether or not to call Ballard, but he needed the money and Josh's scheme was the only way he was likely to get it. With the absence of a regular paycheck, he could measure in weeks the time before rent, alimony payments, club dues, car payments and the incidentals of daily life would eat away what little security he had left and he would be flat broke. He needed to be somewhere where time would pass more rapidly. The Indians were playing a night game with the Yankees and there was still time to get down to the ballpark. He drove toward a circle of light that hung like a dusty halo over the stadium, bought a scalper's ticket for a hundred bucks and climbed to a seat on the third base line where, for the next few hours, he tried to forget the dismal shambles he had made of his life.

*   *   *

Max Jessel had invited Pamela Dawes to join him in his skybox. He heard that she was being let go from the station and had decided that it would be a nice gesture to invite her to one of the final games of the season. They stood together staring down at the crowds of people streaming in.

"You're just two games away from the playoffs, Max. You should be smiling."

"How can I smile when that schmuck junior rabbi of ours is giving me a hard time and I can't do a damn thing about it."

"Why don't you come on my show and tell your side of the story?"

The station had given Pamela an extra fifteen minutes on each of five consecutive nights for her final week of broadcasts. If they were going to dump her she would go out in style. She had scheduled a series of interviews that would leave her audience with indelible memories of what had made her thirty-six years as a television reporter so special. The governor had agreed to appear. Bobby G. was coming on. She had tried to get Max on her show for years but he always refused.

"How about it, Max? It's my last week on the air. It'd be a feather in my cap to have you as a guest. Say 'yes' and I'll let you in on some interesting news. Something that will make you wish you'd been nicer to me all these years."

Max put his arm around her. "Okay, hon, for old times's sake. Now what's so special it can't wait?"

The Indians were at bat and Bobby G. was fouling off pitches. On the seventh pitch, with a man on base, he drove a ball deep into the left field stands, tying the score at two all. The crowd went crazy and Pamela had to shout to make sure that Max could hear her.

"Rabbi Winnick has been seeing someone at Carnavale."

Max never took his eyes off the field, but Pamela could tell from the way he chewed down on his cigar that the news had taken him by surprise.

"Her name's Liz Aurelio. She's the hostess there. Mark comes down to visit her in the afternoons when the place is empty."

"You sure about that?"

"It's what I do for a living, sweetheart."

"How'd you find out?"

"You know I never divulge my sources. All I can tell you is that he's been dropping in there two or three times a week. I have no idea what else is going on, but I'm sure if there's anyone who can find out, you're right up there at the top of the list."

*   *   *

The Indians won and were only a game away from a spot in the playoffs. Brian started down the road from the stadium to Carnavale. He would have a couple of drinks and maybe, if he was lucky, Liz would be there. Then he began to think that he would run into people he knew and he didn't want to have to start explaining why he wasn't working at Petrie anymore. He turned his car around and headed home. When he got back to his apartment there was a message on his answering machine from Peter Freling. "Come for breakfast tomorrow morning. We need to talk." He listened to the message a second time. Peter's voice was cool and guarded. Whatever he had to tell him, it wasn't likely to be good news.

CHAPTER
TWENTY-FIVE

Brian turned his car down the long driveway leading to Milles Fleurs and pulled in next to a gray Mercedes with a uniformed driver behind the wheel. Peter met him at the door and led him into the den. Ballard was there, tan and relaxed, wearing gray slacks and a blue denim work shirt open at the collar.

"Hey, Brian. Good to see you again," he said. Brian's mind grappled with the possibilities. Ballard had flown in to see him. That much was certain. None of this would be happening unless they were worried. Maybe Josh's strategy was paying off. He needed to be firm. Ballard needed to understand that he was prepared to reveal everything unless he got his money.

A maid came in with coffee. "What is it that you want, Brian?" Ballard asked, his thin lips parting in the facsimile of a smile. "What would make you happy?"

Brian took a long deliberate sip of coffee. "I want to get paid."

"I understand that."

"And if you don't pay me I'm going to release a statement about what happened in New York."

"It's not that easy, Brian. It's not just you anymore. It's you and Josh and you both want something different."

"All I want is what you owe me."

"Money's just a part of it." Ballard continued. "Josh wants us to terminate our tender offer." He caught the look of surprise on Brian's face. "Didn't he tell you? Well, that's what he wants. He wants us to back out of our tender offer. We're not sure exactly why, but whatever the reason is, he's using you as an excuse to kill the deal."

Brian stumbled. "I'm not involved in any of that."

"Getting you paid was never the problem, Brian," Ballard continued, his tone turning softer and more confidential. "I always intended to pay you. It was just a matter of when. What did Josh tell you? That I didn't intend to honor my obligation? That's bullshit. Of course I'll pay you. Josh has turned this whole thing into a bargaining chip to get us to back out of our deal to buy the company. Saying he would get you paid is just a cover. God only knows what he has in mind. Maybe he's made a deal with someone else. I wouldn't put it past him. He figures if you're dumb enough to go public with what happened, we'll back out and someone else will get the deal. I don't want to see you get hurt, Brian. I'm not interested in lawsuits and I certainly don't want to see you go to jail."

Brian was confused. Josh had misled him again. The invitation to meet with Ballard had been a ruse to suck him in. Now Josh was using him to kill the deal. He felt like a man who had fallen overboard and was watching the ship steam out of sight.

"We're going ahead with our tender offer," Ballard continued. "If you want to stick with Josh, then go ahead But I'm prepared to do whatever it takes to protect my reputation. Josh has roped you into blackmail, Brian. Blackmail's a nasty business. It takes a steady hand to pull it off. You got a steady hand?"

Ballard paused to give Brian a chance to contemplate a bottomless pit of legal expense and the possibility of time behind bars. "There is a way for you to get your money."

"What's that?" Brian asked in a hoarse whisper.

"You give us an affidavit that you came down to New York to discuss the possibility of a job and that was all we ever talked about. You swear that you were never offered any money or any other kind of compensation and that no one ever asked you to do anything connected with the Fabrico deal."

"And then what?"

"And then you get $250,000."

"It was supposed to be a million."

"You'll get two fifty when you sign. When the tender offer goes through you'll get another two fifty."

"And if I don't?"

"Then you're on your own."

"How do I know you'll pay me?"

Ballard shed his smile with the ease of a snake slipping its skin. "Be in Peter's office by three this afternoon. He'll have papers ready for you and a check. If you don't show, I'll take it that you're not interested. I haven't called Petrie yet, but that's the first thing I'll do if you don't show." Ballard got up to leave. "I know the way out, Peter. Let me know what Brian decides to do."

"Does he mean it?" Brian asked as the sound of Ballard's car faded away.

"He doesn't screw around," Peter answered. "If you're not in my office by three, that's the end of it. You don't show, he'll take his chances on what comes after."

*   *   *

Josh glanced at the clock on his bedside table. It was after eight. He hadn't slept this late in years. On the street outside, a garbage truck was grinding its way through yesterday's trash. He walked to the window and stared down into a church courtyard, where rows of cardboard boxes were lined up like paper coffins. A man climbed out of one of them, yawned, scratched himself, folded his cardboard boxes into a neat pile, then lit up a cigarette and sat on the church steps and watched the world go by. The sight unnerved Josh. Like the homeless man who had no place to go, he had nothing to do but wait around and hope for the best.

The light on his answering machine was flashing. Brian had called. He called him back but there was no answer. And there was a message from Stacey. "Hey, you said you'd show me around when I got to New York. Well, I'm here. Don't chicken out on me."

*　*　*

Brian was elated. He had escaped a train wreck. Two hundred and fifty thousand dollars was better than nothing and the way things were going, nothing was what he would end up with if he wasn't careful. He would take the two fifty. If the tender offer went through, he might get another two fifty but he wasn't counting on it.

He arrived at Peter's office a few minutes before three. Peter was there with a lawyer he had never met before.

"Is Mr. Ballard coming?"

"He's back in New York."

The lawyer handed him some papers. "Here's the affidavit. You might want to read it. When you're ready, sign four copies and I'll have them notarized."

Brian read the document carefully. It stated that he had been invited to New York to meet with Ballard for the purpose of discussing a job with Parallax. Josh Stone had been with him. Parallax had paid for his round-trip ticket and for his lunch at the Regency Hotel. No other payments of any kind had been made or promised and no matters other than a possible job offer had been discussed. Since that date there had been no further conversation or contact with anyone at Parallax.

Brian signed four copies of the affidavit and a young woman came in and notarized them. Peter handed him a certified check for $250,000. "You've done the right thing, Brian. It's going to save all of us a lot of headaches." Brian fingered the check nervously. The lawyer picked up the affidavits, slipped them into his briefcase and left the room.

"Hang around for a minute," Peter suggested as soon as the lawyer was gone. "How about a drink to celebrate? It's not every day someone hands you a check for $250,000. What are you going to do with it?"

"Live off it until I can find another job."

"You can hang out here if you want," Peter suggested. "You can have an office and a secretary while you're figuring out what you want to do." Even with the affidavit tucked safely away, Peter knew that Brian was a loose cannon. He would keep an eye on him until the tender offer was over. "Move your stuff over any time you want. You can have the office Josh was working in. It's right down the hall from mine."

*   *   *

Josh picked up Stacey at the Broadway gate to the Columbia campus. She slid into the seat next to him and gave him a quick hug. "I bet my roommate five bucks you wouldn't show." As they headed downtown on the West Side Highway, she filled him in on her life. "I room with a couple of other girls in an old apartment they've turned into a dorm. Carla's from Boston. My other roommate's a drag. Carla and me are looking for a place off campus for next year. I signed up for art history and I'm auditing a course on eighteenth-century English poets. The survey courses suck, but next year I can take what I want."

"You meet any guys yet?"

"Some."

"Any one in particular?"

"You sound like my mom. Where are we going?"

"Where would you like to go?"

"I want to see where you work."

Josh told her that he had been fired.

"Working with my dad must have been tough."

"Tough enough," Josh answered and decided to leave it at that.

"How's your dad doing?" Stacey asked. "I read up some on ALS. There's no cure for it, is there?"

"It's just a matter of time, I guess."

"I'm really sorry. I loved your dad. We all did."

Stacey slid her arm around his neck and left it there. They drove past the Battery and up the FDR Drive. On Second Avenue he pulled into an empty parking space across from an aging tenement building. It was the same building he had seen in the photograph Stefan Belzer showed him. A hardware store had replaced the hat shop on the ground floor and the store signs were all in Spanish. Otherwise nothing had changed.

Stacey was watching him. "What's so special about this place?"

"My dad grew up here."

"Oh my God! We're going in aren't we?" Stacey pulled at his arm. "C'mon. You want to see it, don't you? I want to see it."

They entered a tiny vestibule with paint peeling off the walls and a row of letter boxes with some of the lids sprung open, others missing. Narrow stairs led up to the fourth floor, where Josh knocked on a door at the back of a dimly lit hallway. The door opened just enough for an old woman to peer out.

"My father lived here," Josh said. "I wonder if I could look around."

The old woman didn't seem to understand. "*Su padre vivio aqui?*"

Stacey said. "*Podreiamos mirar un poco.*"

"*Quien es, mama?*" A young woman with a baby in her arms opened the door a bit wider and stared at them. "What chu want?"

"My father used to live here," Josh explained. "I was wondering if we could look around."

"My husband is no home. You come back later, okay?"

Before the door closed Josh caught a glimpse of a small room with two narrow windows that looked out on a brick wall ten feet away. The furniture consisted of a battered couch, an armchair and a TV on a metal stand. Down a narrow hallway he could see a single bedroom. His father had lived here with his parents, two sisters and a brother.

Once, while he was in college, he had asked his mother if she had ever seen where his father grew up. "Right after we got married we were in New York and I asked him to show me where he was born. We took a cab downtown and we walked along and stopped in front of this run-down tenement building. I wanted to go in but he wouldn't, you know how stubborn he can be, so we just stood outside for a while and then we left. I guess it was a part of his life that he didn't want to remember."

When they were back in the car, Josh sat for a moment staring back at the building, wondering about the conditions that had shaped his father's life.

Stacey sensed the effect the experience was having on him. "Your dad sure has had an amazing life," she said. "You must be very proud of him."

*   *   *

They had lunch in Chinatown. "I don't have any classes until tomorrow," Stacey said. "You gonna take me to see your apartment?"

"Some other time, Stacey. I've got a lot of work to do."

Stacey smiled. "I know a brush-off when I see one. Anyway, I had a great time today and if you ever change your mind and feel like calling me . . ."

Josh drove her back to her dorm and waited until she had run up the steps and disappeared inside. He checked his watch. It was still too early to call. He watched some boys across the street toss a football around, and then, promptly at four, he called Jess Ballard.

"It's Josh Stone. Is Mr. Ballard in?"

"Yes he is. He's been expecting your call. I'll put you through."

A moment later Ballard came on the line. "What's up, mate?"

"I was wondering what you decided to do."

"We're going ahead with the tender offer. I'm surprised you couldn't figger that out for yourself."

There was a click at the other end. Josh knew that was the way deals ended. No apologies. No small talk. It was over. He dialed Brian's number and after a few rings, Brian picked up.

"We got shot down."

"What did he say?"

"He didn't say anything."

Josh had expected Brian to be devastated but he seemed almost relieved. "I sort of figured that would happen."

"Well, I'm ready for the next step, Brian. You got your statement ready?"

Josh could hear Brian take a deep breath. "I don't know, Josh. Everything's been moving so fast. I was thinking of maybe going down to Florida for a couple of days. Give myself a chance to think about what happened. I appreciate what you tried to do. You stuck your neck out for me. I'm sorry it didn't work out."

CHAPTER
TWENTY-SIX

Peter had just come in from his morning run and was sprawled on a couch reading the *Wall Street Journal* when Linda entered the sunroom. For the first time in years she was feeling mellow. She had put her life on hold for him and after endless boring dinners with his business associates, stupid skiing trips, his dalliances, her recriminations, and his inevitable apologies, he was finally behaving like a proper husband. He was making a serious effort to be more attentive and seemed genuinely interested in her efforts to get Mark elected senior rabbi. Her campaign was moving smoothly. Brian Patzer and Bill Palevsky were on board. So were Sally and Bobby G. and Renee. Her remaining concern was with Antonia.

"Put down the paper, honey. I need to talk to you. How are things going with the museum?"

"I talked to the director yesterday. He understands that we're considering funding Antonia's outreach program."

"Did you ask him to talk to her?"

"I let him know we hadn't fully made up our minds. I'm sure he'll talk to her. He'll want her to do everything she can to bring the money in."

With the affidavits signed and Brian safely tucked away in his office, Peter was now fully involved in helping Linda. He realized that once Mark became the senior rabbi, she would be busy at the synagogue and he would have clear sailing with Cindi Li. Linda hadn't found out about Cindi yet and he intended to keep it that way. He scheduled their meetings with the precision of a missile launch. Last night they had driven in separate cars to a small restaurant fifty miles away in a suburb of Akron where no one would recognize them. Over dinner Cindi complained bitterly about Pamela. "She's still trying to poison people at the station against me. I wouldn't be surprised if she has a doll of me in her office and sticks pins in it."

"Don't worry," Peter reassured her. "She'll be gone in a week. I promise."

After dinner they checked into a nearby motel. If Peter had any qualms about their lovemaking it was that Cindi always seemed in a rush. "Let's take it slow and easy this time," he urged as they undressed. She slipped into bed and ran her lips lightly over his bare chest and slowly down his stomach. "Oh god," he whispered as her mouth closed around him. He was on the verge of ecstasy when Cindi suddenly sat up.

"Oh shit," she exclaimed, glancing at her watch, "I lost track of time. I've got to be back at the station in less than an hour. They've scheduled a run-through of my show. I'm sorry, honey, that's going to have to be it for tonight."

*   *   *

Leo Bookman measured four tablespoons of Colombian coffee into his electric coffee mill and watched the tiny blades grind the beans into a fine dark powder. He emptied the contents into an old-fashioned coffee pot that his mother had given him and set it on the stove to percolate. Then he poured cereal in a bowl, added milk and sugar, squeezed the juice of two oranges into a glass and sat down to read the morning paper. He followed the same routine every day. It gave him a comforting sense of control as he prepared to deal with the uncertainties that he knew would be waiting for him the minute he stepped out the front door of his apartment.

He turned to the business page of the paper. A two-column story revealed that a number of institutions that held blocks of Fabrico stock were waiting until the company's third-quarter earnings came out before making up their minds whether or not to tender. At the bottom of the page there was an announcement that Brian Patzer had resigned as general manager of the Cleveland office of Petrie & Company to "pursue other interests." No details were given.

He called Brian immediately.

"I quit," Brian told him. "I got fed up working for Petrie, that's all. I've been thinking about going on my own for a while."

"There's an article in the paper that says that some of the institutions aren't sure they're going to tender."

After the initial burst of activity following the tender offer, Fabrico shares had moved down a few fractions each day. Yesterday the stock had closed at $6.25 a share, still well above Leo's purchase price, but Leo knew that if the tender offer failed, the price was likely to collapse.

"That's bullshit, Leo. Ballard's got it locked up tight. I'm close to those guys. As a matter of fact I'm working out of Peter Freling's office right now. I talk to him every day." Brian was eager to keep Leo from selling his shares. With the end of the tender period approaching and the outcome still in doubt, he could be the white knight who brought in Leo's three million shares to help close the deal. That would earn him Ballard's gratitude and nail down the $250,000 that he was counting on. "Hang in there, Leo. I'm on top of it. This deal is absolutely going to happen. And I wouldn't be surprised if the price goes up again. I know for a fact there are other bidders out there in the wings. Trust me, Leo, there's no way you can lose. If anything goes wrong you'll be the first to know."

*   *   *

Eli glanced across his desk at the troubled faces of Marty Franklin, Max Jessel, and Sam Broad. Marty held a copy of a letter in his hand. Through the closed door they could hear Roz McIver fielding calls. She had been on the phone all morning. Every call was about the letter, typed on synagogue stationery, signed by Linda Freling, and mailed to every member of the congregation.

> *Dear Fellow Synagogue Member:*
>
> *I am writing to you as president of the congregation to bring you up to date on the status of our efforts to secure a replacement for our beloved Rabbi Stone when he retires.*
>
> *We remain concerned about Rabbi Stone's health and the extent to which his health may have an impact on the congregation and its future. I and several other members of the board feel it is essential, given the gravity of his condition, that he announce a specific date for his retirement so that we can make further progress in selecting someone to replace him.*
>
> *Rabbi Stone has been reluctant to set a date for his retirement. While we understand his desire to remain as active as his health will permit, his unwillingness to provide your board with a fixed date for his retirement has led to special problems. Specifically, we have been unable to secure interest from qualified candidates. Most of the rabbis that we hoped might apply currently hold down important positions with other congregations. They are understandably reluctant to indicate their interest since we are unable to tell them*

when the position of Senior Rabbi in our congregation might open up.

In the opinion of many of us on the board, the reluctance of Rabbi Stone to set a fixed date for his retirement has placed the future of our congregation in considerable peril. We have asked him to reconsider his decision and we have encouraged Rabbi Winnick to remain with us for the time being. Rabbi Winnick has consented to do so. Many of us feel that Rabbi Winnick's willingness to help us through these troubled times, as well as his dedication to the congregation over the past five years, qualifies him for consideration as a strong candidate to lead this congregation into the future.

No decisions have been made. We will continue to keep you informed of all significant developments.

Yours very truly,
Linda Freling
President, Congregation Shaaray Emunah

"How did she get hold of the membership list?" Eli asked.

"We're not sure," Marty said. "She came down to the synagogue office a couple of days ago. Leo was out to lunch when she showed up. There's one list in his safe. The only other copy is on one of the computers in the front office and she got hold of it somehow. From what I understand, she's going to ask for a vote at the next meeting of the board to approve the selection of a doctor to examine you to see if you're physically fit to keep on working."

Just three days ago, Eli had been to the doctor for another checkup. The weakness in his right leg had spread to his left. He now used a cane in public, but at home he used a walker and needed the stair lift to get upstairs and down. He had been able to get through the last two weeks of preaching and pastoral visits, but it was only a matter of time until he would no longer be able to handle a full range of rabbinical responsibilities.

"How is the vote likely to go?" he asked.

"There's a good chance the vote will go against you," Marty advised. "She'll have Sally Minton voting with her. Bill Palevsky and Brian Patzer for sure and probably Bobby G. and Renee. That's half the board. All she needs is one more vote."

"This whole thing is bullshit," Max exploded. "I'm sorry, Rabbi, but that's the way I feel. No one is going to force you to resign."

Max's outburst made Eli smile. "I know how you feel, Max, but I don't own the congregation. I'm just a hired hand. If the board votes her way there's not much I can do about it."

"Get your own letter out to the congregation," Max urged. "Tell them what's going on. Unless you do something, they're all gonna believe what her letter says and we're going to end up with that putz as our rabbi. No one wants him except Linda and a couple of her cronies. She gets the votes to have a doctor examine you and the next thing you know she'll have the votes to get him elected."

"What about you, Sam?" Eli asked. "What do you think?"

Sam knew how much Eli detested the idea that Mark might succeed him. But he also knew the physical toll that Eli's illness was taking and how anxious Rachel was for him to retire.

"The letter is definitely going to strike a chord, Eli. Lots of people were at the country club."

"Don't even consider retiring," Max pleaded. "Show her who's boss. Get a letter out to the congregation."

"I can draft a letter for you, Rabbi, if you'd like." Marty said. "A simple statement of your position. Nothing inflammatory. Just so everyone knows what's going on."

Eli glanced across his desk. All these men had been his friends for years and he knew the advice they were giving was motivated by a desire to protect him. But he also knew that once the hiring or firing of a rabbi got beyond the closed doors of the boardroom it would become a free-for-all. In every congregation there were people who loved their rabbi and others who felt they had been insulted or ignored. Someone's wedding couldn't be squeezed into a rabbi's tight schedule. Somebody else was angry because a sick relative had died without a final bedside visit. Getting the entire membership of the congregation involved in the selection of a new rabbi would be a disaster. Should it be a man or a woman? The candidates were either too young or too old, or someone had heard that their sermons were boring or that their positions on social issues were too conservative or too radical. Once the full membership of a congregation got involved in synagogue politics, it was like throwing gasoline on a fire.

"I appreciate what you've all been saying," Eli concluded, "and I know you have my best interests at heart, but I'm not prepared to have the congregation get into a fight over this. Let the board vote on her resolution. Let's find out where everybody stands."

* * *

Josh stood at the window of Marty's office and watched a solitary freighter churn through the choppy waters outside the breakwater. How naive he had been to think that Ballard would succumb to pressure. Men like Ballard lived their lives straddling high-voltage wires, absorbing any unexpected jolts of current that came along. He was free of Ballard now and eager to set things right with his father and Sam and anyone else who would listen to him. He wondered if they would trust him. He was damaged goods. If they thought they had a chance without him, they wouldn't touch him with a ten-foot pole.

He had called Marty the moment his plane touched down in Cleveland.

"Marty, I need to talk to you."

"What about?"

"It's complicated. I'd rather talk to you in person."

"I've got a meeting out of the office," came the cool response. "I'll be back at eleven."

It was almost eleven-thirty when Marty walked in. "What's on your mind, Josh?"

"I've left Parallax."

"You quit?"

"I was fired."

"I thought you enjoyed working there."

"I did for a while. I don't anymore."

"What went wrong?"

"I'm not sure I can explain it all that easily."

"Why don't you try?"

"They promised me a chance to tell my father what I was working on before the news of the tender offer got out, and they let me down. And I got Brian Patzer involved in this thing in ways I'm not proud of."

"What happened with Brian?"

"Petrie was short a bunch of stock and Ballard didn't want them to cover. He offered Brian a lot of money to keep them in the dark. Brian agreed and then Ballard stiffed him."

The ease of their first meeting had been replaced by a cool prosecutorial intensity. "What was your involvement?" Marty inquired.

"I got the two of them together. I'm not proud of what I did. I've made more mistakes than I can count and I want to try to make up for them. I want to help."

Josh was sure his explanation sounded like sour grapes.

"Will Brian testify to what happened?"

"I doubt it. I'm pretty sure they got to him."

The secretary buzzed to say that Sam Broad had arrived. Sam barely greeted Josh, brushing by him and settling in a chair across from Marty. They talked about him as if he wasn't in the room. What had prompted him to come to see Marty? What were his motives? Was he trustworthy or not?

"Well, what do you think?" Sam asked Marty after a full five minutes had passed.

"I think he can help us."

"Okay, then," Sam said, staring at Josh with the look of a person forced to do business with someone he doesn't like, "Tell us what you know."

Over the next two hours Josh told them everything. Marty asked the questions and Sam absorbed the answers like a giant sponge. With each new bit of information he would grunt and shift in his chair.

"Parallax owns ten million shares," Josh said. "Twenty million more have come into the depository. They already control more shares than you do, Sam. The rest of the stockholders haven't made up their minds. A lot depends on what the bank decides to do. Where do you stand with them?"

"They want me to personally guarantee the overruns on the construction loan and put more money in the company. I'm not in a position to do that. I've offered them more stock but they've turned it down."

"What about the company's line of credit?"

"They said they'll pull it if I don't work something out with them."

"Have you talked to other banks?"

"We've talked to all of them," Marty answered. "None of them is willing to step in."

"Here's the way I see it," Josh said. "Peter and Ballard are willing to put twenty million of fresh cash in the company and pick up half of the bank's construction loan. In return they want the bank to issue a statement that they intend to pull your line of credit. If the bank buys their package, you're through. Anyone still on the fence will tender. They plan to wrap up their deal with the bank over the weekend so that the bank can issue its statement by the middle of next week."

"What do you suggest?" Sam asked.

"You've got to cut a fast deal with the bank. If you can do that, you've got a chance. If you don't, it's over."

They spent the next two hours discussing strategy. Sam put in a call to Max Jessel, who expressed an interest in being helpful. Josh called McCarthin at the bank and set up a lunch for the following day. As they broke up, Sam pulled Josh aside.

"Your dad told me that you came to see him. What happened?"

"I tried to tell him I was sorry. I don't think he cares one way or another anymore."

"Talk to him again."

"I don't think it will accomplish anything."

"You're his son, goddamit," Sam exploded. "Go talk to him again. That's not a suggestion. I'm telling you to do it."

*   *   *

RAPHAEL D. SILVER

Bruno Leppelmeier settled his substantial bulk in a chair across from Max Jessel. He took a cigar from a box that Max held out in front of him, bit off the end, spit the cap into a nearby wastebasket, lit up, and took a long leisurely pull, watching the smoke curl up toward a grille in the ceiling. In his early sixties, he had been hired to handle the baseball club's private security detail. He'd been a beat cop in the neighborhood where Max opened his first scrap lumber yard, had done a lot of favors for Max over the years, and now waited for one of the little parables that always preceded a request for something special that Max wanted him to do.

"The wife and I were in Cuba a while back," Max began, "before they made you feel like a goddam criminal for going there. We went to this cigar factory where the workers sit on hard wood benches. If they're lucky they get a couple of bucks for ten hours work. Half hour for lunch. Bread, cheese, maybe a piece of fruit. The lowest paid ballplayer on my club makes three hundred grand just for showing up. They get a pension and health insurance and they bitch if the water in the shower isn't hot enough."

"What's on your mind, Max?" Bruno asked.

"I got a favor to ask. Something I don't want anyone to know about."

"Shoot."

"I want you to put a tail on somebody," Max said.

"Who?"

"Mark Winnick."

"The rabbi? The guy who writes all that stuff about baseball? What's he been doing, stealing from the collection box?"

"I think he's having an affair with the hostess at Carnavale."

"He fucking her?"

"That's what I want you to find out."

Max got up from behind his desk, grabbed a fistful of cigars, stuffed them in Bruno's pocket and walked him to the door.

"If it gets out that I put a tail on him it could be embarrassing, not to say expensive."

"Rest easy," Bruno said. "I'll give this my personal attention." The assignment would be interesting. You didn't get to tail a rabbi every day.

CHAPTER TWENTY-SEVEN

Josh opened the curtains in his hotel room. It was early and the city was just waking up. An unexpected storm had dumped an inch of snow on the streets. It would melt by noon but for the moment the city sparkled like a diamond. His meeting with McCarthin was set for eleven-thirty so he had most of the morning to kill. He got dressed, had breakfast and drove around for an hour, down half-deserted streets, past abandoned storefronts, revisiting places he hadn't seen in years. The city had been a powerhouse once. Along the banks of the narrow river that divided the city in two, giant lake freighters off-loaded iron ore for hungry blast furnaces that worked three shifts a day. Now foreign mills stoked the world with cheaper steel, and the furnaces, banked and silent, stood like ghostly reminders of the past. The city had become a quieter place, drifting into a dignified old age like a dowager on a respectable pension.

He drove east for twenty miles to a small community bordering the lake where he had lived as a small child. When he was ten, his family moved to be closer to the synagogue.

He had always suspected that it was his mother who insisted on the move. His father had enjoyed the isolation.

The road dead-ended on a bluff overlooking the lake. He parked his car and pushed through a sagging section of wire fence with a sign that warned, DANGER, in fading red letters. The house he had expected to find had collapsed into the lake. Only a part of the foundation remained, barely visible among the tall weeds. He walked to the edge of the bluff and looked down. Waves had broken through the breakwater and carved away huge chunks of the cliff. A staircase that descended to the lake lay splintered below, its weathered boards scattered like matchsticks in an eddy of brackish water.

He could still visualize the house. His father's study faced the lake, its curved bay windows catching the rays of the setting sun. There was a screened-in porch where he would sit at night and watch fireflies sputter in the darkness. One night he stayed up late watching sheets of violet light race in shimmering patterns across the sky.

"Take a good look, son," his father said. "You don't often see the northern lights this far south. You may never see them this close again." Whenever his father spoke to him in this way, like a teacher, it bothered him. But now, as he stood at the edge of the bluff and gazed out across the lake, the memory of those days was strangely comforting.

Sometimes on warm summer nights, he would walk with his father to a railroad crossing a mile away. Occasionally the safety barrier would drop down and a long line of freight cars would rumble by. Next to the tracks there was an abandoned switch tower with a ladder that his father let him climb. The room at the top was filled with levers that a switchman pulled to move trains from one track to another. He would stand there, staring down through the broken glass of the switch tower window at the empty tracks, and imagine himself sending a train on its way to some distant place. Then, feeling suddenly insecure, he would climb back down. He could still remember the long walks home, struggling to keep up with his father's lengthy strides, and the reassuring feeling of his small fingers curled in his father's hand.

*   *   *

Tom McCarthin sat across from Josh in the dining room of the Founder's Club, his manicured fingers twirling the stem of a wine glass, his eyes fixed on the pale liquid swirling inside. He took a sip and indicated with a nod to the waiter that the wine was satisfactory.

"I hear you jumped ship," he said.

"I'm not with Jess Ballard any more, if that's what you mean."

Josh didn't feel like going into a lengthy explanation. McCarthin was simply letting him know that he was aware of what had happened. That was the thing about bankers. They were never judgmental. They had no interest in who was right or wrong, but only in how what happened might affect the bank and their own careers.

"I understand you're planning to come out with a negative report on Fabrico," Josh began, "and I'd like to find out if there's some way we can persuade you to hold up on it."

"I'd like to help, but there's not much I can do," McCarthin responded. "Sam had a relationship with the old bunch. Accommodations were made and the bank's lending policies got out of whack. When they gave me this job they told me to clean things up. Sam's a great guy and I appreciate that he's a friend of your family, but my hands are tied. The guys you used to work for are willing to put twenty million of fresh cash in the company and take part of the construction loan off our hands. I've run it past our people in New York and they've told me to grab it. Frankly, it would be a blessing for us if their tender offer went through."

"Is there anything we can do that would make a difference?"

"At this point, I'd say no. We're pretty far down the line. We're planning to close with them next week." McCarthin poked his index finger in the back of his mouth, dislodged a morsel of food that was stuck between his teeth and wiped the offending particle off on his napkin.

"Would you be willing to hold off for a while?"

"For what?"

"For a better offer."

A flicker of interest traced itself around the corners of McCarthin's eyes. "How long would you need?"

"How much time have we got?"

"We're set to close on Friday. We plan to make an announcement that afternoon. If you've got something to offer, get it to me no later than Wednesday morning. I'll need some time to review it with New York."

*   *   *

Linda, Sally, Bill and Brian were crowded together in Mark's small office. "I want this meeting to go off like clockwork," Linda announced. "Bill, you'll make the motion and Brian, you'll second it. If there's any discussion, I'll handle it. And Mark, since Rabbi Stone has decided not to come to this meeting, it's probably not appropriate for you to be there either. Why don't you wait in your office. If we need you, I'll let you know."

Mark sat behind his desk, barely listening. On the way back from New York he had decided to accept the consulting job without asking for anyone's permission. When he told Susan she was appalled.

"Aren't you even going to ask Eli if it's okay?"

"Why should I? It's no different than when he makes a speech and gets paid for it. I wish you'd stop questioning everything I do."

He called the commissioner's office the following morning. A ten-page contract arrived by FedEx the next day. He hadn't read it carefully, noting mainly the section that stipulated that he would receive $8,333 a month for a period of twelve months with a renewal to be negotiated at the end of a year, but only if both sides wished to extend. He had just returned from taping an interview with Pamela Dawes. She had asked about his trip to New York. He was evasive, saying only that he and the commissioner had met and had a productive discussion. As the interview was about to end, Pamela asked him what he thought about Bobby G.'s chances of staying with the team. He knew he was supposed to avoid commenting about controversial matters, but what was controversial about Bobby G.? He was the best thing that had happened to the Indians in years.

"Just look at the numbers," Mark responded. "He's batting .319 for the season. He's hit .420 in the last twelve games. He hasn't made an error since July 19th and he's driven in the winning run in four of our last twenty-one ballgames. Management would have to be out of their minds not to sign him up again."

* * *

By eight-fifteen, all the members of the board were present except for Bobby G. and Renee. There was an uneasy tension in the boardroom, the sense one felt just before a storm when there was an excess of ozone in the air. Everyone knew about the letter that Linda had sent to the members of the congregation but no one seemed to want to talk about it.

Max turned his cell phone off. An assistant had just filled him in on Mark's interview. He'd call Colin Steadworth in the morning and raise hell. Someone better read Mark the riot act. The little prick couldn't keep his mouth shut, and just when he and Bobby G. were getting close to a deal. "We gonna get started or what?" he snapped.

Linda looked up from her notes. "I want to wait a few more minutes, Max. This is an important meeting and I'd like everyone to be here."

"The rest of us got here on time," Max grumbled. "I don't see why we got to wait for stragglers."

There was a peal of laughter from the hallway and Bobby G. and Renee walked in. Bobby glanced around the room. "Looks like our locker room after we blew a big one. Sorry we're late."

Linda was eager to get the meeting started. "Now that we're all here, there are a number of important matters we have to cover. Most of you were at the country club last weekend. You all saw what happened. We simply have to come to some agreement on how to move forward with a replacement for Rabbi Stone." She glanced around the room. "If there are no objections, we'll dispense with the reading of the minutes of our last meeting. Bill, you have a resolution to propose."

"Before we get to that," Max interrupted, "There's a couple of things I'd like to know."

"Can it wait until after the resolution, Max?"

"No, it can't. I'd like to know how you got hold of our membership list?"

"I went to the front office and asked for it."

"From who?"

"From whoever was there at the time. I don't remember."

"That membership list is private. It doesn't belong to you. It belongs to the synagogue. You had no right to use it for private purposes."

"There was nothing private about what I used it for," Linda answered, trying to stay calm. "I sent out the letter so that everyone would know what was going on. I thought it was appropriate to keep the membership informed."

"That's bullshit and you know it," Max shouted, jumping to his feet. "All you want to do is smear Rabbi Stone and force him to retire."

"That's ridiculous," Linda snapped. "I'm offended that you would suggest I would do such a thing and I'm offended by your language."

"How I talk is my business," Max's eyes narrowed to angry slits. "Leo said you told one of the girls in the office that if she didn't give you the list you'd have her fired. Isn't that what you told me, Leo?"

Leo didn't want to be drawn into a fight with Linda. She could make his life miserable.

"Speak up, Leo."

Leo spoke so softly that it was hard to hear him. "I came back from lunch and one of the girls said that Mrs. Freling had threatened to have her fired if she didn't give her a copy of the membership list."

"That's a bald-faced lie," Linda shouted, throwing away all pretense of civility. "I did no such thing. It was on her computer. I asked her for it and she ran a copy off for me."

"Why didn't you wait for Leo to get back?" Max demanded.

"First of all, if there's something the congregation needs to know about, it's my job to tell them and I don't need some little nobody in the front office telling me what I can or can't do. I'm president of this synagogue and there was nothing wrong with what I did and I resent the implication that there was."

"This whole thing stinks," Max said, sitting down abruptly. "If it happened in my business I'd call the cops and have you arrested. I know what you're after and so does everybody else. I'll quit this congregation before you jam Mark Winnick down my throat."

The rest of the board sat in stony silence. "I'm willing to overlook your outburst, Max," Linda said after an appropriate pause. "The fact of the matter is that Eli is no longer capable of doing his job properly and the sooner we get around to recognizing the fact, the better. Marty, you're our counsel. How do we proceed?"

"The proper way is a resolution. But before you get to that, I met with the rabbi at his home this afternoon. His position is that he is still able to do his job. He acknowledges that his mobility is restricted and that he doesn't have the same amount of energy that he used to have, but his mental faculties are absolutely intact. I can attest to that. And he knows that he's had some difficulty speaking from time to time, but he feels that the problem is manageable for now."

"Did he give you any indication of when he might retire?" Sally asked.

"He's waiting for the board to decide on a suitable candidate to replace him."

"Suitable to whom?" Linda demanded.

"A 'suitable candidate' were the words he used."

"That's precisely why I called this meeting," Linda said. "We're never going to be able to agree with the rabbi about who is suitable and who isn't. Our contract gives us a way out of a situation like this. Marty, you're familiar with our contract with the rabbi. Isn't there a clause in there that allows us to select a qualified physician to examine him if there is a disagreement about his ability to do his work?"

"Yes, there is such a clause."

"I got one of those clauses in my contract," Bobby G. said. "Something happens to me, the team has a right to take me off the roster and bring someone in to replace me."

"Jesus Christ, Bobby," Max grumbled. "We're not talking about your goddam contract."

Linda pressed on. "It's not unusual for a congregation to have a contract like that with its rabbi, is it, Marty?"

"No. It's not unusual. There's something like that in most congregational employment agreements, but it's seldom invoked. It's pretty much a last-ditch kind of thing. Most congregations find other ways to work through the problem."

"Marty, please tell us what our contract with Rabbi Stone says, specifically." Linda was in full control again.

Marty was the synagogue's attorney and had no choice other than to explain. "Our contract with the rabbi says that if there is a disagreement between him and the board about his physical or mental ability, then, subject to the approval of a majority of the board, one or more qualified physicians can be called in to determine whether or not he can still do his job. If, in their opinion he can, he stays. If they say he can't, then the board can force his retirement."

"That seems fairly straightforward," Linda said. "Since there doesn't seem to be any other way to get this matter resolved, I propose that we allow Bill to make his motion and then take a vote on it."

Sam Broad had been quiet until now. "There's no reason to submit Eli to that kind of treatment. It's disgraceful. Why don't we just find a rabbi we can all agree on and put this whole business behind us?"

"It's not that simple," Linda continued. "We haven't exactly had a lot of candidates apply for the job."

"How many?" Antonia asked.

"Five."

"Is Rabbi Winnick one of them?"

"No. Out of courtesy to Rabbi Stone he hasn't submitted a formal application. The applications are all from relatively inexperienced rabbis. I've sent Rabbi Stone every one of the resumés and he agrees with me. Most of the names we were hoping would come in are holding back because we can't tell them when the job will be available. It's just what I said would happen. Without an agreement from Rabbi Stone about when he's going to retire, we're not going to get anywhere. He either has to give us a date or we need to find a way to force him to retire."

"Can I say something?" Manny Polsky's thin voice trembled as he spoke. "I've known the rabbi longer than most of you. I've listened to him preach every week for the past forty years, and I can tell when he's having an off day and when he's not. He's the only one who knows what's going on inside his body and he'll be the first one to let us know when we should make a change."

"Thank you very much, Manny," Linda said. "We always appreciate your comments. Anyone else want to say anything?" She could feel the momentum slipping away. "Why don't we take a vote and see how many of us are willing to have the rabbi examined?"

"Are you sure that's wise?" Marty said. "It's a drastic step."

Max Jessel struggled to suppress his rage. "You're trying to shove Winnick down our throats. Any of those other rabbis would be better than him."

"We aren't discussing Rabbi Winnick's qualifications, Max. We're just trying to find out if we can agree on a way to move forward. If there's no more discussion can I have a motion?"

Bill Palevsky raised his hand. "I move that in accordance with the terms of our contract with Rabbi Stone, a committee of the board be authorized to select one or more qualified physicians to examine him and determine whether he is physically capable to carry on with his rabbinical duties."

"Is there a second?" Linda asked.

"I second the motion," Brian said.

"It's been moved and seconded," Linda said. "Is there any further discussion?"

"I want to say something before we vote," Sam said. "It's a sad day when the board of this congregation is willing to embarrass itself and its senior rabbi by proposing something this offensive and demeaning. I think we will all regret having taken this vote, whether it passes or not."

"I sympathize with what you're saying, Sam. We all want to protect Rabbi Stone, but this seems to be the only way that we can move ahead," Linda said, looking around the room to see if anyone else wanted to say something. "All in favor of the resolution please raise your hands."

Linda, Sally, Brian, Bobby G., Renee and Bill Palevsky raised their hands.

"Opposed?"

Max Jessel's hand shot up along with those of Sam, Marty, Manny Polsky and Pamela Dawes.

"Antonia, you're not voting?" Linda asked.

"I'm abstaining."

"You have that right."

"If you don't vote," Marty cautioned, "the motion will carry six to five."

"I thought it took seven votes for a resolution to pass."

"We have a quorum and it only takes a majority of those present and voting to pass the resolution. With you abstaining, six affirmative votes is all it takes to pass."

"Then I'd like to change my vote and vote against the resolution."

"You can't do that," Linda shouted, her voice rising half an octave. "You already voted to abstain."

"Anyone can change their vote if they want to," Marty corrected her. "It's perfectly proper."

"Then may I ask why you're changing your vote?"

"What you're proposing doesn't seem right to me. I guess I want us to find another way."

Linda glanced hurriedly around the room. No one else seemed to be objecting to Antonia's change of heart. It was time to regroup and find another way. "I know this is an extremely emotional issue and I understand everyone's point of view. I hoped we'd make better progress. Maybe someone else has a better idea on how to solve the problem."

"I got a better idea," Max said. "Why don't you step down as president. We'll pick someone else to run things and then everything will get solved." He got up to leave. "If we're finished I got a meeting to get to."

"Sit down, Max," Marty said. Marty took a piece of paper out of his pocket. "The rabbi gave me this letter to read if something like this happened. It's addressed to all of us."

"Please be advised that due to reasons of health I am today announcing my retirement as senior rabbi of this congregation. The date for my retirement will be two months from this date or at such earlier time as the congregation will have chosen my successor. Until then, I shall continue to serve the congregation as its senior rabbi to the best of my ability. I have valued my years as spiritual leader of this congregation and I anticipate that my successor, whoever he or she may be, will continue the fine traditions that have made this congregation a vital center of Jewish life."

It was as if a giant vacuum had sucked all the air out of the room. For a long time no one said anything, then Max spoke up. "I don't get it," he said.

"When I met with the rabbi this afternoon," Marty explained, "he told me that unless the vote came down firmly against the resolution, he would announce a date for his retirement. He handed me this letter to read and said the board could make use of it any way it saw fit."

Linda was barely able to conceal her excitement. "I think a copy of the rabbi's letter should be sent to every member of the congregation. Don't you think so, Marty?"

"It's probably a good idea."

"Leo, will you see to it that a copy of this letter gets mailed tomorrow to all of our members? And Marty, please convey to Rabbi Stone our appreciation for this gesture of reconciliation. It gives us all a chance to put the bitterness aside and move ahead with the important job of choosing his successor."

*   *   *

The board meeting broke up and the members hurried to their cars.

Leo caught up with Sam. "Do you have a minute, Mr. Broad?"

"Sure, Leo. What's up?"

"I want to apologize for what happened."

"There's no need to apologize, Leo. You didn't do anything wrong."

"The membership list was my responsibility. I feel I let the rabbi down."

"I'm sure he doesn't feel that way. He knows you would never do anything to hurt him."

"I just feel miserable about what happened. Will you tell him how sorry I am?"

"Of course I'll tell him."

"Can I ask you one more thing?"

"Sure, Leo."

"It's got nothing to do with the synagogue."

"Go ahead."

"I know it's presumptuous of me, but I bought some shares of Fabrico a while back and I'm not sure what I should do with them."

"I didn't know you were an investor in our company."

"I was going to put them away for investment but then the tender offer came along and I thought about tendering my shares but I don't want to do anything that you would consider unfriendly."

"Do you have a profit in the stock?" Sam asked.

"A little." Leo hated himself for lying.

Sam smiled. "Look, Leo. It's your money. You worked hard for it. If you want to tender your shares go ahead. There's never any harm in taking a little profit. If you decide to hold on to them, all I can tell you is that we're doing our best to turn the company around. And don't worry about the membership list. That's water over the dam."

* * *

Linda collapsed in a chair in Mark's office. "I never thought it would be this difficult but it's like Peter says. 'You keep the pressure on long enough, something always gives.' God, I'm beat. Have you got anything to drink?"

"Just some kiddush wine."

"How's Susan doing?"

"She's a little uncomfortable."

"Know what you're having yet?"

"No. We decided to wait and find out when the baby comes."

Mark watched Linda gulp down a glass of port. He wondered how he would deal with her when he became the senior rabbi. He would never be able to ignore her, the way Eli did. "All that's left now, Mark, is one last meeting and then we'll both have what we want. I've got a million ideas about how the synagogue should run. We'll get together soon and talk. Walk me to my car, will you?"

Mark watched Linda drive away. As he got in his car, he glanced across the parking lot toward a group of aging apartment buildings with fire escapes running down their sides. He wasn't sure which one Liz Aurelio lived in. He wondered what her apartment looked like inside. He had been sneaking away in the afternoons, telling his secretary that he was making hospital calls, then driving downtown to Carnavale. The restaurant closed at three and didn't open again until six. He would park his car in the alley, enter by a side door and sit in one of the booths in the back and talk to her. He wanted to talk to her right now. He took out his cell phone and called her. The phone rang a couple of times.

"Carnavale. Can I help you?"

"It's me, Mark. I'm just leaving the synagogue. We had a board meeting tonight."

"How'd it go?"

"It went great. I'll come down tomorrow and tell you all about it."

"Hold on a sec, Mark, the other phone's ringing."

While he waited he thought about Susan. When he got home he would tell her about the board meeting and she would start worrying. How could he be sure? What if something went wrong? The baby was coming and he was taking too many chances. It was different with Liz. She was upbeat, always encouraging him. He imagined what it would be like in bed with her, her legs wrapped around him, her small firm breasts pushing against him, her nipples rubbing against his chest, doing things that Susan didn't like to do. For now he would have to be satisfied with their occasional meetings, but after things settled down and he was secure in his new position as senior rabbi . . .

Liz came back on the line. "Hey, Mark, listen. We're real busy the next few days. How about I come by some day before I go to work? You can show me around. I've always wanted to see what your synagogue looks like inside."

The thought of Liz showing up at the synagogue terrified him. Not now, when everything hung in the balance. "I'm not sure that's such a good idea."

"Why not?"

"It's just that it might be awkward."

"Why? Are you ashamed to show me around?"

"Of course not."

"It sounds like you are."

He could tell that she was angry. If he refused it might be the end of their relationship. "Of course I want you to come."

"You sure don't make it sound that way."

"It's just that you just surprised me."

"Why?"

"I don't know. You just did."

Liz laughed and the warm huskiness in her voice made Mark yearn for her. "You're worried that I won't look right, is that it? Don't worry. I won't wear what I wear down here. You won't even recognize me. How about Tuesday? Three o'clock okay?"

*   *   *

After the board meeting, Leo went straight home to his apartment and warmed up some leftovers in the microwave. Linda had treated him like dirt again. He had wanted to call her a liar to her face but he didn't have the nerve. He despised the way she was always undermining Rabbi Stone. But what he dreaded most was the possibility that Mark might become the next senior rabbi of the congregation. If that happened and Linda stayed on as president, he would quit his job. He went to the medicine cabinet, took a Sominex and tried to go to sleep but the image of Linda calling him a liar in front of the entire board kept him awake. His mind was whirling. He started thinking about his investment in Fabrico. If he tendered his stock now he would make a significant profit. If he held on and the deal fell through, his entire profit would be wiped out. On the other hand, if he held on to his shares . . . It was a mistake to try to decide things when you were tired. Tomorrow he would wake up early and make a list of all his options and their consequences. That was the beauty of being an accountant. He would tote up the plusses and the minuses and the bottom line would tell him what to do.

CHAPTER
TWENTY-EIGHT

Max Jessel leaned back in his chair and blew a cloud of cigar smoke toward the ceiling. He was a contented man. His team had won its last two games. The Indians were a half game away from the playoffs and he was confident that he was closing in on a deal with Bobby G. He had just finished watching Pamela on *Five by Five*. Bobby G. was her guest and she had grilled him in her clever, ingratiating way.

"Are you planning to stay in town, Bobby, or are we just another stepping stone along the path of your remarkable career?"

"I'm not getting any younger, Miss D. Maybe it's time for me to settle down."

"Does that mean there's someone special in your life?"

Bobby grinned. "I'm not thinking about anything but baseball these days."

"Well, if I can't get you to talk about your personal life, what about you and the team? Have you reached an agreement for next year?"

"Not yet."

"Are you going to?"

"I sure hope so."

Max was sure he would be able to sign Bobby up for another year. He might have to go two years to get him, but Bobby was smart enough to realize that this year was a fluke. Even if he had another good year left in him, the odds that it would be anything like this one were a thousand to one. He'd probably have to pay Bobby more than he was getting now, but nowhere near as much as he was asking. They'd sit down in a day or two and have another talk.

"They're here," Amanda announced over the intercom.

Max greeted Sam and Marty and shook hands with Josh, barely glancing at him as they sat down around a small conference table in a corner of his office.

"You were working for Parallax until a couple of days ago," Max said.

"That's right," Josh said.

"How come you left?"

"I was fired."

Max kept staring at Josh with the look of someone who had just been handed a phony hundred-dollar bill. He found it hard to understand how anyone could switch sides in the middle of a game.

"He's okay, Max," Sam said. "We went through all that with him. He has his reasons and I believe him."

Max seemed only partly satisfied. "How can I help?"

"I want to hold on to my company and I can't handle it myself," Sam said.

"What do you need?"

"Josh met with the bank. Let him tell you."

Josh explained that the bank had an offer from Ballard and Freling to put twenty million of fresh capital in the company. "The bank's ready to make a deal. All that's left is for them to agree on how much of the bank's construction loan they're willing to pick up. Once that's done, the bank will announce a reduction in Fabrico's credit line. That'll shake loose enough shares so that their tender offer will succeed. If Sam's got something better to propose he needs to get it to the bank by Wednesday morning." Josh pushed a thick folder across the table. "I did this report for Ballard a while back. It covers pretty much everything there is to know about the company."

"I haven't got time to read this crap," Max grumbled. "What's it say?"

"It says that at $6.50 the company is a bargain. Ballard thinks it's going to be a twenty-dollar stock in a couple of years."

"What do you think?"

"I think the company's a steal at $6.50."

"Would you buy it at that price?"

"Sure, I would."

"You got any money?"

The question surprised Josh. "Some."

"You willing to put it in the deal?" Max chewed down on the stub of his cigar. "Don't look so goddamned surprised. I got a million things on my mind right now and if it wasn't for Sam I wouldn't even be considering this." He shoved the report back across the table. "You're the one says the stock's a bargain at $6.50. I figure if you're willing to put your money in, that's the best protection I can have that this deal won't end up a big fucking mistake." He pushed back from the table. "How much money you got saved up?"

There was no way for Josh to dodge the question. "Three hundred thousand, maybe."

"You willing to put it in?"

Sam and Marty were staring at Josh the way lawyers stare at a jury when it files in with a verdict.

"What's it gonna be?" Max demanded.

"I need some time to think it over."

"You're the one says there isn't much time. Just give me a straight answer. Yes or no?"

Josh knew that if he said "no," Max would pull out and Sam would lose his company. If he said "yes" he stood a chance of losing everything he had saved over the last eight years.

"What's it gonna be?"

"Okay."

"Okay, what?"

"Okay, I'll put my money in."

"All of it?"

"Yes, all of it."

Max grunted and stubbed out his cigar. Over the next hour they hammered out the deal. They would offer to put $25 million of fresh cash in the company. Max would put up twenty million. Sam would put up five. Josh's three hundred thousand would be part of Sam's side of the deal. One of Max's companies would take over the mortgage from the bank. He would own the new headquarters building and lease it back to Fabrico. Fabrico would give Max an option on three million shares of stock at $7.00 a share.

When the details had been settled, Max turned to Josh. "You think McCarthin will shop the deal?"

"He'll try. That's his nature."

"You better figure out a way to stop him," Max said. "If this thing gets into a pissing contest, count me out. I'm not interested in a bidding war."

*   *   *

Peter's secretary buzzed to let him know that Pamela Dawes was waiting to see him. She was becoming a nuisance, constantly imploring him to reconsider the station's decision to let her go. He wondered what she wanted this time.

"You're nice to see me on such short notice. I know how busy you are, but I wanted to personally thank you for trying so hard for me at the station. It's too bad they won't reconsider."

"I wish I could have done more. I understand the station is making you an offer to consult. I hope you'll take them up on it."

"I suppose it's just a bit of jealousy flaring up," Pamela continued. "I've always been so competitive. I can't stand to lose. You of all people can understand that."

Buddy Kaplan had called her that morning. "You must be psychic, darling. I would have sworn that Peter had reformed. He was at a dinner party I did last week and he hung on to Linda like she was the last woman on earth. And then I get this call from a friend of mine in Akron who saw him at a motel with your Miss Li. Akron, for god's sakes! The rubber city. Well, I suppose that's perfect, isn't it? Anyway, they go to this restaurant you never heard of, and after dinner they check into a Motel 6 next door. He registers under the name of Sylvan Williams. They're in there a couple of hours and then they go home in separate cars."

"You sure?"

"I'll eat one of your hats if I'm wrong," Buddy had said.

Pamela wasn't sure what to do with the information. If she confronted Peter with it now, he would find a way to wiggle out. She needed to spring it on him when he was vulnerable. When he wouldn't have time to figure out how to keep her quiet. She pulled her chair closer to his desk. "The station is making a big mistake, Peter. Cindi Li is not going to help your ratings."

"Maybe you're right," Peter responded. "But the station management has made up its mind. There's nothing I can do about it."

"What I really came to see you about is this series of programs I'm doing. My valedictory, so to speak. I'm interviewing some of the people who've had a positive influence on the city in the years I've been on the air and I want you to be one of them. I know you're right in the middle of this big acquisition but I thought you might be willing to take time out to do it. Please say "yes." It would mean a lot to me."

Peter considered. It was late in the game, but an appearance on *Five by Five* might shake loose a few more shares, and they needed all the shares they could get.

"When would you want me?"

"You'll do it? Wonderful! How about Monday night? Oh, I'm so pleased. I have a particularly large audience on Mondays. And don't worry. You'll be great! The last time you were on my show we got so many calls we couldn't keep track."

* * *

Josh stood in front of the closed door to his father's study. It had been three weeks since his father had ordered him out of the house and he dreaded another confrontation. He knocked and entered. Eli was sitting at his desk, a book open in front of him, writing notes in his irregular scrawl on a lined pad of yellow paper. He shifted in his chair, moving his body carefully as if it was encased in a fragile shell that might crack at any moment. Josh found it painful to watch.

"I'm not working for Parallax anymore," Josh said.

Eli greeted the information with a nod. It was as though someone had interrupted him with a weather report or some other bit of routine information. Josh's expectation that his father would react favorably to the news was replaced by the chilling possibility that he no longer cared.

"I'm trying to help Sam hold on to his company. Christ, dad, haven't you ever made a mistake in your life? I'm doing everything I can to tell you how sorry I am."

Eli remained impassive, his face a studied blank, and it occurred to Josh that perhaps his father's illness had progressed to a point where he could no longer control the facial muscles that he needed to register emotion.

"What do you plan to do when all this is over?" Eli asked.

"I haven't thought much about it."

"Will you go back to New York?"

"I don't think I have much of a future there. Jumping ship in the middle of a deal doesn't win you a lot of friends."

"Life is full of surprises isn't it?" Eli said. "Just when you think you've got everything figured out, the ground rules change."

"I've got a friend who puts it another way. He says that just when you think you've got your head screwed on tight, your ass falls off."

The suggestion of a smile crossed Eli's face. "I'll have to remember that. I might use it in a sermon sometime."

And with that brief exchange, the wall of silence that had separated them for years evaporated with the suddenness of a summer shower. A kind of equilibrium replaced it. A shared awareness that life was unpredictable and that the time left for reconciliation was brief.

They talked for an hour. Josh told his father about visiting the apartment where he had grown up and Eli wanted to know who lived there now and what the place looked like. He asked Josh about his life in New York and his career and Josh asked questions about his father's life and Eli answered them. There was no mention of what had gone wrong between them. Eli never said anything to make Josh feel that the past had been entirely forgotten.

"What about the synagogue?" Josh asked. "What's going to happen there?"

"Linda's determined to have Mark succeed me."

"You think she'll be successful?"

"I don't know. I'm mostly worried about your mother. This thing I've got is unremitting. I'm going to end up being a burden to her and there's nothing I can do about it."

"How long do you have?"

"A year or two maybe. Maybe less. It's hard to tell. I can't imagine what life will be like when I can't do anything for myself."

And then, in the way a cloud passes silently across the sun, Eli's mood darkened and the openness between them gave way to silence. Not an angry silence, just the silence between two people who have come together after a long separation and aren't sure how long the reconciliation will last. Eli opened his book and pulled it toward him and started reading and Josh got up and left the room.

Later, in the kitchen, he talked to his mother. "I told dad what I was doing."

"What did he say?"

"I think he was pleased."

"I'm sure he was."

"He's worried about what's going to happen down the line."

"He's always been so strong . . ." Rachel's voice trailed off. A glass she was drying dropped to the floor and broke.

Josh went to get a broom. When he came back, Rachel was holding her hand under the cold water tap. She had cut her finger and it was bleeding.

"You okay, mom?"

"It's nothing," she answered. "Just another one of those things I can't do anything about."

*   *   *

After Josh left his father's house he called Antonia. He had tried her office a half-dozen times since he had come back to Cleveland and each time he was told politely that she wasn't available. This time she picked up the phone and he asked her if she was free for dinner. To his surprise she said she was. She suggested a Chinese restaurant near the museum. "It's nothing fancy."

He got there first and watched as she walked through the doorway, her figure silhouetted against the light. She was wearing a light blue dress that clung to her.

An aging waiter dropped two dog-eared menus in front of them and poured tea from a battered metal teapot into cracked cups. Their conversation started slowly. She was still wary of him. "We had a meeting of the accessions committee today. Max told me you're working with Sam Broad now."

"I'm trying to help him hang on to his company."

"Why'd you change your mind? It's none of my business but I'd like to know."

Josh told her everything that had happened since the last time they were together. Her expression never changed; her blue eyes stared at him, indicating nothing.

"You work out your problems with your father?"

"We had a long talk. That's probably as good as it's gonna get."

Their cups were empty and the waiter refilled them, spilling some tea on the table and wiping it clean with a dirty cloth. Josh made a face. Antonia smiled. "I told you this place wasn't fancy. Linda came in to see me yesterday. She wanted to talk about my outreach program, but what she really wanted to talk about was your father. She's pushing for a vote on Mark. She's got half the board with her and she's making it very hard for me. The director of the museum called me in today. He said that the Frelings are talking about giving the museum $2 million for my program and he asked me if there was anything I could do to help. I'm not dumb. If I vote Linda's way, the museum gets the money. If I don't, it all goes up in smoke. I'd like to tell Linda to shove it."

"Why don't you?"

"I work in this tight little world where I can make small mistakes. I don't think I'm allowed to make a big one."

"Whatever you decide there's no reason we can't get together."

"You know that's not true. If I vote to have Mark replace your father it would be impossible for us. I'd be the one who destroyed everything your father spent his whole life working for. You'd hate me for it and I wouldn't blame you."

"No, I wouldn't," Josh said.

"Of course you would. Anyway, I don't know if I'm ready to give up my career for anyone. I tried it once and it blew up in my face. I don't want to make the same mistake again."

When they left the restaurant, the light was fading and the sky was full of the soft colors of a fading sunset. They walked around the lake in front of the museum. When they got to Antonia's apartment building, Josh walked her to the door.

"Can I come up?" he asked.

"Let's see how things work out," Antonia answered. "That way neither of us will get hurt again."

CHAPTER
TWENTY-NINE

It was almost noon on Wednesday when Josh began spelling out the details of the proposal that Sam and Max had authorized him to communicate. McCarthin sat behind his desk, his fingers tented in front of him. Two months ago, the bank had a shaky loan on its hands. Now two groups were vying to bail him out.

"We'll put $25 million of fresh cash in the company and we'll take the construction loan off your hands."

"All of it?"

"One hundred percent."

"What would you want from us?"

"A statement that the bank is comfortable with the company's prospects and that it intends to renew the company's line of credit. And we need the statement issued before the market closes tomorrow afternoon."

McCarthin responded with the tight smile of a poker player who knows he holds a winning hand. "I don't have the authority to make that kind of a decision, and anyway, there's no way I can get you an answer that fast."

"I know what you're thinking," Josh said. "You're wondering if the other side might offer you something better. My people aren't interested in a bidding war. This is a preemptive offer. I've been instructed to come back with a "yes" or a "no." You shop this deal and it's gone."

McCarthin's face offered nothing. "Give me until tomorrow morning. I'll get back to you with a 'yes' or 'no'."

*   *   *

Reggio's was tucked away at the end of a narrow winding street in Little Italy, an enclave of tidy white frame houses that clung to the slope of a steep hill near the museum. It had turned unexpectedly warm. Linda and Sally sat at a table in the courtyard of the restaurant under an arbor of grapevines that shielded them from the hot sun.

"I'm planning the final board meeting for Friday," Linda said. "There's a ball game tomorrow night that everyone's going to, so Friday's the earliest I figure we can get everyone together."

Sally listened without enthusiasm. She had gone along with Linda so far but she was troubled by the tempers that had flared at the previous board meeting. "Linda, that last board meeting was absolutely poisonous. I tried to talk to Sam after it was over. He turned his back on me. I feel so disloyal to him. I feel that if I vote for Mark, I'll be betraying him."

"I know it's complicated, sweetie, but we're almost there."

"We're treating Eli like he's some piece of rotten meat that we can't wait to throw away. And for what? For Mark Winnick? I never thought much of Mark in the first place. The only reason I've gone along is because you and I are friends. The way this thing is turning out is making me sick."

"I'm as troubled as you are by what's happening," Linda replied, "but we need to get this mess behind us. Mark will be just fine for the congregation. He's not just another rabbi. He's got a reputation now. People know who he is. The congregation has had five years to get used to him. It will be a smooth transition. As soon as he's elected all this commotion will die down."

"And Peter's going after Sam's company."

"What's that got to do with it?"

"A lot as far as I'm concerned."

"Look, Sally, get your priorities straight. There's no connection between what Peter is doing and what I'm doing. I'm trying to get Mark elected senior rabbi. What Peter is doing is what he always does, which is make money. The two things aren't connected."

"In my mind they are."

"Well, they're not in mine. Peter has nothing at all to do with what I'm trying to do for the synagogue. I want to change the way things are run. Open things up. Make the place work the way it should for a change. The board should be running the congregation, not Eli. That's why we got into this in the first place. You're making way too much out of this."

"I can't help the way I feel," Sally insisted. "Sam's friendship is precious to me. He practically saved my life after my divorce. I can't even begin to imagine where I would be if he hadn't given me a hand."

Linda picked at her salad. Peter had always told her there were moments at the end of every transaction when problems popped up unexpectedly, and unless you resolved them quickly, the deal could slip away.

"Sam's not the issue, Sally. We both love Sam. The future of the congregation is the issue. You either see it that way or you don't." She could see that Sally remained unconvinced. "Look," Linda continued, fixing Sally with a cold, tight smile, "This is the most important thing I've ever done in my life and I need you with me. I never said anything to you when you had an affair with Peter. You didn't know I knew about that, did you? Of course I knew about it. You weren't the first and you weren't the last. It hurt me tremendously that you would do something like that behind my back and it took me a long time to get over it. But I decided to live with it so that we could keep our friendship going. There are times when we all have to make choices. Your friendship means a lot to me, Sally. I'd be sad to see it end." The whole time Linda was talking, Sally's expression barely changed.

The luncheon ended in bleak silence. Sally paid her own check and left. The moment she was gone Linda called Peter at his office. His secretary answered. "He's on the phone, Mrs. Freling. He asked not to be interrupted."

"I don't care who he's talking to. I need to talk to him right now."

As soon as Peter got on the line, Linda poured out her problems. "Everything's falling apart. Sally's upset that you're going after Sam's company. She feels she owes Sam something and I don't have the time to straighten her out."

"Slow down, hon, you're getting me all confused."

"I just had lunch with her. She as much as told me that she's not going to vote for Mark. That means I've only got five votes I can count on. Me, Brian, Bill, Bobby G. and Renee. Everyone else is on Eli's side except for Antonia and Pamela. I need both their votes if I'm going to win."

"I'm doing what I can about Antonia."

"I know you are. What about Pamela? She wants to keep her job at the station. Isn't there something you can do?"

"The station made the decision to let Pamela go, not me. How do you know she won't vote for you, anyway?"

"She never has. Every time there's been a vote she's always been on Eli's side." Linda was desperate. "I've worked so hard for this thing, honey, and now it's all slipping away.

*　　*　　*

It had taken Liz a long time to get over the fact that Bobby G. had dumped her. It still hurt. The last time she saw him he had come into Carnavale with that woman from the university and had pretended not to notice her. In the back of her mind she was sure one of the reasons Bobby had lost interest in her was because she wasn't smart, and she was determined to make up for it. Each time Mark came down to see her they would sit in a booth at the back of the restaurant and talk. She asked his opinion about everything—events that were happening around the world that she didn't understand, what was going on in local politics, questions about different religions. She had been raised a Catholic but had stopped going to church long before she left home. Since coming to Cleveland she had attended evangelical services a few times, and she told Mark she was thinking about letting Jesus into her life again. He said if that was what she wanted, it was fine, and she thought how great it was that someone like Mark treated her with respect. Even at a fancy place like Carnavale, most of the men who came in treated her like a high-class hooker. They would ask her out and she could tell they only had one thing in mind. Bobby G. had treated her that way. Mark was different. He was interested in what she thought and wasn't always trying to get her into bed.

She checked herself out in the mirror. She was wearing a dark gray flannel skirt cut just below the knee and a loose fitting blue cardigan over a white blouse that buttoned at the neck. Her hair was combed straight back and tied with a small bow and she had applied just the lightest touch of makeup. Mark would be pleased with the way she looked. Promptly at three-thirty she locked the door of her apartment, walked down three flights of stairs, crossed the parking lot, entered the synagogue and announced to the office receptionist that Rabbi Winnick was expecting her. She sat down on a bench in the front office, waited patiently for a few minutes, and then got up to go to the ladies' room. When she returned, Millie Pelletier was waiting for her.

"Hi, Liz, I'm Millie Pelletier, Rabbi Winnick's secretary. The rabbi was called away unexpectedly. He was so looking forward to showing you around. He asked me to apologize for not being here and hoped you wouldn't mind if I filled in for him."

*   *   *

"I thought we'd be more comfortable in here," Pamela said as Peter settled down in a chair in her small office. It was five-thirty and her show went on at six. "Nobody ever leaves you alone in the green room. They keep popping in and out to see if you want anything. By the time the show starts most of my guests are a nervous wreck. We still have half an hour so let's relax and talk a while. I'm going to miss this place. It's been like home to me."

She watched Peter as he took a call. How composed and self-assured he was. He snapped his fingers and people jumped. People with money had all the power. They could snuff out your career in a minute if they wanted to. She had spent thirty years building an audience and all the thanks she would get when she left would be a pat on the back. Nothing at all for the sponsors she had brought in or the money she had made for the station. She had stared at herself in the mirror that morning. She didn't look a day older than she had ten years ago but her plastic surgeon didn't have a vote and neither did her mirror. The station had decided that she was expendable. She was last year's model and they were trading her in on a brand new foreign sports car.

"We're going to be voting on Mark tomorrow night," Pamela said. "How does Linda think it's going to go?"

"She thinks it's going to be close."

"I'm ambivalent about it," Pamela said. "I hate the way this whole thing has happened with Eli. It doesn't pay to get old, does it? Especially in this business. You get a few wrinkles and they dump you in the trash can."

Peter didn't want to have to go through all that again. "What are we going to talk about tonight, Pamela?"

"Your background. Where you were educated. What brought you to Cleveland in the first place. I'd like my audience to get a feel for how you make decisions. I hope you'll talk about Fabrico. Everyone wants to hear about that. And something about your family. How you and Linda met. How the two of you coordinate your busy lives. You have a daughter in college. Where?"

"Stacey's at Columbia."

"And Jessica? Does she still want to be a rabbi?"

"Yes, she still does."

"Well, that's interesting. You might want to mention that." Pamela was keeping her eye on the clock. "I got a call the other day from a friend of mine. He has this friend in Akron who says he sees you down there from time to time." She waited for Peter to react.

"I get down to Akron occasionally," Peter responded evenly. "I have business interests there."

The door popped open and a scrubbed young face looked in. "Twenty minutes, Miss Dawes."

"Thanks, Charlie . . . From what I understand they're not exactly business interests."

"What's on your mind, Pamela?"

"Look, Peter, I've got a whole bunch of stuff that can make your life miserable. Names, dates, places, room numbers, motel registrations in the name of Sylvan Williams. My audience will eat it up." Peter sat stiffly in his chair. "I know how you're feeling. Like someone just kicked you in the stomach. I felt the same way when they told me I was being let go."

"I'd be careful if I were you," Peter warned. "You're moving into dangerous territory."

"I'm always careful, Peter. That's why I've lasted as long as I have in this business. It's all documented. And I know how to use it."

"What is it that you want?"

"You know what I want. I want my show back."

"I don't have the power to give it back to you, even if I wanted to."

"Then neither of us seems to have much choice, do we?"

Peter glanced at the wall clock behind Pamela's desk. The minute hand jumped ahead. Why had he agreed to go on her show? He had watched the show enough times to know that she enjoyed skewering people. She was angry about what was happening to her and she was taking it out on him. What was the worst that could happen? Somewhere during the show she would claim that he was having an affair with Cindi. He would deny it. What proof did she have? Photographs? Tapes? He shuddered to think that someone had filmed him with Cindi at the motel. Would Pamela actually show something like that on the air? He doubted it. The mere suggestion that she had something on him would be enough. What would Linda do? She would threaten to leave him, but he had dealt with Linda's anger before. Eventually she would calm down. None of it would have any effect on the tender offer. No one in the financial world cared if you were fucking someone who wasn't your wife. You had to strangle your mother before it was the kind of news that would cause anyone to change his mind. It was the embarrassment of an on-air disclosure that bothered him. All his friends would be listening. Jessica would find out about it and so would Stacey.

The door popped open again. "Ten minutes, Miss Dawes."

"Thank you, Charlie . . . If we can reach some kind of understanding, Peter, there's no reason for me to go into any of this tonight or ever. If you feel that's impossible, then I guess we'll both have to deal with the consequences."

The clock ticked off another minute. There were barely eight minutes left until the broadcast. Pamela stared at Peter. "If you're planning on ducking out, Peter, I'll still go ahead and say what I plan to say. I'll carry on my interview with an empty chair if I have to. We're live, so if you're thinking about agreeing now and trying to cancel the show before it airs, forget about it.

Charlie's scrubbed young face peered in again. "Five minutes, Miss Dawes."

"On our way, Charlie." Pamela got up from behind her desk and walked out the door, not looking to see if Peter was following. He caught up with her in the hallway.

"I'll make a deal with you," he said.

"I'm listening." Pamela kept on walking. There was a short stretch of hall before the door that opened into the studio.

"If I get them to extend your contract for another year . . ."

"Another three years."

"Another two . . . but there's something you have to do for me."

"What's that?"

"At the board meeting tomorrow tonight, you have to vote Linda's way. You do that and we've got a deal."

CHAPTER THIRTY

At exactly four o'clock on Tuesday afternoon, Fabrico's second-quarter earnings flashed across the computer screen in Peter's office. The company announced a loss of fifteen cents a share and the closing of fifty-four additional stores, mostly in Asia and Canada. At the same time it announced that it had sold its new headquarters building to a partnership controlled by Max Jessel for an undisclosed amount and leased the property back for a period of twenty years. The company also disclosed that it had secured new financing totaling $25 million from private sources, with the funds to be added to the company's working capital. The terms of the borrowing were not made public.

A moment later a statement from the Central Bank and Trust Company flashed across the screen:

"The Central Bank and Trust Company announced today that it has extended its credit relationship with Fabrico Corporation of Cleveland, Ohio for an additional three years and views the company's prospects favorably."

Peter grabbed the phone and called Tom McCarthin. "Tom, what the hell is going on?"

"I'm sorry, Peter, but they came in with a proposal at the last minute and it was on a take-it or leave-it basis. I submitted it to my board in New York and they instructed me to take it."

"We had an understanding."

"There were still some open points. There was no firm agreement."

"That's bullshit! All we had left were fucking details. We would have worked them out. Why didn't you call me first?"

"There wasn't time. I'm sorry."

Peter slammed the phone down and shouted at his secretary to get Ballard.

Ballard's tone was steely and composed compared to Peter, whose voice was choked with rage. "I thought you said we had it all wrapped up," he said.

"Your pal Josh fucked us over good," Peter said.

"Where do we stand?"

"The market's closed. The shit won't hit the fan until tomorrow morning. The stock's bound to run up. We're dead in the water at six and a half. No one's going to tender at that price. We better think about raising our offer if we want the deal."

"Let's not panic," Ballard said. "Give the market a chance to digest the news. The fundamentals haven't changed. Give it a day or two and see what happens."

*   *   *

Mark stood at the sink with Susan, drying dishes. The pressure of the last few weeks had worn him down. He had tried calling Liz at work, but as soon as she heard his voice she hung up. He knew he had handled things badly, but the risk of being seen with her at the synagogue was just too great. As soon as he was appointed senior rabbi, he would explain everything. And he had called Linda earlier that afternoon. "How does it look for the board meeting tomorrow?"

"We're going to do just fine," she said.

"Any reason to worry?"

"Let me do the worrying, Mark. Relax."

He reached for the glass bowl that Susan was rinsing out and started drying it. "I'll do that," she said, taking the bowl from his hands. "You'll drop it." She was as much on edge as he was. "I bumped into Rachel on the street yesterday. She hardly said hello. It hurt. She's always been so friendly to me."

"Don't you want me to be senior rabbi?" Mark asked.

"Of course I do."

"Then stop bugging me all the time. Eli set a date for his retirement, didn't he?"

"You don't have to snap at me. I was just asking."

A car horn beeped outside. Bill Palevsky had invited him to his box at the stadium for the final game of the season. The game with the Minnesota Twins would decide whether or not the Indians made it to the playoffs. Mark grabbed his coat and gave Susan a quick kiss. "I'll be home late," he said, hurrying out the door. "Don't wait up for me."

*   *   *

Max Jessel and Bruno Leppelmeier stood at the edge of the owner's box staring down at the field. The stands were filling fast. They watched two men wearing Indians' baseball jackets tie a homemade banner to the railing in right field. Painted on it, in Day-Glo colors, was a caricature of Max standing at the end of a gangplank with dollar bills falling out of his pockets. The sea was filled with sharks. An Indian in war paint was prodding him with a spear and a crudely lettered caption read, "Sign Bobby G. or Walk the Plank." Max was embarrassed. The game was being nationally televised and would be seen by millions.

"How'd that goddam thing get up there?" Max fumed. "It's a fucking disgrace."

"I'll have our guys take care of it," Bruno said.

"None of this would be happening if it wasn't for that pint-sized prick. It we lose tonight, he'll be the reason. You find out anything?"

"He hasn't been down to Carnavale since you and me talked. He gets up. He goes to work. He goes home. I've been keeping an eye on her too. She leaves her place around two-thirty to go to work. Yesterday she leaves early. She goes over to the synagogue and I thought, "Okay, here's something," but I talked to one of the girls in the front office and all she wanted was to have a look around."

"Was Winnick there?"

"He was at the hospital. His secretary showed her around. She stayed maybe thirty minutes and then she left and took the bus to work."

Amanda ushered Colin Steadworth into the box. He had flown in from New York for the game. Fuck Mark Winnick, Max thought. Win or lose, he wasn't going to let anything ruin his big night.

* * *

Eli and Sam settled down in front of the TV in Sam's den to watch the game. The cameras panned across the crowd and lingered for a moment on a homemade banner hanging from the right-field railing with a caricature of Max painted on it. A security detail was starting to pull it down.

"Max must love that," Eli mused. He had preached the previous Saturday. His voice had held up but he could sense a growing unease in the congregation. On Monday he had gone to the hospital. Rachel drove him, but he insisted on seeing Dr. Munroe alone. There were some questions that needed answering and he didn't want Rachel there when he asked them.

"How do I take care of myself when it gets really bad?"

"You'll need help, Rabbi."

"Spell it out for me."

"At some point you'll need round-the-clock care. Getting dressed. Being fed. Pretty much everything." Dr. Munroe could tell from the look on Eli's face that the grim prognosis had been anticipated. "Are you having trouble with your breathing yet?"

"Not yet."

"When that gets to be a problem, you may want to consider using an artificial respirator."

"And if I don't?"

"I'll try to help no matter what you decide to do."

On the way home Rachel insisted on knowing what Dr. Munroe had said.

"He told me everything is going pretty much as expected."

"What else did he tell you?"

"That there's a point where I won't be able to do much for myself."

"Then I'll help you."

"I'm not going to let it get that far."

"Let's not talk about that now," Rachel said. "We have a long time before we have to think about it." In bed that night she put her arms around him. He could feel the tears streaming down her face.

* * *

Fireworks exploded over the stadium as the Indians trotted on the field to take their positions for the start of the game. Sam got up to adjust the set.

"I went to see the doctor again," Eli said. "He asked me a lot of questions. How many times could I do this? How fast could I do that? Was I sleeping okay? How was my appetite? He gave me some pills to enhance my mood."

"You taking them?"

"You think my mood needs improving?"

Sam laughed. "You aren't exactly the easiest person to get along with. I remember when you first came to town.

Lots of the board members were upset. They thought you were going to be big trouble."

"I never thought I'd get the job."

"That was about the same time I was getting Fabrico started. I needed to borrow money and the banks all turned me down."

Eli managed a small tight smile. "You're still having trouble with the banks and I'm still having trouble with the board."

"You could stop her if you wanted to."

"There's been too much drama already. If Linda wants Mark that much she can have him."

"We're the ones who'll have to live with him."

"I'll tell you something," Eli said. "The rabbinate is like any other profession. You get a bad apple now and then. It's unavoidable, but after a while a congregation wises up and they make a change. It's better than the alternative."

"Which is what?"

"Which is when a congregation takes sides over the selection of a rabbi. Then the congregation starts to fall apart and the rabbi leaves anyway. Rabbis aren't stupid. They know when there's trouble and they move on before it catches up with them."

"Where do they go?"

"To other congregations mostly. Or they get a job teaching. Or they end up in business somewhere. Some end up doing stand-up comedy."

"Josh has been helping me," Sam said.

"I know. He told me."

"I hope you're pleased."

Sam waited for Eli to respond, but he didn't. "I'm going to tell you something, Eli. I've known you longer than just about anyone and I've got a right to say this. You've been a big shot so long that you've forgotten how tough it is for most people. Josh has done some things he shouldn't have. And maybe he hasn't led his life exactly the way you would have liked him to, but he's admitted his mistakes and he's trying to correct them. If you haven't forgiven him, do it now, before it's too late. I lost my whole family a long time ago. I'd give anything if I could have even one of them back again."

*   *   *

Antonia met Renee at the same Chinese restaurant where she and Josh had eaten a few nights before. The place was empty. "Everyone at ball game," the waiter said as he took their order and hurried back to watch the game on the TV over the bar.

"I can't figure Bobby out," Renee began. "I went with him to the TV station the other night and he's talking about how he wants to settle down and then we go out for dinner and we're having a good time and this cute girl comes over for his autograph and he gives her this great big smile and says would she like him to sign her T-shirt? And I tease him that he was flirting with her and he gets all upset and says we're not married yet and he can do anything he wants. And then he sits there like a wounded buffalo and stares at the menu and I'm thinking to myself, do I want to get mixed up with a man who still flirts with teenagers? Then, after a while, he apologizes and says he's sorry and that he's under a lot of pressure and that he always gets this way before a big game. And then we go back to my place and he wants to come up and I tell him that maybe we should cool it for a while, and he says, 'Fine,' like it doesn't matter to him one way or the other, and he takes off. So I figure, well that's that, and then he calls me this morning and falls all over himself telling me how sorry he is for the way he behaved and how much he loves me. Men! Jesus! What about you? What happening with you and Josh?"

"We had dinner a couple of nights ago."

"How'd it go?"

"I know he cares about me, but he has a hard time saying it. He's all wrapped up in his work and he's got all these problems with his father and anyway none of it will matter after the board meeting tomorrow. If I vote for Mark, there's no way we'll ever get together. He says it doesn't matter, but it does."

There was a roar from the TV over the bar. "Guy from other team hit home run," the waiter shouted. "They winning."

"Linda call you?" Renee asked.

"Every other day. Like clockwork," Antonia said.

"Me too. I hate what's going on. I'll probably vote for Mark, just to get this thing over with. What about you? Have you decided how you're going to vote?"

"What's the difference?" Antonia answered. "Either way I lose."

CHAPTER THIRTY-ONE

The Indians squeezed in a home a run in the middle of the sixth and the game stayed tied at two all. Then, at the bottom of the ninth, with a man on first and two men out, Bobby G. worked the count to three and two, and hit a line drive to right field that rolled all the way to the wall. The runner on first took off the moment the ball left the bat. The right fielder bobbled the ball, scooped it up and threw it to the first baseman, who relayed it to the catcher. The ball and the runner got there at the same time and when the dust cleared, the umpire threw his arms out wide and hollered. "Safe!" The Indians had won. They were in the playoffs.

On a big TV screen over the bar at Carnavale a local sportscaster was interviewing Bobby G.

"How does it feel to drive in the winning run?"

"It was one of the greatest thrills of my life," Bobby shouted over the wild din in the locker room. "Tommy's a fast kid. I don't take a thing away from him. He took a little off his fastball and I was ahead of it and got lucky. But it's the team that did it. We worked our butts off all year long and it paid off."

Liz's eyes were glued to the screen. Bobby looked so happy. She remembered the good times they had together and the bitterness she felt when he stopped calling. Her girlfriends told her that was the way ball players were. You had to be ready for the fact that they would dump you one day and move on.

"You planning to be back with the team next year?" the reporter asked.

"I'm not even thinking about that," Bobby responded as one of his teammates emptied a bottle of champagne over his head. "Tonight, I'm gonna celebrate."

*   *   *

A wild crush of fans pushed against a wall of policemen as Bobby came out of the players' entrance. He signed some autographs and made his way through the crowd toward Bill Palevsky and Mark Winnick, who were waiting for him in the enclosed area where the players parked their cars.

"I'm going down to Carnavale," Bobby said. "Max is throwing a big party. You guys coming?"

"I can't," Bill said. "I promised Kathy I'd get home right after the game."

"How about you, Rabbi?"

"I'm not sure I'd be welcome."

"You kidding? You're with me. Max is probably so happy right now he won't even notice that you're there."

Bobby's red BMW slid down the road leading to the Flats and pulled up in front of the restaurant. He tossed the keys to an attendant and started toward the front door with Mark in tow. A mass of jubilant fans jammed the entrance. Everyone wanted a piece of Bobby. They reached out to touch him. Someone grabbed Mark's baseball cap and it disappeared into the crowd. When they got inside, an even louder roar went up. Max bulled his way forward, ignoring Mark, and gave Bobby a huge hug.

"You did yourself proud tonight, kid. Say hello to the commissioner." Colin Steadworth grasped Bobby's hand, holding it long enough for the photographers to take their pictures.

Mark found himself alone. Loud music blared from a dozen loudspeakers and pulsing strobe lights created the illusion of frenzied motion. He saw Liz sitting at the bar and pushed his way toward her through a crowd of unfamiliar faces. She was wearing a low-cut black dress and her eyelids were tinted with purple blush. She reminded Mark of every girl he had ever wanted and couldn't have.

"Hi, Liz."

Liz barely glanced at him.

"I'm sorry I wasn't able to show you around the synagogue. I got called over to the hospital at the last minute." Mark had to shout to be heard over the noise.

"Yeah, your secretary told me. Thanks for the no-show."

"I would have been there if I could."

"Sure you would."

"How come you're not working tonight?"

"I'm a guest here tonight, just like you are. Look, Rabbi, why don't you just go away and leave me alone?" She spun away from him, ordered another drink and stared off into the crowd.

Bobby G. shouldered his way over. "Hey, Liz. How you doing?"

"I'm doing fine, Bobby."

Bobby draped his arm across her shoulders. "I see you already met Rabbi Mark."

"Yeah, we know each other," Liz shrugged off Bobby's arm. "Where's your girlfriend? The brainy one with the skinny legs."

Bobby laughed. "She had other things to do. C'mon, let's find a place where we can talk. You too, Rabbi. Keep us company."

They pushed their way to a booth in the back. Bobby made room for Liz next to him, but she slid in next to Mark. "I'll have a double scotch with a twist," she said to the waitress who came over to take their orders.

A fan came by and shook Bobby's hand.

"Great game, Bobby. Just fantastic."

"Thanks, pal."

Mark glanced around, wondering if anyone from the synagogue was there. What if they were? All he was doing was celebrating the Indians' victory with Bobby G. and a girl that everyone would figure was Bobby's date.

"Your hit that drove in the winning run? That was only the second time a team got into the playoffs by someone scoring all the way from first on a single in the bottom of the ninth," Mark said.

Bobby was impressed. "You're fucking crazy, Rabbi. How come you know these things?"

"They just stick in my mind. This year you had a .315 batting average. You struck out 57 times and walked 117 times. You had 65 singles 14 doubles, zero triples and 11 home runs. You stole 6 bases and were thrown out 18 times."

"What about last year?"

Mark reeled off another bunch of statistics. Liz was barely listening. She kept staring at Bobby and wondering why he had left her. A tall brunette in a tight red dress walked over. "Hi, Bobby. I'm Lenore. Remember me?"

"Sure, Lenore. How you been?"

"I've been fine, Bobby. You were awesome tonight."

"Thanks, honey."

Lenore hung around for a while, just standing there. Liz knew that if Bobby wanted to be friendly he would ask her to sit down. That was the way it worked. That was the way she had met Bobby. After a minute Lenore took the hint and left.

"What got you started?" Bobby asked.

"My old man used to take me to ball games when he could afford it. I've been hooked on baseball all my life."

"Me too," Bobby said. "I grew up in this little place in North Carolina where we were one of two Jewish families. The other one owned the furniture store and my old man worked for him. I got a baseball scholarship to college but my old man died and my mom needed me to help out so

I took over the job my old man had. Then a scout came around and gave me a tryout and I got a chance to play triple A. If he hadn't come by, I'd still be back in North Carolina selling mattresses."

The waitress brought another round of drinks. An attractive blonde left her seat at the bar and walked over. "Hi, Bobby, I just wanted to tell you what a great game you played tonight."

"Thanks a lot, sweetheart."

"I go to all the home games just to watch you play."

"Take a load off." Bobby slapped his hand on the empty place next to him and the girl sat down. "What did you say your name was?"

"I'm Becky."

"Well, Becky, say hello to Rabbi Winnick. He's the one you've been reading about in the papers. He knows every goddam baseball statistic you ever heard of. Ask him something."

"I don't know what to ask."

Bobby slipped his arm around Becky's waist. "And this here is Liz Aurelio. She's the hostess here."

"Lucky you," Becky giggled. "You get to meet everybody."

Liz brushed her hair away from her face and stared at Becky. What did Bobby see in her? Just another big-titted blonde who would probably go home with him when the party was over. It wasn't fair. She still loved Bobby. The only thing the rest of them wanted was to fuck him so they could tell their girlfriends about it. She knew she was drunk.

The strobe lights bothered her. The noise was drowning out everything. She noticed a small scar on Mark's chin and touched it with her finger.

"Where'd you get that?"

"When I was a kid I climbed up on a storage cabinet in our garage and it fell over on me."

She moved closer to Mark until her body was pressing against him. "I got a scar too," she said, "where I cut myself when I was in high school, but I can't show it to you." She kept staring at Bobby, who had his arm around Becky's waist and was whispering to her.

"Mark and I are gonna take a walk," she announced suddenly, standing up, unsteady on her feet. "I need some air." She couldn't tell if Bobby was even listening.

It was a cool night. A storm was rolling in across the lake. Lightning tore through the dark sky and there was a rumble of thunder in the distance. They walked along the breakwater. Mark put his arm around Liz to steady her.

"You cold?"

"I'm okay." Tears were running down her cheeks.

"What's the matter?"

"Nothing."

"Something's bothering you."

"All they want to do is fuck him so they can tell their girlfriends about it."

"Guys like Bobby have a hard time leading a normal life. The whole world is after them."

"I know that. You think I'm stupid?"

A few drops of rain began to fall. "Maybe we should go back in," Mark said. "It's starting to rain."

"I don't know why he dumped me. I would have been real good for him." Liz leaned against him. "Take me home, will you? I don't want to go back in there." She brushed her tears away with the back of her hand and kissed him and he kissed her back, inhaling the sweet fragrance of her hair. A taxi dropped off a fare in front of the restaurant and Mark waved the driver over. On the way home Liz fell asleep on his shoulder. He knew he'd had too much to drink. His head was spinning. He was on a roller coaster ride and he didn't want to get off.

The taxi pulled up in front of Liz's apartment. There was a flash of lightning in the distance and for a brief moment the dome of the synagogue was silhouetted against the night sky. Then it began to rain hard. Mark put his jacket around Liz's shoulders and they ran to her building. He watched her hips move as he followed her up three long flights of stairs. At the door to her apartment she put her arms around him and kissed him.

"You're nice," she mumbled. She fumbled with her keys and finally got the door open.

She pulled him into the bedroom. He undressed her, his hands wandering over her body.

She pulled him down on top of her. There was a sudden bright flash of light outside the window. Mark waited for the thunder that he knew would follow.

CHAPTER
THIRTY-TWO

Mark's car turned in at the brick pillars that marked the entrance to Milles Fleurs. It was only his second visit. The first time had been for a small welcoming reception five years ago when he was appointed Eli's assistant. It had been a low-key affair with board members and a few friends. He had hoped there would be other invitations but they never came.

It had been after midnight when he finally got home from Liz's apartment. Susan was asleep and there was a note on the refrigerator door that Linda wanted to see him in the morning. As he drove down the long gravel driveway he pushed aside the notion that there might be problems and prepared himself for the demands that Linda would make once he became the senior rabbi.

Linda finished dressing. She had watched Peter on *Five by Five*. His interview with Pamela had been warm and reassuring. He talked about the fact that while his business was demanding, Linda and his daughters were the most important thing in his life and that after the tender offer was over, win or lose, he planned to slow down and spend more time with them. He said that Linda was the most beautiful and accomplished woman that he had ever known. She felt close to him again.

He had called her right after the program ended. "I've got some great news, honey. Pamela's decided to vote your way."

"That's fantastic! How did you ever accomplish that?"

"I didn't do a thing. I just asked her how she was going to vote and she said she had made up her mind to vote for Mark. I didn't have to do any convincing."

Linda was ecstatic. She had six votes locked up. Antonia would be the seventh. She was sure that Antonia understood what was at stake and would vote her way.

She led Mark into the sunroom and poured him a cup of coffee. "Mark," she began, "the meeting tonight will be a formality. You'll be voted in as our new senior rabbi. I've put a lot on the line to get you this job."

"I know you have, Linda, and I appreciate your support."

"What I want to talk about is the future. I'm concerned about the way the congregation has been drifting. I intend to have the board run the congregation. You'll be our spiritual leader, but the board will have the final word on synagogue policy." Mark nodded warily, knowing that this was only the beginning. "The board will decide on all hiring and firing and salary issues and the way our religious school is run. You'll have an opportunity to express your opinions, of course, and you'll be free to speak your mind from the pulpit, but I know you'll take into consideration the position of the board on sensitive social and political issues." Linda paused, waiting for Mark's reaction. "I want to be sure we're in agreement on all of this. I don't want either of us to be moving forward with unrealistic expectations."

"I understand completely."

"There will be a substantial salary increase, of course. We'll leave it to the board to decide how much. By the way, Peter and I are having a few friends over next Tuesday night for dinner. I hope you and Susan will join us. I want the two of you to start getting around. There are so many interesting people for you to get to know."

*   *   *

Linda remained in the doorway of the house as Mark drove away. Only the swirling of dry leaves on the gravel driveway disturbed the perfect stillness of the morning. A flock of geese passed silently overhead. The first years they had lived in Milles Fleurs, Linda had enjoyed the isolation. She hadn't minded being miles away from everything. Peter had chosen the site. He had picked the architects and dictated the design and positioning of the house. She let him decide everything. Now that part of her life was over. By eight tonight Mark would be the new senior rabbi of the congregation and it would be her turn to call the shots.

As he drove away from Milles Fleurs, Mark reflected on his meeting with Linda. She had made demands, but he had expected them. He had a few of his own and he would make them known as soon as the board meeting was over.

Even if it was only a short time until his formal investiture, there was no reason for him to be stuck away in a closet at the rear of the synagogue. Eli was coming to work less frequently. Why shouldn't they switch offices? It would give the members of the congregation more time to get used to the fact that he was going to be their new senior rabbi.

His cell phone rang. It was Sam Broad. "Rabbi, could you drop by my office on your way to work? Is that convenient for you?"

Mark was pleased with the tone in which Sam requested the meeting. It was time to start developing relationships. "Mend your fences, honey," Susan kept telling him. "Once you're the senior rabbi you're going to have to work with everyone."

"I can come by right now if you'd like."

"That would be fine," Sam said. "I'll look forward to it."

Mark took the elevator to the seventh floor of the suburban office building that was the headquarters of Fabrico. Sam's secretary greeted him. "Good morning, Rabbi. Mr. Broad has been expecting you." She led him down a long corridor to Sam's office. Sam was finishing up a phone call. He waved Mark to a seat at a small conference table and came over to join him.

"I appreciate your taking the time to come here, Rabbi. I wanted us to have a chance to talk before the meeting tonight."

"I know you haven't been in favor of my candidacy," Mark said, "but if the board decides to give me the opportunity to lead the congregation, I'll need all the help I can get, particularly from someone like you."

"I appreciate that, Mark. We're all interested in the same thing."

"I wish this was all happening under different circumstances. I owe Rabbi Stone so much. He's been my mentor for the last five years. I certainly will do my best to measure up."

"I asked Max Jessel to join us," Sam continued. "He should be here any minute. We thought we could go over some ground rules that will make things easier for all of us."

Susan was right. They were coming around. It was time to patch up bruised feelings. "I'd like that very much. I don't think anyone benefits from the kind of pressure we've all been under."

"While we're waiting, tell me something about yourself. I really want to know more about you."

Mark was flattered. For the next few minutes he talked about his background. He made no effort to embellish the past. He told Sam that the rabbinate had not been his first choice. "I wasn't sure when I went into the rabbinate that I would be cut out for it, but I've learned to respect the profession and I feel I have a great deal to offer. I won't be able to do it alone. I'm going to need help from people like you. Linda has been my biggest supporter so far and I'm grateful to her, but she's rather formidable and I'm worried about how to get along with her."

Sam smiled. "She's a handful, isn't she?"

"One idea I had was the possibility of switching offices with Rabbi Stone. You know, the way they do with older lawyers when they retire. They get a smaller office so that everyone understands that there's been a changing of the guard. I'm doing most of Rabbi Stone's work already and it would be so much easier for me if I had more suitable space to work from. It might help everyone understand that I'll be in charge."

"That's certainly something we can consider."

A voice on the intercom interrupted them. "Max Jessel is here."

Max dropped heavily into a chair across from Mark, sliding a well-worn briefcase under the conference table. "Sorry I'm late. I haven't been able to get off the phone since yesterday. Everybody and his brother-in-law wants tickets to the playoffs. You'll be interested in this, Rabbi. I just signed Bobby G. to a new three-year contract. Gave him everything he wanted. It killed me to do it. Fifteen million a year for three years. The guy was over the hill a year ago but after what he did for the team last night, the fans would string me up by my balls if I didn't made a deal with him. How'd you like the party last night?"

"I wasn't sure you'd be pleased to see me."

"That's water over the dam, Rabbi. Everything's different when you got a team in the playoffs. What's up, Sam?"

"Mark was telling me about some of the things he'd like to see us do at the synagogue when he becomes the senior rabbi. He'd like to switch offices with Eli as soon as possible."

"You know, Rabbi," Max confided, "I was the last one figured you'd have a shot at replacing Eli. When you wrote that letter and your picture was in the paper wearing that

Indians baseball cap, I thought you were done for. But it turned out to be a stroke of genius. I gotta hand it to you, Rabbi. It put you on the map."

"I didn't really want to pose for that picture. I thought it was over the top, but the reporter kept insisting."

Max snapped open his briefcase and took out a large envelope. "I bet you didn't plan to pose for these pictures either." He pulled out a dozen 8x10 glossies and spread them out on the table. Mark stared at them. There was a picture of him at the bar at Carnavale with Liz. A photograph of the two of them walking hand in hand on the pier. A shot of them getting out of a taxi with the dome of the synagogue in the background. The last eight pictures were of the two of them naked in bed together. Max leaned back in his chair. "Doesn't leave much to the imagination, does it, Rabbi?"

"Where did you get these pictures?"

"Let's just say you got a few more fans than you thought you had. I got to hand it to you, Rabbi. Job pressure getting you down, just pop across the street for a quickie."

"Who else has seen them?

"So far just you and Sam and me and the guy who took them."

"What do you want from me?"

"For starters," Max continued, "you're gonna take yourself out of the running for Eli's job. You don't have to make your mind up right away. The board doesn't meet until eight tonight. If you haven't decided by then, we'll let these pictures do the job for you." He slid the photos back into the envelope and pushed it across the table. "This set's for you, Rabbi. For your memory book."

*   *   *

Mark sat in his car in the Fabrico parking lot and contemplated the tidal wave of scandal that was about to engulf him. For a moment he considered the possibility that Sam and Max were bluffing. They would never use the photos. How would it look if the news got out that the synagogue was considering replacing Rabbi Stone with a married man who was carrying on with a restaurant hostess in an apartment across the street from the synagogue? The congregation would become a laughing stock. They would never let that happen. There would be a quiet reprimand, maybe a brief delay in his appointment, and the suggestion that counseling might be appropriate. Eventually the whole matter would be forgotten. Then reality set in. Of course they would use the photographs. Sam was Eli's closest friend and Max hated him. Half the board would be thrilled if he disappeared off the face of the earth and the other half would run for cover as soon as the news of what he had done became public. Linda would be the first to jump ship. Pamela Dawes would crucify him on TV. What would he say to Susan? She would never understand.

There were barely nine hours left before the board meeting. He needed to talk to someone. Marty Franklin was the synagogue's legal counsel and he would be interested in protecting the reputation of the synagogue. Together they would work up an explanation that would allow everyone to save face. He picked up his cell phone and got through to Marty and tried to explain the situation.

"I was set up."

"I'd say you set yourself up, Rabbi."

"Will you help me, Marty? I don't know where else to turn."

*   *   *

Max and Sam drove directly to Eli's house. Rachel was waiting for them at the door. "Eli's getting dressed. Why don't you wait in the study? I'll tell him you're here."

Several minutes later Eli entered the study, using a walker to steady himself. Rachel closed the door behind him. "You two look like you've swallowed the proverbial canary," Eli said, easing himself into the chair behind his desk.

"We've finally got that little momzer where we want him, Rabbi." Max opened his briefcase and pulled out a set of the photographs. Eli stared impassively at one of the more explicit ones. "There's more, Rabbi."

"I don't need to see more," Eli said. "I'll take your word for it. Who else knows about this?"

"Just the three of us and Marty. He's already called Marty. He wants to meet with him."

"I don't want any scandal connected with his resignation."

"None of us do."

"And I'm not interested in destroying his life."

After Max and Sam left, Eli sat at his desk contemplating what had happened. In the past his intellect and the raw power of his determination was all he had ever needed to defeat his adversaries, but this time it had been different. His illness had made him vulnerable and Linda had been a formidable opponent. She had attacked him and he had been unable to fight back. He walked slowly to the kitchen. Rachel was at the sink rinsing out some dishes. He came up quietly behind her and circled her with his arms. "What was going on in there?" she asked. "Sam and Max looked like they had just robbed a candy store."

Eli told her what had happened.

"Does that mean Mark is finished?"

"We'll have to wait and see."

"Poor Susan. Are you going to go to the board meeting tonight?"

"I wouldn't miss it for the world," Eli said.

"I'm so happy for you, honey. It'll be like old times. We'll drive down there together and when it's over we'll come back here and celebrate."

*   *   *

The chairs in the parlor were set up in a wide informal circle. Mark sat in his usual place next to the chair that Eli would occupy. The events of the day had left him limp. He had met with Marty Franklin that afternoon and agreed to submit his resignation that evening. Until then he was to say nothing. If the news got out before the meeting, Max would be free to release the photographs. Max would give him a signal when it was time to announce his resignation. If he didn't resign, Max would hand a set of photographs to each member of the board. Privately, Mark agreed to leave the city within four months. That would give Susan sufficient time to have her baby and recover. At Eli's insistence, he would continue to receive his full salary for a year or until he found a new job, whichever came first.

"What will happen to the photographs?"

"The negatives will be destroyed a year from now," Marty told him.

"Who will have them until then?

"Max will have them."

"Max hates me."

"They'll only be released if you violate the terms of your agreement. No one here intends to volunteer any information about what happened. I'll have the necessary papers drawn up by five this afternoon. I'll bring them down to the synagogue and you can sign them before the meeting."

"How am I going to find another job?"

"That's up to you."

"I'll have to tell Susan something."

"We understand that."

Mark had gone home immediately after his meeting with Marty. Over lunch he told Susan that he was tormented by the pressures that had been building in the congregation and had decided that it was impossible for him to stay.

"But you're so close to getting what you want."

"It's better this way, honey. I'd hoped I'd get the job without all the crazy stuff that's been going on. I don't want to be the rabbi of a divided congregation. That's not the sort of future I want for us."

Susan asked him a dozen questions, trying to understand. He had an answer for everything. "When will you be resigning?"

"Tonight."

"Tonight! Something happened, didn't it?"

"Nothing happened. I just made up my mind that this is the right thing to do and the sooner I get it over with the better."

Mark held her as she began to cry.

"Will we have to leave town?"

"Not until after the baby comes. We'll put the house on the market. The synagogue was generous when I told them I was leaving. They've agreed to pay my salary for a full year. There are plenty of places we can go. New congregations are starting up all the time."

* * *

Linda had made her final round of calls. Renee had reassured her that both she and Bobby G. would vote her way. She didn't bother calling Brian or Bill Palevsky. Their votes were in the bag. She was a bit nervous calling Pamela, but Pamela told her that she had decided to vote for Mark, and Peter called to let her know that the director of the museum had spoken to Antonia again, reminding her how important the grant was to the museum's future. She had even called Sally one last time, hoping that Sally would change her mind, but Sally wouldn't take her call. On the way into the synagogue parlor she pulled Antonia aside.

"Have you decided how you're going to vote?

"To tell you the truth, Linda, I haven't made up my mind."

"Well, there's not a lot of time left to think it over, sweetie. There's so much at stake. I know you'll do the right thing."

She had done everything she could. It all depended on Antonia. If Antonia voted her way, Mark would be the synagogue's next senior rabbi. One by one she had brought six members of the board around. Antonia would be the seventh. When tonight's board meeting was over, Mark would be the synagogue's new senior rabbi.

Promptly at eight o'clock, Linda gaveled the meeting to order. "Rachel called to say that Rabbi Stone will be a little late. I know we're all pleased that he'll be joining us. We have a number of routine matters to get out of the way before he gets here, so if no one has any objections, I think we should get started."

The board approved bids for a new boiler. A motion passed to add two new teachers to the Sunday school faculty. Twenty thousand dollars was earmarked for refurbishing the synagogue organ. Linda called on Leo who announced that his preliminary budget indicated that the synagogue would incur an operating deficit in the coming year of almost

$40,000. The deficit could be met by a slight increase in dues or by tapping funds that sat in the synagogue's endowment account. A discussion about what to do with the shortfall was brief and uninspired. A decision was postponed. Everyone knew the real purpose of the meeting and they were waiting for Eli to arrive.

*　*　*

Rachel watched for Eli from the bottom of the stairs. This time he didn't use the chair elevator. He came down slowly, holding on to the banister with one hand and using a cane in the other to steady himself. He had never looked more handsome. When he reached the bottom of the stairs she put her arms around him.

"You won, honey."

"I never thought it would work out this way. I was sure Linda would find a way to get Mark in."

"We don't have to go tonight. Why don't we just stay home and relax? They can manage without you."

"I know they could but I want to be there. There are some things that need to be said. I want everyone on the board to understand that it's over. That it's time to patch things up and get on with the job of picking a successor."

Rachel helped him into his overcoat. He had lost twenty pounds and the coat hung like a sack around his shoulders.

"Do I have to wear a scarf?"

"It's cold outside."

Rachel thought about the pleasant drive ahead. Eli would sit next to her and they would look down at the city spread out beneath them and admire the golden dome of the synagogue gleaming in the distance. She helped him down the steps to the garage and watched as he eased himself into the passenger seat. Then she folded his walker and stowed it in the trunk.

"Get my notes for me will you, hon? I left them on my desk."

"Got your glasses?"

He patted his coat pocket. "I have them."

Rachel walked back into the house and into Eli's study. His notes lay scattered on his desk. Pages of them. Words scrawled half an inch high, written in a shaky hand. What would it be like when he was no longer around? She brushed the thought aside. He was with her now. That was what mattered. She gathered his notes together and left the study, closing the double doors behind her. She walked through the back hall to the door that led to the garage and glanced toward the car expecting to see him. He wasn't there. She ran toward the car. His body was sprawled across the front seat, gasping for air. Rachel's mouth opened in a silent scream.

*   *   *

The ambulance raced toward the hospital, siren blaring. Eli lay stretched out on a gurney, an oxygen mask covering his mouth and nose. His eyes were wide open, staring at Rachel with the look of a frightened child. A paramedic bent over him. Rachel held his hand. It was ice cold. "We'll be at the hospital in a minute, darling. You're going to be fine. Don't try to talk. Just take it easy."

The ambulance turned into the emergency entrance of the hospital. The back doors flew open and two attendants pulled out the gurney. Eli tried to raise himself up and the paramedic restrained him. "Take it easy, Rabbi."

"Please get him a wheelchair." Rachel implored. "He doesn't want to go in this way."

They brought out a wheelchair and helped Eli into it. Two attendants hurried the wheelchair through the hospital doors. Eli managed a pale smile. "I'm right here, sweetheart," Rachel said, holding his hand. Eli could feel his chest tightening. The pain was starting again.

* * *

Linda glanced at her watch. It was ten past nine. "I wonder where the rabbi is? Will someone please call and find out."

"I'll check," Sam said. He stepped out of the parlor and called Eli's house. There was no answer. He called his wife, who gave him Rachel's cell phone number. After a few rings, Rachel picked up.

"We're all waiting for you."

"We're at the hospital. Eli's had a heart attack."

"My God! How is he?"

"We don't know yet. I have to get off the phone."

Sam stared at the closed parlor doors. If he told the board that Eli had suffered a heart attack, the meeting would adjourn before Mark had a chance to resign. If he delayed telling them until after Mark resigned, Linda would urge the board to reject the resignation. She would argue that the synagogue would need Mark as its rabbi, even if it was only for an interim period, and a majority of the board would probably agree. Then she would use the time to regroup and the whole sordid mess would start over again.

He opened the parlor doors and walked in. "I called the rabbi at home," he announced in a matter-of-fact way. "Rachel said he wasn't feeling well and he decided at the last minute not to come down. He wants us to go ahead without him."

"I'm so sorry," Linda said. "I was hoping he would be here. Well, I guess we should proceed. Bill, you're the head of the search committee. I believe you have a motion to introduce."

Max caught Mark's eye and nodded. It was time.

"Linda, there's something I'd like to say before you go any further."

"Yes, Mark. What is it?"

Mark pulled a sheet of synagogue stationery out of his pocket. "This letter is addressed to all of you."

> *I hereby tender my resignation as assistant rabbi of Congregation Shaaray Emunah, effective immediately. I have felt for some time that it would be difficult for me and my family to take on the responsibilities connected*

*with an appointment as senior rabbi. I am
therefore requesting that the board withdraw
my name from further consideration. Susan
and I will be leaving Cleveland within the
next few months to explore other opportunities.
I want to thank the members of the board for
their kindness to us during the past five years
and I especially want to express my affection
and gratitude to Rabbi Stone, who I am
proud to call my teacher and my friend.*

He handed the letter to Linda, who stared at it for a long
moment unable to respond. The rest of the board members
were stunned into silence. Linda finally managed to pull
herself together.

"I don't understand, Mark. What happened?"

"I'm sorry, Linda, but I've been struggling with this for
a long time."

"You never mentioned anything to me about it."

"I should have. I'm sorry, but my decision is final."

Everyone began talking at once.

"Just a minute! Just a minute!" Linda shouted. "Marty,
you're our lawyer. Can Mark do this? Doesn't he have a
contract with us?"

"Mark is free to resign at any time he wants, Linda. We
can't keep him from leaving if that's what he wants to do."

"Don't we have to vote to accept his resignation?"

"You can call for a vote if you want to, but it will be a
formality."

Linda was frantic, seeing her carefully constructed world fall apart.

"Maybe Mark will change his mind once he realizes that most of us favor his election. All in favor of rejecting Rabbi Winnick's resignation say 'yes.'"

"Linda," Marty interrupted, "someone needs to make a motion first."

"I'll make the motion," Linda said. "Bill, you second it."

"I second the motion," Bill announced.

"Let's have a show of hands," Linda called out.

Mark interrupted her. "Linda, I appreciate your support, but I'm not going to change my mind. Even if you vote to reject my resignation I'm still leaving. I know that it comes at a bad time for everybody but my decision is final."

"You're not going to give us any more explanation than that?"

"I'm sorry, but I have to get home to Susan. It's been a difficult time for her and I don't want to leave her alone."

Mark left the room. Linda turned to Marty, "What do we do now, Marty?"

"I'm not sure there is anything more you can do," Marty said. "I suggest that someone make a motion to adjourn."

*　*　*

As soon as everyone had cleared the parlor, Sam pulled Max aside. "Eli had a heart attack," he whispered.

"Jesus! When?"

"They were on the way down here. He's at the hospital."

*   *   *

Rachel stared out the window of the waiting room, her thin hands folded in her lap.

Perhaps it was the weeks of watching Eli's steady decline and seeing how resolutely he had determined to accept his fate that allowed her to face this moment with apparent calm. But inside her heart was breaking.

"Was there any warning?" Josh asked. He had been in his hotel room when Rachel called and had rushed to the hospital.

"He was fine this morning. He had a headache but that went away. We were getting in our car to go to the board meeting and I went back into the house to get his notes. I can't remember him ever forgetting his notes before and when I came back he was slumped over in the front seat."

One of the doctors attending Eli came to the door of the waiting room. "We have the rabbi stabilized. You can go in to see him, but don't stay too long."

"How is he?" Rachel asked.

"He's had a serious heart attack."

"Will he pull through?"

"We're doing everything we can."

*   *   *

Linda hurried down the corridor to Mark's office, barely able to control her rage. She found him sitting behind his desk, staring vacantly out the window. "Why didn't you tell me you were going to quit? I went through this whole damn thing for you and all the time you had no intention of taking the job."

"I had every intention of taking the job."

"All you had to do was sit there and keep your mouth shut and they would have elected you senior rabbi. I had it all worked out. What happened?"

"Nothing happened. I just changed my mind."

"Don't lie to me. You were threatened, weren't you?"

"No one threatened me. It was a decision I made entirely on my own."

"Something happened. Tell me what happened, Mark. Maybe I can help."

He couldn't tell her. Instead he tried to explain that over the last few weeks he had started to think about the difficulties of leading a divided congregation. "I wouldn't be good at that, Linda. It would put way too much stress on me and Susan. It's better for everyone if the board finds someone they can all agree on."

"You're a weakling, Mark," Linda hissed. "You always were. You could have had it all. I put it right there on a platter for you."

*　　*　　*

Eli lay on his back, his head slightly elevated, his eyes closed. The sheet that covered his broad chest rose and fell with each short breath. Tubes fed him oxygen. A heartbeat monitor displayed the rhythm of his heart, a constant pinging that punctuated the eerie silence of the hospital room.

Rachel looked at him. She remembered his smile when she got off the train from Providence and the way he kissed her and the way, without either of them saying anything, they had ended up at a small hotel. She had made her mind up that night that she would marry him. She woke up first in the morning and stared at him, wondering how she could be so lucky. Now something told her that he would not recover, and she wanted him to wake up one more time so they could say goodbye.

Eli opened his eyes. Rachel felt his fingers tightening around her hand.

"You had a heart attack, darling. You're going to be fine."

"The board meeting . . ." he whispered hoarsely.

"Mark resigned, dear. Go back to sleep."

"Is Josh here?"

"Of course he's here."

"I want to see him."

When Rachel came out of Eli's room, Josh was in the hallway talking to Dr. Munroe. "Dad wants to see you," she said.

Josh leaned down and kissed his father's cheek. He could feel the stubble of Eli's beard against his face. Eli tried to speak, but Josh could barely hear him. He took his father's hand in his. A brief smile crossed Eli's face. He closed his eyes. Josh wondered if he had drifted off to sleep.

Then Eli opened his eyes and stared at Josh with a look of infinite tenderness "I'm proud of you, son" he whispered hoarsely. "I love you."

"I love you too, dad," Josh leaned down again to kiss his father. Eli closed his eyes and his fingers tightened around Josh's hand.

*   *   *

The floor of the hospital came suddenly alive. A doctor and two nurses rushed toward Eli's room. He lay naked on the bed, a fierce look on his face, his eyes shut tight against the pain that tore at him.

"NOW!"

Eli's body convulsed as electric shock tried to revive his heart. The scanner line barely moved.

"C'mon, Rabbi. C'mon!"

"AGAIN!"

Everyone stood back. The paddles were applied. The current surged and Eli's body convulsed.

"Anything?"

"Not yet."

"AGAIN!"

*   *   *

Dr. Munroe walked down the hospital corridor toward the room where Rachel and Josh were waiting. "The rabbi's had another attack. We have him stabilized but he's been without oxygen for longer than we'd like. There's a possibility that his brain functions may have been impaired. I wanted to consult with you before we go any further."

Rachel knew what that meant. Eli's mind was the one part of him that his illness couldn't touch. If something had happened to affect his mind he would be left with nothing.

"Can you keep him alive?"

"I think we can."

"Can I see him?"

"Yes, of course you can."

Eli lay on his back with a sheet drawn halfway up his massive chest. His breath came in shallow gasps. His large head rested on a pillow. Someone had smoothed down his great shock of white hair. Rachel took his hand in hers. She hoped for some response but there wasn't any. She stayed in the room a long time. When she came out, Josh went in. He stood at the foot of the bed staring at his father. His eyes were closed. His breathing was irregular but he seemed at peace. His body was there but his spirit seemed already to have moved to another place.

When Josh came out of the hospital room, his mother was talking to Dr. Munroe.

"If you keep him alive will he be the same person that he was before?"

"The likelihood is that there's been some damage."

"He wouldn't want to live that way."

Dr. Munroe said nothing. Rachel took hold of Josh's hand and searched his eyes as though seeking his consent. Then she turned to Dr. Munroe. "Let him go," she whispered.

CHAPTER
THIRTY-THREE

Linda struggled to make sense of what had happened. Mark would never have resigned just because he was insecure about his future. Insecurity drove men like Mark forward, not back. They came from nothing and had nothing to lose. Like cactus plants they flourished in hostile environments where more delicate plants perished. Something had happened to make him change his mind. She called Peter from the car.

"I got shot down at the board meeting. Mark turned in his resignation and I . . ."

"Linda!" Peter said.

"Somebody got to him . . . Max, Sam . . . I don't know who. Maybe they threatened him with something. Maybe they paid him off. I wouldn't put it past them. I don't know how they did it. I can't believe I missed the signs."

"Linda, listen!"

"When I find out what happened . . ."

"Linda!"

"What?"

"Rabbi Stone's in the hospital. I just heard it on TV. He's had a heart attack."

"Oh my God! Where are you now?"

"I'm in a meeting. I'll be home as soon as I can."

Peter switched off his cell phone just as Cindi came out of the motel bathroom wearing little more than a slightly inebriated smile. Her contract with the station would be signed tomorrow and she intended to celebrate by giving him one last night to remember. He had been her insurance policy, but now that her job at the station was locked up, there was no need to keep the affair going. Cleveland was just a pit stop on the road to fame and fortune. New York was her pot of gold. She had already met a network vice president who invited her to have dinner with him the next time she was in New York.

Peter was glad Cindi had been in the bathroom when the news of Eli's heart attack came over the TV. He didn't want anything to spoil this evening. It would be their last night together. By tomorrow morning she would find out that her contract with the station would not be signed, and she would be on her way back to Detroit. *Five by Five* would continue with Pamela for two more years. He pondered briefly why his affairs seemed to be getting shorter all the time. Maybe it was a function of age. Or maybe it was just in the nature of things. Affairs were like business deals. Some worked out. Some didn't. You had to be ready to move on.

*   *   *

A meeting of the board was hastily convened in Sam Broad's living room the following morning. Linda could sense the resentment the moment she came in. Everyone stopped talking. She knew that she wasn't responsible for Eli's death, but when things went wrong people always looked for someone to blame. After a moment the conversations started up again. They were all about Eli and the funeral. No one seemed to care that Mark had resigned. Linda realized that she had to move rapidly to reestablish her authority. "Before we start this meeting," she began, "I want to apologize for what I put us all through. I honestly thought that Mark would be a suitable replacement for Rabbi Stone. I thought he cared about the congregation, but I was wrong. He obviously had no interest in anything but his own future. I should have seen that, but I didn't. It was an error on my part and I deeply regret it."

She glanced around the room to see how her apology was going over. "We've got a number of things to decide this morning. First of all there's the matter of Mark's resignation. It couldn't have come at a more inopportune time. We have to decide what we're going to tell the congregation."

"Why don't you just send out another one of your letters," Max's gravelly voice was laced with scorn. "Write it up any way you want. You will anyway. We wouldn't have had this problem in the first place if it hadn't been for you."

"I understand how you feel, Max. You have every right to be angry. We're all upset. I just wonder whether in the light of everything that's happened, it might not be a good idea to hold off announcing Mark's resignation until after the funeral. We want the next few days to be about Rabbi Stone and what he has meant to this congregation and not about Mark. I'm afraid that if we announce Mark's resignation before the funeral, that's all anyone will be talking about, and no one wants that. I was thinking we might ask him to participate in the service in some way."

"That's crazy," Max growled. "He quit. Why reward the son of a bitch?"

"If he's not on the pulpit, everyone will be wondering why."

"What's he going to do up there?"

"Let him handle part of the service," Linda suggested. "He can lead the congregation in prayer. Lots of other people will be there to talk about Rabbi Stone. After the funeral is over we'll send out an announcement saying that he quit. That way everything will be focused on the memorial for the rabbi. If asking Mark is a bad idea, I'm sure we can get another rabbi to come in, if that's what everyone wants."

Eventually everyone agreed that the important thing was to make certain that the funeral service commemorated Eli's years of service to the congregation. Nothing should be allowed to interfere with that.

"Will Mark agree to do the service?" Antonia asked.

"I'll ask him," Linda responded. "And someone should call Rachel to make sure it's okay with her. Will you do that, Sam? You know her better than anyone." Sam nodded. "Well that's settled then. Now let's get on with the language of the letter we want to send out after the funeral is over."

They all agreed that the letter should be brief and would be signed by all the members of the board. Marty wrote out a suggested draft:

> *This letter is to advise you that Rabbi Mark Winnick has tendered his resignation to the board of our congregation. His resignation has been accepted, effective immediately. Rabbi Winnick leaves us at a difficult time and with no advance notice. We wish him and his wife well. A new senior rabbi will be chosen shortly.*

The letter was unanimously approved and a motion was passed to issue a new call for applicants for Eli's job. Sam Broad and Max Jessel were appointed co-chairmen of the committee that would screen the applicants.

The funeral was scheduled for Sunday morning in the sanctuary. The assembly hall in the basement would be open to receive the expected overflow. The governor, the mayor, and the state's two senators would speak briefly. The eulogy would be delivered by Stefan Belzner, Eli's boyhood friend. Leo agreed to oversee the preparation of the printed program. Roz McIver and Millie Pelletier and some of the front office staff would handle the phones.

Manny Polsky suggested that he meet with Adam Burwell and settle on music for the service. "Adam knows the music the rabbi liked," Manny said. "I'll work the program out with him if that's all right with everybody."

Linda was pleased with the way things were going. No one was challenging her authority. Even Max agreed that having Rabbi Winnick lead the service made sense. She was mending fences faster than she had thought was possible. After the meeting she pulled Sally aside. "I had no right saying those things to you, Sally, and I owe you an apology. I hope you'll forgive me. We've been friends forever and I want us to stay that way."

*   *   *

Mark sat at the kitchen table with the morning paper open to Eli's obituary. The past twenty-four hours had been a nightmare. He had heard the news of Eli's death on his car radio driving home. The proper thing would have been to go over to the hospital but he knew that his presence there would be unwelcome. When he got home he told Susan that Rabbi Stone had died. After she got over the initial shock she wanted to know if Eli's death changed anything. Mark told her that nothing had changed and that he had handed in his resignation.

"Why did you have to push so hard?" she cried. "If you'd only waited a while it would have all worked out."

At ten o'clock the following morning a FedEx letter arrived from the Office of the Commissioner of Baseball informing Mark that his consulting agreement had been terminated. If he had any questions he should contact Marty Franklin, who would be handling matters for the commissioner's office. An hour later the doorbell rang again and Susan went to answer it. When she came back, Linda was with her.

"Susan, could I have a minute with Mark alone? There's some synagogue business we need to discuss. You don't mind, do you?"

As soon as Susan left the kitchen, Linda sat down across from Mark.

"How is Susan holding up? I know she had her heart set on staying here."

"It's been very difficult for her."

"I can imagine. Look, Mark, the reason I came over is that the board was wondering if you would handle the service at the funeral. It's an unusual request considering everything that's happened, but we thought that as a matter of respect for Rabbi Stone you might be willing to do it. It's up to you of course. You don't have to do it, but we'd be obliged to you if you would."

For a moment Mark wondered if this was a reprieve. With Eli gone, the congregation needed a rabbi. Maybe Sam and Max had relented and he would be allowed to stay. "Has there be some reconsideration of my role at the synagogue?"

"No, Mark, there hasn't. Your resignation has been accepted. It's just that there's a feeling that it would be appropriate for you to lead the service. The congregation still sees you as their rabbi. We think they would be comfortable with you on the pulpit during the funeral service. It's up to you, of course."

Mark decided that he had been right about Linda all along. He had failed her and she was determined to inflict one final humiliation on him before she discarded him for good.

"I don't think I want to do that, Linda."

"It's your decision, Mark."

"It's not a good idea."

"I can understand the way you feel."

"With the baby coming, Susan and I have plans to make and I have to find another job."

"Have you spoken to anyone about your resignation?"

"Not yet. Susan is the only one who knows."

Linda pulled her chair closer to the kitchen table, reached across and dug her fingers into Mark's arm. "Listen to me, Mark. The entire congregation will be at Eli's funeral. Everyone in the whole city who matters will be there. You'll be up on the pulpit all alone. You'll handle the ritual part of the service. After the eulogies are over, you'll ask everyone to stay for some brief announcements. Then, when everyone is settled down, you'll have a chance to speak."

Mark was utterly confused.

"You'll say how fortunate the congregation was to have a great leader like Rabbi Stone and what a privilege it's been for you to serve under him. Not a word about your resignation. You'll talk about the congregation's illustrious past and your hopes for its future. You'll say how hard it is to accept the loss of someone as beloved as Rabbi Stone and how important it is to preserve his legacy. You'll make your remarks warm and personal. Everyone will be in a sober, reflective mood. By the time you're finished, every single person there will wish they had someone like you to follow

Eli. If the reaction is what I think it will be, we can still turn this thing around. There's not much time, Mark. Think it over. I need to know by two this afternoon. That's when the programs go to the printer."

As soon as Linda was gone, Susan confronted Mark. "What did she want?"

"She asked me to conduct the service at Eli's funeral."

Susan was appalled. "You're not going to do it, are you? You don't owe them a thing. All they want is to avoid the embarrassment of having to acknowledge publicly that you've had the courage to resign. Why would you want to humiliate yourself like that?"

"How would I be humiliating myself?"

"They're using you. Can't you see that? Promise me you'll call and tell her no."

But the possibility that even the smallest chance remained to salvage his career raced through Mark's mind with the speed of a train roaring through a tunnel toward a pinpoint of light at the other end.

"I hear you, honey," Mark said. "Just give me a little time to think it over."

CHAPTER
THIRTY-FOUR

By nine-thirty Sunday morning all 2,200 seats in the sanctuary were filled. An overflow crowd of several hundred had been directed to the assembly hall, where they could watch the service on a large television screen.

Leo Bookman had been one of the first people to enter the sanctuary. He sat unobserved in one of the highest rows of the balcony. The last few days had been the most difficult he had ever experienced. His beloved rabbi was dead. The synagogue, the source of stability in his life, was in turmoil. And his financial affairs, which he had spent his whole life protecting from prying eyes, were no longer a closely guarded secret.

When the bank announced its decision to renew Fabrico's line of credit, the stock had surged briefly before sliding back to settle at around six and a half. With no white knight showing up to bid against them, Ballard and Peter decided not to raise their price. Over the next few days, shares kept trickling into the depository, but more slowly than expected, and with the tender offer due to expire in less than a week, the three million shares that Leo owned suddenly loomed as a major prize. Brian played his trump card. He walked down to Peter's office and told him about the shares that Leo owned.

"Get him in here," Peter ordered. "If his shares put us over the top, I'll personally guarantee you get the next two hundred fifty thousand that Ballard promised you."

Brian called Leo immediately. The switchboard operator wanted to know if he was calling on synagogue business. Leo made it a point of avoiding calls that had anything to do with his personal affairs, but Brian insisted that it was urgent and the switchboard operator put him through.

"What is it, Brian?" Leo asked.

"I just got out of a meeting with Peter. There won't be any competing bids coming in, so they've decided not to raise their price. My suggestion is that you tender your shares. Six and a half is the best you're going to get."

"I'm not sure yet what I want to do."

"Don't be a jerk, Leo. If the tender offer fails, the stock will drop so fast it'll make your head spin. You'll get two or three bucks a share if you're lucky. I want you to talk to Peter. It might help you make up your mind."

"You told Mr. Freling that I owned shares in Fabrico?"

"All I told him was that you owned a few shares. I told him that you're a friend of mine. I'm trying to do you a favor, Leo. I'll send a car for you and have you back at the synagogue before anyone knows you're gone."

Leo left the synagogue without telling anyone. The minute he entered Peter's office he knew he had been deceived. Brian stayed by the door while Peter draped an arm around Leo's shoulder and walked him to a window facing the lake.

"I don't have to tell you how surprised I was when Brian told me you owned three million shares! That's absolutely incredible! You're one of the company's biggest shareholders," Peter said. "We both know all that stuff in the papers about new money coming. Fabrico doesn't mean a thing. The company's fundamentals haven't changed. They're still bleeding cash. Sam Broad's over the hill and his management team is ineffective. Nothing's going to change unless our tender offer is successful. Tender your shares, Leo. You'll be glad you did and I'll be indebted to you."

Leo wasn't listening. He was thinking how effortless it was for someone like Peter to manipulate other people's lives. The only difference between Peter and Linda was that Peter was more polite about it. Leo was tired of being pushed around. He was fifty-three years old and he had been taking crap from people like Peter and Linda all his life.

"To tell you the truth, Mr. Freling, I have no intention of tendering my shares. Sam Broad has been good to me and I'd be an ingrate to abandon him. I hope your tender offer fails. To be more precise, I hope it falls flat on its ass. Now, if you'll excuse me I have to get back to the synagogue. I have a budget to prepare for the board meeting tonight."

Brian walked Leo to the elevator. "That wasn't very smart, Leo. You just made an enemy of a very powerful man."

As the elevator doors closed silently between them, Leo felt an indescribable sense of relief. He had stood up for what he knew was the right thing to do and he was proud about it. When he got home that night he would microwave his favorite TV dinner, uncork the most expensive bottle of wine in his small collection, watch *Gone with the Wind* on Turner Classics for the ninth time, and celebrate the fact that, like Clark Gable, he had finally summoned up the courage to tell someone exactly how he felt.

*   *   *

Linda stopped by Mark's office just before the memorial service began. "You ready, Mark?"

"As ready as I'll ever be, I guess." A gray pallor had settled over Mark's face and his eyes had deep shadows under them. He had spent all night preparing his remarks.

"You're going to do a brilliant job, Mark. We're going to pull this thing off. I know we are."

*   *   *

Liz Aurelio stared down from the window of her apartment and watched the endless flow of mourners pouring into the synagogue. She had decided to pay her last respects to Rabbi Stone. It would give her a chance to see Mark again. She remembered very little of what had happened that night at Carnavale except that she got drunk, Mark had taken her home, they made love and when she woke up he was gone. She was sure he would call the next day but he didn't. The following morning, when she learned that Rabbi Stone had died, she tried to call him but couldn't get through. She wanted to tell him he didn't have to worry. She would never tell anyone what had happened. He had been sympathetic when she was feeling low and that was more than Bobby G. had ever been. She found a seat on the aisle, halfway back in the sanctuary, where she hoped Mark would notice her. While she waited for the service to begin she admired the stained-glass windows that circled the sanctuary dome. They reminded her of St. Margaret Mary's back home. All religions were pretty much the same, she thought. They gave you this place where you could come and feel like you were a part of something important and not just some glorified cocktail waitress at a fancy downtown restaurant.

Then the memorial service started and Mark walked out on the pulpit in his long black robe. Liz was sure that he noticed her as he crossed the pulpit, but he moved rapidly to his seat and avoided looking in her direction again. By the time the organ prelude was over, Liz realized that Mark no longer wanted to have anything to do with her. Like Bobby G., he had gotten what he wanted and he was moving on.

*   *   *

Renee and Antonia sat together near the front of the sanctuary and watched Mark as he rose from his chair and came forward to begin the service.

I lift up mine eyes unto the mountains. From
whence cometh my help? My help cometh from
the Lord who made heaven and earth.
He will not suffer thy foot to be moved. He
that keepeth thee will not slumber.
Behold, He that keepeth Israel doth neither
slumber nor sleep.

"Would you have voted for Mark if you'd had the chance?" Renee whispered.

"I'm not sure," Antonia answered. She had struggled with the decision during a sleepless night and had gone to the board meeting uncertain of which way she would vote. If she voted no, there would be no grant to the museum and she would have to think about moving on. If she voted yes, her relationship with Josh would be over. She was in love with Josh but he was unpredictable. No matter what he said, she knew he would never forgive her. Her career was the only thing she could count on. It had never let her down.

* * *

Pamela sat in her accustomed seat midway back in the center section of the sanctuary. She wore a wide-brimmed black straw hat that she kept for these occasions. The station manager had called her late yesterday to tell her that her contract was being renewed for two more years. He conveyed the news as gracelessly as he did everything else, but she didn't care. Cindi Li was gone. *Five by Five* would be back on the air on Monday. On her way into the synagogue that morning she had exchanged an awkward greeting with Peter, and Linda had pulled her aside and suggested that she keep her eyes open because something interesting might happen. She wondered what Linda meant. A parade of speakers extolled Eli's accomplishments, managing at the same time to draw attention to their own. Nothing surprised her anymore. Everyone tooted their own horn, even when they were burying somebody.

Eli's simple oak coffin, banked by flowers, rested on a stand in front of the pulpit. Josh sat next to his mother and listened to the words of praise being lavished on his father. He marveled at how little the speakers really knew him. His father remained a mystery, as remote and inaccessible as a distant moon circling an alien planet. The only one who spoke knowingly about him was Stefan Belzner. Stefan talked about his father as a man who revealed only as much about himself as was necessary. "He was three different people," Stefan said. "The first, someone the world knew through his accomplishments; the second, a more private person, known only to his family and a few close friends; and the third, a man known only to himself, someone whose life was defined by forces that only he understood."

Then it was Josh's turn. He climbed the four short steps to the pulpit, stood behind the lectern, and gazed down at the closed casket that held his father's body and then out across the crowd that filled the sanctuary. He had written a few words on a sheet of paper. They had not come easily and he hoped he would be able to get through them without breaking down.

"My father was a very private person. He didn't share much about himself and he wasn't the easiest person to get along with. When he saw things that bothered him he spoke out and he didn't worry about the repercussions. He expected the best from people. It didn't matter who you were. If you disappointed him, he let you know. But he understood that people can change and if you changed he was prepared to forgive. He was a great father. I know that now. I think I always knew it.

"I ran across something my father wrote years ago, before he became ill, about the inevitability of death. But it really has to do with the way he viewed life and I thought it would be appropriate to read it here.

"'Death,' Dad wrote, 'is sad only when we have missed all the meaning and all the beauty of existence. Death is sad only when we go to our graves without having climbed the heights which we might have climbed, without having become what we might have been, without having raised the banners which we might have unfurled. Death is sad when we go down to our graves with regrets: for joys which we might have shared, for love which we might have given, for beacons which we might have kindled. Death is sad when the portals of the grave close over us and we leave no memory behind . . . no one to ask and no one to answer who and what we were . . . no trace to mark our passage through time . . . no echo to hold, if only for a moment, the ardent song of our heart. Then death is sad. Otherwise death is not sad. It is the consummation of our days, the harvest which follows the seed time, the fall and winter which follow the spring and summer.'

"My father was not afraid of death. For him, life and how you lived it was all that mattered. That's the way I hope he will be remembered. That's the way I will always remember him."

When Josh was finished the cantor chanted the *El Mole Rahamin*, the traditional mourner's prayer, and it was time for the closing prayer. Mark came forward to the lectern. "Following the conclusion of this service I would appreciate it if you would remain in your seats for one or two brief announcements." Mark raised his arms and 2,200 mourners rose. He closed his eyes and, extending his arms outward as the priests of ancient Israel had done in biblical times, he intoned the traditional closing benediction.

> *May the Lord bless you and keep you.*
> *May the Lord let his countenance shine upon*
> *you and be gracious unto you.*
> *May the Lord grant to you and all your loved*
> *ones the everlasting gift of peace.*

The service had been everything Linda had hoped for. Josh's remarks had brought many in the congregation to tears. The cantor's chanting of the *El Mole Rahamin* had provided the fitting climax to a moving service of remembrance. Now, if Mark would add the proper grace note, she might still come out a winner. She stared at Mark, trying to gauge his mood. He seemed relaxed and confident and she thought she saw him smile.

With the benediction over, Mark waited for the congregation to settle down. He pushed his arms through the folds of his robe, grasped the sides of the lectern with both hands and gazed out across the congregation. Every single seat was filled. He was alone on the pulpit. Twenty-two hundred pairs of eyes were focused on him. He laid his brief speech out in front of him. He had no intention of delivering the kind of speech that Linda wanted. He would tell the congregation exactly how he felt. He would tell them that Eli was no saint, but just an ordinary mortal whose inability to let go had prevented him from turning over the congregation to someone younger who would have led the congregation to even greater heights.

He would single out Max Jessel as a man whose greed was helping to destroy a great American institution and who had determined to destroy him in the process because he had dared to challenge his authority. And he wouldn't spare Linda. The congregation needed to understand the nature of the person they had selected as their president. She was devious and untrustworthy. She had used him as a tool to promote her own interests. She didn't care about the synagogue. All she cared about was herself. When he was finished, everyone would know what a great injustice had been done to him. He would be vindicated and he and Susan would move on and make a new life for themselves somewhere where his talents would be properly appreciated.

Manny Polsky stood in his accustomed spot at the back of the sanctuary. As he watched Mark standing where Eli used to stand, he was barely able to suppress the rage he felt at the way this insignificant little man had managed to make the last few months of his beloved rabbi's life so miserable. He had wanted to object when Linda suggested that Mark conduct the service but he had kept silent. Instead, he met with Adam Burwell to discuss the music for the service and to warn him that with Mark on the pulpit anything might happen.

"It has been my privilege to serve as assistant rabbi of this congregation for the past five-and-a-half years," Mark began. "They have been wonderful years. Years that Susan and I will always cherish." He glanced at Linda who was sitting in the front row next to Peter and smiling up at him. "But as we all know, life is unpredictable and there have been bitter moments along with the sweet. A few days ago, after weeks of mounting pressure . . ."

Manny had heard enough. He ripped the white carnation out of his lapel and threw it on the floor. Adam Burwell was watching through the curtains in the organ loft. It was the signal they had agreed on. He spun around on his stool, his hands reaching for the keyboard, and suddenly the throbbing chords of a Bach recessional reverberated through the sanctuary, drowning out Mark's words.

". . . I decided to resign my position as rabbi of this congregation. My decision to leave was not my own. It was forced on me by . . ."

But no one could hear a word that Mark was saying. A great tidal wave of organ music flooded the sanctuary, echoing off the walls. Mark reached for a button on the side of the pulpit. A buzzer sounded in the organ loft, a signal for the organist to stop playing, but Adam ignored it. His hands raced across the keys, his feet flew across the pedals, and the thunderous chords of the recessional filled the sanctuary with waves of majestic sound. Several more frantic bursts of the buzzer sounded but Adam kept on playing. At the rear of the sanctuary Manny Polsky rose on the balls of his feet, a wide smile on his wrinkled face. "Try talking over that, you little putz."

There was no point trying to continue. Mark glanced briefly in Linda's direction, picked up the pages of his speech and started for his seat, then changed his mind, crossed the pulpit and hurried through the door on the other side.

After some minutes of confusion, the rest of the congregation began to leave. Row after row of mourners jammed the aisles. The sanctuary emptied out. Linda and Peter were among the last to leave. As they reached the parking lot, organ music could still be heard, echoing through the open doors of the sanctuary and drifting up into the cool afternoon air.

CHAPTER
THIRTY-FIVE

A few days after the funeral, a letter announcing Mark Winnick's resignation was sent out under Sam Broad's signature to every member of the congregation. That same day the Indians began their playoff series with the Boston Red Sox. The news of Mark's resignation was relegated to a tiny notice at the bottom of page seven of the morning paper and the event drifted unnoticed into the dustbin of history.

The following Monday, the depository in New York released the results of the tender offer for Fabrico shares. Only 41 percent of the shares had been tendered. Peter Freling and Jess Ballard abandoned their efforts to take control of the company. In the sell-off following the collapse of the tender offer, the stock fell below two dollars a share and Leo's portfolio lost more than half its value. Six months later, the company announced its first quarterly profit in three years, the stock soared, and Leo was suddenly worth more than $20 million. The news of his windfall leaked out and he found it awkward to keep his job as secretary of the congregation. He resigned and the board elected him secretary emeritus for life. Members of the congregation began to seek him out for investment advice and he was in touch with Marty Franklin to find out what legal steps were necessary to become a registered financial advisor.

After an intensive three-month search by a committee of the board, a new senior rabbi was chosen. He was a tall, intense young man with a shock of thick black hair who reminded many of Eli when he was young. Within a week of his arrival he had locked horns with Linda and let her know that he would be running things. She resigned as president of the congregation, and at a brief ceremony, her photograph was added to the gallery of past presidents that lined the walls of the synagogue parlor. In her departing remarks she expressed the hope that the feeling of goodwill and common purpose that the congregation had enjoyed under her leadership would continue under the tenure of the new rabbi. At her request, her remarks were printed verbatim in the synagogue bulletin.

Mark and Susan left town shortly after their baby girl was born. Mark found a job as the rabbi of a new congregation in south Florida and began working on a memoir called, *Rounding Third and Heading Home: My Years as a Baseball Rabbi.* Brian Patzer also moved to Florida. With the $250,000 Ballard paid him, he made a down payment on a condo in Coral Gables, got a broker's license, and sold real estate. He joined Mark's congregation and the two of them occasionally played golf together.

Five by Five soared in the ratings. Pamela Dawes treated herself to another face-lift and continued her weekly conversations with Buddy Kaplan to keep up with the city's social whirl. It was from Buddy that she found out that Bobby G. and Renee had been secretly engaged, but that the marriage never happened. Bobby still had a roving eye. From time to time he dropped in at Carnavale, where Liz Aurelio was still the hostess, but she kept a mile away from him. Liz gave up on Jewish lovers, moved to a new apartment, joined a Pentecostal church and began dating the born-again Christian quarterback of the Cleveland Browns.

Peter Freling's dalliance with Cindi Li proved to be the last straw for Linda. She filed for divorce, and after a long and acrimonious negotiation, Milles Fleurs was transferred to her name, along with $40 million. Peter's promised gift to the museum fell through.

Antonia moved to New York, where she took a job as the assistant to the director of the Whitney Museum. She and Josh stayed in touch, but the events leading up to Eli's death had dimmed the intensity of their relationship. They talked on the phone from time to time, but the calls seemed only to widen the gulf between them.

Josh took a job managing investments for Max Jessel, but soon realized that working for Max was no different than working for Jess Ballard. The $300,000 he had invested in Fabrico grew to more than a million, and he decided to go back to New York and try to make it on his own. The day he got there he called Antonia. They met at a small downtown restaurant. Their conversation drifted aimlessly for a while but eventually came around to Linda's effort to force Mark on the congregation.

"How come you never asked me how I would have voted?" Antonia asked.

"I guess I didn't want to know."

Josh thought how often his relationships ended this way, with issues unresolved and conversations drifting into silence.

"I sure made a mess of things," he said.

Antonia's eyes held him in their steady gaze. "That's getting to be a habit with you," she said.

"It won't happen again."

"Why's that?"

"Because we belong together. We get along."

Antonia's throaty laugh reminded Josh just how much he missed her. "I get along with my cat," she said.

"I can't imagine living my life without you."

Antonia reached across the table. Her fingers caressed his face. "There," she whispered, "was that so hard to say?"

* * *

A year after the funeral a small group of mourners huddled under umbrellas in a corner of the cemetery to commemorate the setting of the headstone on Eli's grave. Rachel, her eyes dry and clear, stood between Josh and Antonia as the new rabbi read from the Book of Psalms. A light rain was falling and there was a chill in the air. A large granite boulder had been found at the edge of a glacial moraine east of the city and trucked to the cemetery, where it was placed at the head of Eli's grave. The boulder was irregular in shape, rough in texture. Tiny quartz crystals imbedded in its surface glistened in the rain.

The brief service concluded with the recitation of the Kaddish. The mourners drifted off. Antonia took Rachel by the arm and they walked away. Josh stayed behind, staring at the massive boulder that marked his father's grave. The light morning rain had ended and the sun had come out from behind the clouds. Josh placed his hands on the granite boulder. The cold stone felt unexpectedly warm to his touch.